EL PASO

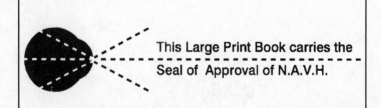

This Large Print Book carries the
Seal of Approval of N.A.V.H.

EL PASO

WINSTON GROOM

THORNDIKE PRESS
A part of Gale, Cengage Learning

GALE
CENGAGE Learning·

Farmington Hills, Mich • San Francisco • New York • Waterville, Maine
Meriden, Conn • Mason, Ohio • Chicago

GALE
CENGAGE Learning®

LIBRARY OF CONGRESS CATALOGING-IN-PUBLICATION DATA

Names: Groom, Winston, 1944– author.
Title: El paso / Winston Groom.
Description: Large print edition. | Waterville, Maine : Thorndike Press, 2016. |
  Series: Thorndike Press large print basic
Identifiers: LCCN 2016041098| ISBN 9781410495952 (hardback) | ISBN 1410495957
  (hardcover)
Subjects: LCSH: Villa, Pancho, 1878–1923—Fiction. | Kidnapping—Fiction. |
  Outlaws—Fiction. | Frontier and pioneer life—Southwest, New—Fiction. | BISAC:
  FICTION / Historical. | GSAFD: Historical fiction. | Western stories. | Adventure
  fiction.
Classification: LCC PS3557.R56 P37 2016b | DDC 813/.54—dc23
LC record available at https://lccn.loc.gov/2016041098

Published in 2017 by arrangement with Liveright Publishing Corporation, a division of W.W. Norton & Company, Inc.

Printed in the United States of America
1 2 3 4 5 6 7 21 20 19 18 17

To the memory of Edwin D. "Eddie" Morgan

Marine Corps hero of the Pacific War, fine friend, and raconteur of this expansive tale.

And

To Carolina Montgomery Groom — age eighteen.

When you were seven you would come into my office and ask what I was doing — I was writing your book, Patriotic Fire, *a tale of pirates, soldiers, Indians, heroes, and scoundrels at the Battle of New Orleans in 1815.*

When you were twelve I wrote another story for you, Kearny's March, *about the Mexican War of 1848 — about explorers, mountain men, Indians, presidents — and always the heroes and the scoundrels.*

It's ever the same — in history, novels, life, and in this book for you — those heroes and those scoundrels provide the grace and disrepute that makes our species, above all animals, at once interesting, and unique.

— Your loving papa

PREFACE

Novels don't usually need forewords but in this case it seems useful that the reader know the background of the events depicted herein.

Beginning in the late nineteenth century the Mexican government — in eternal social and financial turmoil — started selling off vast tracts of land in its desolate northern provinces on the notion that wealthy American entrepreneurs would exploit the land by building infrastructure that the government in Mexico City could not afford. Accordingly, the Guggenheims began to develop large mining operations in Northern Mexico, Harrimans built railroads, Morgans, Hearsts, and Whitneys developed enormous livestock ranches, and so on, employing thousands of Mexican citizens until, inevitably, the revolution moved northward.

The gist of this story — the kidnapping of children by the legendary revolutionary general Pancho Villa, and the manhunt through the Sierra Madre — was suggested to me by a dear friend, the late Edwin "Eddie" Morgan, of the New York Morgans, whose grandfather owned an immense cattle ranch in Chihuahua, Mexico, that in 1916 was attacked by Villa's army and later confiscated by the Mexican government during the revolution. Eddie regaled friends with stories of his grandfather and entourage riding in his private railcar from New York down to Chihuahua, the purchase of the bear in Nashville, and the great cattle drive to El Paso. Pancho Villa actually strung up Morgan's ranch manager and had him sabered to death — the same manager who, when once asked by a large Chicago meat packer if he could supply thirty thousand head of cattle, wired back: "Which color?"

Those were strange and romantic times for the new century, with the Great War raging in Europe and the Mexican Civil War threatening to spill over into the United States. Colorful American characters, from the journalist-socialist John Reed to the misanthropic satirist Ambrose Bierce, soon found themselves tangled up in the thing, for better or for worse, and although this is not a "historical novel," I couldn't resist throwing them into the story. Serious students of the period will find that I have tampered with the evidence from time to time to present the more interesting tale, which — as I am also a writer of history — I usually try never to do.

8

But in this case, as a novelist, I think I can get away with it.

Winston Groom
Point Clear, Alabama
January 2016

PART ONE:
INTO MEXICO

ONE

Often, when he was anxious or depressed, Arthur Shaughnessy would stand behind his large desk in the First Vice President & General Manager's Office of the New England & Pacific Railroad Company's operations headquarters in Chicago, looking through the plate-glass window at the rail yards. From his vantage point three stories above, endless miles of rail track led into and out of the yards as far as the eye could see. Abutting the coal piles — each its own mountain of black with a towering metal crane and shuttle jutting out from the top — were hundreds of outdated and rusting boxcars, flatcars, passenger cars, and locomotives parked on sidings, waiting for the scrap heap. But closer, the scene was more animated. Engines of all types were arriving and departing; hauling freight, passengers, and in some cases other engines — yard locomotives pulling or pushing a big sixteen-sprocket beast to the roundhouse or repair sheds.

The trains came from all points of America: up through New Orleans and the South with cotton, fruit, and the spoils of the Caribbean; down from Wisconsin and Michigan with dairy and wheat; from the Pacific with lumber, the Southwest with livestock for the packing houses, the Midwest and Great Plains with corn and grain, coal from Kentucky and West Virginia; from Pennsylvania, steel; from the Rockies with metal ore for the smelters; and from the Atlantic Coast, finished goods — clothing, furniture, glassware . . .

And some not-so-finished goods: great unwashed hordes of emigrants from Europe.

Chicago in 1916 was the hub of everything that moved by rail across America.

Arthur Shaughnessy stood at the window with a telegram in his hand. He'd already read it, and merely let it dangle by his side as he surveyed the scene below, where scores of men moved in every direction.

They came in motor trucks and mule-drawn wagons, handcarts, man-carts, and on one platform a gang of black men unloaded green bunches of bananas by hand from a freight car just in from the Gulf Coast.

Somehow, all the activity had the effect of taking him away from his troubles, which were many.

Since the window was closed, Arthur could

barely hear the cacophony rising toward him, a din that screamed up day and night: the blaring of whistles, the roar of engines letting off steam, the hissing blasts from air breaks, the clanging of bells, the rumble of the locomotives, the creaking of railcars. And awash in it all was the shouting of flagmen, switchmen, oilers, brakemen, fire-men, signal-men, porters, conductors, and the cursing and yelling and chanting of the freight gangs and yardmen of all stripes — many of them were on the payroll that Arthur was somehow supposed to meet by the end of the week.

That dreary afternoon, clouds of gray smoke billowed into the air from scores of engines, uniting with a low bleak autumn sky that could either mean rain or the season's first snowfall. Arthur's mood matched the ominous weather. He put the telegram on his desk, sat down, and looked at it again.

WILL BE ON AJAX TO IRELAND STOP
SEE IF YOU CAN HANDLE IT — FATHER

Something sagged in Arthur.

He despised that damned yacht — boat — ship — whatever-you-called-it — and the fortune it cost the company. And to Ireland, of all places, just as the whole business might go to pieces. How could the Old Man not?

John Shaughnessy, Arthur's father, had built the railroad up from a dinky two-

15

hundred-mile passenger and freight line all the way out to Chicago and had been headed west fast as he could until construction stopped cold on the Dakota plains. And he was even going to overcome that until . . . Arthur cleared his throat and fingered the telegram, moving it around on the desk as though wiping up dust with it. The Old Man might have picked up the phone and called him so they could discuss things. But Arthur knew the reason he hadn't was precisely because he did not wish to discuss it.

SEE IF YOU CAN HANDLE IT

Arthur had been working at New England & Pacific — NE&P — ever since he was old enough to be an office boy in the Boston headquarters. Summers between day school and college he worked in the rail yards or on the trains themselves, while his friends — at least those from the upper-crust Shaughnessy connections — whiled away their time in Bermuda or Newport or sailing on Nantucket Sound with girls manning the yards.

The Old Man was a stern taskmaster, especially in those days, but to Arthur he once said: "Son, someday this will all be yours, and your children's and their children's children's. The only way to learn it is from the ground up." This Arthur had done, with a sense of duty, if not always cheerfully, because if Colonel John Shaughnessy and his wife, Beatie, had not plucked him out of an orphanage in South Boston one winter morning twenty-three years earlier and taken him into their home and given him their name and the considerable benefits of their considerable wealth, he might right now be peddling apples from a cart on Boston Common or eating out of a garbage heap.

Arthur wadded the telegram and tossed it into the trash. His plan, his hope — the thing he had perceived to get the company back on stable financial footing — was to take it public and acquire an influx of stockholder cash and a sensible board of directors who could put a lid on his father's extravagances, such as the *Ajax* and other costly fancies that he knew were draining their assets.

He was proud of the NE&P and the progress that it stood for. But the Colonel didn't want to be troubled by the whims of stockholders or the controlling votes of any board of directors — or for that matter the snooping of newspaper reporters that would come with a public company — and after many futile discussions Arthur felt bound to honor his father's wishes.

After all, he didn't just owe him a lot; he owed him everything.

Beatie Shaughnessy had given birth to one daughter, Alexa — and could bear no more children. The news made Arthur's father — the Colonel, as he was known — more heart-broken than his wife, but not over worry or concern; like every man, he simply wanted a son.

Then one afternoon a decade later, while doing charity work for the church, Beatie found herself in the stark environs of the Laura Bostwick Foundlings' Home. Every Christmas she delivered presents to the orphans — candy, cookies, hand-me-downs, and worn-out toys. Though she seldom went into South Boston, where Irish Catholics lived, the Bostwick orphanage was not limited to Irish Catholics only. It was a nonsectarian institution and Beatie felt it her duty to help the most unfortunate. All children deserved Christmas, and certainly those who were made orphans through no fault of their own.

That same afternoon, the custodian told Arthur to help get the things out of the carriage as usual. Right away he put on his most charming demeanor for the tall, handsome lady, and when Beatie asked his name, he replied, "Arthur."

Without thinking, Beatie asked, "And what is your surname, Arthur?"

To which he replied with his most bashful, poignant expression, "I don't have a last name, mum." Beatie bent down and hugged him and apologized, her eyes misty and his glistening, too. While Arthur did in fact have a last name, Gray, he was never sure if it related to his true father or mother or was just something given to him at the orphanage so he wouldn't be embarrassed at school.

Nevertheless, the real Christmas presents soon arrived. Two days before Christmas Eve, the custodian told Arthur what every child in the foundling home wanted to hear more than anything else. To wash up and put on clean clothes: Arthur had visitors.

As he came downstairs, Arthur saw the handsome lady again. With her was a burly man, with blue eyes, graying hair, and an easy smile, dressed as a true gentleman, with a black top hat in his hand. "This is Mr. and Mrs. Shaughnessy, Arthur," the custodian said. "They want to speak with you."

The three of them then sat in a little drawing room the orphanage used for important visitors. There the burly gentleman gently questioned Arthur. He asked if he knew who his parents were. Arthur replied that he did not. He asked how Arthur liked going to school. Arthur told him he did. It was the truth. He liked learning. The man asked Arthur if he liked the orphanage. Unsure how to reply, Arthur said nothing. The man asked again.

"Yessir, it's nice."

"Good," replied the man. "That's what I like to hear." He smiled at his wife.

There was a silence for a moment. Arthur

hadn't known what to think. If he said he didn't like the orphanage, they might think he was a troublemaker; not grateful for what he had. If he said he did . . . well, why would they ask that? Had they come just to find out if he liked living here? As he forced a smile, he began to choke back a sob that rose in his throat.

"Yes, sir," Arthur repeated. "They're . . . they're . . ." He hadn't been coached, but heard from others that crying could sometimes get you what you wanted. Beatie rushed to the sofa where the boy sat and embraced him tightly as he fought back the tears. The man over Beatie's shoulder shifted awkwardly, something between a frown and pity on his face. Beatie turned to him.

"We're taking him with us right now!" she said.

"Well, my word, Mother, we can't just —"

"Yes, we are!"

"Well, I think we ought —"

"No," Beatie said firmly. "He is going home with us."

But Arthur did not go home with the Shaughnessys that day. The orphanage wouldn't permit it, no matter that the Shaughnessy name was among the most influential in Boston.

By Christmas Eve, however, and under a most unusual arrangement, Arthur went to the Shaughnessy home for something of a trial period. Shaughnessy had worked it out with the orphanage people. Arthur would stay with them over the Christmas holiday. If it worked out, they would discuss the matter further. The orphanage didn't like such things because there was always the chance the child would be returned — more hurt and confused than ever — but this was John Shaughnessy, owner, president, and chairman of the New England & Pacific Railroad Company. He was not a man to disagree with, especially if donations were in the air.

Turning away from the window and the hustle-bustle of the Chicago rail yards, Arthur gazed at the large oil painting that dominated the opposite wall. In the picture, the Colonel stared down at him, at anyone who entered the room. His features seemed larger than most men's: high wrinkled forehead, thick dark hair slicked back, a great black brushy mustache, full lips, aquiline nose, square jaw, and a strong, masculine chin that could take, and had taken, many blows. Then there were the same deep-set, penetrating blue eyes that Arthur first noticed at the orphanage so many years before, and on this day the painting reminded him of the morning he first entered into the Shaughnessy household.

Arthur had been nine when the Colonel and Beatie removed him from the Laura

Bostwick Foundlings' Home. At the time, the boy had all but given up hope that his fate would be any different from that of the countless other boys who turned sixteen without finding a home. Like them, he dreaded the day when he would be sent out into the world with nothing more than a hand-me-down suit and some pocket money. Aside from what he wore on his back, the only things Arthur owned were his collection of butterflies and a glass cutter. He had always wanted to collect coins or stamps, but they cost money. Butterflies were for the taking.

He'd amassed an impressive lot of specimens from nearby parks and along the waterfront, and after finding one would make his own plate frames from scrap wood and cast-off glass from a window manufacturing business down the block where one of the workers had given him a glass cutter. On that strange day when he moved to the Shaughnessys' fabulous Beacon Hill home, he proudly lugged with him a little cardboard box of neatly labeled insects, which included moths of all descriptions, dragonflies, and a number of large aerial biting creatures such as the horntail wasp, the giant cicada, and robber flies.

Beatie and the Colonel had come for him on the morning of Christmas Eve.

TWO

Up in his third-floor room in the foundling house, Arthur had carefully packed his butterfly collection into a cardboard box and said good-byes to his roommate, Michael Martin, who was off to the last day of school before the holiday. Arthur was especially fond of "Mick" Martin, who, even though only a year older, was vastly mature compared with himself. Mick was fearless, daring, and mischievous, and a natural-born leader.

He also looked the part, with his dark hair and eyes, impressive height, and a full, strong mouth that made him look more like an adolescent than a ten-year-old. That same year he had gotten Arthur into trouble — or, better put, Arthur had gotten himself into trouble, by letting Mick persuade him to run away from the orphanage together. It had been summer and they were just returning from a two-week camp at the other end of the state. For the most part, it had been a memorable experience, except that Mick, who everybody believed was the bravest and strongest of all the boys, had managed to develop an unreasoning fear of snakes after stepping on one in the woods. It was just a large harmless black racer but, startled, had hissed and struck Mick several times on his bare leg before racing off. From the marks on his leg, no one knew but that it was not a venomous copperhead. They put iodine on the bite and confined Mick to a bed in the camp infirmary, where they watched carefully for swelling that never developed.

They'd been back at Laura Bostwick for a week after camp when things began to go sour for Mick. Until the snakebite he'd never known pleasures like those at the camp, in the wilds of the countryside, and coming back to the city depressed him. Summer at the orphanage was drudgery anyway. The boys were made to scrape paint and white-wash walls and scrub floors and kitchen equipment — clean out the jakes. The chores weren't so bad but there was half a summer to go and Mick was fed up. Late one after-noon, as Mick and Arthur were walking down a hot filthy street, Mick stopped to look at his reflection in a shop window. He studied it for a long time, as Arthur stood patiently by.

"Arthur," Mick said finally, "we can do bet-ter on our own."

"What's that mean?" Arthur asked.

"We can do better. I met some fellers a few

days ago on Dorchester. They were just like us, but living their own way. They got a shed to stay in and nobody tells them what to do or to go to school or when to go to bed and all that. Why, they're free as birds."

Arthur was puzzled. "How do they eat? Who —"

"They got jobs, see, when they want them. They feed themselves."

"What kind of jobs?"

"All kinds." Mick told Arthur that if a guy at the barbershop wants a pint of cold beer, one of the street guys runs and gets it for him — and gets a tip. Or if somebody wants some numbers run, "You stop in the shop and get the money and the guy picks his number — and all you got to do is take it back to the main runner. There's lots of things like that."

The notion made Arthur hesitate, but it was exciting, too.

"The beauty of it," Mick continued, "is you don't gots to do it unless you want to — work. You want to go down to the river and fish, it's up to you. Way it is now, we work all the time and don't gets a dime for it."

"We got a home," Arthur answered.

"A home? Yeah, a damned orphanage! Nobody's gonna take us, Arthur. We too old. All they want is babies — you've seen that. I figure we need to get started in life. Those guys, some of them, they even got girls."

A few days later, Arthur and Mick took a few of their things in paper bags, planning to sneak back into the orphanage later and get the rest, what there was of it. The first night they used a few of their saved-up pennies to buy a loaf of bread and some bacon, and when the sun had set they made a fire and cooked over rocks in a park along the shore.

The night was deep and starlit, until a pumpkin moon eventually rose up over the water. It backlit the islands in the harbor and the two of them speculated that many of these might not be inhabited and that maybe they could find a way out there on a fishing boat. Once they arrived, they could build themselves a cabin and fish all summer; winter was not discussed. At dawn the next day, they set out, full of hopes, for Dorchester and the streets paved with gold that awaited them.

It turned out, however, that the Dorchester Avenue boys Mick knew were part of a vicious Irish teenage gang that didn't take kindly to strangers. Even with Mick's toughness, the Bostwick lads were no match for these thugs, who chased them off their turf all the way north to Summer Street. After three days of squandering their tiny hoard of coins, Arthur and Mick were reduced to hanging around the docks and fighting rats for the spoiled vegetables left on the piers.

Still, they fished in the harbor and Arthur

was usually able to scrape up some kind of dinner of flounder, clam, or crab stew. Once Mick killed a seagull with a stick after tempting it with a piece of moldy bread and even that went into a stew. But, within a few weeks, Mick seemed to be getting morose and lost so much interest in fishing or scavenging that these tasks were left to Arthur, who had constructed a little shed for them out of washed-up boards he found along the beach.

They stole a pail from behind a butcher's shop and Arthur would fill it with water from a fountain in the park and lug it back to camp for drinking, eating, and washing purposes. But at his lowest, Mick basically lolled around and stared out across the water and rarely spoke. The biggest excitement came when Arthur caught a little green grass snake and brought it back to camp. Mick pitched such a fit that for a moment Arthur thought he was going to hit him unless he let the thing go, which he eventually did.

Then, one morning, Arthur finally said, "I'm going home."

Mick looked at him with an air of disappointment, but both of them realized that at least *this* great adventure was over. When they got back to Bostwick, the two of them spent the next several weeks of their spare time cleaning out the jakes — a typical punishment for what Mick quickly began referring to as their "daring escape."

■ ■ ■ ■

Arthur sat by the window of his room in the orphanage, looking out on an iron-gray Boston morning. The sun had barely risen, and the streets already bustled with traffic and noise. His life at Laura Bostwick had not been miserable; since it was all he could remember, he felt no anger or even hurt that he was an orphan. But all of Bostwick's children, Arthur included, were taught to harbor a hope that someday a family would come and take them in.

When it so suddenly appeared that this might happen, Arthur couldn't help but wonder if it was no more than a wispy dream about to burst. Would they show up? The beautiful lady and the big handsome man; Arthur looked again at the piece of paper Mrs. Walters had given him: "Mr. And Mrs. John Shaughnessy (Beatie). He owns a railroad."

Then, out of the corner of his eye, Arthur saw a shiny open car round a corner and turn down the street. It moved slowly and deliberately among the regular traffic of South Boston — vegetable trucks, coal and ice and milk wagons, fish carts, trolleys, and ox-drawn bread vans mixed with a few dilapidated private vehicles and a spray of pedestrians.

The motorcar halted while a woman wearing a shawl around her head crossed the street, then moved slowly toward the orphanage. The motorcar attracted attention; people stopped and stared. Arthur's heart began to race. When it stopped in front of the building, he picked up the canvas bag and cardboard box.

They were standing in the dimly lit foyer of the Bostwick Home when Arthur descended the staircase into the room. Mrs. Walters had told him to smile. Beatie did not rush to him, but remained by her husband, holding his arm with an anxious, expectant look on her face. The man smiled broadly with big strong teeth. The matrons came in soon after and filled the foyer, where there were oohs and aahs and everyone bursting into conversation. Arthur stood there, alone in the corner, feeling forgotten. And then it was time to go. Mr. Shaughnessy took Arthur's cardboard box and carried it to the car, where he handed it to a man standing beside the open door. He was a young dark-skinned man enormous as a statue and dressed in chauffeur's livery — gray suit with brass buttons, salmon tie, high-topped polished brown boots and a cap, perched on a head of bushy hair. He seemed to scowl. The man reached for Arthur's bag, too, but Arthur took a step backward.

"It's all right, Arthur," Beatie said. "This is

Bomba, our driver. He will put your things in the trunk."

Arthur handed him the bag and, after Beatie got in, stepped up into the large open motorcar, followed by Mr. Shaughnessy, who stepped inside like a king ascending his throne. Arthur had never been in an automobile before and it was more magnificent than he ever could have imagined. When Bomba cranked the engine it seemed to come alive, like the sudden purr of a sleeping beast.

The seats were of deep, pleated walnut-colored leather that smelled of polish and saddle soap. The floor was covered with a lush gray pile of carpet that his worn-out shoes seemed to sink into. Behind the front seat a gleaming mahogany table folded down; built into it was a bar with crystal glasses, decanters, and a silver ice bucket. The car began to move with a low, breathy snarl, and Beatie handed Arthur a soft wool lap robe. He wasn't sure what to do with it, but she tucked him in. Light snowflakes swirled past the windows.

"Well," said Mr. Shaughnessy, "what would you like for Christmas?"

Arthur looked at him, stupefied. It was a question he'd never been asked before.

"Haven't you anything in mind, Arthur?" Beatie asked.

Arthur shook his head.

"All right, then we'll just have to find

something, won't we?" Shaughnessy said merrily.

Arthur stared straight ahead, not knowing what to think.

The motorcar slowly wound its way out of South Boston, crossing a river, and through the city proper. Arthur had never actually seen the city — the *real* Boston — with its stately stone buildings and men in expensive chesterfields and top hats. A place of big parks with enormous trees and manicured lawns. He unabashedly looked around as Mr. Shaughnessy pointed things out to him: the State House, the Revere Monument — and before he knew it, they were . . . home.

Bomba pulled the car up to the front of a tall, elegant brick house five stories high. It had an enormous bay window in front and the other tall windows were flanked with shiny green shutters. Bomba seemed to scowl as he opened the car door, but as Arthur stepped out and faced the house his mouth dropped open and Bomba beamed like a harvest moon. A set of white marble steps led to the front door, which was adorned with gleaming brass.

"Bomba will put your things in your room, Arthur," Beatie said as they climbed the steps. Arthur could see his reflection in the plate of the brass entrance knocker. A maid opened the door and they stepped inside. Arthur didn't realize his mouth had dropped open, but he had the presence of mind to remove his cap. The hallway was illuminated by a great crystal chandelier that was gaslit. To the left was an elegant parlor room covered with a tremendous Aubusson carpet; elegant and plush chairs and sofas were scattered around among tables of highly polished wood. To the right was a room with a grand marble fireplace flickering warmly. On the floor sat a richly colored Persian rug, upon which stood deep leather furniture and plush chairs with ottomans. Trophy animal heads were affixed to the walls, along with hung paintings of racehorses, yachting events, and shooting scenes; African spears and shields adorned the desk, as did the bleached skull of something: ape — possibly human.

"That is Mr. Shaughnessy's room," Beatie explained. "He goes in there to smoke cigars."

They walked farther through the house, past a tremendous dining room, marked by three sparkling chandeliers and a table that could have seated fifty. They passed other rooms, too, including what Arthur observed through a slightly cracked door was an inside toilet. Seeing that Arthur had taken notice, Beatie asked cheerfully, "Would you like to freshen up?"

Arthur nodded, not knowing exactly what this meant, but Beatie opened the door to the toilet and showed him in. Arthur stood inside the little room, lit by gas lamps, which made it warm and inviting, unlike the outdoor jakes of the orphanage. He stepped up to the toilet and relieved himself. When he finished, he buttoned up and stood staring into the bowl, so different from the black holes into which lime was poured every day or so. This bowl held the water — all of it. There was a pipe leading behind the toilet to a porcelain tank on the wall and a velvet cord with a pull attached to it. Arthur wondered what it was for. He stood for a long time until he heard Beatie outside:

"Arthur — are you all right?"

He stepped back into the hall, hat in hand. "Yes, ma'am."

Beatie understood. Since she had not heard the toilet flush, she stepped into the lavatory and pulled the cord. The sound startled Arthur.

"See?" she said.

THREE

The next morning, Mrs. Shaughnessy awakened Arthur and got him properly dressed for Christmas, the likes of which he had never experienced even in his wildest fantasies. He'd never seen a tree like the one in the center of the Shaughnessys' great back room. The room overlooked the Charles River, and the tree stood in front of a broad bay of windows. Silver and brass ornaments, shiny glass balls, and strings like pearls were draped from every branch. The tree at the orphanage only had candy canes, apples, and strings of popcorn — all things that would be eaten later. But atop the Shaughnessys' tree was a fine porcelain angel with real white bird's wings, the whole thing lit by dozens of tiny candles in clip-on brass holders, and there were presents for Arthur under the tree.

Sitting impatiently in a chair and eyeing the presents under the tree was a girl, Alexa, the Shaughnessys' ten-going-on-fifteen-year-old daughter who, per her mother's instructions, was restrained from starting Christmas as she always did by rushing to the tree and tearing into the loot. She looked distinctly unhappy about having to wait, but also about Arthur's intrusion into her life; still, she smiled as she'd been ordered to do when he was introduced.

Soon enough Colonel Shaughnessy entered the room and word was given to open the gifts. Beatie had gone to the Jordan Marsh department store and bought for Arthur several lovely suits of clothes: a tweed jacket, a soft cashmere scarf, a black velvet cap, polished leather shoes, wool knickers, a belt with a silver buckle, cotton shirts. More than he had ever had in his life, or had hoped to get. There was also a bone-handled African throwing knife that Shaughnessy had picked out from his own collection.

But this was not the present that Arthur had asked for. On Christmas Eve night, when the Colonel had asked him again what he wanted the next morning, Arthur had stammered before finally asking, "Could Mick come for Christmas?"

"Who is Mick?" Shaughnessy asked.

"My friend."

"From the orphanage?" Beatie prompted.

"Yes, ma'am."

Her husband shot her a disapproving glance.

"Well," Beatie said, "won't he have a Christmas of his own there, then?"

"Yes, ma'am,"

"So wouldn't it be best if he enjoyed it there," Beatie said, "with his friends?"

"Yes, ma'am," Arthur replied, "I guess so."

"Then why do you want him here?" asked Shaughnessy. "Instead of with his friends?"

"I . . . I . . . guess I just wanted him to see it," Arthur said hesitantly; he felt the beginnings of a stammer. Another glance was exchanged between Beatie and her husband, but this of a different sort.

"Well, I think that would be all right," Shaughnessy had said expansively. "I'll send the car around to have him picked up tomorrow."

If possible, Mick Martin was even more flabbergasted than Arthur with the Shaughnessy opulence. His mouth actually gaped as he walked inside. He forgot to remove his cap as he immediately gravitated toward Mr. Shaughnessy's grand study, with its trophy heads and spears and sporting prints and the big tiger-skin rug. Arthur stopped him before Beatie could.

"No, no, it's all right," Mr. Shaughnessy said, suddenly appearing around a corner and ushering the boys inside. "It's Christmas." The tall man led them through the room, explaining in detail how the tiger was shot, and what the trophy head with the twisted antlers was, and where and when he had bagged it. They were most impressed with a big stuffed piranha fish Shaughnessy had caught in the Amazon. He showed them a deep, ugly scar on his wrist where the thing had bitten him as he tried to take it off the hook.

"Well, Mick," asked Shaughnessy, "what do you want to be when you grow up?" The Colonel had seated himself behind his desk with his feet up on it and lit a cigar.

Mick looked at Arthur, who had gone to a cushy leather chair and sat down, already beginning to feel a little comfortable after only a day in this mansion. Arthur had no advice in his eyes.

"A policeman? A fireman?" pressed Shaughnessy.

Mick remained mute. No one had ever asked this sort of question before. It had always been as if life was lived a day at a time. At the orphanage, there had always been the dream that someone like the Colonel — some wealthy person — would swoop in and whisk him away, though Mick had long since given up hope of it. And yet now, with Arthur . . .

"Well, come, boy, have you got fur on your tongue?"

"No, sir," Mick said.

"Perhaps you'd like to own a railroad, like I do?" Shaughnessy said.

Mick, who had finally taken off his cap,

nodded stupidly, like a bird drinking water.

"Marvelous!" Shaughnessy thundered. "Well, now, when you get old enough, and get out of school, you come and see me, all right? There are jobs for good men on the NE&P."

"I want to be an engineer," Mick said.

"An engineer! Grand. My word, grand! We have lots of engineers running our trains," said Shaughnessy.

"No, a real engineer. To build buildings," Mick said.

That revelation shocked Arthur. He wasn't even sure what an engineer was.

"Well, well — a boy with ambition!" said Shaughnessy. "That's what I like to see. Now, you come and see me anyway, boy, when you're finished with school. I have plenty of those kinds of engineers working for me, too." Arthur and Mick looked at each other almost furtively; all this simply seemed too good to be true.

Christmas dinner was a feast of a kind that Mick and Arthur had only imagined. Cold sliced roasts and poached salmon and soups, hot and cold, and then a fat suckling pig with an apple in its mouth glistening in the gaslights. Neither Arthur nor Mick understood all the various utensils beside their plates. Mick picked up a salad fork and speared an oyster. All day Alexa had tried to ignore them but now could not resist becoming their mentor as Mick lifted an oyster to his mouth.

"No, that's not it — it's the one to your front," Alexa rebuked him, holding up her oyster fork.

With the oyster already to his lips, Mick stopped dead in his motion, put the oyster back on his plate, scraped it off the fork, and let it sit there. Beatie shot a hostile glare at her daughter, who looked back, appearing self-satisfied and smug.

When the servants cleared away the next set of china and brought in bowls of steaming artichokes, the boys had no idea what to do with the strange vegetable. Alexa drew the boys' attention by plucking off an artichoke leaf and putting it in her mouth, pretending to eat the entire thing. The boys followed suit.

As Shaughnessy wound up a story about elk hunting in Alaska, Beatie looked over to her new charge and his friend. Both had stuffed whole leaves of artichokes in their mouths and were chewing, almost red-faced, their cheeks bulging desperately, while Alexa sat with a beatific smirk on her face.

"Oh, I'm sorry, boys!" Beatie cried. "Let me show you how this is done." She demonstrated the method of artichoke-eating to the boys, who stopped chewing and were watching her intently. Mick finally put his hand to his mouth and removed the huge wad of the 'choke.

"No!" Alexa cried exuberantly. "Same way

39

in, same way out. Use your spoon."

"I didn't put it in with a spoon," Mick said sullenly. "I put in with my fingers, like you showed us."

Beatie immediately got up from her chair. "All right, Alexa!" she said sternly, storming toward her daughter. Beatie's footsteps pounded around the edges of the rug. Knowing what was about to happen, Alexa clouded up as if she were going to cry. "Go to your room. I warned you!" Beatie seized Alexa by the arm and was towing her, whimpering, out of the dining room.

"Now, Mother," Shaughnessy declared after things had gotten quiet again. "I suppose someone's got to administer a little discipline in this household."

The boys looked at each other. Mick smiled bravely.

"She ought to come eat where we do," he said. "They don't even give us a knife."

At this, Shaughnessy roared, "Yes, my word, yes! Maybe she should at that! Here," he said, "I will carve up the pig myself. I take pride on being the finest pig-cutter west of the Hebrides! Do you boys like pig?"

At these reassuring words the feeling of embarrassment that had overcome the boys suddenly blew away as flakes of ash from a hearth. Arthur looked at Mick, who was grinning, studying the pig. It was one thing he had no doubt he knew how to eat.

■ ■ ■ ■

For the very first time in Arthur's life, the entire world spread out around him like a gift, one he was determined not to lose. Never even to let from his sight. He was enrolled in a day school and, as the years passed, his new situation settled on him mostly in ease. Arthur received a generous allowance of a dollar a week that was raised to two dollars when he turned twelve, and not only kept up his butterfly collection but also, at his father's suggestion, took up collecting coins and stamps as well. The elder Shaughnessy taught him how to sail on small boats in Newport, and on vacations in Maine they saw bears and moose along the roads.

Still, Arthur hadn't made any really close friendships with the other boys of the day school. They seemed different, and though they didn't tease or make fun of him for where he came from, they always seemed apart and let Arthur alone. He kept in touch with Mick Martin, though, and every so often Mick would stay over for a weekend at the Shaughnessy house in Boston and sometimes even be invited down to their place at Newport. Mick was Arthur's lone tie with his past and both his father and Beatie thought it best to let him deal with this in his own way. And so the years slipped by and Arthur grew up, a happy boy, if a little shy.

Then came the ordeal at Groton.

As soon as young Arthur had arrived from the orphanage into the Shaughnessy family, the Colonel began to pull strings to get him into the Groton School, just as the Colonel's own father had pulled strings to get him into Harvard. When the time came, at age fourteen, Arthur was packed off, with the Colonel's tales of boarding school grandeur ringing in his ears. Arthur, however, had reservations, not the least of which was that only five years earlier he had finally arrived in the most magnificent household imaginable, only to be shipped off to a place full of strangers, no matter how wealthy and sophisticated they might be.

Colonel Shaughnessy had arranged an imposing entrance into Groton for Arthur. That morning, he timed it precisely so his private railcar would deliver his son to the rail station just as the other boys were arriving on the public trains. For a few moments the ploy seemed to work. Arthur stepped down from the gleaming railcar, with Bomba carrying his bags. A hush came over the throng of Groton boys on the platform while they gaped at this strange person arriving as if from another world, a world different and even more exalted than their own. Then from the back of the crowd someone started it.

"Would Mr. Astor wish his bags to be taken

for him?" came a loud voice.

Everyone took up the cry.

"Would Mr. Astor like his shoes shined?" somebody said to great laughter.

"Could someone arrange for flowers in Mr. Astor's private suites!"

Bomba put on his fiercest expression and parted the derisive crowd, with Arthur tagging behind, mortified.

"Will someone please call Mr. Astor's personal motor coach!" a shout went up.

It was not a good beginning for Arthur Shaughnessy at the Groton School. And in time, no matter how Arthur tried, it only got worse.

When they learned his name, Shaughnessy, there was more mockery. They called him a harp and a bog-trotter and a fish-eater. All the Irish slurs to hurt and embarrass. When Arthur protested that his family was not Catholic, they ridiculed this, too, saying behind his back that this was no better than the Jews changing their names so as to take over the country.

Hazing became an art form.

They short-sheeted his bedclothes and put toads and beetles in his desk drawers in his dorm room. Someone even taped a piece of Limburger cheese to the back of his closet — it took him a week to find the source of the odor. Once he returned from class to find lace curtains put up around his window. Ar-

43

thur became a loner, which of course made it worse. Boys often got the treatment from the Groton elite and were expected to be good-natured about it. But Arthur kept sullenly to himself, thinking that at the orphanage at least they all tried to get along. Then one day the dam burst.

It was the end of the first term, and so far Arthur had made good marks in all of his studies. But when he was called on and stood to read a class paper on the history of the Ostrogoths, he discovered his hands were black after he reached into his satchel. Someone had poured ink into it, ruining the work. Arthur turned red; his breath caught in his throat. He thought he was going to choke. Tears welled in his eyes as his classmates smirked at one another and the instructor stood waiting impatiently. Finally Arthur burst out, "I hate all of you! You're wicked bastards! You're . . . you're . . ."

People began laughing. The instructor marched to Arthur and snatched his wrist and led him from the room to the dean's office for punishment. Arthur could hear the scathing laughter from the classroom all the way down the stairs and out of the building. Back in his room, he stared out of the window until it was dark and even afterward. He envied the birds he saw wheeling in the air and wished he could be like them. When he got back to Boston for the holidays two days later, Arthur informed his father that he would not be returning to Groton.

"You cannot quit, Arthur! It's the worst thing you can do. All boys get hazed at boarding school." They were sitting in the study, the Colonel behind his desk, distressed, Arthur in his chair.

Arthur merely looked at him. The Colonel knew that when Arthur made up his mind it was hard to change it, and tried a different tack.

"Look, son, why don't you think about it over the holidays? Just think about going back for the last term. It might be bad, but then, next year, you'll be an upperclassman. It will let up, I promise you."

Arthur said nothing. He could not begin to explain the indignities he felt had been heaped on him at Groton. He had told his father only that the other boys were rude to him, but could not bear to go into details.

"All right, Arthur," the Colonel said at last. "Just promise me you will think about it — is that fair? It's your decision to make." Even though the Colonel knew Arthur well enough to believe that the situation was bad, he did not like this business of quitting. It could be habit-forming.

Arthur nodded, appreciating this concession by his father. He'd always felt he was treading on thin ice in the Shaughnessy home. To make matters worse, Alexa made

45

him feel like a leper at every opportunity. She declined to introduce him to friends she brought over to the house and, recently, when the Colonel had asked Arthur if he might want to get a dog, she loudly complained that fur made her sneeze.

Beatie and the Colonel, however, were warm, obliging, and kind: the Colonel told him that what he did mattered; Beatie complimented him on his curiosity, and told him that he had a destiny to fulfill, though she had not ventured what it was.

Still, Arthur felt a little knot of anxiety deep down inside him. He'd developed a hunger for a place of his own in the world, and ever since the first day at the Shaughnessys' there was that little lurking fear that it could all be taken away just as fast as it had come. Even though there wasn't a whit of evidence that such a thing might happen, Arthur seemed incapable of severing relations with the harshness of his past, a past weighted with his childhood loneliness.

Next afternoon he went to the Laura Bostwick Home to see Mick Martin. Mick had quit school and at the age of sixteen looked almost like a grown man, tall and muscular, with a handsome rugged face set off by a chiseled nose and a short mustache. Now he ran a lathe in a shoe factory and on the side he had a rather murky job that he didn't much talk about. But from what Arthur guessed, it had to do with one of the gangs that controlled the gambling, shakedowns, and prostitution in Southie.

They took a walk around the old neighborhood. Mick told Arthur he was going to move out of the orphanage pretty soon and find a place of his own. Soon as he got up enough money. He told him he had a girlfriend, too, who worked in the shoe factory. After a while, Arthur told him his own story.

"And so these punks are really laying it to you?" Mick said.

Arthur nodded.

"And you ain't going back."

Arthur shook his head.

"Well, just suppose," Mick said, "that I go up there with you when the classes start again. I don't think any of those little snots are going to fool with you after I give them a talking-to."

Arthur shook his head again. "It's not worth it, Mick, but thank you," he said. Arthur just couldn't see it, not after what they'd done. How they'd treated him. He felt sick to his stomach every time he thought about it.

"So let me ask you this," Mick said. They were stopped at the curb to let a trolley rumble past. "Who's the one who's the ringleader? The one who gives you the most trouble?"

"They all do," Arthur said dejectedly. "I'd

rather be back in Southie than to go back there."

"C'mon, there's got to be a ringleader. There's always a ringleader."

"I don't know," Arthur said. "I guess if it's anybody, it would be Hawkins. He's from Ipswich."

"And you don't want me to go and say hello to Master Hawkins?" Mick asked.

"No, Mick, like I said, it's too late, at least for me."

Mick looked at his friend. He felt terrible for him. With all Arthur had now, all the things he himself could only dream of, and now this unhappiness.

"Well, bucko," Mick said, draping a thick arm over Arthur's shoulder, "you do whatever you think best. That's the thing — the only thing. And now I'm going to take you to a place and buy you a beer."

When school resumed two weeks later, without Arthur's knowledge or consent, Mick Martin boarded a train to Groton. It did not take him long to find Hawkins after he'd asked around. Mick caught Hawkins just outside his residence hall and yanked him behind a tall long hedge, where he administered a fearful beating to the boy, making sure Hawkins fully understood the reason. Hawkins told the headmaster; a search was launched for Hawkins's assailant, and the Boston police came to the Shaughnessy home and questioned Arthur, which was the first time he learned what Mick had done, but he told them nothing. He didn't really lie; besides, all he had were his own suspicions. Still, Arthur did not return to Groton that year or any year, enrolling instead at day school in Boston. His father never let him forget it.

Now, at his desk at the rail yards in Chicago, Arthur sat with a pencil and a pad, trying to compose a response to his father's wire that would convey the mounting crisis at NE&P. Since his father was now aboard *Ajax* where there was no phone, the telegram would have to be worded cautiously, since the worst thing that could happen was some loose-lipped telegraph operator letting it get out that for the second time in its history under the Shaughnessys, the New England & Pacific Railroad Company might not be able to meet its payroll.

The first time this had happened, three years earlier, Arthur's father wriggled off the hook by selling a considerable piece of company property in western Connecticut. He'd realized so much money from the sale that the company was not only flush, but the elder Shaughnessy was able to order the construction of the *Ajax,* which Arthur felt was a wild extravagance.

But his father was always extravagant: the

49

big house in Newport, the enormous ranch in Mexico, the place in Maine, the lavish parties, the safaris and trips to Europe. All that might have been fine while the company was making money. And indeed it had made a great deal of money for a while; so much so that John Shaughnessy was able to fulfill at least his *second*-most ardent wish, which was to be included in that rarefied class of barons such as Gould, Harriman, Hearst, Rockefeller, Stanford, Huntington, Guggenheim, and even J. P. Morgan himself. Although John Shaughnessy was on the outside tier of that august bunch, he was nevertheless a member of the club, which he would not have been had he merely been content to own a codfish fleet and not a railroad company.

The *first* most ardent wish of the elder Shaughnessy, however, would never be realized, and Arthur knew it.

This was that the Old Man would be included in the circle of the Boston Brahmins — Sedgwicks, Lowells, Cabots, Adamses, Lodges, Saltonstalls, and so on — all those elite Yankees with blue blood dating back to the *Mayflower* who would never accept a second-generation Irishman into their class, no matter how much money he had, or that he had adopted the Protestant religion, or even the fact that he had gone to Harvard.

Oh, they were polite enough, all right, when they had to be, at places like the Harvard

Club. But to their own clubs and dining tables Arthur's father was not invited, no matter how large his yacht or grand his parties, which, Arthur understood, was why the Old Man indulged in all this ostentation in the first place. So the elder Shaughnessy had to content himself with the companionship and admiration of the New York, Pittsburgh, and Chicago lords of commerce, whom proper Bostonians considered vulgar. But when the Old Man looked at his social circle, while he wasn't ashamed of it, he was deeply frustrated — perhaps hurt wasn't the word — that no matter what he accomplished, this avenue to the old-line society of Boston would be forever shut off to him.

Arthur's father had actually won the railroad company in a dice game. At that point it was little more than a broken-down two-bit enterprise organized in 1862 to transport munitions and men across northern New England so they could connect up with a major line headed down South where the fighting was. After the war, the New England Northern, the old name of the company, had turned into a milk train, transporting milk from the dairies of western New England to Boston and fish from Boston back across the region. About that same time, however, New England farmland was playing out and the farmers were migrating by the thousands to the Midwest. As a result, less and less milk got to be transported and there was a much-diminished demand for Boston fish. The owner at that time was a man named George Mudd from Hartford It was from Mudd's son, who had become filthy rich from his mother's inheritance, that John Shaughnessy acquired the railroad in the dice game several years after he graduated from college in 1882.

John Shaughnessy didn't much care for fish, or his father, either, for that matter, and so instead of going into the great codfish fleet business as was expected of him, he threw himself full-time into his own railroad enterprise. When he took over, there were ten decrepit locomotives, the aged rolling stock, mostly left over from the Civil War era, and the company was in debt. With loans from his father and several friends, Shaughnessy began rebuilding the New England Northern and expanding it at the same time.

The great rail moguls of the day — Vander-bilts, Harrimans, and Huntingtons — had created their wealth by bringing the railroads to the towns and cities. But now that they had done this, there was no room for competition. So Shaughnessy had the expansive notion that if he could not bring his railroad to the cities, he would bring the cities to his railroad. He quickly grasped that the land and lumber of New England was running out after two hundred years of colonization, and as the farmers began to be forced westward into new territories, he built his track in that same direction. By the 1890s, after his father died, the younger John Shaughnessy had sold the codfish company, invested its proceeds in the railroad, and had pushed the New England Northern out past Chicago, intending to take it all the way to the West Coast. Thus he renamed it the New England & Pacific.

As he laid track across Iowa toward the Dakotas, a fortuitous thing began to happen. Another vast wave of immigrants arrived on American shores, these from Northern Europe: Norwegians, Swedes, Finns, Latvians, and some Germans, too. Shaughnessy, quick to see an opportunity in this, had his people place ads in foreign-language newspapers in New York, Boston, and even in Europe, telling of the great fertile prairies waiting to be homesteaded in America.

The NE&P offered transportation across the country free of charge to any family that would settle on the plains. Not only that, he threw in a free cow, bags of seed, and a handbook on cultivating the land. There were accommodations in the boxcars, along with the families' belongings, the cows, and the seed. By the time Shaughnessy's tracks had reached the Dakotas, there were homesteads and towns all along their wake and the big money soon began rolling in, just as he had expected: the crops and stock the immigrants produced came east and the implements and items they needed as they prospered went west — all on the NE&P. The gamble had paid off.

Arthur had stopped trying to word his telegram and simply sat tapping his desk with the pencil. He looked at the picture of his wife Xenia and thought about phoning Boston, just to talk to her. She'd seemed unusually distant in their last conversations and he couldn't understand why, except he might be spending too much time in Chicago. But more pressing things were now in the air.

His father's cavalier attitude about the company's predicament upset him. Even though his father was known in certain circles as a "man of action," Arthur had observed over time that he could sometimes be paralyzed when confronted with large difficulties — such as the time a few years back when he seemed to come apart after a racehorse stable he owned in upstate New York went bankrupt.

Everybody could see it coming, bad buys in horseflesh and the manager secretly pocketing stud fees for himself, but the Old Man wouldn't act. Wouldn't sell horses or fire the manager. Just said, "One good season at Saratoga and we're back in business." Change seemed beyond him, the older he got. At the time, Arthur thought it would have been smarter if the Old Man had invested in a glue factory or a rendering plant, for all the horses were worth. More and more, the elder Shaughnessy seemed to devote himself to social hobnobbing, lavish entertaining, and improvident travel instead of applying himself to the company. Yet when the big decisions were made, he insisted on being the one to make them.

Except now, this: SEE IF YOU CAN HANDLE IT, the telegram had read. How? Arthur thought. They had a payroll of $388,000 to meet by week's end, plus a $428,000 loan payoff to the National Bank of Boston. Cash on hand was less than $900,000. The Old Man had been in Boston — why for chrissakes wouldn't he go to the president of the bank and get an extension? Arthur knew the answer. The Old Man was embarrassed that it should be known around town — especially in the circles that shunned him — that the great rail mogul Shaughnessy was actually short of cash. So what does he do instead? He goes to Ireland!

Recently Arthur had been doing much reflecting on what had gone wrong with the NE&P, rolling it around in his head like a man rolling a ball bearing on a table. Things certainly had been rosy until the past several years, and then events that were far beyond anyone's control overtook them. For one, Washington politicians had begun to object to the giving away of millions of acres of public land to railroad companies for their rights-of-way. All sorts of outrages found their way into newspaper headlines — railroads owing millions to the government, then demanding insulting extensions of the loans while the owners cavorted around in private Pullmans or disported themselves with the kings and queens of Europe. The entire nation was suddenly up in arms over such abuses of the public trust.

Arthur's father had been the recipient of nearly a thousand miles of free track land until, as the route reached westward through southern South Dakota, he was, quite literally, stopped in his tracks.

The weather in those climes was not being cooperative, either. The first years were good, all considered — including the usual blizzards and droughts — and the sturdy Scandinavians stuck it out, being used to the cold, if not the heat. Then, during the first decade of the new century, the droughts became more frequent and the winters more severe, killing sheep, cows, and pigs.

Worse, tremendous winds blew up out of the Midwest, bringing clouds of choking dust to the Great Plains. Plagues of grasshoppers appeared, devouring every growing thing and in many cases halting the trains because their wheels could not make traction over the hordes of squashed grasshoppers. Soon, a few people began leaving; giving up, turning back. At first it was a trickle, but recently there were more uprooted settlers returning eastward on the company's trains than meat and produce, and many of the little towns the NE&P had spawned, nurtured, and depended upon began to wither and die.

How maddening, to watch all this and not really know what to do. Arthur faced a task of almost heroic proportions. As operations manager he was responsible for everything that went on at NE&P: right-of-way disputes, building track, repairing washed-out track, maintenance of rolling stock and locomotives, acquisitions of new equipment, planning and strategy, the hiring and maintaining of thousands of men, theft from freight cars parked on sidings, loading and unloading, scheduling, payrolls, lawsuits, train wrecks, and, yes, even grasshoppers on the tracks.

And now: SEE IF YOU CAN HANDLE IT.

Arthur snapped the pencil in two. They needed an infusion of cash, and quickly. Sure, the Old Man had assets, but these were now in great part reduced to his playthings — the yacht, the damned cattle ranch in Mexico where he'd go to get away from Arthur's mother and everybody else, the "cottage" in Newport with its thirty-six rooms.

The times Arthur had tried to talk to his father about taking the company public, the Old Man invariably changed the subject. In fact, NE&P was one of the last privately owned railroads in the country. But the Colonel was vehement: "The moment we begin selling shares in this company," he'd railed, "buzzards like Morgan and Harriman and Stanford and Gould will be all over us, secretly buying up our stock until they add us to their private collections, and we'd both be out on our ears. They'd pack the board of directors with their own people and squeeze us out. Then they'd issue more and more stock shares until the value was worthless. I've seen them do it! No, sir! My word! No, sir!"

"But I thought those people were your friends," Arthur had reminded him.

"They are, Arthur, they are. But you know the saying: 'All's fair in love and war.' And business, my boy, *is* war! Besides," he added, "I'd do it to them, if I could."

In this, at least, Arthur conceded that his father was correct. And if the Old Man considered the men he had just mentioned "friends," he truly needed no enemies. Since they had not been able to buy the company out from under him publicly, those great tycoons seemed determined to ruin the NE&P in every way possible. In the great war that was exploding across Europe, the British and French needed all the munitions and supplies they could get from the United States. Obviously these would be transported to the Atlantic ports by rail — but did the

NE&P have a single contract? No. They had been deliberately underbid across the board by such as the New York Central, Union Pacific, Great Northern, Illinois Central, Central Pacific, Southern Pacific, Lackawanna, B&O, and even the lowly Wabash and Rock Island. A single contract was all Arthur needed at the moment to put his company back on track. But no — thanks to the very same people his father had just included as his "friends"! And now he was going to have to go and kiss somebody's ass at the National Bank of Boston because his Old Man didn't want to sully what he considered his reputation by doing it himself.

SEE IF YOU CAN HANDLE IT. Yes, Arthur concluded, I suppose I can; at least for now, but you're not going to like it.

Arthur went to the trash basket and retrieved the telegram. He smoothed it out on his desk and studied it again. It did say, exactly: SEE IF YOU CAN HANDLE IT. And so it in fact gave him the authority. He placed the telegram in his top desk drawer and locked it and rang for his secretary, whom he told to book him a berth on the next train to Boston.

Three days later, when Arthur went to the bank in Boston to renegotiate the loan, the officers balked. He'd expected it.

They wanted to see the company books;

Arthur didn't want that.

They persisted.

He figured they would. But he had come to them with an alternative that from the instant he came up with it in Chicago seemed crazed — he would offer them collateral instead: a new note with the Colonel's prized *Ajax* as security.

The stiff-collared old men were struck silent by this suggestion. They all knew of the Colonel's famous yacht, "grander than the one owned by the King of England"; its picture had been in the newspapers and whenever it sailed into Boston it was the talk of the town. None of them had been invited on it, of course, because none of them ever invited the Colonel into *their* private domains, but they knew it was a very magnificent piece of property, worth more than the loan. After a short whispering conference in a corner, the bankers accepted. Officially, the *Ajax* was owned by the NE&P; Arthur had brought the title with him. Papers were signed. As Arthur was leaving the room, one of the bankers thought to ask: "Where is the boat now?"

"On its way to Ireland with Father," Arthur replied.

Again, the room fell into a sort of electrified silence.

"But he cannot remove the collateral property outside the country," the man gasped. "The agreement specifies it."

Arthur stood facing the man, who seemed as though his collar were beginning to choke him.

"You must cable him and tell him to return at once."

"You tell him," Arthur said, handing the man a slip of paper with the *Ajax*'s wireless call signals. Then he smiled, bowed politely, and left the bankers in their boardroom.

FOUR

Late in the afternoon of the same day, and thousands of miles to the south, deep in the Mexican state of Chihuahua, General Francisco "Pancho" Villa nudged his horse over the top of a gently rolling ridge to survey a wide expanse of green that spread out from him as far as he could see. Grazing on the plains below, tens of thousands of brownish red cattle, practically motionless, appeared as figurines placed in a painting.

General Villa was not thinking at this moment about stealing these cattle. Instead, his mind was on Halley's Comet, which had appeared to him in 1910, the very evening he crossed the Rio Grande at El Paso with his pitifully small band of followers to join the Great Revolution.

They had all heard of this spectacular comet, but, seeing it then for the first time, Villa took it as a bad omen, for reasons he did not himself fully comprehend. And as he reflected on this now, after five more years of killing, it seemed he'd been correct. His Grand Army of the North, once fifty thousand strong, was fading away to nothing, like the comet that had arced briefly across the sky, never to return again in his lifetime.

As these disturbing notions passed through Villa's mind he heard a horse come up slowly behind him, then stop.

"You want me to give the signal, General?" asked a voice belonging to his most trusted aide, General Rudolfo Fierro, known by everyone as "the Butcher," a sobriquet that by rights should have belonged to Villa, since he had actually owned a butcher shop in Chihuahua City before the Great Revolution. But Fierro came by his nickname honestly, too, as a butcher of men, not beef, and trouble seemed to follow him like a cloud of flies on a steer.

Villa nodded, and a few moments later a pistol shot rang out. From his vantage point Villa watched as a dozen of his horsemen trotted out from behind a swale and crossed the green plains toward a large herd of the cattle.

"Well, General Fierro, tonight at least we won't have to eat beans again."

Villa was a big, stocky man with huge shoulders, a thick neck, and a bushy mustache, and it was said that when you looked into his eyes you could see the lights of a freight train bearing down on you.

"No," Fierro said. "You know whose cows it is we are taking here?"

"Some rich gringo named Shaughnessy. I guess it's still him. He stole this place from the people twenty-five years ago. We should have brought more men and got the whole herd."

"I was just thinking that myself. But that's a lot of beefs," Fierro said. "How many you suppose?"

"Who knows? Hundred — two hundred thousand? How can you count them? They're moving all the time. You can't see far enough to see them all, either. This place goes on nearly to the mountains."

"You know what that many beefs would bring in El Paso?" asked the Butcher.

"*Would* have brought," Villa reminded him.

Another reason he was sour on things today. All through the years the Americanos on the border had left him a free hand, allowed him to ship millions of rounds of ammunition and boxcar loads of rifles, machine guns, cannons, cars, and even airplanes and coal for his railroads. They had been betting on him in Washington in those days, but now the times had changed. The border was closed both ways.

In the beginning, the general's acrimony had been visited on the Spanish, because they were the symbol in Mexico of all the stinking foreigners since the days of Cortés. For the four hundred years they'd been in power, the Spanish and their descendants treated the people as if they were beneath contempt, which to the Spanish they were. So Villa's first move was to get rid of the Spanish, first by threats, then by carrying out the threats and confiscating their vast properties and even killing them — at least the ones who raised objections. There were also the *latifundistas,* the rich Mexicans. The *latifundistas* had allied themselves with the Spaniards, and so they came next.

And then there was the matter of the Chinamen.

Villa did not like the Chinamen any more than he liked the Spaniards or the rich Mexicans. In fact, he liked them so little that he had corralled and slaughtered more than six hundred in one afternoon in the state of Sonora. The Chinamen had been brought in by the Spanish, rich Mexicans, and Americans to work in the gold and silver mines, thereby displacing even the poorest Mexicans, but after a time most of the Chinamen quit the mines and began opening restaurants and laundries. But Chinese food made the Mexicans sick, which didn't help matters. In any case, there were now six hundred fewer Chinamen in Northern Mexico.

But so far as Americans went, Villa's attitude had been more or less "live and let live."

That is, until recently.

He had not wished to rile the Americans because, after all, he needed the military equipment that the U.S. arms factories such as Colt, Remington, and Winchester had been so willing to sell him at the El Paso border. Besides, Villa had even come to be on good terms with the American general in command there, who thought Villa was a splendid fellow and communicated this opinion personally to President Woodrow Wilson in Washington, D.C.

But in the past few months everything had changed. The Americans recalled the good old general and replaced him with a stinking customs agent named Cobb, and the honeymoon was over — no arms shipments, no selling stolen cattle across the border, no —

Fierro pointed ahead. "Look there!" Fierro was a tall, swarthy man, with a mustache that drooped down almost to his chin and beady weasel eyes. Furthermore, one of his eyelids sagged, which gave him a curiously untrustworthy look. He was the kind of man who exuded meanness. When he looked at you it was through mean eyes, and when he smiled it was through mean lips, and when he laughed, there was meanness in his laughter.

Down on the plains, Villa could see his men beginning to round up the cattle. They must have had a hundred head or so cut off and were herding them back up to the low hills.

Far to the southeast they could barely make out the sprawling hacienda that, from this distance, appeared to the lens of the eye as a frozen configuration of miniature buildings set amid a miniature copse of trees. In fact the hacienda covered more than half a square mile, employed more than two hundred people, and some of the trees were actually a hundred fifty feet tall. But Villa could clearly make out the dust of a number of horsemen, apparently barreling full-tilt toward Villa's cattle rustlers.

"Well, now," Villa said, "there's some vaqueros in for a big surprise."

FIVE

Two thousand miles to the northeast, the owner of the Mexican cattle stood aboard a great yacht that lay at anchor in the harbor of Newport, Rhode Island. It was one of the largest private yachts in the world. John McGill Shaughnessy had named his ship *Ajax,* after one of the recently built British dreadnought-class battleships. In fact, if the Colonel had it his way, he would have preferred that it *had* been a battleship.

The Colonel stood on the bridge of *Ajax,* smiling with pride while his guests debarked from half a dozen motorized tenders belonging to the ship. He watched with satisfaction as they were piped aboard with the same military formality that might have attended the real battleship *Ajax.*

The blue-green waters of Newport shimmered in the setting sun. The Colonel resisted an urge to step up to the glistening varnish and polished brass of the bridge panel and begin barking orders down the tube. Too grandiose a gesture even for him, since the captain, second officer, and several of the bridge crew all stood on deck watching the guests board.

The Colonel's guests for this evening's formal stag dinner represented the titans of American industry: steel barons, steamship owners, railroad magnates, mining czars, automobile and manufacturing kings, as well as practically every major broker with a seat on the New York Stock Exchange.

That he could command the attendance of such a stellar audience was a source of continuous conceit for the Colonel, because only one generation earlier his father, Shamus McGill O'Shaughnessy, had stepped off a cheap boat fleeing the Irish potato famine with a handful of royal crowns in his pocket. The timing was perfect — smack at the beginning of the American Civil War. After exchanging his coinage for what amounted to fifty dollars, the Colonel's father used most of his American money to purchase things he believed U.S. troops might want in the field.

Before long he established himself as one of the most prominent sutlers with the Union Army. Afterward, with wads of greenbacks in his back pocket and after dropping the *O* from O'Shaughnessy, he became a lawyer, then a United States senator, and the owner of a vast codfish fleet. "Only in America," the Colonel was fond of saying of his father, old

Shamus McGill. And to hell with the so-called Boston aristocrats!

In 1898 that same son of old Shamus, the son who was standing now on the deck of the *Ajax*, raised a squadron of Massachusetts cavalry and led them hell-for-leather afoot up San Juan Hill with Theodore Roosevelt's Rough Riders in the Spanish-American War. And follow Shaughnessy they did, struggling up as Spanish lead came raining down. Teddy Roosevelt may have ridden a horse, but the rest slogged up the hard way.

That was how he came to be called the "Colonel" — even though Shaughnessy was never officially ranked higher than captain. Nowadays, like all other upstanding industrialists, the Colonel detested Theodore Roosevelt and his Bull Moosers for their suicidal trustbusting and other inconveniences. His former friend and comrade-in-arms Roosevelt was definitely not one of the guests on the *Ajax* this evening, or any other evening, for that matter.

But the Colonel was still a Rough Rider and always would be. In his younger days he played polo but now contented himself with riding the Myopia Hunt. A crack shot, he went on African safaris for lion, rhinoceros, elephant, and practically every other type of game, large or small — from gnu to eland to dik-diks — and the stuffed heads of all these adorned the remarkable room in his Back Bay

70

home. The Colonel believed in fair play, hard work, bravery, and practical jokes.

Once, from Zambia, he had shipped a friend a pair of live twelve-foot-long crocodiles, with instructions for an accomplice at home to have them placed in the friend's swimming pool in Newport. When it was discovered that the pool had been drained for repairs, the crocodiles had to be stored in their crates in the basement of the Colonel's club in Boston. There the stewards washed them down daily with pails of water and fed them raw meat until the pool was finally filled and the joke played out.

And so as this marvelous assemblage of American capitalism marched up the gang-plank and onto the decks of the *Ajax* the Colonel's breast swelled with pride and authority. If a bomb were to blow them all up right now, he thought — not inconceivable, since there was a lot of bombing going on just then — half the wealth of the United States would sink to the bottom of Newport Harbor. In any case, Colonel Shaughnessy was looking forward with the greatest delight to the joke he intended to play upon the gods of industry and society that evening. If his scheme went as planned they'd be writing about it till Christmas.

SIX

In Chihuahua the cattle rustlers were already driving their booty back toward the rolling hills where Pancho Villa and his detachment sat watching them. The band of horsemen from the hacienda were closing in fast, but the rustlers seemed unperturbed and continued driving the cows at a leisurely pace.

"Please send for Señor Mix," Villa said. Fierro barked an order, and presently a tall, lean, good-looking young man with slicked-black hair and dark flashing eyes rode up on a palomino and saluted Villa. Six months earlier Tom Mix had been just another bored cowhand back in Arizona. In his idle moments, Mix harbored visions of someday becoming a movie-star cowboy but, along with a handful of other American soldiers of fortune, he'd thrown in with Villa's army hoping to come away with enough cash to get his start in Hollywood.

"Take two machine gun squads and cut off those vaqueros," Villa instructed. Mix saluted and wheeled back down the far side of the hill, where about four hundred of his Villistas were resting, grazing their animals, lying on the ground, drinking mescal, smoking, joking, and engaging in other leisurely pursuits. Mix spoke to them in a combination of pidgin Spanish and sign language and the men began to rise and collect their weapons.

It made Mix feel important that he could command obedience from this mob. He'd joined Villa with little more than a second-hand revolver, a dented Winchester .30-caliber rifle, and a trick horse, but in a short time his industriousness, bravery, and pleasant manners got him promoted as a key aide to the general.

Villa called him "my gringo fireman."

The little band of hacendados riding from the ranch was now about halfway between the cattle rustlers and their path back to Villa's position, but the distance to them was closing fast. Then off to his right Villa saw Tom Mix's detachment of machine gunners with an escort of a dozen riflemen tear out from the swale, the horsemen leading four big mules that carried the German Schloss machine guns and ammunition in their packs, so that now there were three groups of horsemen, seemingly converging on one another.

Although the hacendados were farthest away, they were much faster than the rustlers and the machine gunners with the pack mules in tow, but the little situation below was developing just as Villa expected. The hacendados must have by now seen the new detachment but they did not slow down. The sun had sunk low on the horizon and reflected off a bank of big gray clouds to cast an infernal glow over the entire landscape.

"They better hurry," Fierro said, but it was unclear whether he referred to the rustlers or the machine gunners. Suddenly the cloud of dust behind the hacendados quickly enveloped them as they drew to a halt. Nothing stirred in the air, not even the faintest breeze. The machine gunners continued and the rustlers were shouting, waving, and trying to get the cattle to move faster. Then, quite suddenly, the hacendados got on the move again, split into two groups; one rode directly for the rustlers, the other arced toward the machine gunners, the two groups acting as a sort of pincers.

Now a new figure arrived at Villa's side. General Vargo Santo — "the Saint," as he was known in the army. Santo was one of Villa's principal military advisors, having grown up in France and been educated at Saint-Cyr, the French version of West Point.

Vargo Santo had been faithful to Pancho Villa and the revolution since the beginning, all through the fabulous victories of the early years and even now through the recent defeats, and, as a military scientist, had taken a keen interest in the tactical developments in the great war in Europe, particularly in the use of defenses such as trenches and barbed wire and the machine gun.

"Well, General, a nice little show coming along down there," Santo commented. An unremarkable-looking man with a graying mustache and light green eyes that betrayed him as a mixed-Creole and probably of the aristocratic classes, both of which Villa despised. But Villa was not one to look a gift horse in the mouth, and when Santos resigned from the Federal Army and offered his services to the revolution, he was glad to have him.

"We haven't had a fight in more than a month," Villa replied. "Not even a bloody fuss like this. I'm looking forward to it."

Santo nodded. Villa had many pithy mottoes, which Santo had endured over the years, and one of them was: "Try to eat a little shit every day, just so you don't lose the taste for it."

The first group of hacendados now closed quickly on the flank of the rustlers.

Mix had evidently seen the hacendados split up and shifted his course to get between them and the cattle herd. Now the cowboy slowed and began to unload his mules, the machine gunners rushing to unlimber their guns. The riflemen, most of them still on their horses, began pointing their weapons toward the approaching hacendados, and soon little puffs of white smoke could be seen, followed by the faint echoes of gunfire.

"Now we teach these vaqueros something," Fierro said with relish, as if he wished to the highest heavens he were down in the fray. Whatever else had created Rudolfo Fierro, war and killing enhanced and refined it until it was commonly said he could kill a man with no more qualm than swatting an insect. Once, in the early years, he shot one of his own soldiers through the eye while sitting in a street café at Chihuahua City. He had done this on a bet from someone that he could not hit a man in the eye with a single shot from a pistol at the distance of across the street. Fierro generously donated the proceeds of the bet to the victim's widow.

Suddenly it was apparent to Villa and the other two generals that Mix had gone wrong.

The American cowboy had set up to block the pincers movement of the hacendados but failed to defend his rear. Surely he must have seen the split-up; obviously the first prong of hacendados would reach the rustlers and their catch momentarily, which was just what happened.

While Mix's men frantically toiled to assemble and operate the machine guns, the hacendados pitched into the band of rustlers and, outnumbering them three to two, began a small battle. Unable to both fight and control the herd, the rustlers tried to assemble themselves into something like a fighting unit, but by now it was too late. The hacendados were upon them.

"Shit," Villa spat. Four or five of his men either dropped from their horses or the horses toppled over.

Meanwhile, the pincer prong of the hacendados came within firing range of Mix's machine guns, which opened up on them with devastating effect. The gunners were aiming low so as to cut down the horses, and after a few brief bursts only three or four hacendados remained in their saddles. Finally realizing the firepower they faced, they beat a hasty retreat. Mix had forestalled defeat in five seconds and five hundred rounds.

"Must've thought they were dealing with a bunch of scruffy bandits," Villa remarked with an air of relief, turning his attention back to the herd and the fight going on there. Fierro wheeled his horse and was waving and shouting something to the main band below, but Villa interceded.

"Too late," he said. "Don't worry about it. We can take all this gringo's cattle whenever we want. Don't waste the time."

By now the hacendados had driven the rustlers back toward the hill in a sort of running battle and, perceiving their job as finished, they broke off and began trotting back toward the ranch. The herd, panicked by the gunfire, was stampeding, twisting and turning like a swarm of bees. Mix and his men were watching the action but were too far away to be of help.

"Your Señor Mix don't seem to appreciate an envelopment tactic," Fierro commented disgustedly.

"No," Villa replied, "he's young. He's got a lot to learn."

"We can teach him," Santo offered.

"We can," Villa sneered. "But first I'm gonna teach those gringo hacendados something they won't forget for a while. And I guarantee you, we will not be eating beans tonight."

SEVEN

Huge generators hummed and electric lights shone brightly aboard *Ajax* as the festivities got under way. A hundred or more business potentates in their dinner jackets drank from crystal glasses of rye, scotch, champagne, and the finest wines of France. Stewards dressed in the distinctive salmon-and-gray uniforms the Colonel had tailor-made for his yacht served Russian caviar and smoked fish and duck pâté on silver trays.

The Colonel stationed himself on the promenade deck leading to the grand salon, profusely greeting and mingling with the host of Harrimans, Goulds, Rockefellers, Fords, Guggenheims, Vanderbilts, Mellons, Whitneys, Hearsts, Dodges, Lehmanns, and other luminaries, who, in their turn, complimented the Colonel on his fine ship and splendid hospitality. His guests also knew that his favorite baseball team, the Boston Red Sox, had just won the World Series, and since the Colonel had always made such a big thing of it, they congratulated him on that, too.

One of those on board was a man named Claus Strucker. Tall, immaculately dressed in a dark spruce-colored velvet dinner jacket, charming, and with a platinum-rimmed monocle fixed in his left eye, Strucker was a wealthy German industrialist and member of the New York Yacht Club, which was where the Colonel had encountered him some years before. He was also a commissioned captain in the German Naval Intelligence Service Reserve, and was on his own mission that was closely held business between him and his country.

Of course, the Colonel knew nothing of this; he and Claus Strucker had a long history of association ever since Strucker turned up at the Yacht Club in a handsome, varnished thirty-two-meter sloop — suave, debonair, and impressive with the "ladies." In those days the Colonel was sometimes — perhaps more than sometimes — apt to be seen in private — and sometimes in public — with a woman not his wife. Strucker often not only enabled these trysts by making introductions, but also served as a "beard" in case word should somehow get back to Beatie.

It was not an entirely foolproof ruse, however, and caused a terrible row in the Colonel's family eleven years earlier when he was caught conducting an affair with an actress.

Beatie stopped sleeping with him then and joined the temperance movement, and now she occupied a place in his life not unlike the *Ajax*. All that notwithstanding, the Colonel had maintained his acquaintance with Strucker because he usually found the German quite entertaining in an obsequious kind of way, and they would often reminisce in private over their former exploits.

For his part, Strucker had ulterior motives in joining the affair that evening, to which he had in fact invited himself. His country was at war in Europe — all over the world, in fact — and Strucker's interest in Colonel John Shaughnessy had more to do with his big spread down in Mexico than any damn yachting party. Truth was, a Junker like Strucker could make trouble even while he was just sitting there.

Seeing Strucker board the *Ajax* brought much of the past back to the Colonel and, as all the guests were aboard, he went up to the ship's bridge with a cigar and glass of scotch to watch the casting-off operations. The scotch went down smoothly and warm and, for some reason, on the dim outskirts of the conversational buzz below, he began to consider his life and times.

Never mind the chilled relations between them now, Mrs. Shaughnessy had provided the Colonel with two children, the first of whom, Alexa, turned out a disappointment.

Now thirty-four, she had never married and led a dissolute life in New York City. The adopted one, Arthur, who had come to them at age nine and was now thirty-two, had married and sired him two grandchildren, which made the Colonel exceedingly pleased.

But Arthur was in many respects all the things the Colonel was not, and it often pained him. What he had hoped for in Arthur was a mirror of himself, but he might have known it wouldn't happen, since the boy wasn't his own flesh and blood.

Those things the Colonel enjoyed, Arthur did not, and either buried himself in his collections of stamps, coins, and, yes, *butterflies,* or, more recently, devoted himself to tinkering with the *Grendel,* that infernal flying machine of his. Once, when Arthur was no more than eleven and had lived with the Shaughnessys for two years, the Colonel had tired of his excuses for not wanting to ride or box or shoot or play rough sports and determined to get to the root causes.

Shaughnessy had demanded of the orphanage that they turn over the names of Arthur's true parents so that he could investigate them himself. The orphanage refused, even in the face of veiled threats to cut off his generous donations, but in the end Shaughnessy was somewhat relieved.

What if he had discovered Arthur was the child of a thief or prostitute or spies or worse?

No, he would work with what he had, and work Arthur he did, trying without success to remold him in his own image. The boy was maddening sometimes; he tried hard to please, yet let you know his heart wasn't really in it.

It became apparent that Arthur had developed his own personality while in the orphanage and changing it would be difficult, if not impossible. Still, the Colonel had to pay a kind of grudging respect to his adoptive son. Even though he quit Groton, which, for all intents, removed him from consideration for Harvard, he'd worked hard at Boston College (though Beatie went into conniptions because it was a Jesuit school) and slaved at the railroad business until the Colonel began to depend on him for sound decisions and advice. Yet he remained disappointed that Arthur had not turned out to be the companion he needed in his later life, someone to ride and hunt and fish with, someone who shared his views, political, economic, and social.

The mirror, a perfect mirror, of himself.

Presently, dinner was served. The well-oiled guests, including Claus Strucker, who had consumed half a dozen glasses of schnapps, trooped into the ship's dining hall, where a huge feast had been prepared. Strucker took note that the tables were set in the finest Irish linen and the mahogany chairs were covered in salmon and gray velvet with a big *A* for *Ajax* embroidered on the backs. The columns were strung with fresh green smilax and bright drooping ferns.

Following the elegant soups, salads, oysters, scallops, and crab meat, enormous trays of roast venison, partridge, pheasant, duck, hams, Atlantic salmon, mountain trout, halibut, swordfish, and lobster were offered. The wine flowed freely, as usual. At last, when coffee and desserts were being delivered, the Colonel took to a podium and over a newfangled broadcast system opened a speech.

"Gentlemen, we are gathered here this evening for a bit of relaxation," he began, then hesitated. "While our ladies are at home, devising ways to spend our hard-earned dollars."

There was much applause and the Colonel continued. "However, we must never forget that the price of liberty to conduct our affairs in such a way to make this great nation prosper is . . . eternal vigilance!"

Strucker, sitting twelve guests away, put down his dessert fork and made a mental note of this remark.

More applause, as the Colonel warmed to his subject. He inveighed against the current horrors that were on everyone's lips: the infernal federal income tax, Mexico, socialism, unionism, anarchism, trustbustingism, notions of alcohol prohibition and women's suffrage — but nothing, Strucker observed, about the war in Europe. The speech had gone on for half an hour when the *Ajax* began a low vibration and a deep shudder emanated from far belowdecks. At this, many of the dinner guests seemed alarmed and looked at one another. Signaling a crew officer, the Colonel leaned off the podium for a moment, then addressed his audience.

"Gentlemen," he said reassuringly, "there is no problem to concern yourselves with. I have just been informed that a severe storm is reported off Nantucket Island, headed this way. I have been advised by the harbormaster to weigh anchor and remove *Ajax* to the open seas so as not to run the danger of grounding. We will put in safely at Boston Harbor first thing in the morning."

Immediately there began a low mumbling from the guest tables, since many of these men had important duties to attend to at their offices — duties that involved millions of dollars, contracts, mergers, businesses to run. But the Colonel, smiling, waved them silent.

"There are comfortable cabins aboard for all of you, and when we arrive at Boston one of my trains will be on hand to carry you back to Newport, New York, Pittsburgh, Philadelphia — wherever you wish to go. The harbormaster has already notified your drivers ashore of the situation, and any of you wishing to send telegraph messages may use the wireless station on the bridge deck. So please, let us finish with the evening's program. Have another drink and enjoy a comfortable night on the high seas, courtesy of the New England & Pacific Railroad Company!"

This information seemed to calm the guests as the *Ajax* steamed past the rock-perched beacons guarding Newport Harbor and out toward the dark Atlantic Ocean. The guests relit their cigars, drained their brandy glasses, called for more, and settled back for the remainder of the voyage and the Colonel's address. A little past midnight Shaughnessy finally wound up to thundering applause from the dining room coterie, which to a man agreed with everything he said — even the German spy Strucker, who, in his drunkenness, had dropped his monocle into a dish of custard.

Before the Colonel closed the ceremonies he asked that certain members of the guest party remain behind. He ticked off their names: Whitney, Hearst, Harriman, Guggenheim, Buckley, and others. They were singled out for this distinction because, like the Colonel, they had a vested interest — a very large vested interest — in the present goings-on in Mexico.

These families and a few more owned practically the entire northern part of that country that adjoined the United States — millions and millions of acres that, for a quarter century and more, they exploited for ranching, farming, mining, railroads, and the like. Now the Colonel had some news he wished to give them.

Shaughnessy led the way to a smaller parlor in which a fireplace had been lit, and more brandy was poured. The Colonel had the select group seated when, just before the doors closed, Strucker appeared in the companionway and lurched in without asking if he could join them. "I am always interested in Mexico," the German said, "and perhaps I can be enlightened by your information. I have thought of buying a house there somewhere, perhaps on the Pacific Coast." This seemed harmless enough, and Colonel Shaughnessy showed him to a seat, into which he plopped unceremoniously. Then he noticed on a small bar several bottles of whiskey and liquor. He began to rise toward them but his arms failed him and he sank back resignedly into the deep leather chair.

"Something is happening down in the state of Chihuahua," the Colonel told them in slow, measured words. "My reports are not precisely clear, but I have a man — a nameless man, mind you — who has access to the office of Mr. Bryan," the Colonel said, referring to the U.S. Secretary of State, William

Jennings Bryan. "And he tells me there is going to be a shift in our Mexico policy.

"As you know," the Colonel continued, "we have all tried to get along with this fellow Pancho Villa. We have arranged for shipments to be made to him for his military operations. We have repaired his railroad trains in our yards at a discount and with credit. We have freighted him millions of tons of coal for his engines. We have loaned him money for medical supplies. We have paid taxes and duties to him — bribed him, if you will — for the oil and minerals and timber and cattle we raise down there . . . and we all know that in exchange for this, he and his men have left our interests in Mexico alone. So far . . ."

The Colonel looked at a scrap of paper in his hands and cleared his voice. "Now, however, because some military reverses have befallen General Villa, it seems as if President Wilson — our *schoolteacher* in the White House — may have decided to recognize General Carranza as the legitimate president of Mexico. What will happen now?" the Colonel asked. A grumbling of disbelief filled the room as this news sank in.

The Colonel answered his own question. "I fear," he said, "that Villa may no longer be willing to respect our position vis-à-vis our property. We all know he is a bandit at heart, even though the press portrays him as a great revolutionary savior, or some such nonsense.

Now, I have met Mr. Villa personally on several occasions and our discourse was always pleasant and conciliatory. And yet I ask myself, what is to stop him from looting our interests? He still commands an army of some sort. I tell you, gentlemen, I own nearly one million acres of ranchland down there, upon which there are some hundred thousands head of cattle, and I shudder — *shudder* — at the idea that Pancho Villa and his people have had their eyes on them for quite a while now. My word, gentlemen, this calls for action."

In other, less auspicious gatherings, this news might have provoked a panic of sorts, but these were cool men. The captains — no, admirals — of industry in the greatest industrial nation on earth, and they did the only sensible thing that might have been expected of them. To a man, they got up and ran to the bar for another drink.

Herr Strucker was astonished by their reaction, these so-called American tycoons who went for whiskey at the first sign of trouble. Strucker had known some of these men socially, but this was his first inside glance at how they behaved when the chips were down. What, he thought, would they do when the helm was hard down and water coming in over the lee rail — scramble down to the cabin like scaredy-cats and take a drink? He knew what his own countrymen would do in similar circumstances. They would immediately demand war! And have this Mexican's head on a pike at the end of a week.

When some attitude of calm had been restored, the Colonel continued his address.

"I think we all understand what the destiny of Northern Mexico finally must be," he told them. "We must bring it into American hands. Why, my word, we own most of it by deed already, but we're constantly frustrated and even threatened by some tinhorn dictator-of-the-moment down in Mexico City. This is no way to run a business enterprise, is it?

"Naturally," Colonel Shaughnessy continued, "the left-wing press will scream that we're just a bunch of jingoistic imperialists. Well, let them — they're right! We proved that when the great Texas patriot Sam Houston kicked the bloodthirsty dictator Santa Anna back to where he came from, and again seventeen years later when we had to send our army to capture Mexico City. What would be the fate of Texas now, or for that matter Arizona, New Mexico, and California, if the Mexicans were still in charge of it? Same as the fate of the rest of Mexico, which is a state of eternal war! We must stand together in this, no matter what it takes, no matter what the sacrifice, personal or financial. What is at stake here, gentlemen, is nation-building!" the Colonel thundered.

"And nation-building is what America is about!"

These remarks by Colonel Shaughnessy were much more to Strucker's liking, though he noticed that most of the others did not applaud, and some seemed to look dismayed, but even through the haze of smoke and gin at least he thought he'd found in the Colonel a man of action, a man who might be useful — to the *German* cause.

In the early morning hours, after everyone else had gone to bed, the Colonel poured himself a nightcap in a very private little anteroom off his private suite on the ship. Only two or three of the *Ajax* crew even knew the room existed, and no one was let in without permission. The room was quite small, with but a single port. On the walls hung personal mementos from the Colonel's life and career: military photos from the Rough Rider days, college baseball and football pictures, scenes from a safari, and a shot of the Colonel on his favorite horse. The only furniture in the room was an overstuffed black leather chair, a side table, and a lamp.

He sat in the chair sipping his drink and wondering what Arthur's reaction had been to his telegram: SEE IF YOU CAN HANDLE IT.

He knew their situation was critical, but neither, to the Colonel's way of thinking, was it grave. He was being squeezed, both professionally with the NE&P and personally. He had been extravagant lately and his personal finances were quite thin right now. But there were many ways out — the most immediate and obvious of which was to postpone the note due to National Bank of Boston. But be damned if he'd go over there, hat in hand, and reveal his predicament to those pompous bastards.

It would be all over town. Of course, it would get all over town, too, when Arthur went there — as the Colonel knew he must — but Arthur had a way of explaining things that the Colonel did not enjoy. Say what you would, the boy *could* handle it.

When the Colonel went in for a loan, he simply marched up to the president of the bank and said, "Phillip, I want you to put a million in the NE&P account tomorrow," and it would be done, and later the legal papers would follow. The Colonel greatly delighted in this kind of power and pull. Now it would have to be explained why NE&P needed an extension on such a loan, and that would be sticky business. Questions would be asked that could lead someplace he did not wish them to lead. Arthur was far better at explaining such things, while he himself would probably just harrumph around and maybe even get belligerent and cause a row.

As far as the long-term went, Shaughnessy

was confident things would work themselves out. They always had. Building the railroad up he'd experienced many reverses, yet when things seemed darkest, something always intervened to pull them through. What it would be this time, he did not know — the munitions contracts, perhaps; another wave of immigrants to whom he could resell the notion of western homesteading, just as he had to the others. Or perhaps something else he hadn't even considered. The Colonel had always been lucky in his life.

After all, didn't he win the railroad in a dice game in the first place?

In the center of the room was a polished walnut stand upon which sat a complicated mechanical device housed in a large glass dome; it was silent now but by ten a.m. would begin spouting out ticker tape with quotations from the New York Stock Exchange. The Colonel sat in his chair and stared at the ticker tape machine and sipped his final brandy of the night. By the time the machine began clattering out its first morning messages, the dinner guests would be shaking off their hangovers to the realization that they had become the latest victims of the Colonel's most elaborate practical joke to date. They would have arisen expecting to look out their portholes to see Boston Harbor or at least the sight of land. But all that would greet them would be the ocean swells of the North

Atlantic.

He was relishing this prospect when there came a hesitant tapping at his door. He got up and unlocked it to find the captain of *Ajax* standing there, hat in one hand and a piece of message paper in another.

"Sorry to disturb you, sir," the captain said, "we just received this. You told me you insist on hearing controversial news immediately."

Colonel Shaughnessy took the piece of paper and shut the door, leaving the captain outside. He read it in disbelief, face turning beet-red, feeling first a wave of panic, then anger surge over him. He slammed his fist against the bulkhead wall and crumpled the paper in his hand.

"Goddamn it!" he spat, throwing the wadded-up message paper on the floor. He paced around for a few moments, once looking out of the lone porthole, where all he could see was empty ocean. He flung open the door to find the captain was still standing there, hat still in his hand.

"All right, damn it!" he muttered. "Turn us around. Take us to Boston. And say nothing to anyone about this!"

EIGHT

Johnny Ollas had spent the afternoon skinning a cow at the Hacienda Valle del Sol,
Colonel Shaughnessy's preposterous ranch in
a remote part of the Mexican state of Chihuahua nearly two hundred miles from the
American border at El Paso, Texas.

Johnny Ollas did not often occupy himself
in cow-skinning, but he needed a new set of
chaps and this was the most convenient way
to get them. Around Valle del Sol, Johnny Ollas was something of a *gran hombre*. In addition to being a cowhand, he aspired to be a
great matador. A decade ago, the Colonel had
decided to enter the bullfighting business by
acquiring one of the premier stud fighting
bulls in all Mexico; Toro Malo was his name.

Toro Malo weighed nearly sixteen hundred
pounds, large for a fighting bull, and had so
far sired four hundred ninety-eight progeny,
the sale of which had earned the Colonel
nearly three hundred thousand dollars. Toro
Malo now occupied a pasture to himself and

was in the sole charge of Johnny Ollas, who loved the old animal like a pet.

Johnny Ollas was also the personal ward of the Colonel himself. Three years after Shaughnessy purchased the ranch from the Mexican government — at the going rate in American money of fifteen cents an acre — the manager had found a naked day-old baby boy lying in a drainage ditch, surrounded by dogs.

Word was that the mother had fled to Texas in disgrace after having the illegitimate child. The manager brought the baby to Valle del Sol, and during one of the Colonel's visits there he took compassion on the infant and instructed the manager, an Oklahoman named Callahan, to see to it he was reared and schooled in a proper fashion.

Manager Callahan took this task upon himself and he and his wife raised Johnny Ollas along with the rest of their brood — even named him after Colonel John Shaughnessy, his patron. From then on, the Colonel always took an interest in Johnny's development, and on his annual visits to Valle del Sol he spent time with the boy and over the years grew quite fond of him.

Several years earlier, Johnny had taken a wife, Donatella, whom everyone called Donita. She was a true beauty whom Johnny had met in San Miguel de Allende, where he had gone to buy saddles. She was a Creole of

Spanish descent, of a social class well above an orphaned Mexican ranch hand, but, despite her parents' objections, Donita became taken by Johnny's handsomeness and charm and the rumor that he would one day become a great matador.

But it had not all worked out the way she wished. First, she discovered that being a bullfighter meant being away most of the time, and often Johnny did not take her with him. In a way, this was a relief, because she found herself increasingly fearful when she watched him in the ring. But neither did she like being left alone for such long periods. She felt it would be better if he stayed on at the ranch and she was certain that if he did, one day the Colonel would make him ranch manager. That was a good, solid job. Being outspoken, Donita and Johnny could be heard arguing on many occasions, and it was generally agreed around the hacienda that she usually had the better of it.

That morning, lying in bed, he had wanted to make love, but, still angry over one of their arguments the night before, Donita had pushed him away. In any case, Johnny had gone to skin his cow in the courtyard of Valle del Sol when the warning sounded that rustlers were on the premises.

Johnny Ollas the matador was no *pistolero* and so did not respond to Callahan's call for arms to rout the cattle thieves. Nobody, especially not Callahan, thought less of him for this. Matadors, even aspiring ones, were considered to be above rough gunplay.

When Callahan's party saddled up and rode out to drive off the rustlers, they had no notion of encountering anything but ordinary bandits. Even while the revolution raged up and down Chihuahua, there were always some outlaws who conducted depredations in either Villa's name or one of his generals', but nobody much believed them because Villa was a certified hero to much of the population.

From time to time Callahan had to ride out against cattle thieves and his policy was to go in force and with unmistakable determination. Usually, when they saw Callahan's men coming straight at them, the thieves ran off. But this time, when Callahan saw the second party of men — Mix's — emerge from the fold of ground, he became wary, which was why he split up his posse. He had not, of course, counted on the machine guns.

By the time Callahan got everybody back to the ranch it was nearly sundown. The machine gunners had hit seven horses and three men. The horses had to be destroyed; the men were injured but not badly. Women were tending the men's wounds and the conversation was heated in the plaza of Valle del Sol when word came that more trouble was on the way.

Callahan climbed to the bell tower and his heart began to pound. Spread out across the plains, coming toward him, were hundreds of horsemen, in large formations, carrying flags and banners. He knew the hacienda was about to be paid a visit by some part of Pancho Villa's army, a very sobering thought, and it made him wish he'd stayed in Oklahoma.

Callahan's apprehension was well founded. Johnny Ollas was among those standing in the courtyard when Villa's vanguard rode in through the walled gate. Fierro rode in first, just behind two guidons with red and white serpent flags on lances. Next came Pancho Villa himself with half a dozen bodyguards and staff, their horse's hooves clattering on the brick pavings. The women of the hacienda gathered nervously on the balconies and beneath the columned porticos that surrounded the courtyard. Among them was Johnny's wife, Donita.

No one was quite sure what to do with the arrival of the famous Pancho Villa.

Callahan, the manager, stood in the courtyard with the rest, waiting for somebody else to make the first move. The Villistas' horses clopped around on the paving stones while the general surveyed the hacendados for a leader. Finally Señora Parnadas stepped forward, twisting a handkerchief in her fingers. She was the house manager of Valle del Sol, a sort of mother figure to everyone, who arranged the meals and housekeeping duties, and she had been there longer than anyone could remember.

"May I get you something, General?" Señora Parnadas asked.

"Do you have any lemonade?" Villa answered.

"I can make some," she said, turning with instruction to one of the women to start squeezing lemons.

"So who was it led those *cabrones* against my men?" Villa said loudly.

Everyone knew. No one wanted to say. No one dared meet Villa's gaze. At last Callahan reluctantly stepped up. "General," he said, "I ordered my people to go after cattle rustlers."

"And who are you?"

"The ranch manager for Mr. Shaughnessy," Callahan replied, figuring that his minutes on earth might be fast ticking away.

"Well, we are not cattle rustlers," Villa informed him. "We were requisitioning beef for my army. I am governor of Chihuahua and I can requisition beef when I need it for the revolution."

"We didn't know it was you," Callahan said. He knew it sounded feeble, but it was true.

"You should have asked."

Since he hadn't been shot by now, he figured he could be a little bolder, but was careful not to sound argumentative. A maid brought a large glass of lemonade to Señora Parnadas, who handed it to Villa.

"*Gracias,*" responded the general, taking a large swig, then returning his attentions to the man before him.

"My men haven't had any fresh beef in a while," Villa said. "It is not good for an army to be underfed."

Callahan had the feeling the general might be toying with him, but, emboldened merely by being alive, he plunged ahead.

"General," he said, "all these years you've left us alone. All us Americans down here, we wish you the best. We don't want to get in your way. If you want some cows, we can let you have them."

Villa had a way of twisting his mouth to the side so you couldn't tell if it was a grin or a grimace. Callahan thought it was a grimace.

"You want me to send my boys to cut out some of the herd for you?" Callahan offered.

"I didn't know your hospitality would be so generous," Villa said. "We were all looking forward to having a big beef supper tonight. Just a little while ago I promised this to General Fierro myself."

"Well, then," Callahan said hopefully, "let me get my people working."

"I don't think that's necessary," Fierro interrupted. He had been glaring at Callahan all during the conversation. "You see, on the way here we picked out a very fine beef for our dinner. He's old and tough, like us. We're not used to your good grain-fed cows. We been fighting and on the march too long."

General Fierro motioned one of his aides to come forward. On his saddle horn the aide carried a large burlap sack. He walked the horse slowly until he came up beside Callahan, then pulled out a knife and slit the sack open. The severed head of a bull tumbled out of the sack and onto the paving.

"In the bullring," Fierro sneered, "they just cut off the ears and the tail. We in the army cut off the entire head."

It took Johnny Ollas a moment or so to realize what this was. It hit him like a kick to the gut. "You bastards!" he roared, bursting through the crowd. "No, no!" He lunged for Fierro but was cut down by a savage flat-of-the-blade saber blow to the back of his head from one of Fierro's men.

There was stunned silence in the courtyard. Women clapped their handkerchiefs to their mouths. Everybody knew how Johnny cared for Toro Malo, how even as a kid he'd get dressed in the middle of a lightning storm and lead him to the safety of a barn. How he always used to say he didn't understand how the old bull could produce such fine fighting stock, since he was really as gentle as a lamb. How proud he was to show him off to visiting ranchers. In fact, even though Johnny killed bulls for part of his living, he had grown so attached to the beast he would never have thought of meeting him in the bullring.

Donita had run up by now and was kneeling over Johnny and screaming profanities at Fierro. Johnny was bleeding badly from his wound but was still conscious. Fierro smiled at her, his mouth twisted in disdain.

"Big *macho*!" she spat. "Big man! You say you're a man helping the people, huh? You're a criminal. A bandit!"

Villa motioned for two men to restrain her.

"This your boyfriend?" he said.

"My husband."

"Well, well." He took a final swallow of lemonade and flipped the rest to the ground. "I think I'll invite you to dine with us this evening, señora. We need an ornament for our table."

Callahan's anger overcame the fear in him.

"The lady's just trying to help her husband. Why don't you let the señora take care of him?"

"She called us some pretty bad names," Villa said. "You want to defend her?"

"Look, General," Callahan said, "we're peaceful people here. We ain't done you any harm, and won't, if you'll just let us alone."

"Yeah, I let you alone too long, I think," Villa retorted. "You and Señor Hearst with his millions of acres down here in Mexico and Mr. Guggenheim and Mr. Whitney and

Mr. Buckley and all the rest of you Americanos that have stolen the people's property and turned them into slaves on their own lands with your stinking mines and stinking oil wells and stinking railroads and stinking cow ranches. And now your stinking government has closed the border to us so we can't even buy coal for our military trains or ammunition or even rations, so we go hungry, huh? And you want me to let you alone?"

"I don't know nothing about any of that," Callahan said.

"Well, Señor . . . what was your name?"

"Callahan."

"Well, Señor Callahan, you don't know nothing about that, huh? So I think maybe I'll make you understand. Maybe I make an example of you for your gringo Señor Shaughnessy, so maybe he will go to your president Woodrow Wilson and get him to change his mind about us. Your Señor Shaughnessy is a powerful man, right?"

"He owns a railroad. A *muy* big railroad. And that boy you just cut down there, he is the Colonel's favorite. And the Colonel don't take to this kind of thing very lightly, either."

"Do you value your life, Señor Callahan?"

"Yeah, I value it."

"Well, that's too bad," Villa said, "because all you gringos have got to know that you are here at our pleasure in Mexico and not because you claim you own a bunch of land that those crooks like Díaz and the rest of them in Mexico City said they sold to you for a few stinking pesos. And maybe the message will finally get through that we aren't fooling around down here."

Villa turned to a lieutenant at his side and said something, and three or four men jumped off their horses and seized Callahan roughly. Villa gave more instructions to the lieutenant, who barked orders to the men to carry Callahan to the courtyard gate. They put a rope around Callahan's wrists and hoisted him to the bridge of the gate so that he dangled eight or nine feet above the ground while everybody watched in fearful silence.

"Now we will have a little saber practice," Villa said. "My men have gone too long out of battle. They're getting rusty." Several men, wearing sabers at their sides, fell out and backed their horses in a line some distance from Callahan, who had stopped struggling and was hanging there, with his eyes on Villa.

"God save me," Callahan said.

"Why not let the crooked priests do that for you?" Villa replied.

The women on the balconies or under the eaves either turned their backs or retreated into the hacienda. Villa gave a nod and the first horseman drew his saber and made a gallop toward Callahan. His blow struck a leg as he passed beneath the gate and out into the open lawn. The leg was half severed by the gash and blood spurted through Callahan's torn pants leg. The second swordsman tore a hole in Callahan's side and part of his intestines spilled out. Callahan kicked, and his cries became pathetic and feeble. Several other riders had joined the line. After the fourth or fifth pass, Callahan fell still. They kept on, though, as if they were sabering a straw dummy. It was rare these days to have a live person to practice on.

Outside the gate, in the gathering darkness, half a dozen men were skinning Toro Malo. They took good care to do it right, too, fully aware of Villa's high reputation when he'd been in the butchering business himself. Large cooking fires had cropped up all through the fields surrounding Valle del Sol, and other soldiers were skinning more of the Colonel's cattle for their own dinners. But the skinning of Toro Malo took precedence and the hacienda's barbecue pit had been lit with good-grade charcoal. They understood this was to be a very special bull-roast.

Meanwhile, Villa had allowed some of the women to carry Johnny Ollas off to a bedroom to be looked after. He was lapsing in and out of consciousness, and after they cleaned his wound they sat beside him, doctoring his wound with agave juice and pepper sauce.

Donita, however, remained in the charge of Villa's aides. They hustled her to the long dinner table that had been set up in the courtyard, opposite the end where Villa had installed himself. When slabs of Toro Malo were served, Donita gagged at the plate and spat on the ground and glared at Villa with a look of almost unimaginable contempt.

"You know, señora," Villa said, wiping the meat grease from his mouth and mustache with the back of his hand, "I like you. I think I'm gonna bring you along with us in the morning, just so this Colonel Shaughnessy gets the notion that I am a serious man. Maybe he'll even make us a deal to get back the wife of his pet boy, huh?"

She wished she and Johnny hadn't argued with each other last night. Damned old bull, she thought. Johnny could have just kept quiet. But he was still a matador, and matadors don't get to be matadors by being cowards. As that thought struck her, she repeated it to herself with a renewed respect for Johnny Ollas: *Matadors don't get to be matadors by being cowards.*

NINE

It was midmorning two days later when Arthur and his family turned down the long gravel drive to Cornwall, the thirty-six-room stone "cottage" his father owned on the Newport bluffs, overlooking the Atlantic Ocean. Like the naming of *Ajax,* the naming of Cornwall had been another futile attempt by John Shaughnessy to anglicize himself. As they drew nearer, Arthur could see the Colonel standing on the wide slate steps, arms folded, head back, a posture Arthur recognized too well.

The Old Man had steamed into the harbor the night before, after his aborted trip to Ireland, and Arthur knew, when he was summoned down for lunch, that a confrontation was going to erupt over Arthur's mortgaging of the *Ajax.*

When they drove up in front, the children, Katherine, twelve, and Timmy, nine, hopped out and went to their grandfather, who gave them hugs and smiles, but when Arthur got out he was greeted with a disapproving look that was just this side of a scowl. Arthur went straight up to his father.

"Shall we talk?" he asked.

"Not now," the Colonel replied. "Bomba has set up the traps and we need to shoot before the sun moves into our eyes. We'll be done in about an hour. I'll see you then, in the library."

With that, the Colonel met Arthur's wife Xenia with a hug and ushered Timmy and Katherine around to the lawn overlooking the ocean. Xenia and Arthur went into the house, she to their upstairs room and Arthur to the library. He figured he might as well stake out his territory, and besides, there was a bar where he could fix the drink he thought he'd need.

The first thing that struck anybody entering the Shaughnessy library at Cornwall was the stuffed head of an enormous African bull elephant the Colonel had killed on safari a year after Arthur had come into the Shaughnessy household. The Colonel had taken him along on this expedition, and all the way from Nairobi to the plains of Kilimanjaro goaded him at every campsite while throwing clay pigeons from a hand trap: "Don't flinch!" "Stick your behind out when you set up for a shot!" "Lean into the gun!" "Be flexible, you're tensing up, *don't flinch!*" Until, after a week or two, Arthur became a reasonably good shot, however reluctantly.

When the time came for the elephant hunt, Arthur was not allowed to go, but was instead sent out with a tall African man to shoot Thompson's gazelles. Elephants were too dangerous, his father said, but late one afternoon a wagon pulled up in camp and a native driver told Arthur the Colonel had said to fetch him. Several miles later they arrived at the site of the elephant kill. Arthur had never seen an animal so large, not even in zoos. The elephant lay in a sitting position, its rear legs tucked beneath the massive body and its front legs splayed out in front. The elephant's trunk had coiled on one of its sprawled legs and provided a prop-up for its enormous head and tusks. Its eyes were open and between them was a small hole from which a surprisingly tiny amount of blood oozed out. The eyes were sad and wistful, with an almost bewildered stare. Several bearers in native dress stood around while one of the half dozen hunters in the Colonel's party set up a tripod for a photograph.

The picture itself, now hanging in the Colonel's trophy room back in Boston, showed one of the hunters perched on the elephant's back. Another sat on a leg, his foot on the trunk. The Colonel posed beside the elephant, his rifle crooked in one arm, with the other arm resting around a great ivory tusk. All the hunters were wearing high boots, tweed jackets, and shirts with ties. They had removed their pith helmets and held them in their hands. The Colonel insisted on proper dress while shooting elephants.

"These are dignified animals," he said, "and we must show our respect by hunting them in a dignified way." When they stuffed the old elephant's head to hang on the Colonel's wall, the taxidermist inserted artificial amber eyes that made the creature's countenance seem glaring and fierce. It was not at all the way the dead animal looked in the photograph, or the way Arthur remembered it.

Arthur poured his drink, a gin and tonic, and stood looking out the big bay window of the room, away from the elephant out toward the sea. He watched his father setting up Timmy with a shotgun. The boy seemed reluctant to take it, but the Colonel patted him on the shoulder, talking animatedly, though Arthur could not hear what was being said.

Timmy's learning to shoot wasn't a bad idea, but Arthur had never pushed the boy to do anything he really didn't want to — which was what the Colonel had done with *him* after they had taken him in at the same age Timmy was now. After Arthur had come to the Shaughnessy household, the Colonel constantly pushed for him to become an athlete and horseman and hunter and ball player, but it had backfired. He tried those things

111

and he either didn't like them or wasn't good at them; later he became a pretty fair tennis player but that was about it — the New England & Pacific was the crown of his life's work, and in what spare time he had, Arthur studied business journals — and then there were his collections: the stamps, the coins, the butterflies. And, of course, the flying.

Over the years Arthur became one of the major amateur lepidopterists in America. He had long ago observed that men of wealth generally divided themselves along two lines: the first were sportsmen and raconteurs with great country houses: the polo players, hunters, yachtsmen, mountain climbers, and explorers — or in some cases, drunks.

The second assortment, to which Arthur belonged, were more or less introverts — at least introspective — content to sit in their town houses reading, listening to music, painting, or studying art, all the while becoming collectors of everything under the sun. And because these tended to be solitary pursuits, in some cases they became drunks, too.

It had been three years since Arthur discovered flying, and it opened up an entire new world to him. Aviating was the one truly exciting thing Arthur did in his spare time; he didn't mind at all the mechanics of it, either, coming home greasy and oil-smeared from pulling props, changing magnetos and firing plugs, pulling engine heads, cylinder rods, cowlings. In fact, he exulted in it. It was the sublime feeling of flight that mattered: loosed from the earth, that one grand thrill when the machine cleared ground, looking back to watch the other world fade away while he was in the broad sky free as a bird, free almost as God Himself, a thrill beyond anything Arthur Shaughnessy had ever imagined. Sailors and yachtsmen must somehow feel some of the same things, but Arthur was beyond that now; flying had spoiled him.

The Colonel loathed flying. He could not understand why a man would want to go up in a silly airplane when there were railroads, yachts, horses, and motorcars in his immediate life, and that, of course, was precisely the reason Arthur enjoyed it so much.

Arthur knew his father disapproved of his lifestyle, considering it bohemian, if not bizarre. Xenia often conducted a kind of salon in their home, a refuge for writers, poets, musicians, painters, and a collection of wits and free thinkers around Boston, of which there were not many, but some from New York passed through. The thing was Xenia's idea and he just went along for the ride, though he found much of the talk interesting, to a point. There were not many Bolsheviks, anarchists, or perverts, which was a measure of outré by New York standards —

just the occasional socialist, Harvard professor, or women's suffragette — this last a volatile issue that Xenia wholeheartedly embraced.

Arthur's main contribution, at Xenia's behest, was to sponsor a literary review, with the help of company money, where new and controversial ideas were published that rankled the Colonel and embarrassed him in front of his friends. Arthur wasn't particularly sorry for this; in fact, it gave him a perverse satisfaction.

But for the past couple of months, Xenia had become alarmingly distant with him and closeted herself alone after meals. Sometimes he thought he heard her crying in her room, but whenever he asked about it she said nothing was the matter, that she had been "tired" lately. She had become almost antisocial, suspending her salons, and declined many social invitations. Clearly something was wrong; and he even wondered if she was having an affair. He refused to believe this, of course, and had decided that when they returned to Boston he would insist that she see a doctor.

Up in her second-floor room, which also overlooked the ocean, Xenia sat by the window watching from a different angle the same scene that Arthur was witnessing. She felt sorry for Timmy, because she knew how much he hated shooting, and Xenia knew something about hate, since for the past two months she had been hating herself.

Xenia Shaughnessy was a tall, graceful woman in her prime at the age of thirty-two, with bright bluish green eyes, dark lustrous hair, full lips, and an aristocratic aquiline nose — a classic Anglo-Saxon beauty. And yet she wasn't that at all. Xenia was in fact of Polish extraction; her parents had emigrated to Pittsburgh a quarter century earlier and her father, after laboring in a foundry, scraped up enough money to start his own coal and ice delivery business, which grew into one of the few success stories that could be told by Polish immigrants.

Arthur had met her in the north of England while climbing in the hills near the Scottish border on the only true vacation he'd ever taken. The Colonel had presented him with a summer in Europe after his college graduation. Xenia was there with her mother and they were next headed to Paris, a gift, like his, for graduation, in her case from finishing school. One day he came to a country inn where Xenia and her mother were having lunch. They fell into conversation and Arthur was quickly smitten. He canceled his plans to go to Scotland, took the Channel ferry to the Continent, and followed her to Paris, where they secretly met in afternoons or mornings when Xenia managed to slip away from her mother. Paris became their enchanted city.

"Oh, Arthur," she'd said with a laugh one day as they lay on cool sheets with the breeze blowing a translucent curtain through the window of Arthur's rooms near Xenia's hotel off the Champs-Élysées, "it's impossible!" Paris was beautiful in June, before the sun of July and August turned it into a sweatbox. The parks were full of flowers and the skies deep blue and cloudless.

"Why? I think it's perfectly proper. Besides, it'll give us an excuse to see each other in the evenings. For dinners, I mean."

"Tout au contraire!" she exclaimed almost condescendingly in her finishing school French. They were lying spoonlike, he pressed tightly against her, absorbing her smells and feeling the pulsing of her blood against his skin.

"Why not? Why wouldn't your mother be glad to find an American in this city, one whom she's already met? What could be the harm if I took the both of you out to dinner now and then?"

"She'd suspect something immediately," Xenia replied. "Oh, she might acquiesce once, but then she'd watch me like a hawk. No more freedom to go out on my own on afternoons like this." She turned and made a slicing motion with her hand across Arthur's nose. *"Nez coup! N'est-ce pas, mon cher?"*

"Because you've done this kind of thing before?" he said peevishly.

"No, silly, but I know Mama. She's shrewd. There's no way you could disguise the look in your eyes if we were to meet with her — nor I in mine. She would see you looking at me *tout nu,* and it would all be over. Mama is a noticer — she notices everything. She'd put me on the leash."

They had all been in Paris for three weeks, and it was the longest and grandest three weeks of Arthur's life.

He'd found out from Xenia where she'd be staying before they left England and upon arriving in Paris had immediately taken rooms a few blocks away from her hotel. He'd hung around there in the shadows for several days until he spied her and her mother at an outdoor café, which he correctly concluded was where they went in the afternoons. After several days of this, when her mother once left the table, he gave a waiter ten francs and a note he'd kept in his pocket since arriving, telling her his address and asking her to leave a note of her own at another café near his apartment if she would like to meet him sometime. She did, next morning.

"But I can't stand it," Arthur said, "just seeing you for an hour or so — and not even every day, at that."

"It will have to do, darling," she told him. "And now I must go." She got up from the bed, stripping the top sheet with her and wrapping it around her figure like a Greek goddess. Her bright eyes gave Arthur a shimmering thrill of excitement, as if she were the only woman in the world for him, which of course she was. He wanted never to let her from his sight.

"We're going back to the Louvre in the morning," she said. "Mama will be tired after that. She'll take a nap after lunch. I'll say I'm going out for a walk on the Champs. I'll meet you at the Rive Gauche between two and three — *à la bonne heure!*"

"Yes, but —"

"You must stay out of the picture for now," Xenia said firmly. She was seated on a chair next to the bed, picking up her underclothes, and gave him a loving squeeze on his wrist. She had thought of all the Polish boys she had known back in Pittsburgh — nice enough, for Polish boys whose families had also made something of themselves other than fruit-stand peddlers or garbage men — but they were rough-and-tumble compared with Arthur Shaughnessy of Boston, Massachusetts.

What Miss Walton's School had taught Xenia Kzwalskci was that there was more to life than what her parents had had in mind for her, and in her four years there she'd developed a fierce determination to become something better than what was expected, which in her case was to find a nice Polish boy with a career and to bear a succession of Polish Catholic grandchildren so her parents would have a legacy of little ones bouncing on their knees for the rest of their natural days.

That was not for Xenia, and she felt that this handsome, shy American, this collegiate man who she could tell was from an important and cultured family in the fabled and cultured New England stronghold of Boston was like a dream come true for the daughter of an ice-and-coal man from Pittsburgh. She had read of the great New England aristocracy, and Arthur seemed certainly to be one of these. His father owned a railroad company! It never occurred to her that his name, Shaughnessy, was one that, simply on the face of it, wouldn't have allowed him to be a part of that rarefied class of Bostonians she'd read so much about.

Dressed now, Xenia bent to Arthur in the bed and gave him a long kiss. She could scarcely believe she had actually given herself to him — and after only ten days. But it all seemed right and true, and so she did not stop to dwell on the horror with which her parents would have greeted her behavior, let alone the Church.

"*Bonjour,* darling," she said, blowing a kiss, opening the door.

"I don't know why you so worship the language of these people," Arthur said as a parting shot.

"Qu'est-ce que c'est?"

"Well, for one thing," he said, "how can you have any respect for a man who, when his house catches on fire, he starts running around in the street shouting, 'Foo, foo, foo'?"

She stuck out her tongue at him.

For his part, Arthur had never met anyone like Xenia, either.

In his time with the Shaughnessys, he'd attended tea dances with the daughters of Boston's lace-curtain Irish, smiling, snappy colleens who giggled and shrank back to their mothers and later, as they became adolescent, into the Church, so he could barely manage a kiss on the cheek. There were of course Protestant girls whom he'd met at day school or at his father's bathing club near Gloucester, but they seemed stuffy and shy.

Then, during his short, dreadful experience at Groton, when they'd had swaps with Miss Porter's and other boarding schools, the girls not only ignored him but in some cases most obviously whispered about him — tuned in, as they were, by his ruthless and mean-spirited classmates: "He's Irish," they'd say. "He's an orphan and a mackerel snapper," they'd say. "He was left in a basket on the Irishman's stoop."

In time Arthur managed to develop friendships with others like himself — the sons and daughters of wealthy Bostonians who were on the fringes of Yankee society like the Shaughnessys were and, because they weren't born into it, would never be invited in, no matter how witty and charming they were, and so they formed their own outer circle with their own parties and dances at their own clubs.

But in all of this, Arthur had never met a girl to fall in love with. Perhaps he was too busy to fall in love — or even have a girl-friend. Mostly, what hours he did not spend studying or working at the rail offices of the NE&P he spent in a top-floor room of the Shaughnessy mansion with his collections.

When finally Xenia and her mother de-parted Paris several weeks later, Arthur promised to visit her in Pittsburgh on his return. When he got home to Boston the next month, there were numerous letters from Xe-nia, the last announcing that she was preg-nant.

The Colonel and Beatie had had great plans for Arthur that did not include the daughter of a Polack from Pittsburgh. For her part, Xenia was faced with the nauseating prospect of informing her parents of her condition. Arthur, being the gentleman he was raised to be, visited Pittsburgh as soon as possible and on his return announced to the Shaughnes-sys his intention to marry Xenia Kzwalskci without delay. In the uproar that followed, Arthur stood his ground for one of the few times in his life with his father. Beatie, if not happy, at least resigned herself to the event, and two weeks later, they all journeyed down to Pittsburgh in the Colonel's private railcar to attend a Polish wedding.

It became an awkward affair for all concerned, in no small part because, beforehand, Beatie had told everyone that Xenia was the daughter of a Polish count, which was not exactly the truth. At the reception, as the groom's small party stood aside from the throngs of Polish guests, Colonel Shaughnessy coarsely wondered aloud whether they should have brought a pound cake. Beatie felt grateful that Mr. Kzwalskci had ordered an orchestra to play classical music (even if it was Chopin) and she managed a nice chat with Mrs. Kzwalskci about tatting lace. Afterward the couple took a brief honeymoon to New Orleans, which neither of them had seen. Then he and Xenia went back to Boston, where he joined the company full-time. All this occurred in 1903.

Seven months later, Katherine Shaughnessy was born, and two years afterward Timothy Gray Shaughnessy came into the world. Arthur never regretted his decision, and as the years went past considered himself one of the world's lucky men. Xenia's finishing school in Pittsburgh had given her an abiding interest in literature, music, and the arts. They were a good fit, the Polish girl and the orphaned descendant of whatever-kind-of-immigrants, both just a generation or so removed from poverty and servitude. "Only in America," as the Colonel was fond of saying.

TEN

In the drawing room Arthur tired of waiting. He walked outside just in time to hear Beatie, who had returned from a walk on the beach, cry, "Oh, no, John! Not before lunch!"

"Pull!" the Colonel shouted, and snapped off two roaring shotgun blasts, powdering a double of clay pigeons out over the water. Beatie clapped her hands over her ears and Timmy Shaughnessy put his hands to his own.

"Now you try it," said the Colonel.

The Colonel wasn't at all satisfied with the way his grandson was developing, which he long ago concluded was a direct reflection on Arthur. The Colonel's granddaughter, Katherine, going on thirteen and a true blond beauty, was coming along just fine. She rode with distinction, shot, fenced, and played a spectacular back on the girl's field hockey team. Katherine was immensely well poised for her age — everyone said so — and, except for her blondness, it was easy to see the resemblance to her mother. She was going to be tall — was already tall, in fact — a "leaf-eater," as the Colonel was fond of saying. She had gone immediately to the stables where one of her two black geldings was kept.

"Pull!" the Colonel shouted again, and Bomba, who was wearing a seersucker suit and a Panama hat, let loose two more clay targets. Colonel Shaughnessy easily blasted them into little wisps of black dust.

"John — must you?" Beatie wailed. "We were so enjoying the quiet of the morning."

Bomba glanced back, noticed Arthur standing on the terrace, and broke out into a big grin. Arthur had long ago concluded that Bomba understood everything on earth.

Bomba had been hired — if that was the word for it — thirty-three years earlier when Colonel Shaughnessy fell off his yacht while drunk one night during a marlin-fishing trip in Samoa, and Bomba, then a sixteen-year-old dockhand, jumped in and rescued him. For this the young Samoan was rewarded with the splendors of the Boston world.

The Colonel had read too many stories about anarchist assassinations in Europe and figured it wouldn't be long before the practice reached across the Atlantic. As the owner of a railroad, he feared he would be a prime candidate, so he felt he needed someone around to act as a bodyguard.

Bomba wasn't his real name but the Colonel bestowed it on him because whatever he was called in Samoa was unpronounceable in English but one part of it sounded like "Bomba," the name of one of the old-time kings of Naples.

Bomba's countenance was remarkably fierce but belied a more genial disposition. His grandfather had been a cannibal but Bomba's favorite food was ice cream. He spoke little English, but understood more and, when he had to, probably could say a lot more than he let on.

At meals at home, Bomba often sat on the Colonel's left, breakfast, lunch, and dinner. He never used a fork, though he did use a knife and spoon, except for soup — which to Beatie's disgust he drank from the bowl and the Colonel forbade her to correct him. Around Bomba's waist was always strapped a holstered revolver and he kept a variety of throwing knives in the lining of his jackets.

Colonel Shaughnessy was stewing about young Timmy's reticence with the skeet shooting . . . such a reclusive boy, bookish and tentative about horses and guns and other manly things . . . wouldn't do — just wouldn't do. If the Colonel hadn't succeeded in making Arthur a mirror image of himself, he was determined to have a go at his grandson. He shouldered his gun.

"Pull!" the Colonel shouted.

■ ■ ■ ■

Arthur, standing on the terrace with his drink, thought for some reason about Mick Martin, and wished he'd had his old friend down for weekend. He couldn't understand why, when he mentioned inviting him, Xenia had burst out the way she had and paled. Arthur had kept his friendship with Mick through the years, though there were times their lives diverged and they didn't see each other for months.

Two years before Arthur entered Boston College, a depression closed down a shoe factory where Mick had been working and Arthur talked the Colonel into giving Mick a job in the railroad's freight department. In summers, they worked together; evenings, they went to the boisterous saloons across from the yards to drink beer, play darts, and on more than one occasion to chase girls, an occupation in which Mick succeeded and Arthur often failed.

Once Arthur met a girl, Betty, who was a secretary at a life insurance company. He took her out on a date to a show in the park and later they met Mick at one of the saloons.

Then one afternoon Arthur was returning from school early on the trolley when he saw Mick and Betty walking on the Common, arm in arm, she leaning against his best friend's shoulder and petting his hair. The trolley had turned a corner by then, so Arthur had to crane back to see them, not knowing what to think. The office where Betty worked wasn't far from there; maybe they'd just met on the street and decided to take a walk. But obviously they weren't walking like simply good old friends.

Arthur quit seeing Betty after that, and didn't blame Mick; he blamed her instead — she was just a passing fancy, anyway. Mick's life had been hard and his own was soft, and he'd always felt a little guilty about it.

One day, however, Mick made an astonishing announcement to Arthur.

"I'm going to become a lawyer," Mick said.

"Why, for heaven's sake? How . . ."

"You leave the *how* to me," was the answer. "And the *why*, well, it's because lawyers have the power, you see. If you're a lawyer, you can do anything. You know all the answers. You're above it all. The only thing better is being rich."

To Arthur's amazement, Mick managed to find a Boston law firm that let him "read" the law for four years and he managed to pass the bar exam. Arthur never knew exactly how Mick accomplished this moneywise, but suspected it had something to do with his employment with the Irish gang. Arthur heard rumors in the old neighborhood that Mick was in thick with a very rough bunch and part of his job was serving as a strong-arm man. He was said to be extremely handy with fists, knives, and even guns, but he was also said to have earned a reputation for fairness. It was even rumored that he'd killed a man.

The year after Timmy Shaughnessy was born, Michael Martin hung out his shingle in a small office across from a small park in South Boston.

By now Mick had become a fixture in the Shaughnessy families' households. He wasn't invited to the fashionable parties and dinners the Colonel and Beatie threw, which Mick good-naturedly understood, and even joked about. But he soon became a regular at Xenia's intellectual salons and the free thinkers delighted in his good looks, irreverent wit, and a few even used him as a lawyer when they had a problem. Every few weeks he had dinner with Arthur and Xenia, and became "Uncle Mick" to Katherine and Timothy, always bringing them delightful little gifts when he came to the house. He brought presents for Xenia, too — flowers, perfumes, "whatnots" he'd picked up along the way. It had pleased Arthur that even his father would occasionally remark to him, "Say, where's old Mick? We haven't seen him lately."

Then Arthur would call Mick and invite him down to Cornwall on slack weekends.

As the years passed, Mick began to establish

himself as more than just an ordinary lawyer. Mick's background excluded him from joining any of the old-line Boston firms, and even more naturally his first clients were people from the Irish gangs who found themselves in difficulty with the law. Eventually the gang leaders themselves began to use Mick for counsel. Then, in the summer of 1910, the same year Pancho Villa had seen Halley's Comet, an event occurred that propelled Mick into a new and highly profitable area of the law.

A leader of the principal Italian gang in Boston had kidnapped one Bobby "Bobbin Boy" O'Reilly, a onetime spinning-mill worker, whose numbers racket the Italians felt was spilling into their territory. A ransom of ten thousand dollars was demanded. Bobbing Boy O'Reilly was popular and also first cousin to the head of the main Irish gang and, with paying the ransom out of the question, the Irishmen went to Mick Martin for advice. He counseled them to negotiate and they agreed, but the first meeting nearly ended in disaster, with guns drawn and threats hurled and the Irishmen storming away in a huff. Mick then offered to conduct the negotiation himself.

It took nearly three weeks, but in the end Bobby O'Reilly went free and the Irishmen had parted with only two thousand and a promise not to encroach on Italian turf. Two thousand was about the average man's yearly salary in those days. Mick got paid a hefty fee of five hundred and a party was thrown in his honor by the gang. After that, he became firmly entrenched as official arbiter for the Irishmen, and in time his particular services were in demand from other quarters as well. Kidnapping had become a popular pastime, and during the years that ensued he negotiated the release of kidnap victims from Trenton to Chicago. In time he arbitrated for everybody as well: Irish, Jewish, Italian, and even a Chinese gang in San Francisco. The U.S. Department of State even employed Mick's services in a secret deal to secure the return of one of their diplomats in Guatemala.

"Would you believe it," Mick once said to Arthur, "I've carved me out a new niche in the law!"

"Yes, I've heard you're more in demand than Clarence Darrow," Arthur told him. They were having a late lunch at McSweeny's Restaurant and Mick was on his eighth highball. For several years, Arthur had been concerned that Mick drank too much, but his success in the law was undeniable. He now had a fine set of offices, a powerful Stutz motorcar, and a fine set of rooms at the Copley House.

"Way I see it," Mick told him, "if everybody goes away a little unhappy, but not really mad

— then I've accomplished my purpose."

"That's an interesting way to look at it," Arthur said. "Just like King Solomon."

"You see, all it comes down to in my business is trust. When these guys try to work something out, nobody believes anybody. But when I step in, they know they'll get what's promised. Everybody knows Mick Martin can be trusted."

Mick was wound up and Arthur noticed he was slurring his words a little. To placate him, Arthur said, "I'd trust you with my life."

"I know you would, my bucko," Mick replied. "But let's hope it never comes to that."

Arthur had returned to the library when his father came in.

"Well, Arthur, your boy's not afraid of that gun anymore. He's hitting things, too."

"Thank you," Arthur said.

"Your mother thinks I'm crazy, but the boy's got to learn to shoot sometime — just like you did."

"I don't shoot very well, Papa," Arthur said.

"Because you never do, anymore," replied the Colonel.

Arthur turned for a moment and looked out the window. A cloud bank had gathered and the sea was gray and running high. Arthur really didn't mind that his father was teaching Timmy how to shoot; in fact, he thought it was a good thing. The boy needed pursuits like that — manly amusements that Arthur hadn't really taught him.

"Maybe you're right, Papa." Arthur stood by the window with his hands behind his back, ready to get on with it. It was always the same; when the Colonel got angry about one thing, he began with a prelude over something minor — like skeet shooting — then built it up so that eventually the real anger burst out. This time it wasn't long in coming. He closed the pocket doors that led to the foyer and spun around.

"All right, Arthur, all right, dammit!" the Colonel growled. He pulled the rumpled piece of paper out of his pocket and thrust it at Arthur. "Just what in tarnation is this?"

Arthur glanced at the wireless message and was annoyed at what it contained: "Bank of Boston holds collateral on steam yacht known as *Ajax,*" registry such and such, description thus and so; "under agreement per," blah, blah, blah . . . "said vessel may not be removed from Territorial United States waters while agreement still in force," etc. "Imperative vessel return to said U.S. waters immediately," and so on. A lawyer had evidently drawn up the cable. Arthur had hoped the bank president himself would have sent a more friendly, personal telegram. But what the hell, maybe this was what the Old Man needed.

133

"I'll have an explanation!" the elder Shaughnessy seethed.

"Isn't it plain, Father?" Arthur asked calmly.

"Goddammit, Arthur, do you realize what you've done?" He pointed toward the cable as if it were a serpent. "What have you done?"

"Done? I got us a six-month extension. I had to sign papers."

"By signing exactly what kind of papers?" the Colonel demanded.

"I had to put up *Ajax* as security. Would you rather I'd signed over our rolling stock and rights-of-way? At least if the worst happens and we have to default, the company could still operate without having a bank as our partner. It was the only way they'd do it, Papa," Arthur told him.

"They've never done this before. They're aware of our assets."

"Maybe you have assets, but I don't," Arthur countered. "And you told me to handle it. They wanted to examine the company books. My action avoids that," Arthur said coldly.

The Colonel just looked at him, the contempt slowly draining from his face. He, too, realized what failure to get the loan would mean: Word leaking out all over the country of the precarious condition of the New England & Pacific Railroad. Vultures swarming in; people whispering, maybe even the newspapers getting hold of it — contracts canceled, creditors alerted. The Old Man shook his head. "Well, I don't want this hanging over us. I'm going to pay the thing off myself."

"From your personal funds?" Arthur asked cheerfully. "Well, it's what made the Rothschilds so successful — they pledged their own fortunes."

"Hell with the Rothschilds," the Colonel spat. "Besides, I don't have any personal funds anymore."

"What?" Arthur said. In fact he'd wondered over some of the remarks his father had made during the past year, but he'd always been careful not to be too inquisitive about the Old Man's private affairs. Still, he found it astonishing.

"Do you mean that you're broke?"

"It's too true," the Colonel replied. "There've been some reverses in my investments. I'd counted on company profits to make them good, but then these past few years . . ."

"Completely broke?" Arthur asked, alarmed.

"Well, no, of course not. But I'm in a pinch and it's getting pinchier by the day. It's expensive to run all this, the houses, the yacht, my place down in Mexico . . ."

"Well, how broke, then?" Arthur pressed.

"I stopped giving money to the charities six months ago," the Colonel said by way of explanation.

"But Father, how on earth then could you have planned to take all those people to Ireland or wherever? That must have cost —"

"Because I'm borrowing money from some of them," the Old Man cut him off. "I can go to Harriman or Whitney or Vanderbilt and ask for a little personal loan, you know? A friendly private matter. But I can't appear to be indigent. Besides, I wasn't going to take them to Ireland if they protested. It was just a little joke." He jabbed his finger at the message. "And then when this thing came, I was made to look like a fool. We were way out in the ocean when they woke up, while I was supposed to be taking them up to Boston! Now they laugh and say I can't even navigate my own yacht!"

Arthur looked out the large bay window to where a few sailboats were negotiating their way through the rolling, windy seas. He rubbed his forehead and reflected with dismay on how his father had refused to take the NE&P public all those years when it had made a stunning profit. Now it was a sticky question because the company was operating nearly in the red. Still, it was crazy in this day and age for a railroad to be run by a single owner.

The Colonel had collapsed into a chair. He seemed deflated.

"Listen, Arthur, we need to talk a moment.

While you were in Chicago and I had all these people on *Ajax,* some of them are in our same fix down in Mexico and I had to give them disturbing news."

"What's that, Papa?"

"This Pancho Villa fellow. That country's in a hell of a mess. They change presidents every month or so and every time more fighting or revolution or whatever they call it breaks out. We've got some pretty large investments down in Chihuahua, but so far, Villa's stayed out of our affairs."

"We've been lucky," Arthur said, perplexed at his father's change of subject.

"Well, what I'd been thinking was that I can sell off some of the cattle in Mexico, maybe all of them," his father continued. "Which is why I bring up this matter. There's close to two million and a half dollars in beef on the hoof at Valle del Sol. Enough to put NE&P on some kind of footing until we can get the company back on track. Just one of those munitions contracts from the English or French will do it. I've been working on it."

"I considered the cattle myself," Arthur said. "But I was worried it might not be a good time, with all that's going on down there."

"Well, you better start worrying more," the Colonel told him, "because Villa's talking about nationalizing everything or just plain stealing it, and kicking all the foreigners out of Mexico and giving it back to the Indians and peons or something. I don't know if he can do it. I don't even know who's in charge down there and nobody else does, either. Anyway, it's created a situation."

"I can only imagine," Arthur said. He suddenly felt a peculiar pang of something like fear rush through him from his gut to his brain. All these years he'd felt financially secure, not just because of the railroad, but because of what he thought was his father's wealth — the family fortune. He'd simply assumed that, whatever happened, the Old Man had stashed away enough to keep everyone comfortable. It had never occurred to him that the Colonel could actually go broke.

"You know," the Colonel said, "I met Pancho Villa once when he was running a butcher shop in Chihuahua City and came to the ranch to buy a few cows from us. He seemed pleasant enough, but I don't put it beyond him to impose some sort of sanctions."

"What did the others say when you told them?" Arthur wanted to know.

"Took to strong drink," said the Colonel. "Then they wanted to know how to handle it. My word, together we own most of Northern Mexico. Old Man Guggenheim almost dropped his false teeth on the floor. He's got millions tied up in those silver mines. Harriman, the same; he owns railroad right-of-way franchises for six thousand miles of track.

And there's Hearst, with all his ranching operations."

"Was anything decided?"

"We can't reach Valle del Sol by telephone; the lines must be down. The only way we're going to get a handle on this thing is to go ourselves and get a look firsthand."

"Mexico?"

"Exactly. I haven't been to Valle del Sol in nearly a year. And you haven't been at all. We need to find out what's going on. Get a good feel for the situation," the Colonel said conspiratorially. "I think it will be instructive. And if the situation looks clear, we can drive the cattle up to Chihuahua City and load them into stock cars and bring them across the border at El Paso. That ought to solve our sticky little financial problems for a while. Hell, Arthur, a cattle drive, one that big! Can you imagine it?"

"But Papa, We can't leave the railroad to run itself. Not now. We've got a major problem that's beyond just short-term patch-ups with cash. We need to talk about this — about the whole business."

"We can talk about it later," said the Colonel. "On the trip."

Arthur saw where the conversation was going to lead, and knew in the end he would not win, and that in fact it might even be a good thing for him to go to Mexico and do his own surveying of the assets down there.

Arthur had known for a long time that the Old Man was not quite balanced; that he was mercurial and sometimes rash. Even though the Colonel called him son, had given him his name and all that went with it, Arthur had always felt subservient, far more than most sons with their fathers — real fathers — and with his sense of gratitude, mixed with an apprehension he could never articulate, Arthur almost always deferred to his father's wishes and demands, even when he believed them wrong. The *Ajax* business was an exception. But this . . . this seemed a reckless. He didn't want a part in one of the Colonel's grandiose schemes. What he had heard during the past few minutes had done more than startle him.

"With all you've just told me," Arthur said, "don't you think it might be dangerous to go into Mexico now?"

"Oh, hell, no. We're not going to get any kind of trouble from Villa and his bunch. They know where their bread's buttered. I'll write him a check for five or ten thousand or something — been thinking about doing that anyway. That'll keep him happy," the Colonel said with calm assurance.

"But that's a war they have on down there," Arthur said. "War is . . ." Arthur was getting that nervous feeling he always got when he saw his father becoming wrought up about something — there was often no stopping him. It had been that way ever since Arthur could remember. His childhood had been an unbroken string of jolts and fears of what the Colonel would come up with next; when Arthur was thrown by a horse, his father traumatized him by making him get back on. In Maine his father once took him deep into the woods and left him there alone, telling him he must learn to find his way back home. For his first swimming lesson the summer he arrived at the Shaughnessy household, the Colonel simply brushed him off a dock into icy water that was over his head. Looking back, Arthur realized his father hadn't meant to be cruel; he'd only meant to be instructive.

But all these impressions were indelibly stamped in Arthur's mind.

"Don't talk nonsense," said the Colonel. "They've never had fighting anywhere *near* Valle del Sol."

"Well, how would all of you like to take a vacation down in sunny Mexico?" the Colonel announced. They were seated for lunch at the elaborate rosewood dining table in the dining room overlooking the sea. The Colonel sat at one end in a huge ebony chair carved like a throne, and Beatie sat at the other. Next to her was Timmy, and opposite was Katherine. As the older, at twelve, Katherine exerted a kind of supervisory position over Timmy, who, at nine, followed her around like a puppy when she wasn't out riding or fencing or playing field hockey. He wasn't frail, but somehow he seemed lost, though Katherine attributed that to his age. He could talk to her about things, and did, and she knew he was no dummy. Xenia sat to the Colonel's right and on his left was Bomba, dressed in a tuxedo that everyone knew had half a dozen throwing knives hidden inside.

"What did you say?" Beatie asked. "A vacation? In Mexico?"

"You've never even seen Valle del Sol," the Colonel said. "After twenty-five years, it's high time you did."

"All of us?" Arthur asked, incredulous. "I thought it was just you and me."

"I've never been to Mexico," Katherine said innocently.

"Papa, I didn't know this was to be a family excursion," Arthur said. "They've been having a war in Mexico for three hundred years. It's not a war like what's going on in France," he continued, "but it's a war."

Xenia broke in. "I've never seen the ranch," she said. "I think it might be nice."

Arthur was stunned. For weeks she hadn't said much of anything at all, let alone something positive. Xenia gazed across the table toward the ocean with a wistful expression, which to Arthur was when she looked the most beautiful. He didn't know whether to be glad, but if her melancholy might be cured by a trip to Mexico, he'd certainly go along with it.

The Colonel's suggestion about going to Mexico had set off a spark in Xenia's soul. Until that moment, sitting at the Shaughnessys' dining table, with the vast ocean and all the trappings of grandeur spread out around her, Xenia had been utterly miserable. She was carrying a secret darker than she could ever have imagined, and carrying it deep inside herself. She was pregnant, and not with Arthur's child.

To explain such a thing was beyond her, but she knew she must, because she loved Arthur without compromise. There was no denying the fact, however. The doctor had said she was two months gone.

What problems they'd been having before, between Arthur's long business trips and the sort of gentle lassitude they'd slipped into during the past year, foreclosed any possibility she could convince him it was his child. She thought about ending the pregnancy, but though she'd heard whisperings of doctors who might perform such an operation, personally she knew no doctors who would. That would have been the easiest way, but it was also something completely against Xenia's own sense of self-respect and honor. When the Colonel mentioned Mexico, something clicked inside her. Somehow there was a ray of hope — a new country, far away from Boston and the disgrace and humiliation the very name of its society implied.

"But Father, really," Arthur said. "After all, we should at least think this out."

Xenia cut in, "It's going to be fun." Her eyes seemed suddenly alive and bright; she was even smiling.

Arthur again was floored that such a change that had come over her.

"There's the spirit," the Colonel chimed in. "You'll see deserts and prairies and mountains — it's a big country. Why, Valle del Sol is nearly the size of Belgium!"

Turning to Tim, who'd been silent during the conversation, the Colonel enthused, "Why, you'll even get to meet my young compadre Johnny Ollas, who's going to be a great matador someday. And old Buck Callahan, my ranch manager — who will show you how to carve a Toltec idol out of a piece of cottonwood, or teach you how to rope and tie a steer one-handed. You'll see things you never dreamed of," the Colonel said.

ELEVEN

The morning after Pancho Villa's butchery at
Valle del Sol, General Vargo Santo looked in
on Johnny Ollas. He found him semi-delirious
from the saber gash but his color was good
and he looked like he would live. He was surrounded by several women, who changed his
oozing bandages every few hours.

"Well, amigo, you seem better than when I
last saw you," Santo remarked.

"Where's Donita — my wife?" Johnny
asked weakly.

"She's with the chief. She's in good hands."

"What do you mean?"

"General Villa wants to take her with us for
a while. Sort of an insurance policy."

"Insurance? What insurance?" Johnny put
his hand to his temple and looked up at Santo
blankly.

"You're lucky to be alive," Santo told him.
"It's unwise to try to attack the chief."

Johnny's memory of the evening before
began to return. The head of Toro Malo on

the paving stones. The sneer of Fierro.

Johnny looked at the women. "Where's Buck?" he asked. The women looked away.

"Where is he?" Johnny said again. "He needs to deal with this." Two of the women immediately left the room.

"That is your ranch manager?" Santo asked.

"Buck is my . . . my father. He raised me."

"I see," Santo said. "I just wanted you to know about your wife. Many difficult things will happen during this revolution, you know. We are not kidnappers. We are soldiers. I wanted to tell you personally not to worry so much. I hear you are a matador, huh? I enjoy the corrida myself."

"Donita . . . where is she?" Johnny repeated. The remaining woman looked darkly at Santo. "You ought to leave him alone," she said.

"*Adiós,*" Santos said, and abruptly left the room.

Johnny turned to the woman. "Please go get Buck," he said. "Something's happened."

They had already buried Buck Callahan when Johnny Ollas finally felt up to getting on his feet. He had been told what had happened but for three days lapsed in and out of consciousness as his wound slowly healed, leaving a nasty reddish slash from his right ear to the crown of his scalp. Johnny's adoptive brothers helped him to the grave site, where a small wooden cross had been erected. It was under a big oak on a sharp knoll near the ranch.

Buck's widow, Rosalita, accompanied them. A blue-gray thunderstorm was gathering down the valley and lightning flashed against the looming Sierra Madre foothills. Johnny's four younger brothers stood on one side of the grave with their sombreros in their hands as the storm spread over the foothills. Little gusts of wind spun dust devils over the fresh mound. Even though his companions were only stepbrothers, they were Johnny's closest family and insisted on helping in his bullfights.

Johnny stood over Buck Callahan for a long moment.

Finally he said, "I guess there's nothing left but to go on."

"Go on where, Johnny?" asked Rosalita Callahan.

The rumble of thunder echoed and Johnny shook his head. "Somebody's got to go and get this finished."

"Finished?" Rosalita said. "It *is* finished. Buck's dead."

"And Donita's been kidnapped." Johnny Ollas had no clear idea of what to do, but he had to do something; this he knew. It wasn't just Donita, though that was most of it. The rest had to do with the fierce Mexican pride instilled since the time of the Aztecs; the more they were beaten down — by the humiliations of the Spanish conquest, by the rapacious Americanos, by the unrelenting hand of their own corrupt government — the prouder, the more defiant the people had become.

Johnny Ollas was no different from anyone else.

"Johnny, Pablo goes every day to the telegraph office. Colonel Shaughnessy will come as soon as he hears."

"Well, then he hasn't heard, has he?"

"Villa's cut the lines, they say, but they'll be fixed," Rosalita told him. "And we also sent a man up to Chihuahua City with a message yesterday. They'll get it through, and even if they can't, we sent a man with instructions to go all the way to El Paso. Why don't you wait and see what happens?"

"No time," Johnny said. "Villa can disappear, maybe in those mountains, and nobody can catch him. What happens to Donita then?"

The evening sun lit up his face, and he squinted beyond the wooden cross that marked the grave. Johnny was delicately built, somewhat like a lady's wristwatch, thin and slight, yet his wrists were thick with muscle from so much practice in the bullring with the sword. A bullfighter needed strong wrists to drive the blade deep into the big hump on the bull's neck.

Johnny's hair was straight and black but his eyes were blue and deep-set. His nose was straight, too — not flat like an Indian's; his chin was somewhat pointed and dainty, his lips thin, and his canine teeth large and pearly white, all of which gave him a lean, wolfish look.

"Oh, Johnny," Rosalita said, "Buck wouldn't have wanted you to do this. Buck was a practical man. He'd wait for the Colonel. Buck always did what the Colonel wanted."

Johnny stared down at the mound of dirt. A few drops of rain fell.

"Look what it got him," Johnny said.

Twelve

The Colonel's private train, NE&P No. 1, sat
huffing on a siding in Providence, Rhode
Island, under the curtain of night when
Bomba drove them up beside it in a black
Mormon motor coach. The headlights reflected on the glistening dark green cars and
polished black engine, their sides emblazoned
with the big salmon-and-gray NE&P emblem.
Another automobile followed with baggage.

"Splendid, splendid!" cried the Colonel,
rubbing his hands together. "Just look how
she shines!"

The train was made up of the engine and
five cars — collier, baggage, diner, salon, and
sleeper — plus a special car Arthur had
added. Bomba and two other men from the
baggage auto began loading everything
aboard. Through the windows of the dining
car they could see white-jacketed cooks working inside in the galley and smell the fresh
aromas of supper wafting out on the cool
night air.

The engine's bell clanged and every so often fantastic clouds of white steam belched onto the siding as the engineer eased off his boiler pressure. A dark-skinned porter helped Beatie and Xenia onto the salon platform, then ushered Timmy and Katherine aboard. The Colonel started to go forward to speak to the engineer when Claus Strucker turned up in a taxi. He was dressed in a black three-piece suit set off by a gold watch chain, and his hair was slicked back like a New Orleans bartender's.

"Well, well, Colonel," said the German, "what a fine-looking train." He ran his fingers over the glistening side of the Colonel's private salon car, which was named *The City of Hartford.* It was painted in the company's colors: a deep lacquered gray with a salmon stripe down the length of the car.

"Good to see you, Strucker," replied Colonel Shaughnessy. "Glad you're coming along. I'll have my people bring your bags."

Three days earlier, Strucker had called the Colonel to thank him for the voyage on the *Ajax.* More than the others, Strucker had gotten the joke, and when he learned the Colonel was headed to Mexico, Strucker immediately asked to come along. The Colonel was glad to accommodate, grateful to have the company of someone other than women and children on the long trip. Besides, the German's presence reminded him of some wild

151

times of yore.

It was just the sort of break the German had been waiting for. Strucker wasn't sure how it would play out, but going down to Mexico under cover of accompanying a man of Colonel Shaughnessy's stature could offer endless opportunities.

Everybody in the family had met Strucker at one time or another, so there was no need to reintroduce him around. Presently they were all aboard and snug in the elegant leather-and-velvet-clad parlor car.

For his part, Strucker was secretly contemptuous of the kind of American democracy that produced such bourgeois creatures as Colonel Shaughnessy and his family. His supreme value was the Prussian hierarchy, in which one kissed ass upward and defecated downward, and even though he enjoyed the company of the Colonel, Strucker actually despised Americans in general, the same way he despised anyone in his own country who was subservient to him.

"This feels good," Xenia remarked to Beatie, "a trip into the night to a foreign land."

"Yes, I imagine," she replied, "provided we don't get tangled up in their war." Beatie chanced a look at Strucker, who was seated at the end of the car near the bar. She didn't like the man, mainly because in the old days he was always around when the Colonel seemed to be, well, up to something, though she couldn't prove it. Nevertheless, he was an old friend of her husband's, and it would do no good to protest now anyway.

Colonel Shaughnessy had overheard the exchange between Xenia and his wife and interrupted with a gravelly roar: "Now, Mother, Chihuahua's a huge state and all the papers are saying now that Pancho Villa is all the way over in Coahuila. It would be like me saying I'm afraid of going from Boston down to New York just because somebody's fighting a war way out in St. Louis."

The children, Timmy and Katherine, had already opened the game locker and were setting up a Parcheesi board, while the Colonel headed back to the end of the car to speak with Strucker. Neither of the children liked the mannered Teuton, though they would be hard-pressed if asked to say why. There was something officious in his manner toward them, as if they were an impediment in his company. Katherine especially didn't like the way he looked at her; almost, but not quite, a leer.

The Colonel told Alvin, the salon porter, to bring him a scotch and sparkling water. At this, Beatie launched into her familiar diatribe, scolding him for drinking in front of the children, and, in fact, for drinking at all. She was still at it when the servant returned with the cocktail.

"Now, now, Beatie," the Colonel said, shaking his head and waving his hands. "We don't want any of that on this trip. If people want to drink on this train, I don't want them to have to go skulking around out of sight."

"Just as you always do, I suppose," Beatie said sourly.

"That is all too true," replied the Colonel, "because of those carping temperance women whom you associate with."

"And without regard to my feelings, either."

"Well, if your feelings are hurt by seeing a man having his drink before dinner, I imagine they will just have to stay that way," replied the Colonel. "My word, woman, we are descended from Irish warriors!"

"You might be, but I'm not," Beatie huffed.

She settled into the plush rear sofa of *The City of Hartford* while Xenia hovered over the children, who were engrossed in their game at the other end of the car. The dimmed electric lamps gave the polished-mahogany-and-velvet decor of the car a warm, friendly glow, the kind of glow the Colonel liked to get from his whiskey.

Katherine looked up from the Parcheesi board and caught Strucker watching her. He stood now by the door to the observation platform, drinking a double rye and taking in this scene. No German would ever put up with his wife bickering at him that way; in fact, no German wife would even think of such bickering. These Americans were a weak people, despite their material wealth and the vastness of their lands and resources. If Germany owned this country, it would rule the world — and might just wind up doing so anyway, depending on the outcome of the war. Katherine ran her fingers through her hair and offered a quick smile at the German, before wrinkling her nose and returning to the game, which left Strucker looking puzzled. These Americans! he thought. Even the children are weird.

"It all comes from the liquor," Beatie continued resentfully. "From the moment you took up with that wretched woman. And, of course, it was your drinking that caused it!"

"She wasn't wretched," the Colonel corrected his wife, "she was perfectly nice, but you have continued to assume the worst. We were simply acquaintances."

"Wasn't *wretched*!" Beatie huffed. "Why, she ran stark-naked through the lobby of the hotel following the Belmont Stakes!"

"She was merely returning to her room," the Colonel answered dismissively.

Strucker was appalled at being a witness to this conversation, but was not surprised by it; once, long ago, he and the Colonel had taken a pair of women on the yacht then owned by Strucker and sailed them out to Bermuda. Oh, the things that went on! In recent years, however, Strucker was left with the impression that the Colonel had reformed himself, though Strucker couldn't see any reason why he himself should.

From somewhere up the tracks a voice cried out, " 'Boarrrrrd! 'Boarrrrrd!" and the train lurched as the air brakes unlocked. Strucker, who had also ordered a double rye, had been looking around and seemed puzzled, as the Colonel stepped out on the rear platform. "Where is your son, Arthur?" he inquired.

"In Chicago, tending to company business," the Colonel replied sharply.

"And so he is not coming with us?" Strucker asked, surprised.

"Yes, he's coming, but in his own way and his own time. He's *flying* down," the Colonel spat, as though he had a mouthful of ashes.

"Flying?" Strucker repeated, as though he had not understood the answer correctly.

"In that abominable flying machine you arranged for him to get."

"The Luft-Verkehrs?" the German said, astonished.

"None other. Arthur insists that without the guns and ammunition and extra crew member it was designed for, he can take on enough fuel cans and spare parts to stay in the air eight hours at a time and — do you know what he said? He actually said he would *beat* me to El Paso!"

"A race, between train and plane!" Strucker could hardly contain himself.

"That's what he said," the Colonel sniffed. "I told him he was nuts, because my train can run twenty-four hours a day and he can only fly that thing during daylight."

"Well, that Luft-Verkehrs does have a great range," Strucker observed. "It can stay in the air four hours at least, with a full armored load, and who knows how long when it's lightened."

"Arthur says eight." The Colonel shook his head in apparent disgust and motioned for the servant to bring him another scotch. He didn't blame Strucker for getting Arthur the plane; as a matter of fact, he was somewhat beholden to him for doing it. When Arthur first began flying, about all that was available of American aircraft were the Curtiss Jenneys, which were unreliable, slow, and prone to crash. On the other hand, the Europeans — the British, French, and Germans — had made amazing advances in aircraft production and design, since they had actually been at war with each other.

Arthur had set his eye on a sleek little Deperdussin monoplane manufactured in France, but the French War Ministry had forbidden aircraft manufacturers from selling any of their products except to the military. He had almost bought a Blériot E.2 from an owner in Spain, but it turned out to be underpowered and in bad shape.

The subject of airplanes had come up one day the previous year when Strucker was down to Cornwall for a weekend. Sensing an opportunity to ingratiate himself with the American rail baron Shaughnessy, the sly German knew that in his position he could pull strings. Four months later Arthur went to the dock at Boston Harbor and took possession of a brand-spanking-new Luft-Verkehrs, crated up on a Swedish steamer, along with an extra engine and a variety of spare parts. The manufacturer had not put the German Iron Cross on the machine. Instead, at Strucker's direction, he'd painted it a deep candy-apple-red.

"Arthur told me he needed to get back to the company operations headquarters in Chicago and mind the store," the Colonel went on, "but I'll bet it was just an excuse to do this flying stunt."

"Well, it will certainly be interesting to see who wins," Strucker declared. "That's a long distance from Chicago to El Paso, isn't it?"

"It's fifteen hundred miles," the Colonel replied.

The whistle blew in the chilly night air as NE&P No.1, with a plume of steam roiling back over it and vaporizing along the tracks, pulled out of the Providence rail depot and plunged into the inky darkness, toward Mexico.

"He'll be damn lucky if he doesn't crash the thing," the Colonel added. Strucker found himself musing over Arthur's flight. If he could make that distance, why couldn't the Germans power up the Luft-Verkehrs and use them to bomb the cities of England? He'd have to get a message on this revelation through to his superior in the consulate at the first opportunity.

THIRTEEN

Johnny Ollas had been gone only a day when his troubles began in earnest. He got lost.

Mexico was not a hard country to get lost in. Aside from a few rail tracks, main roads, and towns, that part of north-central Mexico was a trackless wilderness of desert, plains, forest, and of course the sinister and seemingly impenetrable Sierra Madre. Every so often one might come across a village of Indians or the occasional adobe hut of a farmer, but mostly the country was a waste.

After leaving Valle del Sol with his four stepbrothers, Johnny tried to track Villa and his army but lost the trail even before he left the property. The fact that one had to go more than twenty-five miles just to *get* off the property was of little consolation, because losing track of an entire army is an embarrassment, even for amateurs. The Callahans were ranch hands and bullfighters, not plainsmen or man-hunters, and the only times Johnny had been this far away from Valle del

Sol he had been on a train or in an automobile.

In any event, they were lost.

Villa's path had been easy enough to follow at first. Not only were there the hoofprints and droppings of thousands of horses and cattle, but also the residue and droppings of five hundred men: campfires, mescal bottles, cigarette and cigar butts, wrapping papers, food tins, and other discarded things. But somewhere the Callahan brothers had gone wrong. The first and second nights, they had camped confident that they were overtaking the four-day-old tracks of the kidnappers. On the third day they arose by a creek and ate the last of Señora Pardenas's beans and by-now-stale bread.

Two hours later, they lost the trail.

The smart way, Johnny realized now, would have been to backtrack, but the path ahead looked so likely, they went on toward the northwest, hoping to pick up the tracks again, and by late afternoon they were, basically, nowhere. In the distance they spotted a settlement of sorts, graying and pinkish in the last shadows of the sun. Dejected, they headed for it.

It was a small Mestizo village, a couple of dozen adobe huts, framed by tall cacti and fica trees. The dusty street that ran through the center of the village was pitted with slime-filled watery holes, and chickens, ducks, turkeys, and a pig or two wandered aimlessly in the thoroughfare. But far from being the kind of sleepy one-horse town they had envisioned, to their surprise the place seethed with activity. At first, Johnny thought some sort of fiesta was in progress.

Then they saw the woman.

She was hobbling on a cane, followed by a donkey loaded with straw brooms strapped to its back and pursued by a crowd of men, women, and children hurling insults, stones, rotten eggs, and spoiled fruit. She was barefoot and wearing a filthy rebozo, the traditional Mexican shawl, and was obviously frightened as she plodded away down the rutted street, occasionally glancing back to see what was to be heaved at her next.

"What town is this?" Johnny asked one of the mob.

The man eyed the horseback-riding strangers suspiciously and shrugged.

"The name — what is the name of this place?"

"No name," the man said.

"What do you mean? You live here, don't you?"

The man nodded.

"So what is the name of this town, then?"

"It hasn't no name," the man said. By now several other ragged-looking men and some children abandoned their persecution of the woman and had come to see the strangers.

Johnny addressed another of them.

"What is the name of this town?" he demanded. "Where are we?"

"You are here," the man said.

"I know I'm here. Where is this?"

"It's just a place," the man replied. "We live here."

"I see that," Johnny said. "You mean there's no name for this town?"

"We've always lived here. There is a river over there." He pointed off toward some trees.

"What is the name of the river?"

The man shrugged.

At first Johnny was beginning to believe the men were making fun of him, but finally it sank in that the village didn't in fact have any name.

"Why were you molesting that woman?" Johnny asked, which had also been on his mind, more out of curiosity than anything else.

"She's a *bruja,*" the man said.

"A witch?"

"And a bad one, too. She makes the melons die, and little children, too. She wouldn't leave, so we run her off."

By this time the woman was past the place where the street stopped and was hobbling across a dusty prairie toward some scrubby-looking willows. The donkey plodded after her. The crowd had straggled back to the village and was milling around in the street

163

among pigs and chickens.

"Have you seen an army?" Johnny said. "Pancho Villa's army? Has it come anywhere near here?"

The man looked at him uncomprehendingly. Johnny suddenly realized that if this man lived in a town that didn't even have a name, he probably didn't know what an army was, either. If in fact Villa's army *had* come through the town, the man would certainly have been impressed enough to remember it, and would have told him.

"Well, let me ask you this," Johnny said. "Where is the nearest big town from here?"

The man shrugged again.

"What direction? Huh? How long does it take to get there?"

The man just gawked at him openmouthed. This man, and all the rest of them, most likely hadn't been more than a couple of miles outside this village in their whole lives. Johnny was not only lost, he was lost among a whole village of lost people who didn't even know they were lost.

He shook his head and wiped the dust from his eyes.

"Well," he told his companions, "we might as well keep on going. See if you can buy some food from these peons. I figure we just stay headed north and maybe something'll turn up. If Villa got to those mountains already, I don't guess there's much we can

164

do anyway. But if he's still out on the plains, there's a chance we can catch up."

Johnny was getting disgusted, mostly with himself, for letting Donita get kidnapped and for being so helpless in tracking her down.

He had married Donita four years ago this month, and already he had failed her. She'd pressed him to begin bullfighting in earnest up at Chihuahua City, which was a day's train ride from the ranch. He wasn't ready and knew it, but she didn't. A man doesn't just get into a bullring with fifteen hundred snorting pounds of horns and hooves unless he knows exactly what he's up to. Not if he expects to get the kinds of ovations and praise a matador needs — let alone avoid being killed or maimed. But everybody at the ranch said Johnny was a natural, that he'd be *número uno* someday, and nobody had believed this more than Johnny Ollas himself.

He had the moves, the brains, the touch.

But there was style to consider. Style was all of it.

One wrong sweep or false move and the aficionados would have him undone. The newspapers would be full of it the next day: "This Johnny Ollas can fight a bull, but he himself is an ox." That kind of thing. And now Donita was in the clutches of the most fearsome and legendary bandit and revolutionary general in the entire nation, a man who would line you up and shoot you with no more provocation than perhaps a gnat bite; the man who had strung up Buck Callahan and eviscerated him for mere amusement. And Johnny Ollas, himself no pistolero, and with a still-festering head wound and so followed by flies, was chasing after a whole army of Villistas with four men and no particular plan in mind for how to retrieve his wife from this monster. I must be nuts, concluded Johnny Ollas. A leading candidate for *un castañazo.*

A little way out of town, Johnny and his brothers came to a small muddy stream lined with swamp willows which looked like as good as anyplace to camp for the night. Johnny's brothers Julio and Rigaz had purchased some beans and dried corn and bacon in the village and they set up a fire to cook on. Luis and Rafael went to the stream for water but sheep had apparently been using it for a toilet. They dipped a pot in and skimmed off the muck as best they could, then set up the pot over some rotted limbs. Everyone was uneasy, since none had the faintest idea of where they were.

But Johnny's cuadrilla inspired his faith. More than once they had saved his skin at the risk of their own. When he had been lying in bed with the head gash they had gathered around and Luis said to him, "Whatever you want to do, Johnny, we'll be with you." He'd appreciated that more than words at the time could express. So here they all were: five men against an army.

Once they'd begun cooking their meal, they beat down the thick wiregrass to make a comfortable place to stretch out. The sun had been down for an hour when the woman appeared. They had been discussing what to do in the morning when they heard the rustling of her donkey in the brush, and then the woman emerged from some low shrubs, the firelight flickering on her face, hooded by the shawl. Her eyes were dark and hollow. Rigaz had already drawn his pistol at the sound of the donkey and he had it resting on his lap, pointed in the woman's direction. Out here, at night and lost in presumably hostile territory, the first instinct of all five of the men had been to take cover when they heard the rustling of the animal, but just as quickly they reassessed this urge on the grounds that a completely defensive posture might tend to aggravate the situation — especially if the intruders were a larger force.

"Buenas tardes," said Johnny Ollas.

"You want some bread?" the woman asked.

"Bread?"

"I got some corn flour — yeast. You got a fire. I smell something cooking. Maybe I could make some bread for you," she said.

Johnny looked at the others. They seemed none too comfortable to have a bruja in their camp, but here they were out on the desolate llanos, and she was alone and seemed harmless, and the notion of bread with their supper was appealing.

"That all you got, bread?" Julio said.

"That's it. I thought maybe we could share a little meal. I have a long journey tomorrow."

"You know where we are?" Johnny asked.

"Sure," she said. The donkey had wandered into the campsite by now and began grazing on the edges of the firelight.

"Where?"

"Plain of the Winds," she said.

"Yeah, well, where is that?" Johnny asked.

"You go west, you be in the barrancas, east is the llanos," she said, signifying either the canyons or the barren plains. "North is the great desert. I guess you come up from the south, but I suppose you know where you come from."

"That doesn't tell me much," Johnny said. "We got a compass. We know where the mountains and everything are. We need to know where is the nearest town — city, you know what I mean?" It wasn't exactly the truth, but it saved them some face.

"Well, there is a big town, Chihuahua City. Maybe two, three days from here."

She wasn't telling Johnny anything he didn't know. He'd fought in the bullring there. But, in fact, from here he didn't have the foggiest notion of which way Chihuahua was. "Where's the road to that?" he asked.

"There isn't one from here. You follow the morning sun, day or so, there'll be a road."

"We're looking for a man with an army," Johnny said. "General Pancho Villa. You heard of him?"

"Of course."

"Yes? Know where he is?"

"Yes."

"Where, then?"

"He's in Creel."

"Where's that?"

"North. On your horses, four days."

"How do you know this?"

"The bones tell me."

"Bones? What bones?"

The woman reached into a pocket of her dingy dress and produced a handful of some kind of bones, mixed up. Looked to Johnny like chicken and pig and sheep and maybe a cow bone or a bird's, all bleached white as sand. Johnny had seen people throw the bones before. Fortune-telling, or some such. Just old women's superstition.

"So what is it you're trying to tell me? You threw those bones and figured out where Pancho Villa was?"

"I don't need to throw them. I keep them in my pocket. Now, you want some bread with your dinner?"

Johnny looked at his brothers. The woman

seemed harmless enough. Probably crazy, but she obviously knew something about what she was talking about. At least more than those ignoramuses back at the no-name village. And bread sounded good.

"Okay," Johnny said, "let's have some bread. The beans are almost done." He motioned for her to join them and sit on a log. She went to a ratty-looking canvas sack on the donkey and pulled out a paper bag of flour, then pulled up a log by the fire.

"You got some water?"

"In that tin there," Rafael said.

The woman got the tin and began mixing the flour with the water inside the paper bag, just a little at a time so the bag didn't burst, and then took out a little tin of yeast. She took off her shawl to reveal a head of long straight black Indian hair that had an almost deep indigo sheen to it. Actually, in the firelight, she wasn't bad-looking. She was tall, slender but supple. Maybe forty or so years old, much younger than they'd first thought. And she had strong, high cheeks and a straight nose like his own, a "Spanish" nose, not Indian at all. In fact, after a while they could see a certain ageless beauty to this woman, even if she was a witch.

"What's your name?" Johnny asked.

"They call me Gourd Woman."

"They also say you're a *bruja.*"

"Maybe. Sometimes I suppose I am a

bruja."

"Witches aren't very popular anymore," Johnny remarked.

"It depends on who you're with."

"The people in that village said you made their children sick and their fruit die."

"How? I was only there four days. I came to sell them brooms."

"Brooms?"

"Yeah, I make them out of straw I pick up." She pointed toward the donkey and the load of brooms strapped to its back. "Right time of year, you can find the straw in just about any place; just have to keep moving. The handles, I make them out of branches. Strip off the bark and polish the wood with oil. Makes a nice broom. Better than store-bought, huh?"

"Where do you come from?" he asked.

"No place. I never had a home."

"Nobody comes from no place," Johnny remarked, but he was on the verge of taking it back after he suddenly remembered the people of the no-name village.

"You did," she said.

"What makes you say that?"

"Bones tell me. You were born in a ditch."

Johnny Ollas sat up, startled. Nobody on the ranch had ever talked about this with him since they'd first explained it when he was a small boy. Gourd Woman continued to knead the flour and water inside the paper bag while she stared at the fire. Up above, the night had become dark as ink and stars were twinkling brightly. There was no moon and a chill had settled over the plains.

"Gourd woman . . ." Johnny said. "You don't have another name?"

"Everyone called me Lurie when I was little," she said. "And I'm not really a *bruja,* I think I'm a *curandera* — I heal people."

"Then why do they call you Gourd Woman?" Johnny asked.

"I don't know," she said. "I sell brooms."

FOURTEEN

The city of Juárez had always been an annoyance to Pancho Villa. It sat directly across the Rio Grande from El Paso, where Villa received his arms and supplies from American munitions companies. Three times he had taken the city from the Federal forces, but he couldn't hold it and was forced to withdraw. And each time the Federal forces reentered the city they strengthened its defenses. In the past this had been a mere inconvenience, but President Woodrow Wilson had done him the discourtesy of officially recognizing his sworn enemy, Carranza, as the legitimate leader of Mexico.

Now that his arms and munitions shipments from America were cut off, Villa needed to go to El Paso and talk to his old pal, the U.S. army commander Scott, to find out what was going on and whether the situation could be restored. After due consideration, he concluded the strongest case he could present to Scott would be to recapture

Juárez from the Carranza men and prove he was still in charge of Northern Mexico. First, however, Villa would have to take Chihuahua, because he couldn't leave the Federal garrison there in his rear.

Furthermore, Juárez was more than two hundred miles away, across the largest and most hostile desert on the American continent. He had last taken the city a year ago by a trick he remembered from the fable of the Trojan horse.

A Federal train arriving at Chihuahua City from Juárez was seized by Villa's men. Using the name of the train's commander, and with a pistol at the head of the telegraph operator, Villa sent a message to the general of the Federal force at Juárez saying that his locomotive was broken down and he needed a new one, plus a dozen more boxcars. The new train was dutifully sent and Villa loaded nearly two thousand of his soldiers aboard. Villa now sent a second wire to Juárez, addressed to the train's commander: "Large force of rebel troops approaching from south. What should I do?" Presently the answer that Villa was waiting for was tapped out: "Return at once."

Juárez was duly captured next day from the stunned Federales and this feat gained Villa worldwide recognition. But that was then, and nobody was going to fall for such a ruse again, so Villa occupied himself tearing up railroad tracks, cutting telegraph wires, and moving slowly through the countryside on horseback.

It was unseasonably hot as the general's caravan, with Donita Ollas in tow, plodded north.

At the small town of Denardo they came across the scene of a horrendous massacre Villa's men were in the process of finishing. Some of his troops had gone there earlier and determined that many of Denardo's citizens now favored the Federal government of Carranza — a position that had been indelibly impressed upon the villagers during a recent visit by some of Carranza's men. A second lesson-teaching was in order, Villa's captain in charge had decided, and now, as the travelers rode past the macabre site, Donita Ollas was sure she would be sick.

She was riding in a wagon, escorted by Tom Mix. It was a warm, pleasant morning, with gentle breezes and a pastel-blue sky. Donita was thus doubly unprepared for what she saw when they reached the village. It seemed like half the town had been wiped out. Bodies of men, women, and children lay scattered in the streets, many being picked apart by dogs or *zopilotes.* Others were hanging from trees and doorways, some flayed alive and their skin hanging down in strips. Fires had been lit under some of these, and the bodies smoldered. Small children stared in shock or wept over their dead parents or relatives. Many of the horses became unnerved by the strange sight, their ears laid back, and they became skittish and shivery.

Donita gasped. Mix himself had been looking straight ahead so as to avoid seeing the carnage.

"It's a rough war," Mix told her.

"You call this war?" Donita buried her face in a handkerchief. The stench of death hung heavily over the place.

"It's the way the Mexicans fight it, ma'am," Mix replied. "They don't give no quarter or ask for any."

"It is not war, it is revolution," came a voice from behind them.

Villa had ridden up, the silver on his saddle jingling, and overtaken the wagon. "You think these people wouldn't do the same to us if the chance came?"

Donita waved the handkerchief in front of her nose to snuff out the smell. "You must be monsters, to kill people this way," she said.

"Revolution is different," Villa continued. "Nobody likes this kind of thing. But it's necessary. We learned this from the Spaniards. You got to kill people twice: once to make sure they're dead, then to make sure their souls are dead. That's the way the stinking Spanish started doing things here four hundred years ago. We were just taught too well, maybe."

"To kill women?" Donita said disgustedly.

"You don't think women kill us, too?" Villa said. "Women can shoot a rifle like anybody else. Matter of fact, somebody shot at my men as they rode into town."

Donita knew he was right and had heard of numerous women in Villa's army, armed to the teeth.

"The citizens must learn to understand that unwise choices of loyalty can have bad consequences. I bet next time my men come into this town they get a more polite reception."

Villa ordered the wagon stopped. They were in front of a church where several of his men were manhandling a priest through the portals. The church was an adobe building two hundred years old with beautiful oriental-looking cupolas. The priest was a short, balding Mestizo man with tears in his eyes. They brought him before Villa.

"Well, Padre," Villa said, "do your people see now the error of their ways?"

"Why, you've killed most of them," the priest said. He looked frightened, but belligerent, too.

"Yes, I imagine you'll have a smaller parish now. Not so many alms to collect, eh?"

"How can you commit such things in the face of God?" the priest cried bitterly. His face was a purple mask of anger.

" 'Face of God,' you say? Why, we've done

nothing more than recreate the murals on the walls of your own churches. This is what those stinking Spaniards brought over here with them — your Holy Inquisition. Huh?" This had been a theme of Villa's for many years. Paintings in the churches showing people suffering horrible torture at the hands of the Inquisition, which in Villa's view was only to intimidate the churchgoers, especially the little children. The Church itself naturally supported whatever government was in power, which Villa concluded was only so it could keep operating smoothly and keep collecting alms from the peasants.

"It is murder," the priest said. "God will punish you."

"It is revolution," Villa retorted. "And don't talk to me about God. What kind of God lets this kind of thing happen in the first place, eh?"

Villa could feel the old rage rising up in him and he welcomed it, the rage slowly encompassing everything, welling from deep within.

" 'What kind of God,' you ask?" cried the priest. "There is only one God, and he is watching. God doesn't forgive murder," said the priest. "Murder is a mortal sin."

"Don't you worry that I will have you stood up against a wall and shot to rags for talking to me like that?" Villa asked.

"Everybody dies," the priest replied, looking Villa in the eye.

Villa took a deep breath and sighed, looking out past the fields that surrounded the town. He stretched his shoulders and bit his lip, and slowly shook his head back and forth, as if trying to clear some evil impulse, before turning back to the priest. The rage had mercifully receded.

"Well, Padre, maybe your God answers you today, huh?" said Villa. "I was within an inch of giving the order, but I had a man hung once I ought not to have, and it bothers me still."

He nudged his horse down the street; Mix and Donita followed in the wagon.

"He's a maniac," Donita Ollas said under her breath. "You're all maniacs."

FIFTEEN

The race began at precisely seven a.m.

The Colonel's railcar, *The City of Hartford,*
arrived in Chicago the night before. It had
been agreed that the train would start from
the Chicago yards, while at the same time
Arthur would take off from a flying field near
the lake. There were no rules to speak of.
Whoever got to El Paso first would check into
the Toltec Hotel; the desk ledger would prove
the time.

Arthur had been in Chicago for five days,
getting into the office at the crack of dawn
and not leaving until well after dark, tending
to all the myriad little details that he could
before an absence of who knew how long.
His second-in-command, a vice president
named Smith, was a capable man in whose
trust Arthur placed the immediate future of
the NE&P.

After work, Arthur would drive out to the
flying field and work on the Luft-Verkehrs,
which he had named *Grendel,* after the

monster in *Beowulf.* It didn't matter to Arthur that Beowulf had killed Grendel in the end, Arthur just liked the name. It was a nice flying ship, much faster and more maneuverable than the Jennys, although it was large, with a wingspan of forty-two feet two inches, and was twenty-five feet seven inches from propeller to tail. The *Grendel* was a two-seater biplane designed by the Germans as a reconnaissance aircraft, which was why it had a four-hour airborne endurance capability, double that of most airplanes. It was powered by a 160-horsepower Mercedes D.III six-cylinder in-line engine, water-cooled, and had an airspeed of eighty-one miles per hour. It could climb to a maximum altitude of 16,405 feet and, more important, had a reinforced landing gear that would allow it to set down in a farm field or other rough surface. It was the envy of every aviator at the Aero Club in Chicago.

Without the added weight of its normal two machine guns and their ammunition, and the gunner, Arthur was able to rearrange the fuselage to carry eight twelve-gallon jerry cans of fuel, which he had instructed the machine shop to connect by copper pipes with a faucet tap in between each can. When the main fuel tank was running low, Arthur could simply reach back and turn one of the taps to add another twelve gallons of fuel, thus doubling his capacity. He also found room for thirty quarts of oil, spare magnetos, firing plugs, cylinder rods, gaskets, hoses, belts, strut wire, grease, an extra propeller, and an expanded tool kit.

All of this preparation in a single week was a stupendous achievement for Arthur Shaughnessy, given that he also had to be in his office twelve hours a day. But it paled in comparison with the acclaim he would receive if he completed his cross-country flight in the time he anticipated. Only a few years earlier a man named Cal Rodgers had set out on a cross-country flight in a Wright biplane from the East Coast to the West Coast. Rodgers had arranged for an entire railroad train to follow him, filled with spare parts, fuel, and a machine and woodworking shop, and, some said, a coffin, just in case. It still took him eighty-two days and seven crash landings before he arrived. The fact that Arthur could now contemplate making a fifteen-hundred-mile journey such as this in three days was a tribute in itself to the lightning advances that aviation was making since the Wright brothers first flew a heavier-than-air craft not much more than a decade earlier.

In the dim light of the hangar, Arthur surveyed *Grendel,* and it had never looked so magnificent. Her candy-apple-red fuselage and wings seemed almost translucent in the light. He had already stowed tins of canned beef, raisins, prunes, apples, oranges, peanut butter, cookies, a large Polish salami, hot mustard, two gallons of water, several bottles of beer, a side of cheddar cheese, and some crackers. In the morning he would stop by the bakery to add two loaves of freshly baked bread and pick up a hot roasted chicken at a delicatessen.

Arthur had stayed up night after night planning the voyage, poring over maps until past two a.m. Regular landing fields were few and far between, especially after Wichita, Kansas. The next one he could hope to make in a day was at Amarillo, Texas, and after that there would only be the vast and empty spaces of Texas and New Mexico before he reached El Paso on the Mexican border.

It was a daunting challenge, but Arthur felt up to it. In fact, he'd been planning such a trip in his mind ever since first setting sight on the Luft-Verkehrs when it arrived in its crate from Germany. It had been his notion to outdo the aviator Rodgers's feat by flying over the Rockies in a single leap, but now this seemed even better. Nobody had ever flown from Chicago to El Paso, especially single-handed. While he still had worries about the Colonel's intention to bring his family into the turmoil across the border, Arthur also thought he might set some kind of flying record. And besides, he thought, an airplane might somehow come in handy down in Mexico.

Colonel John Shaughnessy had also been figuring out his game plan. He was not going to be outdone by a son of his who had almost thrown it in his face that a flimsy flying machine could beat a sturdy railroad train operating on its own inexorable timetables. Nevertheless, Shaughnessy had taken precautions. He had arranged with the dispatchers that *The City of Hartford,* NE&P No. 1, would have a through route, no waiting for freights and milk trains.

Through his pals in the business, he secured his clearances and, after studying his routes, concluded that his train would travel directly from Chicago to Memphis, where it would cross the Mississippi and head southwest though Little Rock, Dallas, and on into Big Spring, Texas, to El Paso. There were shorter ways to go — though St. Louis, for instance — but then he would be stuck with trunk lines, and who knew how well they were kept up?

The Colonel calculated that even if Arthur could manage five hundred miles a day in the aircraft, daylight to dusk, he would probably have to set down well before that to refuel, since flying fields weren't located so conveniently as rail depots. And that was also assuming Arthur didn't have any mechanical problems or weather that would put him out of action earlier.

Naturally, in the back of his mind the

Colonel wished Arthur well. In a sense, it was a no-lose situation for the Colonel, but he still loved a good fight, and wasn't about to slack off. As he sat at his desk on the train, making mathematic figurings on foolscap and calculating the train speed, route, and downtimes for recoaling, Colonel Shaughnessy was actually proud of his son. Might just be he'd raised a chip off the old block after all. But he wasn't about to give Arthur a hint of this.

The night before the race began, they all dined in Chicago at the Palmer House, with its huge Corinthian columns, marble-tiled floors, and giant, bulbous chandeliers.

"Well, at least the weather looks good for you," the Colonel told Arthur. He had checked with the U.S. Weather Bureau and learned that skies were forecast to be clear over the entire section of country that they'd be traveling; perfect autumn days, with a Pacific high lingering over the midlands. Arthur nodded. He'd been checking it himself twice a day.

Claus Strucker was seated at the opposite end of the table, wearing a high formal collar that appeared to be chafing his neck. "So?" Strucker said expansively. "Who am I going to be pulling for?" He tried adjusting the collar but it seemed to do no good. "Will I bet on the man I arranged to receive this extraordinary German aircraft, or my gracious host on his train down to Mexico?"

"If you're betting money," Arthur said, "I'd put it in the air."

"Ha!" the Colonel responded. "My wheels may be slow, but they turn day and night. Haven't you heard the fable of the tortoise and the hare?"

"Papa will win," Katherine said emphatically.

"Ungrateful child," the Colonel responded. "I suppose the lot of you are against me!" They all laughed. Katherine wasn't against the Colonel, she loved the Old Man and his nutty ways; in fact, she sensed she was like him in his impetuosity, his zaniness. She brushed a long curl off her forehead and said:

"No, Grandpapa, we're just *for* Papa." Shaughnessy truly loved this golden child; what beauty, what poise, what . . . *Shaughnessyness*. And oh, how she could ride a horse.

"Trains go to El Paso all the time," Beatie put in. "But aeroplanes don't. I think that's what everybody's trying to say."

"And there's a reason for that," answered the Colonel. "Reliability. We make our own stock in pure reliability."

"It's a new and different world," Strucker exuded. "Great changes are overtaking us." He tried shrugging his shoulders but the collar was getting the best of him. A red mark had appeared on his neck.

Arthur looked at the German. True,

Strucker had arranged the aircraft purchase, but there had always been something about the man he didn't exactly comprehend. His manners were almost too polished; his eyes were unreadable, and if the "great changes" he was speaking of were embodied in what the Germans were up to in Europe these days, Arthur felt he could do without them. He might have said something about that, but instead he just smiled.

"And when we get into Mexico," the Colonel continued, "you can bet we'll all be on steel wheels and rails, because they don't even know what a flying machine is down there." He was so confident in winning that he had tipped off an executive at his pal Hearst's newspaper, and the morning news was full of the train-plane race.

Arthur answered, "I still think we should let the situation that we find once we get to El Paso dictate whether or not we actually go into Mexico. Things can change very quickly in the kind of war they're fighting."

"Oh, please don't start that up again," his father groaned. "We aren't quitters."

Arthur sat looking at his father, trying to meet the man's eyes with a defiant stare, but the Colonel gazed at the napkin in his lap, paying Arthur no attention. The table was suddenly silent, then everyone heard Strucker try to stifle a belch. He had fiddled with the collar so much it had sprung open and framed his neck ridiculously like a set of white wings.

Despite the weather report, when Arthur took off next morning the skies over Chicago were gray and thick. He climbed the *Grendel* to eight thousand feet and broke through the overcast. The sun shone brightly as he scanned the dusky bank of cloud beneath him that stretched from horizon to horizon. He wished it had been clear, because he'd hoped to locate the Colonel's train and give it a barnstorming buzz, but since that wasn't possible, Arthur concentrated on his tasks at hand. Navigating by compass was the most difficult; he felt the tug of a westerly wind and knew it would push him off course. He kept the needle of the compass south-southwest, but since he was above the cloud ceiling there were no reference points. He could dip beneath it, but no telling what he'd find; the soup might go all the way to the ground. Kansas City would have been the better destination but it was too far. A little town called Kirksville lay about two hundred miles closer and it had a landing field. Arthur had earlier arranged by phone to have someone meet him there and refuel the plane. He would rest that night beneath the wings, in a sleeping bag.

He wondered how his father's part of the race was going. The Old Man was always a determined competitor and Arthur knew he'd have *The City of Hartford* at full steam. As he floated near the heavens, he recalled the time at a dinner party years earlier when the Colonel, after having a few, bet the owner of a Muncie steel mill fifty thousand dollars he could hit the bull's-eye of a target with a hatchet thrown from fifty feet. Next morning, instead of eating crow and calling the thing off, the Colonel phoned the man and told him to bring his fifty thousand. The Colonel won it, too.

About noon the cloudbank dropped off, a relief to Arthur, since the land below was now clearly visible, large patches of farm fields dotted with the occasional house and barn. Below he could see the Illinois River and followed it until in the distance he got a glimpse of the vast Mississippi, shimmering in the bright autumn sun. After he'd flown across it, he descended to about three hundred feet to get his bearings. Surprisingly, a road sign told him he was on Route 6, which ran right into Kirksville.

After another hour he spotted the landing field on the south side of the town and was astonished to see a host of automobiles and a huge crowd of people. Arthur circled the strip twice, noted the wind sock, then brought the Luft-Verkehrs in for a smooth landing on a grassy field. When he taxied up to the flying shack, the mob surged around the *Grendel*.

"You the feller going to El Paso?" asked a man in a grease-monkey suit.

"That's me," Arthur said as he climbed down from the cockpit. A cheer rose from the crowd.

"Well, mister, we're all proud of you," said the grease monkey. "I'll get you gassed up right now." He went to a fuel truck and pulled it beside *Grendel,* put the nozzle into the fuel tank, and began pumping with a hand lever. Meantime, everyone wanted to shake Arthur's hand. He received so many invitations to dinner and a warm bed he was not only stunned, but perplexed about how to handle the offers.

Finally it was agreed there would be a dinner in Arthur's honor at the town Elks Club, and afterward he could decide whose bedroom he wanted to sleep in. He knew from the map that he had come 489 miles.

Next morning, Colonel Shaughnessy's NE&P Train No. 1 had stopped at the Memphis railroad depot, waiting for coal to be loaded on. In twenty-four hours he had made 550 miles. Saturday was bright and many people crowded the station, including peddlers and vendors of newspapers, pies and cakes, hair tonics, and straw hats. There was also a clown walking on stilts and a man with a performing bear.

Timmy and Katherine pressed their faces

to the windows of *The City of Hartford,* drinking all of it in. Even though they'd sailed with the Colonel on *Ajax,* this was the greatest adventure of their lives. Timmy, who had more of his father's temperament than the Colonel's, was especially excited when the Colonel described for him Buck Callahan's superb ability as a craftsman and woodcarver. Timmy's current interest was in building wood models — ships, airplanes, automobiles — all of which came in kits with glue, paper, and balsawood. But Buck, the Colonel said, would show him how to make things out of real hardwood, substantial things with heft and strength: animals, birds, things with curves and depth. He nearly couldn't wait.

Strucker was amused by the bear, which was doing a sort of dance with a cane while its owner, a dressed as a gypsy, cranked out a tune on a hurdy-gurdy. For most of the morning, to the disgust of Beatie, Strucker had indulged himself in orange juice and gin and by now was basking in its glow.

"That bear is quite a sight," exclaimed the authoritarian Junker. "It looks almost human, does it not?" Strucker was wearing an expensive-looking dark green vicuña smoking jacket with a yellow silk ascot. When he arose from his parlor chair to get a better look from the window, Xenia could have sworn she heard him click his heels.

"Maybe it's just a man in a bear suit," Xenia remarked hopefully. Like Arthur, she didn't like Strucker much, despite the man's reputation as a cultivated internationalist and despite the Colonel's high opinion of him as a yachtsman. Strucker represented himself as a businessman who professed to be appalled with the stupendous bloodletting recently unleashed by what most Americans commonly assumed was German greed. But Xenia's experience with Germans was that they rarely turned on their own kind — even the Americanized ones, which Strucker was not — and she found the urbane Saxon a bit too suave to be true.

The Colonel had gone to the telegraph depot in the train station to see if his Boston office had transmitted him any messages of importance. As he was returning to the car, the performing bear act caught his eye.

"Look," Timmy said, "there's Grandpa."

"Your grandfather certainly enjoys animals," Xenia said.

The Colonel was transfixed with the bear act, sporting a strange sort of smile on his face. The bear was not a particularly large specimen, but standing on its hind paws, it was nearly tall as the Colonel. It was unmuzzled and, with its mouth open, appeared to be smiling.

The organ grinder quit grinding and began feeding the bear peanuts, which it ate shells and all. The Colonel stepped forward from the small crowd and began petting the bear on its head. The bear responded by licking the Colonel's fingers. The Colonel was talking to the gypsy, who began nodding his head.

Out on the platform the Colonel was still speaking to the gypsy, who was now waving his hands and shaking his head. The Colonel pulled something out of his coat pocket and displayed it for the gypsy, who began emphatically shaking his head.

"My God!" Xenia said. "He's going to have it in here with us. He's trying to buy it!"

"Buy what?" Timmy asked. It never occurred to him the Colonel would go so far as to *buy* the bear, but he wouldn't be surprised if he somehow *invited* the bear onto the train.

"The bear, you dummy," Katherine told him. Xenia shot her a disapproving look but said nothing, and Katherine was sorry she'd used the word.

"What?" Strucker inquired. "The Colonel is going to buy this bear?" He was watching Katherine appreciatively from the corner of his eye. Before long . . . he thought, she would be a very handsome woman.

Katherine caught his glance and it made her uncomfortable. She was caught in a transformation she did not really understand. A year ago she had stopped wearing her blond hair in pigtails and now let it fall around her shoulders. And she had noticed lately the way boys and some men looked at her. She knew she was pretty — she'd certainly been told it enough ever since she could remember — but she didn't comprehend all that it meant, and thought about it from time to time. In any case, for now, to the great relief of her father, she was mostly interested in horses.

"The bear is for us?" Timmy wondered. He suddenly imagined in some way the bear sitting in one of *The City of Hardford*'s plush parlor chairs, with a bib around its neck, drinking a glass of milk . . .

Now the Colonel was waving more money in front of the gypsy's nose and the man was clearly wavering. His gestures now included shrugging of the shoulders.

"What's going on here?" Beatie said, emerging from the bedroom section of the car.

"We think father is trying to buy that bear," Xenia said.

"What bear?"

"The one out there on the platform."

"That's absurd. What would we do with a bear?" Beatie huffed, peering out the window.

"Look," Xenia said. Out on the platform it appeared a deal had been struck. The gypsy was now nodding his head and had accepted a wad of paper from the Colonel. In return, the Colonel accepted the bear's leather rope leash from the gypsy.

"He's done it," Xenia groaned.

"You must be mistaken," said Beatie. "We

can't have a bear. Bears are for zoos."

"Wanna bet?" Xenia said.

"He must have been drinking again," Beatie wailed. "Has the Colonel been drinking this morning?"

The Colonel led the bear toward the train on its leash while the gypsy watched with his hands clasped. His face seemed a long mask of sorrow, but every so often he glanced down at the wad of bills the Colonel had given him.

Arthur took off from Kirksville just after sunrise. At last he had a fine, clear day, and his spirits soared with the *Grendel*. He wondered to himself what his life would have been like without flying, and as the day went by reflected on the bittersweet memories of his first rendezvous with ethereal things.

It had been, most oddly, nearly five years earlier at a dance in New York and a chance encounter with a beautiful woman, *not his wife,* at the Astor Hotel. Arthur had stepped out of the ballroom for a moment to smoke a cigar when he saw walking toward him from the lobby entrance an exquisite female accompanied by the famous actors John and Ethel Barrymore. She was tall and breathtakingly beautiful and Arthur managed a slight bow as she passed by. He thought for a moment she hadn't noticed him, but she suddenly stopped her laughter with her companions and gave him a smiling nod. The

Barrymores stopped, too, and in the awkward moment Arthur said, "I am a great admirer."

Barrymore began to say something, but the young woman cut in, "Of mine, I hope."

"Yes, certainly," said Arthur. Her smile, her lips, her blue eyes all dazzled . . . "But I . . ."

"I am Harriet Quimby," she said, "and these are — oh, but of course you know."

"Yes," Arthur said haltingly. "And I am Arthur Shaughnessy."

"Miss Quimby is the theater critic for *Leslie's Weekly,*" Barrymore said by way of introduction. "We have all just come from one of Georgie Cohan's silly farces."

"We're going to the lounge for a supper. Would you join us?" Harriet Quimby said.

Arthur was stunned at the brazenness, but somehow, coming from her, it did not seem untoward. After all, these were theater people. He suddenly felt brazen himself. "Well, I am in here," he said, nodding toward the door to the ballroom. "Why don't you come and join me? There's plenty to eat and drink, and grand music, too."

"A dance?" Ethel Barrymore said.

"Yes, the Nine O'Clocks," Arthur replied. "But we're quite sociable. After all, this is New York. And it would be a grand coup for me to introduce your party to my friends."

"It's not a costume ball, is it?" intoned Barrymore, who in fact was dressed in evening clothes.

"Heavens, no," Arthur replied. "Just a little get-together of friends. We do it twice a year."

"Well . . ." Ethel said. "You are so kind . . ."

"Oh, let's!" Harriet Quimby injected, taking them both by the arms. "We might get to meet fashionable people."

Barrymore looked mischievously at his sister and Arthur led the trio into the grand ballroom of the Astor, where five hundred people were dancing away. He threaded them toward his table, where Xenia was seated with their friends, and made his introductions. The rest of the guests were duly impressed by the Barrymores because even if they *were* theater people, they were presently the most famous theater people on earth. Barrymore danced with Harriet, Arthur danced with Ethel, and when they had all settled back down at the table and champagne and various canapés and caviar had been brought and consumed, Arthur found himself next to the beautiful Harriet Quimby, who asked, "And so, Mr. Shaughnessy, what is your profession?"

Arthur told her — at the time, he was not first vice president and general manager, but simply vice president in charge of freight operations in the New York office.

"How interesting," Harriet said politely.

"No, not really," Arthur replied. "Not unless you find the moving of all sorts of things all over the place interesting. I would think your work at *Leslie's Weekly* far more fascinating than what I do."

"That's not the half of it," Barrymore interrupted. He quickly swallowed a mouthful of Beluga caviar to finish his thought. "Harriet is the rarest of avis — she is an aeroplane flier, as well."

"You . . . are an aviator?" Arthur asked.

"The only female in the world to drive a flying machine," Barrymore declared cheerfully.

"No, that's not so," said Harriet. "There is another, my friend Miss Moisant. Her brother was killed in an exhibition near New Orleans last year. You might have heard of it."

"Well, that's just . . . well. I think it's wonderful," Arthur said.

"Why don't you come out to the aerodrome and see us sometime?" Harriet said.

"Where is the aerodrome?" Arthur asked.

"Near Mineola, on Long Island," she replied. "We'll be flying tomorrow afternoon."

Next morning Arthur had put Xenia on the train back to Boston and went straight to a motorcar agency, where he rented a long red Chrysler convertible and drove it to Mineola and the Moisant aerodrome. He arrived at about two, just in time to watch Harriet Quimby glide to a perfect landing on a lush grass strip in her new two-seat Blériot monoplane, painted pure white. Arthur had seen airplanes before, but never a monoplane —

all the rest had two or three sets of wings. Harriet emerged from the cockpit in a peach-colored flying suit and white silk scarf. She looked stunning.

"Oh, Mr. Shaughnessy, you're here!" Harriet cried. "What a delight!"

"Well, yes," Arthur said a little sheepishly, "I thought it would be smart to see what the competition is up to."

Harriet Quimby laughed heartily. "Oh, I don't think your big railroads are going to have to worry about us in our little flying machines," she said. "We only do this for a pastime. To soar with eagles . . ."

"That's a handsome machine of yours," Arthur ventured.

"Would you like to go up?" It seemed to Arthur an especially warm invitation.

"Well, I . . ." Arthur hesitated. Would he?

"Oh, do! I promise I won't do anything rash. No loops or anything. Just straight and level — the *first* time."

Arthur shuffled a little. He had in the back of his mind thought this might happen and that he would find himself sailing through the skies with the beautiful Harriet Quimby, but now . . . and a woman . . . but if she would do it, how could he . . .

"They've fueled me up," she said, glancing over her shoulder. Arthur stood mute. It's now or never; carpe diem, Arthur . . .

■ ■ ■ ■

So Arthur Shaughnessy climbed into the cockpit of Harriet's airplane and began for himself an experience that, to his mind, changed his life forever.

Harriet was an expert flier. She had performed acrobatic stunts at the inauguration ceremony of President Madero in Mexico City in 1911, and only a few months before had become the first woman to fly across the English Channel. She was a marvelous instructor, patient and good-humored. In four weeks' time, Arthur was flying solo, first in a little Curtis biplane trainer, and then Harriet's own Blériot.

Arthur went home to Xenia in Boston on Fridays and returned to New York on Mondays, but during the week, as the spring days grew longer, he would drive out to Mineola with Harriet in the afternoons for a few hours of flying time. Afterward, they would ride back to the city and often dine together. Sometimes Arthur wondered what his reaction would be if she moved to take things to a different level. She was a joyous, freespirited woman whom most men would probably find irresistible, but, at least in Arthur's company, she blithely reversed her occasional advances, reaching out and touching his arm sometimes during an animated exchange, but then withdrawing her hand immediately.

For her part, Xenia did not attempt to strip Arthur of his interest, either in flying or in Harriet Quimby; he talked freely with her about his flying experiences. Quimby she could understand, but flying she could not. It seemed to be constantly on Arthur's mind, a preoccupation she hoped would eventually wane. Then, one day in mid-May 1912, Arthur announced to Xenia that he had invited Harriet to come to Boston to stay with them while she was participating in a big flying exhibition over Boston Harbor.

Xenia was gracious and even grateful, because she assumed that if an affair had been in progress, Arthur would not invite the woman in question to stay in her home. Both Harriet and her flying machine arrived a week before the air show, courtesy of the NE&P, and Xenia gave a big dinner for her and, when the evening was done, had satisfied herself that she in fact liked Harriet Quimby very much and hoped they, too, might become friends.

Moreover, Arthur had arranged for Harriet's date at the dinner to be Mick Martin, who arrived full of fun and stories and dressed in a fine tuxedo with a gold wolf's-head collar piece that had sparkling rubies for its eyes — gaudy, but Mick could bring it off. When Harriet left the room for a moment, Mick had whispered to Arthur,

"Thanks for this, bucko. She's a stunner, all right."

In the beginning, Mick and Harriet hit it off grandly. He not only took her to lunch next day, but went flying with her later, and then took her to dinner by themselves that night. Xenia remarked to Arthur that this might be the start of serious intentions and he agreed, although he felt somewhat slighted, since he himself was attracted to Harriet. Somehow it still bothered him that Mick was getting the girl, as usual.

Several nights later they were all going to the theater but Mick wasn't present. When Arthur asked if he was coming, Harriet said, sharply, no. Xenia later asked Harriet, but her answer was vague, and when Xenia persisted, Harriet made it plain she didn't wish to pursue the subject. Arthur asked Mick about it, too, and got a similar reaction. Clearly something had happened.

On the afternoon of the aerial show Harriet flew a number of stunts before a crowd of thousands, and as her finale she was to fly all the way out to circle the Boston Light, twenty miles to sea and back. She had asked Arthur to fly with her, but he was busy in the crowd with his parents, Xenia, and the kids, and so Harriet took along the organizer of the event, a man in a straw boater and an ice-cream-white suit. The two took off in a clear late afternoon sky and the throngs cheered as her plane faded to a black speck on the horizon. Not long afterward, after circling the lighthouse, Harriet's plane reappeared, the sun glinting golden on its white gossamer wings.

Then, just as the Blériot returned over the tidal flats toward a landing, it seemed to tip downward. The tail rose, higher and higher, until it looped beyond vertical, and to everyone's horror a body suddenly was ejected from the aircraft, clutching what appeared to be a hat, legs and arms thrashing as it headed thousands of feet downward toward the flats — and then another; they could just get the glint of the sun on the peach-colored flying suit. The plane, pilotless now, slowly righted itself and spiraled down in ever-decreasing circles as the two bodies smashed into the mud of the inner harbor shore.

It had happened so suddenly. People rushed from the shore out onto the flats, floundering knee-deep in the gray mud toward where the bodies had landed. The airplane inexplicably glided to an almost perfect landing way out on the flats, its wheels sinking into the mud and the engine still running until the propeller dug into the muck and stopped.

They hauled the crushed, mud-covered bodies of Harriet and the air show organizer to shore, but Arthur had already hurried off a stunned Xenia, the kids, and his parents as quickly as possible. He spent the next days under a cloud of despondence, and wondered if he would ever fly again. He was among the mourners at Harriet's funeral and joined the sad cortege to Woodlawn Cemetery in the Bronx.

That had been nearly five years past, and Arthur Shaughnessy the orphan-tycoon had continued to fly. Now he had long since flown past Kansas City and was headed for Wichita. The reception he found there was far greater even than the one he'd received in Kirksville. There must have been a thousand people on hand to greet him, and again he was feted and bedded in style and comfort. He figured he was winning the race by now, though by what margin he could not tell. He calculated he had flown about eight hundred miles.

Meanwhile, the NE&P No. 1 was rolling along through the flat Arkansas farmlands from Memphis south and west toward Dallas, heading into a huge red setting sun that reflected through the windows on the Colonel's face as he declaimed over the situation in Mexico. A layer of haze from Strucker's cigarette drifted across the salon, almost like a fog. Beattie fanned her nose at it.

"I do not exactly understand these communications," said the Colonel, holding up a telegram that had been received from his Boston offices at the Memphis depot. "There's been some sort of trouble at Valle del Sol, some kind of cattle rustling. People were . . . well, it's garbled."

"My stars!" Beatie cried. "Cattle rustling? I thought that went out with the last century."

"I don't know why they can't be clearer about these things," the Colonel grumbled, shaking his head. The family had all gathered in the parlor section of the dining car, waiting for dinner to be served. From the galley, pungent aromas of roasting beef floated through the car. The children had occupied themselves with a Ouija board, while the others listened to the Colonel's assessment of the situation in Mexico. They had spent the afternoon playing with the bear, which they had named Sherman in honor of the late Union general. Timmy had wanted to name it Teddy, but the Colonel wouldn't hear of it — he'd name nothing of value after what he called "that four-eyed backstabber."

After a while, the bear had been banished to the baggage car and the Colonel sat at his elegant walnut desk in *The City of Hartford* and spread out several telegrams that had been waiting for him at the station. Strucker was sitting in his great parlor chair methodically soaking up gin, but was witty and charming, at least by his own lights.

As the train rocked and clattered into the twilight, Colonel Shaughnessy was lost in his own thoughts about his crumbling empire. He had his people all over Washington working feverishly to secure even one of the lucrative government war contracts that the other roads seemed to come by so easily. Maybe his attitude toward Woodrow Wilson had something to do with it; maybe Wilson had heard that the Colonel had referred to him as a "namby-pamby" during a poker game in Philadelphia a few months back. Maybe it had gotten out that the Colonel had secretly given money to the walrusteen former president William Howard Taft in hopes he might run against Wilson in the next election. Or perhaps it was someone else in Washington whose toes he had stepped on. In any event, just one of the contracts to ferry munitions, grain, clothing, and other war items to Great Britain and France would be enough to dig him out of this present hole. It was infuriating — but he was not done yet. Not by a long shot.

Scanning his communications from Boston, the Colonel found most of them routine until he came to the several messages concerning the general situation in Mexico.

"A fine kettle of fish," said the Colonel. "Someone's stealing my livestock and, from what I can make of it, sounds like they're blaming it on Pancho Villa."

"Sounds pretty serious," said Xenia.

"Well," the Colonel replied, "he's supposed to be way over in the state of Coahuila, and that's a lot of miles from Valle del Sol."

"Cattle stealing," Strucker observed. "It appears you have a delicate situation on your hands, my dear Shaughnessy." Strucker was secretly delighted by the news.

"Yes, well, if it's so," the Colonel replied. "But these people get hysterical — especially the Mexicans. They see Villa everywhere down there. Think he's some kind of Robin Hood character — steal from the rich, give to the poor — that kind of nonsense. They even believe he can actually change himself into animals to thwart his enemies — dog, owl, wolf — and disappear into the wilderness. It's getting to be ridiculous. Every time some two-bit bandit wants to steal something, he pretends to be with Villa. Goes on all the time. Villa's never bothered us before. Let's be sure our facts are straight before we go making a lot of assumptions."

"Where will we get these facts?" Strucker inquired.

"El Paso," the Colonel replied majestically. "They know everything at El Paso."

At dawn, Arthur put *Grendel* into a sky so clear blue it looked drinkable. A pale full moon hovered on the western horizon. *Grendel* left Wichita behind, with Amarillo ahead, where Arthur would put down about midday to refuel, then take off again to land in desert scrub for the night. So far Arthur had only had to change oil, clean the firing plugs, and tighten two hose clamps. The machine was performing marvelously.

But above the plane's monotonous drone, something had been eating at him ever since the farewell dinner at the Palmer House in Chicago — that remark by his father about being a "quitter." The more he tried to put it out of his head, the more it returned, like a sour rhyme or idiot tune. Groton. Well, he decided, to hell with it, maybe his Old Man hadn't been thinking of that at all.

In the dining car of *The City of Hartford,* just before pulling into Dallas, there suddenly arose a great commotion. The steward had set up a fine table of the Colonel's NE&P china and was placing crystal glasses when the door to the kitchen burst open and three shouting, wide-eyed cooks and the Chinese chef named Ah Dong tumbled out into the parlor and dashed past the astonished Colonel and his party.

"What's this?" Colonel Shaughnessy demanded.

"Bear!" hollered one of the cooks.

From behind the swinging galley doors there came the sounds of heavy snorting and the breaking of glasses and dishes.

"Bear got into kitchen!" Ah Dong said. "Got loose when Pearly went into baggage car for wine! Must have smelled roast! Chew through rope! All teeth and claws!"

"I'll see to this," bellowed the Colonel.

"Children, let's go into the salon car," Xenia ordered. "You can take your Ouija board with you. Close the door and don't let anyone in."

"We'll all go to the salon car," Beatie said. Katherine took her grandmother's arm and helped her across the agitated, racketing steel scuttle that joined the two cars; Timmy leaped across without touching it. It frightened him, the jiggling piece of metal that seemed as if someone or something down beneath it were alive and evil. He wished he had his sister's poise. He wished he had at least — at least her laugh.

"My, my, this is an exciting trip," Strucker remarked, staggering to get up. "Lucky this is not on my yacht, but I keep a pistol in my suitcase. Anyone want to use it?"

"I don't need any pistol," answered the Colonel. "That bear is as tame as a lamb. The gypsy told me so himself."

"The gypsy doesn't own the bear anymore, Father," Xenia said, to the crash of more broken dishes. "You do."

"Yes, and I'll deal with him," the Colonel told her. "Besides, Bomba's armed." He removed his dinner jacket and hitched up his suspenders. "I've dealt with bears before. Shot a few in my time, too. Bomba, let's go have a look."

Xenia, Beatie, Strucker, and the children,

along with the kitchen staff, were safely behind the door of the salon car, peering through the glass, as the Colonel and Bomba strode confidently into the galley.

"Your husband is brave man," said Ah Dong. "But bear get crazy when smell roast beef."

"Yes," Beatie said, "so does the Colonel."

Suddenly the galley door burst back open and Bomba, followed by the Colonel, fled down the aisle toward the safety of the salon, the bear in hot pursuit. Strucker quickly opened the door for them, and closed it just in time to shut off the snarling, clawing bear.

"Why, that thing's wild as a tiger!" the Colonel panted. "I've been tricked by the gypsy!" The bear was pressing hard with its hind legs, its breath making big smudges on the glass door separating the cars, its teeth and claws bared.

"Why, it's ripped out my trousers," the Colonel growled, reaching behind, and finding his hands covered in blood. "My word, I think I'm wounded!"

"Let's see, dear," Beatie exclaimed, stooping to examine the situation.

"I think we will not have much of a dinner tonight," Strucker remarked. "It's a good thing the bar is back here."

"Oh, be quiet, please," Beatie said.

The German, unaccustomed to such a rebuke, plopped into his chair, incensed at being spoken to that way by a female. These Americans, to Claus Strucker, were a strange, rude people; a ridiculous people.

It turned out the Colonel was not badly injured. The bear had only scratched him, but the family and the kitchen staff spent the rest of the trip in the salon car while the bear enjoyed their dinner in the diner. At Little Rock that evening the Colonel took everyone to eat at the Peabody, a fashionable hotel. He also telegraphed the Memphis depot to locate the gypsy and place him on the next available train to come and reclaim the bear, which he had at last had removed from the dining car kitchen by men from the local sheriff's office, and chained to a metal lamppost at the train station. First thing next morning, the party got under way again.

The bear scratches were painful enough to put the Colonel in an edgy mood, plus he worried whether Arthur was all right. His train had come more than a thousand miles from Chicago and they would reach El Paso within another long day. But Arthur was alone in a flimsy flying machine. The Colonel knew in his soul that Arthur was no "quitter," and regretted his remark at the dinner table in Chicago, though he never apologized, since he considered it a sign of weakness.

"You would think," Colonel Shaughnessy said, "that bunch we have in Washington —

now that they've got us in this predicament — would have the guts to stand up to Pancho Villa. Don't they have a duty to protect American citizens' interests? Hellfire, if the government can regulate the rates I charge for my train transportation, then they can help protect what I transport. It's only fair."

"You are certainly right, sir," Strucker agreed enthusiastically. Today he was dressed in a red silk kimono and parlor slippers, and munching on half a head of lettuce he had procured from the kitchen. In his other hand was the eternal drink. "It's a disgrace for a country as great as the United States to be shoved around by a villainous bunch such as they have in Mexico. It makes your people look weak and silly."

The more thievery, murders, and kidnappings the Mexicans carried out — even if they were at the expense of his old friend — the better, so far as he was concerned. War was about war, not about friendship. After all, the king of England was the kaiser's first cousin, and look what family ties got in that case.

"Maybe your country will intervene," the German continued, placing his platinum-rimmed monocle back into his eye. Several years earlier during a strange diplomatic tangle the U.S. Army had been sent to occupy the Mexican port of Veracruz, which nearly touched off a war.

"I wish we would," said the Colonel. "Teach

those greasers a lesson."

By early morning they had crossed from the hill country of Arkansas into Texas and were on the seemingly endless dusty plains, with only an occasional cowboy on a horseback or a telegraph pole to remind them that they were on the same planet as the day before.

"We need to get Hearst and his blasted newspapers behind us," Colonel Shaughnessy said. "He owns more land than I do down there! Now, that man knows how to start a war. If it's war they want, it's war they'll get."

"You're exactly right, Colonel," Strucker exclaimed, "War — can you imagine it!" The monocle dropped out again as the German's eyes widened. He took out a handkerchief and began polishing it in a way that somehow annoyed Xenia.

"War's not an answer for anything," Beatie interjected. "If this Villa's a bandit, why doesn't the Mexican government just arrest him?"

"My word, woman," replied the Colonel, "you don't just go out and arrest someone who has an army. He might arrest you, instead."

"Colonel," Beatie said firmly, "now, I don't want you going and starting any wars. I simply put my foot down. We've been lucky to stay out of the one in France. It's not our affair."

"Many times war is the only answer," the Colonel replied.

At the other end of the car the children were playing with the Ouija board, which after repeated passes over its letters had spelled out two words that could be taken as a warning:

"BE WEAR."

The train rolled on toward another night, while to the west Arthur was having the fight of his life in the air high above the Jicarilla Mountains in southeastern New Mexico. *Grendel* seemed unable to buck the dangerous headwinds of the only pass through the bleak treeless peaks, and darkness was also coming his way.

Sixteen

Three hundred miles deep into Mexico, Johnny Ollas and his cuadrilla were headed into the scorching morning sun, while Gourd Woman tagged along behind, prodding her donkey. Even though Johnny didn't trust the opinion of someone who divined information from a handful of bleached bones, they had decided to go to Creel anyway because they needed both provisions and to find out if anyone there had news of Villa's whereabouts. It was the only game in town.

Johnny stopped for a moment to get his bearings and Gourd Woman caught up with him. "So what do you do when you're not out hunting after a man like Pancho Villa?" she asked.

"I fight bulls," he said. He was actually glad to have somebody to talk to.

"You're a matador?"

"Yes, and these are my cuadrilla," he said, nodding to his brothers. People thought they were quadruplets, but in fact they'd been born each a year apart from the other, beginning twenty-four years earlier. But like twins or quadruplets, they looked and even thought alike, which kept conversation to a minimum. Johnny, on the other hand, liked to talk; it was what kept him sane.

"What's that?"

"The men who fight with me. My picadors, my banderilleros . . . they are also my brothers."

"Your stepbrothers," she corrected him. Johnny was astonished.

"How do you know that?"

"Family resemblance," Gourd Woman replied. "You don't look like them. Anyway, why are you trying to find this Pancho Villa?" It was true; the four brothers might have been cut out of a cookie cutter: short, slim, dark brown eyes, each with little pencil-thin mustache and short black hair.

"Because he kidnapped my wife and killed the man who raised me. But why ask me this? Don't your bones already tell you?"

"I'd rather hear it from you. They say Pancho Villa is a friend of the people. That he wants to give them property."

"You ever hear of Pancho Villa giving anybody any property?"

"It's what they say."

They were crossing a broad, rolling plain and the sun already was getting hotter in the late autumn sky. But the air was so fresh and

216

still that Johnny could almost smell the blue flowers carpeting the plain.

"I've never seen a bullfight," Gourd Woman said.

"No? You might enjoy it."

"I don't like killing."

"Don't you eat meat?"

"I just don't like the killing."

"Well," Johnny said, "bulls are born to be killed. If we didn't breed fighting bulls to be killed in the ring, then they would never have existed in the first place. We do them a favor by letting them live three, four years doing exactly what comes natural to them, which is to charge around and tear things apart. Their lives may be short, but they're happy. Besides, it makes me a good living on the side." They stopped to cook beans for lunch.

All morning Johnny had been thinking about Donita, but also his Toro Malo. When the Colonel first brought the bull to Valle del Sol, Johnny was eight years old and could not believe how such a huge beast could be transported in only a cage on the back of a mule-drawn wagon.

Johnny had started up again and Gourd Woman went into a kind of shuffling trot to keep up with his horse. "I still don't see why you want to kill these dumb animals, even when they win," she said, as if she were reading Johnny's mind.

"Wild bulls are not dumb," Johnny said.

"And it's why they must be killed. Bulls figure out things too quickly during the fight. If the same bull were to be used over and over, the contest would soon be unequal. It's hard enough as it is."

"If you're so tough, why don't you become a prizefighter?" she offered.

"They're not so tough," he said.

"No? Why?"

"Because in prizefights one of the fighters doesn't always die."

"I used to sell cider outside the bullring in Jalpa," Gourd Woman said after a moment of reflection. "I'd see them drag the dead bulls out. Dead horses, too. I don't like killing."

"Jalpa? You're a long way from home."

"I don't have a home," she said, "except where I can sell these brooms." She nodded back toward the donkey, its baskets loaded with broomsticks.

Killing, Johnny thought. It was as if she knew something about him he didn't know — or, worse, that he did. The killing had always been the rub with him. His work with the cape was stunning, some said. Some had compared him with a ballet dancer — an artist — a scientist, even. But he never truly enjoyed the killing, the supreme moment of placing the sword between the bull's neck muscles and ramming it home. Why, he didn't know. Maybe it was because he liked animals. Maybe he wasn't a natural-born killer as some matadors were. He could do it competently enough but not quite with great gusto.

"In bulls," he said almost absently, "the killing is the most dangerous part."

"You're just toying," Gourd Woman said. "You're playing with death."

"Playing? Say that to the graves of a thousand matadors who've died in the ring."

After Johnny's goring last spring, when the bull caught him under the armpit and ripped through the muscle and into his lung, when they thought he would lose the lung, maybe even his life, he wondered, lying in the hospital bed, if he would ever be any good again.

At the age of eight he began by fighting calves, then yearlings and cows, and by the age of twenty had fought and killed 109 bulls.

He'd been thrown dozens of times and nicked, too, but never really gored until a bull hooked the wrong way and tossed him with the left horn nearly ten feet into the air. If he hadn't been tossed off the horn and Julio and Rigaz, the banderilleros, had not rushed in to distract the bull, Johnny would most likely be dead.

It took three months for him to heal, and when he finally walked into the arena at Chihuahua the crowd roared their approval because everyone knew he'd been badly gored. But he could not quite seem to keep his feet still. No matter how hard he tried, his feet moved in tiny little mouse steps away from the passing bull, just the distance to give him an edge of safety. It was duly reported in the papers next day by the critics, who politely suggested that perhaps he had returned to the ring too soon. That maybe he needed to take more time off and regain his old style.

Johnny had wished that the bull that had gored him had not been killed, so that he could avenge himself. Still, each Saturday afternoon in the ring he tried to make the little tippy-toe steps more and more imperceptible, but he knew what he felt: the dry mouth, the barely noticeable trembling of fingers. Johnny feared cowardice more than he feared death.

"You gonna kill Pancho Villa?" Gourd Woman asked, breaking Johnny out of his reverie.

"He surely deserves it," Johnny Ollas replied. "He murdered my father and took my woman."

"And what if he kills you first?" she said. "Have you thought of that?"

"Nobody who fights bulls can be afraid of a *man,*" Johnny answered.

■ ■ ■ ■ ■

PART TWO:
THE *DESIERTO*

■ ■ ■ ■ ■

SEVENTEEN

Arthur thought he had the flight licked and the race won, when trouble sought him out. *Grendel* was ticking along perfectly in a dry, cloudless sky over the flat, desolate landscape of southern New Mexico: a few tiny mining ghost towns, clusters of houses here and there, and narrow sandy roads that seemed to lead nowhere, even viewed from up in the air. Ahead, two ridges of tall bleak mountains ran north and south, and between them the pass he'd have to fly through to make El Paso.

Until he reached this pass, Arthur believed it would be an easy go.

It wasn't.

Soon as Arthur put *Grendel* between the mountains, an ugly headwind began to strike him. It bucked and battered the plane upward and Arthur fought to hold on to it; then a downdraft hit him before a crosswind slipped him dangerously in the direction of a mountain peak.

Arthur struggled to keep *Grendel* straight

and level; he flew at about eight thousand feet until suddenly the bottom dropped out. He tried climbing above the mountains, but up there the turbulence was worse. He descended into the pass to about four thousand feet, but there the headwinds had him. Scanning the horizon and the earth below, Arthur figured he wasn't making much more than ten or fifteen knots' headway.

This wouldn't do at all; it was eating up too much fuel and not building enough airspeed. He dropped the manifold pressure and cut back on the RPMs to save gas, but he could see this wasn't going to work for long.

Arthur had been caught in what the Navajo called the Paso del Ventoso, or Pass of the Winds, for nearly two hours and it was too late to turn around, just as it was not feasible to try to climb out over the mountain peaks. He was stuck and turned the taps for the first, second, and third jerry cans of extra gas, with only two more left and darkness on the horizon. Worst-case, the desert below seemed like a relatively good place to put down, and maybe the winds in the morning wouldn't pick back up. On the other hand, he didn't see anyplace where he might find more fuel. In all this time, he'd not noticed a single car, or even a wagon, on any of the roads.

Arthur kept flying as long as he thought prudent.

He certainly didn't want to run completely low on fuel and of course understood the necessity of keeping at least one reserve tank full for taking off in the morning, if nothing else helped him.

He dropped down to five hundred feet and began scanning the ground ahead for a place to put down. The ground seemed all the same: sand, small cactus bushes, desert scrub, and the occasional rock. Arthur dropped lower, making sure to try to keep as close to a gravel road he'd spied as possible. He didn't want to land on it because there were telegraph wires on both sides and he couldn't tell how close they were; the Luft-Verkehrs had a wide wingspan.

There seemed a barer stretch ahead of a cactus patch, and Arthur throttled back and nosed the stick forward. The wheels touched the earth, bounced, touched again, hit something like a cactus, and the plane began a ground loop. Arthur applied the right brake, but by that time the *Grendel* jerked sideways, and when its nose pitched, Arthur heard the sound of the propeller snap as it hit the ground. At the same time as Arthur cut the engine off, the landing gear broke and *Grendel* pitched forward, tail upward, throwing Arthur against the control panel, where he hit his head. Then all was the silence of the desert.

Arthur rubbed his head, relieved he saw no

blood on his hand. He climbed down and surveyed the damage. The smashed prop wasn't a crisis because he'd brought a spare one, but the axle on the landing gear had broken. It was not destroyed, but this kind of repair needed a weld. Arthur had some other choices. The sleeve he'd brought in his spare-parts kit might get him into the air again, but landing would be a problem. Plus he was about out of gas.

He looked around him at the barrenness of the desert.

Here on the ground, no wind blew, not the faintest breeze.

Arthur climbed back into the cockpit and pulled out of his hamper a jar of peanut butter and a slice of bread and made himself a sandwich, which he sat eating on the lower wing. Assuming he replaced the prop, repaired the axle, and was able to take off, and the winds died down in the morning, Arthur figured he had only an hour's worth left of flying time on the last fuel tank, which would put him down only forty or so miles ahead in the same bleak territory, and with no more fuel to take off again.

The sun had almost gone down now, throwing a burnished cast over the mountains and the desert, turning the grayish peaks an engaging color of orange and red. As Arthur contemplated his predicament, the faint sound of an engine began humming through the still desert air. In the shimmering burnished distance, sure enough, a big open car was headed toward him. Arthur hopped down from the wing and ran to the middle of the road. When the occupants of the car saw him and the tail-up airplane, they slowed to a stop. Arthur walked to the car. A man and a woman, nicely dressed, sat in the front seat.

"Have some trouble?" the man asked. He was young and striking-looking, with prominent ears and forehead, a lump jaw, wild wavy hair, and dark probing eyes. His voice was strong and authoritative. Arthur thought it was sort of a dumb question to ask, given the sight of the upturned plane.

"Have you passed by anyplace I can buy some gasoline?" Arthur asked.

"There's a little station back about twenty miles," the man said, "if he's still open."

How could he have missed it from the air? Arthur wondered. "My name is Arthur Shaughnessy," he said, extending his hand.

"I am John Reed and this is Mabel Dodge," the man said. "Are you just out for an afternoon's aviating?"

"No, I came down from Chicago. I'm trying to get to El Paso."

"You're joking?" Reed said.

Arthur glanced over at his plane. Did it look like he was joking?

"Are you out to set some record?" Mabel Dodge asked.

227

"If it happens, it happens," Arthur replied. "Mainly I'm just trying to get to El Paso. But the winds between these mountains almost ran me out of gas. I have some cans in the plane. You're the first sign of civilization I've seen out here. I'd be glad to pay for your time if you'd drive me back to that gas station."

"We'd be happy to help you in any way we can," said Mabel Dodge. She was a handsome woman in a prickly sort of way, with large brown eyes and rouged cheeks, and she was wearing one of those little felt hats that looked like an overturned flowerpot. "We're on our way to El Paso, too," she said pleasantly, "and we know what it is to be stranded. Our train got stopped by a landslide back in Alpine, so we rented this car."

Arthur and Reed went to the *Grendel* and Arthur began unfastening the jerry cans; Reed helped him carry them to the car before going back and uprighting the plane.

"What are you going to El Paso for?" Arthur asked Reed, as the car puttered north.

"I'm a reporter for the *New York World*. El Paso's just the jumping-off point. I'm going into Mexico to cover the revolution."

"The Pancho Villa revolution?" Arthur said.

"He's the man of the hour," Reed answered. He had a toothy grin and his teeth shone in the dusk as though they'd been radiated.

"And you, Miss Dodge, are you going with him?"

"Certainly not. Mexico's no place for a lady," she said, "at least not in these days and times."

"Do you know where Villa is?"

"No," Reed replied, "but I expect he won't be hard to find." They rode on in silence for a while, darkness closing across the glowing mountains.

"What about you, Mr. Shaughnessy?" Mabel asked. "Why did you choose El Paso as a destination?"

"Oh, I don't know," Arthur told her. "I guess you could say I have family there." He wondered if this could be the infamous Mabel Dodge, whose New York salon was the talk of the times. Unlike Xenia's mildly scandalous gatherings in Boston that sometimes set the old blue noses gossiping, Mabel Dodge's gatherings included real bomb-throwers of the radical left, such as "Big Bill" Hayward, Max Eastman, and Emma Goldman, among others. He remembered that the Colonel had known Mabel Dodge's father, a wealthy banker from Buffalo who was utterly traumatized by her behavior.

"And where are you from, Miss Dodge?" Arthur inquired.

"New York City," she replied, as if she'd lived there all her life.

"I thought so," Arthur said.

Presently they arrived at the little shack where a hermit-looking Mexican with a hunched back sold gas and groceries. Arthur filled the cans, making sure to filter the fuel through a small mesh strainer, as well as a piece of porous matting he kept in the plane. When they returned to the desert site, Reed helped Arthur carry the cans to the plane.

"You're certainly welcome to come along with us," Reed said, eyeing the broken axle. "You might not be able to take off again."

"Thank you," Arthur replied, "but I imagine I can fix it enough to get into the air. Landing might be a little dicey, but I think I can make it all right."

Reed shook his hand. "It's a bold thing, coming all this way in that," he said.

"Good luck, Mr. Reed," Arthur told him. "I hope you get your story."

When Reed and Mabel Dodge had gone on their way, Arthur fastened the gas cans back in place with the help of an electric torch, opened a bottle of beer, laid his sleeping bag out on the wing of *Grendel,* and stretched out under the hard desert stars. He wondered if the landslide that held up Reed's train had also held up his father's. He hoped it had.

Even before the sun began to break over the eastern escarpment Arthur had laid out his tools and spare-parts kit and found the metal sleeve to work over the broken axle. It was fashioned with flanges every six inches that bolted together, and when he finished, the thing seemed almost good as new. Next he removed the splintered propeller and replaced it with the spare one. He could feel no wind at ground level and, watching a hawk or buzzard soaring above, decided there didn't seem to be much turbulence on high, either. With no wind at all, it would be difficult if not impossible to take off, because there'd be no lift on the wings. The desert remained so quiet it was almost spooky. Arthur went into the cockpit, switched on the magneto, eased the choke, and pulled the throttle out one-quarter. He got out and sprayed the carburetor with a can of ether, then took his best pull on the prop.

The Mercedes engine coughed once, then caught.

A more experienced aviator had once told him that if there was no wind, you could possibly stir up just enough yourself by revving the prop. Arthur tried it and, as he'd hoped, it caused a little breeze to come fluttering down the valley and he turned into it and up he went. Arthur climbed to five thousand feet and cruised southward as the sun climbed over the mountain range. The headwinds had abated.

By midafternoon he began to see signs of civilization on the horizon, little villages scattered off the main road, and by two p.m., with only a single can of fuel unused, he saw the spread of El Paso, nestled beneath tall, gray, jagged mountains, with the Rio Grande shimmering to the south.

The landing field was north of town; Arthur spotted it without trouble, disappointed that it was not a grass strip, but graded yellow dirt. He hoped for the sake of the axle it was smooth and not too hard. He circled twice to make sure there weren't any wire poles in the way, then came in as slow as he dared. This time no crowd was there to greet him, but at least the axle held, and Arthur pulled the *Grendel* up to the flight shack and cut the engine. A grease monkey emerged and looked him over.

"You the one that come down from Chicago?" he asked.

Arthur nodded.

"That's what I figured," he said. "Your old man's waiting for you at the hotel in town. He sent a man out this morning to say if you got in, to call him on the telephone and he'll send a car out to pick you up."

Appalled, Arthur asked where the telephone was. He might have been late, but he was no quitter, he thought disgustedly. Now he'd probably have the Old Man lording it over him the whole damned rest of the trip.

Eighteen

Ambrose Bierce was nearing the end of a long and distinguished career and welcomed it. He had been among the most popular story writers in America and his cynical newspaper columns brought him fame and fortune. But he was seventy-one years old, while most of his family and his contemporaries, friend and foe alike, had long since gone to the grave, and on a fine winter day while visiting New York City Bierce determined to put all this behind him and leave America forever. America repelled him now.

First, however, the old Civil War veteran decided he wanted to see one more war before he died, and the conflict presently raging in Mexico seemed like a perfect opportunity. He would probably die in Mexico, and that was all right with him, too. Before leaving, he wrote to one of his few remaining friends that he would most likely be "stood up against a wall and shot to rags — but isn't that a lot better than dying in bed?"

To put himself in the mood, Bierce arranged that on the way down he would revisit the battlefields of his youthful service with the Union Army fifty years earlier. In Macy's Department Store on Fifth Avenue, he bought himself a gold-embossed leather journal to record his adventures and withdrew from the Morgan Bank the sum of ten thousand dollars, cash.

He left by a night train to Chattanooga, Tennessee, and two days later visited Missionary Ridge, where he started a journal in the form of letters to Miss Christiansen, his secretary in Washington. He wrote:

I ascended the Ridge from Orchard Knob, just like we did in '64. Weren't those grand old times! Flags flying, cannon roaring, shot and shell and the smoke descended onto the knob like a blanket of cotton. But we took it then and could take it again today, if needs be. Walked ten miles today.

Next afternoon he visited Chickamauga. He told his journal:

Made a sketch of Grizzly's battery with its inscription and sent it to Grizzly. Stayed at the Hotel Patten and walked fifteen miles. Rosecrans disgraced us here; only great defeat of Army of the Tennessee.

A day later he was outside Nashville:

Rained most of the afternoon. At the Franklin battlefield I walked seven miles. It's not much different now than it was fifty years ago. Lots of corn planted now in the fields where Hood's army had to cross and many of our old fortifications are still there. What terrible slaughter. Still can't believe they tried it.

Finally Bierce arrived at Shiloh — Pittsburgh Landing — the site of his first major battle. Referring to the fact that he was visiting the battlefields in inverse order to when the battles had been fought, he wrote:

I seem to be doing all this backwards, but it's the only sensible way. Poured cats and dogs all day long and the asthma's acting up. I'll be glad to get to Mexico where maybe it won't rain. The steamboat trip from Nashville was long and tedious and we stopped at every landing to put on freight. The landings are not towns, just dirt roads coming down to the water. River is beautiful but at so low a tide you cannot see the countryside over the banks.

Walked maybe twenty miles. Found the graves of twenty of our regiment. Their names are all right in the cemetery record but only half the bodies have been identified. The Confederate dead still lie where buried and none named. The fields across the river are still much the same as described in "What I saw at Shiloh." I wonder if Mexicans fight like this? I expect they die like this, anyway. I've lost about ten pounds.

Next day Bierce took a ramshackle old automobile to Corinth, Mississippi, where he caught a night train to New Orleans. On arrival he was still suffering from asthma but was met by three reporters who wanted to interview him, and he sat up all night with them.

Good to see New Orleans. People in the streets are not in a hurry; corridors of hotels are crowded; men play billiards as they did years and years ago and the bars — oh, you should see a New Orleans bar! The drinks they make, and the trays and trays of them sent upstairs. Talked Mexico all afternoon; it's on everyone's lips here — more so than the war in Europe — since they do a brisk trade through the port. Some say Villa is a bandit, some say a hero. Newspapers print both sides, but I'm looking forward to finding out for myself.

Took a stroll along the river among the cotton bales. All my old haunts are lost to me and excepting the few blocks about the Monteleone Hotel, it is a strange city. Can't find even a few places where Pollard and I dined and drank so many years ago.

Bierce was a man who'd made a career in doomsaying, but he was set in a gloomier mood than usual by New Orleans. He sat on the balcony of his room at the Monteleone, watching the bustling streets below and recording his impressions. After the third drink, he had a sudden premonition that he was on his last roundup and he took his tablet out once again. He wrote:

Dear Miss Christiansen, since it is in no way certain that I will survive the conflict in Mexico, I am sending you these pages of my journal by post and will continue to do so daily if possible. By the way, at Shiloh visiting the graves of the 9th Indiana I found a headstone with the bald inscription No. 411, T. J. Patton. Captain Patton was our adjutant and fell early in the engagement and for more than fifty years has been lying there, denied the prestige of his rank. I have corrected that and though he will sleep no better for it, I will.

Having said this and having mailed the pages to Miss Christiansen, Bierce packed up and caught the train to San Antonio, where he got his first look at Mexicans. He did not think much of them at first blush.

San Antonio is a city of 110,000 but you can cover the Alamo with a hat. Passed an hour there; the name Alamo means cotton-wood trees. It was rather interesting with relics, old documents and bad poetry — the shrine of each Texan's devotion. Outside the wall are large numbers of idle Mexicans. The Mexicans like nothing better than to sit in the sun smoking cigarettes and drinking pulque — their national alcoholic beverage — unless the sun is too hot and, on those frequent occasions, they sit in the shade smoking cigarettes and drinking pulque.

Journeying on to Laredo, Bierce observed it was *"a town of 18,000 of which 3,000 are Americans. English is not spoken by any of the Mexicans, not even the hotel waiters or chambermaids. Mexicans run the city and federal government offices — particularly the Post Office. Took half an hour to buy a stamp."*
He was interviewed by the editor of the only English newspaper in Mexico, who regaled him with the story of a Mexican cabinet member who kept an old copy of *Cosmopolitan* and bored all his friends by reading and quoting from "A Wine of Wizardy," a poem written by George Sterling, whom Bierce had chosen to mentor. It pleased Bierce to be recognized so far south of the border, but after he left Laredo, he went underground.
He assumed the name "Jack Robinson," both to diminish his recognizability by Ameri-

can officials, who he feared might prevent him from crossing the border, and also because he'd heard stories about Mexicans kidnapping anybody they considered rich or famous. He also dyed his snow-white hair with black shoe polish, which turned it more or less to the color of an eggplant, and began growing a beard. There would be American reporters around Villa's army and his picture had been in the papers enough that he needed a disguise. Besides, when he looked in the mirror, he thought it took ten or fifteen years off his age. Total anonymity was his desire.

At El Paso, Bierce linked up with a middle-aged man known as Cowboy Bob, who claimed to have inroads to Villa and his army. After outfitting himself handsomely with horse, guns, and supplies, including a parasol and a roll of Mexican postage stamps, Bierce, Cowboy Bob, and three of Bob's friends set out for Chihuahua, where Villa was then rumored to be holding court.

Bierce wrote Miss Christiansen:

Have regained lost health and about five pounds of lost weight. Am in Mexico at last. Juárez is nothing more than a collection of bars, whorehouses and churches whose bells ring night and day.

In the lobby of the Toltec Hotel before leaving El Paso I observed a man making a scene right out of a Booth Tarkington novel. It was pointed out to me that he was a Colonel Shaughnessy, a muckity-muck from Boston who owns a railroad and has a big spread down in Mexico. He was declaiming wildly over Pancho Villa's alleged crimes and depredations and I was tempted to identify myself and find out more but decided instead to get it straight from the horse's mouth!

At Juárez, I was cordially received by officials and given credentials to accompany Gen. Villa's army. I now weight 165 pounds. No rain in sight.

NINETEEN

"That man looked familiar," the Colonel said. He and Arthur were standing at the bar in El Paso's Toltec Club, which adjoined the hotel.

"Which man, Papa?"

"The old coot with the beard. The one who was sitting there eyeing me in the lobby when we came through. I've seen him someplace, or his picture."

"Well, why don't you ask at the desk when we get back?" Arthur said.

"I think I'll do just that," replied the Colonel. "He looked kind of shifty, didn't you think? You can't be too careful down here. There are spies all over the place. Besides, it looked like he'd dyed his hair with shoe polish or something, didn't it?"

Arthur was grateful that the Colonel in fact had *not* lorded the race over him. Maybe he hadn't felt he needed to — after all, facts speak for themselves. He must have known that flying all the way cross-country from

Chicago was important to Arthur, and while his father could be bellicose and domineering, he wasn't petty. Arthur was proud of that in the Old Man, and rightly so.

The Colonel had been furious all morning, ever since he picked up the newspaper and the lead story said that Pancho Villa had issued a proclamation saying that foreigners, including Americans — especially Americans — could no longer hold property in Mexico and their lands would be confiscated and nationalized. The Colonel was blowing his stack when he saw a second article that said the rail tracks between El Paso and Chihuahua City were still not repaired and there was no telling when they would be.

"So now I imagine we'll have to organize a caravan of automobiles and drive ourselves across the desert," the Colonel groused.

"Are you sure you still want to go through with this?" Arthur asked. "After all, we have the women and children to think about."

"They'll be fine," the Colonel said. "By all accounts he's still over in Coahuila — even the newspaper says it — and he can't bother us from there. Besides, as I've said, I've met this Villa. I don't know what's got into him. I still don't understand everything that's gone on down there. I'm inclined to think there's been some kind of mistake. Nationalize our property, by God! Who does he think he is? I'd like to see him try it! Besides, I'm going to start taking care of things right now."

"How so?" Arthur said.

"I think the smart thing is to go straight to Wilson himself."

"To the president? I thought you couldn't abide him."

"I *can't* abide him. That moron Bryan, either," said the Colonel. " 'Cross of Gold,' and all that nonsense."

TWENTY

John Reed was as excited as a respected and ambitious young reporter could be.

He was on the assignment of his career and knew it. War — not just any war, but revolution. As a devout Marxist, Reed quickly realized he was in the perfect place at the perfect time. Beside him in a big Oldsmobile touring car was the wealthy brunette Mabel Dodge. *The* Mabel Dodge, with whom he was conducting an affair, temporary as it might be. The Texas sun beat down; the sky was blue and the roads were bumpy but dry as they made their way to El Paso after a slide had blocked the rail tracks and Reed persuaded the wealthy Mrs. Dodge to spring for the automobile. They would have already been in El Paso by now if they hadn't stopped to help the troubled airman stranded in the desert.

"You know, Mabel," Reed remarked as they rounded a turn in the Hueves Mountains, "I don't give a hoot in hell about getting in the war in Europe, but this — this is what wars should be about! This man Pancho Villa — a peasant who a few years ago didn't have any other choice than to rob trains and steal cattle — and he's now the leader of the greatest political uprising on this continent since the American Revolution!"

"What about the Civil War?" Mabel asked.

"That was different," Reed asserted. "I'm talking about an uprising of the masses."

"Well, that was a lot of masses in the South that uprose, if memory serves me," she said.

"I'm surprised at you."

"You might have given a little more thought to what Linc wrote you." Mabel Dodge said. Lincoln Steffens had been Reed's mentor at Harvard and, in fact, had introduced Reed to Mabel Dodge and her salon in New York. Steffens was already in Mexico, but down in Mexico City, covering Carranza's side — *the other side* — of things.

Reed kept his hands on the wheel and glared down the road ahead. He had Steffens's number, all right. Steffens didn't like Villa because Wall Street did, at least for the moment. Reed thought it ridiculous to conclude that because Wall Street slightly favors somebody, you automatically take the other side. He figured Steffens was just jealous, and doing his redder-than-thou thing.

"Linc's been a good friend to you — you know that. And I think you should at least value his advice," Mabel said.

Reed felt blissful in the south Texas sunshine, and full of radical politics. He was not only covering the revolution for the *Metropolitan,* one of the leading socialist magazines of the day, but also for the *New York World,* which would give him a huge national following. In his mind, he'd already built up a legend around Villa that would make Robin Hood look like a cheap sheep thief. If Lincoln Steffens thought Pancho Villa was merely a capitalist tool, Reed was there to prove him wrong.

They reached El Paso late in the afternoon and checked into separate (but adjoining) rooms in the Toltec Hotel. He found the city teeming with correspondents, munitions salesmen, pitiful refugees, and spies of all descriptions. Outside a dingy shack stood a line of several hundred Mexican soldiers. Inside, an agent for a portrait company was taking orders for colorized enlargements of their snapshots and photos. All in all, the air was fierce with electricity, as if a storm were brewing over the horizon. Reed took Mabel Dodge down the dusty main street that led to the international bridge. There, as the sun sank over the western mountains, the two of them gazed across the shallow muddy Rio Grande at their first view of Mexico. In the distance was Juárez, its church steeples and adobe walls pink in the fading light. Giant

ancient mesas framed the valley, lined southward like a fleet of great battleships in the
darkening desert. On a plain outside the
buildings of Juárez some Federal troops were
on mounted parade, passing in review in
front of a cadre of officers.

"That's quite a pageant," remarked Mabel
Dodge.

"Those people will lose this revolution,"
Reed declared. "They are conscripts of the
Mexican government and haven't any heart
in what they're doing. Revolution is foreign
to them. But Pancho Villa's people, they have
something at stake."

"You be careful going over there," Mabel
told him.

"I'm not a child, Mabel," Reed said expansively. "I am a foreign correspondent for the
New York World."

Mabel looked into the hazy distance while
fumbling in her purse for a cigarette, and
thought: You're a child in many ways, Jack.
You're a beautiful writer and a handsome
man, and I like sleeping with you. You see
things with such pure, honest passion. It's
one of the reasons why I like you, but I do
worry for you sometimes.

"This is more important than you understand, Mabel," Reed continued. "This is what
we've all been waiting for. I believe it is the
prelude to world revolution. That war in
Europe will destroy all the monarchies, and

there's nothing left to take their place but pure, honest socialism — the dictate of the proletariat. Just consider it, Mabel, world revolution! And here I am!"

"Yes, Jack," she said. "Here you are."

TWENTY-ONE

"A fine kettle of fish!" bellowed the Colonel, pacing the parlor of the family suite at the Toltec Hotel. In the five days they had been there, he had found out everything there was to know in El Paso about the situation across the border. Unfortunately, it wasn't much, and not good news, at that. First, even though the telegraph and phone lines into Chihuahua had finally been repaired the rail tracks were still torn up at least to within fifty miles of Juárez, where a big trestle over a ravine had been blown up. Villa's whereabouts were still put somewhere in Coahuila but the rumor mill had him at places hundreds of miles apart. All in all, the Colonel and his party were in the dark.

"Hell with this," the Colonel said. "I didn't come all the way down here to squat in this garish establishment. So tomorrow we're on our way."

Arthur, Beatie, and Strucker sat in tufted chintz armchairs watching while the Colonel paced. Strucker puffed a cigarette from a long carved ivory holder. Xenia had taken the children for a stroll, escorted by Bomba.

"I've got all the cars arranged," the Colonel announced. "Five Packards and a truck. Bomba, myself, and the children will ride in one. Arthur, you, Xenia, and Beatie will ride in another. Two more will be for the bodyguards I've arranged, and the last one for spare parts. The truck will be for luggage. You must tell Bomba what baggage you will need to accompany you. When the track's repaired, the train will follow us down with everything else.

"I'm not going to be intimidated by some tinhorn bandit. We're American citizens on legitimate business," the Colonel continued.

Arthur realized his father was mostly talking to himself.

"The trip ought to take no more than three days — two nights on the road. There are good hotels in Chihuahua City — at least there used to be. But who knows what's going on down there — I'm taking no chances. In addition to the baggage, the truck is equipped with tents and a field kitchen. Ah Dong is coming along and he's out buying our food supplies as we speak. Why, it's going to be a real adventure, camping out on the open plains under the stars. There'll be fresh Texas steaks cooking over a roaring fire. And beans. Just like the cowboys do it. You'll see

— we need to breed a little of the Boston out of all of us — except for the beans!"

Arthur shook his head slowly. As usual, it would do no good to argue with the Colonel when he was in this mood. Besides, the Colonel had actually been to war and he had been to Mexico, while Arthur had been to neither. Nevertheless, his handling of the affair with *Ajax* had been emboldening. But that had been a fait accompli, not a face-to-face knock-down-drag-out. Arthur wondered how he'd handle that, and then figured he'd find out soon enough.

"Don't shake your head that way, Arthur. I know what I'm doing," his father proclaimed. "That's why I own a railroad."

"I'm sorry I can't go along," Strucker said. "It sounds like an excellent expedition." He was wearing a gray mohair sport jacket with green felt tabs and his hair seemed slicked back more than usual, as if he were using some kind of wax. He had changed his ascot to puce.

"If you change your mind, there's still time to let me know," the Colonel told him.

The German nodded graciously. From what he had learned, the Colonel's party would be traveling far away from the troubles, and besides, he'd concluded it would probably be best to first see Carranza before trusting his mission with a man such as Pancho Villa. He could always catch up with the

Colonel later if he needed to.

During this conversation, Beatie remained silent in her chair with a puzzled, inquisitive expression on her face, as though she didn't quite comprehend what was being said or, at least, was too stunned to appreciate it. At last she raised a tentative hand in the air, almost like a schoolchild wanting to ask a question.

"But John," Beatie said, "I don't understand. Where shall we go to use the facilities? How —"

"Ah, Mother, you leave that to me," the Colonel replied majestically. "You just leave everything to me."

TWENTY-TWO

Ambrose Bierce and his little party had sneaked down across the border in the dark of night. They crossed the Rio Grande unnoticed about ten miles west of El Paso, plunging into the dusty scrub desert under cover of starlight, passing only a few lonely adobe huts lit inside by dim candles. It was unseasonably warm for this time of year on the high plains, and the first night they camped out in a thicket of mesquite.

Cowboy Bob was naturally curious about his mysterious traveling companion who called himself Jack Robinson, but the hundred dollars he'd been paid to take Bierce to Pancho Villa, along with Bierce's taciturn manner, inclined him not to ask too many questions. He did, however, once inquire what Bierce's occupation had been.

"I have spent my entire life making idiots feel uncomfortable," was Bierce's blunt reply. "It has been my life's work. And now I am retired, and living a life of leisure." After that,

Cowboy Bob didn't ask anything else.

"I been thinking about a new plan, Mr. Robinson," Cowboy Bob said. "Tomorrow, we'll head down to the Arroyo Blanco trestle." The five of them were stretched out around the dying embers of a fire. "It's about forty miles from here, southeast."

"And when we get there?" said Bierce.

"We wait for the train. I imagine somebody will have fixed the tracks by then. It'll take a lot longer to rebuild that trestle. But I don't intend to ride a horse all the way down to Chihuahua City if I can help it. That's sort of beyond the call." What Bob counted on was that even with the trestle out, the train from El Paso would run up to the river, then they could cross over and catch a Mexican train that would have run up from Chihuahua.

"Is that where you think Villa is?" asked Bierce.

"Probably, in Coahuila, maybe, or somewhere near it. It's kind of his headquarters, unless the Federales have kicked him out again. Anyhow, there are plenty of people in Chihuahua who'll know where to find him."

"How do you know he'll welcome us?"

"I don't," said Cowboy Bob. Until recently, Cowboy Bob used to scout for Villa's army. But with the Americans closing off the border and all, he assumed that Villa wouldn't be exactly happy to see too many Americans. In the old days, Villa kind of liked Americans —

even had three or four of them on his staff. Had some French and an Englishman, too, and even an Italian. Bob thought it made Villa feel important, having those sorts of people around.

"You think it would help if I brought him a present?" said Bierce.

"Maybe. It's kind of their custom down here. What sort of present?"

"I have something in my bag. Bought it in El Paso. I thought he might like it."

This piqued Cowboy Bob's curiosity even more but since Robinson didn't volunteer any more information, he let it drop.

"What do you suppose Villa really wants out of this business?" Bierce asked.

"That's a good question," answered Cowboy Bob. "He's got this notion of a revolution where the poor people run things instead of the rich folks in Mexico City. It's gotten to be kind of like a religious zeal with him, like he was a savior or somethin'."

Bob had known Villa in the old days, too, when he used to run stolen cows across the border and sell them to the ranch Bob worked for, and Villa hadn't given a damn about much of anything back then.

"Well, that's the thing about revolutions," Bierce said. "Their only purpose is to elevate the poor to the same level of stupidity as the wealthy. Does Villa enrich himself personally in the process of this revolution?"

"He ain't broke, if that's what you mean. Got good horses, good clothes, good guns. I mean, he's a general, if that's what you call it. As far as does he have a stash? I got no idea. But if I was him, I sure as hell would."

"How's his English?"

"Not good, not bad," Bob said. "Speaks it so you can talk with him pretty well. I don't think he writes it or reads it much, though."

"And vices?"

"Women and cigars are about it, if you leave the killing aside. He don't drink. Never seen him touch a drop. Somebody said he use to in the old days but he quit. I guess it didn't agree with him or something. He eats a lot of ice cream. Absolutely loves it. That and lemonade."

"I'm going to give him a sidearm," Bierce said, and produced from his kit a small shiny two-barreled pearl-handled derringer, finely engraved and extremely well made, to the point that the screw covers on the handles were inlaid cut diamonds.

"Well, well, Mr. Robinson," said Cowboy Bob. He was stunned. It was just the sort of gift that would put Villa in an expansive mood. He cradled the pistol in both hands as though he were holding a sacred relic.

"Made in London," said Bierce. "Carry it in your pocket or wherever. I supposed you could wear it in a hatband."

"You're a pretty intuitive feller," Bob said,

using one of the few complex words he knew.

"Does he have a sense of humor?" Bierce asked.

"Well, yeah, if you can call it that," Bob said.

He remembered the time Villa had caught four Federales who had been murdering, raping, and stealing at a village over in Sonora, and lined them up for the firing squad, but at the last minute decided they weren't worth the bullets he was going to shoot them with. So he told them all to do a left face. Then he fetched some big old buffalo rifle about .65-caliber with a barrel four feet long and positioned himself in the line behind them and killed them all dead with one shot that passed right through one to the other in the heart. It looked to Bob like falling dominoes. Villa had seemed very pleased with himself after that.

"Well, everyone needs a sense of humor," Bierce observed. "War and cruelty apart, it's no longer a laughing matter to be a member of the human race."

"I reckon not, Mr. Robinson," Bob said. "Not where Pancho Villa's concerned."

TWENTY-THREE

"Now, folks, this is what it's all supposed to be about," the Colonel crowed. He gazed toward the looming Sierra Madre towering so high in the distance the stars themselves seemed to crown the peaks. Behind him in the hard desert scrub a crackling fire warmed the evening chill and the aroma of savory beefsteaks wafted over the campsite. The Colonel was wearing polished leather boots, riding breeches, a pith helmet, and had a large revolver strapped around his waist in a hand-tooled leather holster he'd picked up at a gun store in El Paso.

Under the big tent fly, Beatie and Xenia sat in canvas folding chairs, while Arthur and the kids sat on leather stools around the fire. Ah Dong was preparing roasted corn in husks on hot rocks and occasionally stirred a pot of steaming chili. Bomba had wandered out into the desert to attend to his needs, and nearby the six bodyguards the Colonel had hired were tending a campfire of their own.

"About the only thing you have to watch out for here is snakes and scorpions," said the Colonel. "So don't leave anything like shoes or boots or open luggage on the ground next to your cots."

At this, Beatie gave an audible gasp and checked the ground around her feet.

"Why not, Grandpapa?" Timothy asked. He was a quizzical boy, slim, towheaded, who always seemed on the verge of asking a question, but rarely did. Arthur, sitting beside him, regretted that his stint in Chicago had been preventing him from spending time with Timmy during the week. He knew the boy was growing up quickly and that time was gone forever.

"Well, once, in Borneo," the Colonel proclaimed, "I jumped out of bed and when I lifted my boot to put it on I thought it felt a little heavy. When I looked inside, why, coiled up there was a blue krait — deadliest snake in the world. Over there they call it the 'two-step snake.' After it bites you, you take two steps and it's all over."

Beatie moaned.

"What did you do, Grandpa?" Timmy asked, unexpectedly. Arthur was delighted. He'd heard the story a thousand times.

"Why, I snatched a thong of leather off a tent pole and tied up that boot tight as I could and ordered the bearers to dig a hole in the ground halfway to China. Then I threw the boot down in it and had them cover it up." He had become theatrical now, lowering his voice conspiratorially for Timmy.

"If that snake had leaked even an iota of its venom into my boot, I didn't want to put my foot in it ever again," the Colonel hissed. "Remember, he was a 'two foot snake.' "

"How did you get around on one boot?" Katherine asked, ever practical.

"I had them make me a sedan chair," the Colonel said grandly, explaining what a sedan chair was. "Out of native bamboo, and they carried me everywhere, and when I needed to get down, I hopped wherever I went one-legged, like a flamingo, or a crippled kangaroo!"

The desert stars shone hard and cold on the Shaughnessy encampment that night; Beatie fidgeted on her cot and let out little groaning sounds at the notion of snakes.

By midafternoon next day, the Colonel's party reached Valle Del Sol.

"My word," the Colonel exuberated as they topped a rise, "it's as magnificent as ever!" Under a cloudless cobalt sky, the valley was ringed by low mountains and foothills covered with dense green pines, while the vast snow-capped Sierra Madre rose imposingly in the faraway distance. Tall green grasses waved in the breeze, and the plains and hillsides were dotted with tens of thousands of cattle. Occasionally, men on horseback would be seen riding among them. At the head of the valley was the ranch, its reddish adobe buildings set amid a copse of trees. An enormous pear orchard lined both sides of the road, and as the Colonel's motorcade wound its way toward the hacienda a red-tailed hawk soared, looking for prey.

TWENTY-FOUR

Ambrose Bierce had been with Pancho Villa's army for a week when John Reed arrived.

Just as Cowboy Bob predicted, the train tracks were repaired to Chihuahua City after a few days and, after crossing the river and loading their horses on boxcars, the party proceeded in that direction by rail. Bob contacted an old Mexican who he knew had been close to Villa in the past, and was given instructions on how to reach the general's encampment in a maze of foothills about thirty miles from the city.

And, again just as Bob predicted, Bierce's gift of the lovely little derringer broke whatever ice there might have been.

To everyone's relief, Villa was a delightful host to "Señor Jack Robinson," who billed himself as a former military officer in the American Civil War, saying he had merely come to observe the fighting.

Bierce expressed surprise that the ambushers had not also closed off the line of retreat for the Federales, thus catching them not only in a crossfire, but bottling them up front and rear as well. This observation impressed Villa to the extent that he sent a messenger down to order the thing done, and when the Federal horsemen eventually arrived they were cut down almost to a man. It was the first fighting Ambrose Bierce had seen in fifty years but the old rush of excitement welled up in him immediately, just as it had on the battlefields of Chickamauga and Shiloh.

"That was as near-perfect a butchery as I have ever witnessed," Bierce commented as Villa's infantrymen began working their way through the fallen Federales, going through their pockets and dispatching any still living with a bullet to the head.

"Thanks in many ways to you," Villa told him. "I'm gonna haul up that young lieutenant down there just as soon as he comes back and let him have it," he said with a laugh. "Imagine, having to be instructed in the setting of an ambush by a man who hasn't seen a battle in half a century!"

"It comes back to you," Bierce replied. "Of course, those machine guns of yours made all the difference."

"They're something," said the general.

"In my day it would have taken a regiment to put out that rate of fire," the old man said.

"It's made killing a lot easier, but we need more of them. They are always breaking down and it's hard to find spare parts."

"Must be harder since my country closed down the border," Bierce said tentatively.

"That's damn true, Señor Robinson," said the general, "but we got other ways. That war they're fighting over in Europe, they got more machine guns than they know what to do with."

"Who from? The English, the French?"

"No, the Germans," Villa said. "English and French wouldn't sell us a cupful of warm spit. But the Germans are trying to be friendly. We'll see."

A few days later, Bierce, Villa, and half a dozen of the general's staff including Santo — "the Saint" — and Fierro — the butcher — were sitting around a campfire on some empty ammunition crates when John Reed arrived. They were watching Tom Mix do some fancy pistol-twirling he had taught himself out of boredom on the range back in Arizona.

"Chief," said the young officer escorting Reed, "this guy says he wants to see you. He's a gringo newspaperman from New York, he says. All the credentials he's got come from this note he carries. It's from that stinking Federale Orozco." The officer extended to Villa a wadded piece of telegraph paper, but Villa waved him off.

"No, no — what does it say? You read it." Reading, even in Spanish, was not one of Villa's strong points.

"Yes, General," the officer began. "It says: 'Dear Esteemed and Honored Señor Reed. If you set foot inside of Chihuahua, I will stand you sideways against a wall, and with my own hand take great pleasure in shooting furrows in your back.' "

Villa looked puzzled for a moment, then burst out in laughter. "If you are Señor Reed, I'd say you must've done something to make General Orozco very unhappy."

"All I did, sir," Reed replied, "was to politely ask his permission to enter Mexico to see you."

"That would have been enough," Villa responded, "but it's not his permission to give, anyway. It's mine. So why are you here and not against the wall?"

"Well," Reed answered, "I'm not sure about that, either, except that I went ahead and waded across the river and I saw General Mercado, who apparently hates General Orozco, and he told me if I minded my business it was all right to stay in Juárez."

"General Orozco is now in Juárez?" Villa inquired. "Commanding the Federales?"

"He was when I was there."

"With his army?"

"As far as I know. He had arrived recently."

Villa pondered this information for a few moments, stroking his chin. "Then tell me, Señor Reed," he said finally, "what brought you here?"

"Well, sir, for a few days I stayed in Juárez, until they repaired the rail tracks, and then I took the train to Chihuahua and somebody told me in a sort of general way of your whereabouts, and I started out, and when I got to the beginning of the mountains these gentlemen accosted me."

"And you are not harmed?"

"No, sir, your people were very proper. Except that they took all my money and my press credentials."

Villa scowled at this revelation. "You give him those back," the general told the young officer.

"We were only holding it for him, Chief, in safekeeping," the escort said sheepishly.

"It will be a lot safer with him than with you," the general replied. The man did as he was told.

"And what newspaper are you with?" Villa asked Reed.

"Sir, the *New York World.* I am sent to write about the war."

"And whose side is the *New York World* on?"

"Nobody's," said Reed. "The *New York World* reports the news as it is."

"Well, Señor Reed," Villa said, "we will see. So what exactly do you want?"

"To write stories," Reed replied, "about you, and your revolution."

TWENTY-FIVE

Rosalita Callahan rushed into the courtyard at Valle del Sol the instant she saw Colonel Shaughnessy step out of the car, bursting into tears as she fell into his arms. She poured out the news of her husband's murder and the pillaging. Shocked by the revelations, the Colonel felt compelled to make a speech and held his arms up for silence. The ranch workers gathered around with anxious eyes. Most of them had seen the terrible scene that Pancho Villa had caused. They had always felt safe with the Americans at Valle del Sol, because neither side in the war wanted to disturb the Americans — until Pancho Villa broke the rule.

"I know there has been evil done and many of you might remain worried," the Colonel declared. "Fear no more. I am here." As this was being translated to those who understood no English, the Colonel continued. "Now, I am terribly saddened by the death of Buck Callahan. He was my friend. And also about the injuries to some of the rest of you. I understand there's been a kidnapping as well. All I can say is, give me some time to get settled and I promise you we will sort things out."

At this there was a chorus of approving voices and nods, and the Shaughnessy family was escorted to their quarters. Bomba supervised the unloading of the baggage with his uncanny way of communicating with people whose tongue he did not speak — a firm series of grunts and gestures that seemed to constitute an international language all its own.

With the Colonel's appearance, normality seemed to return to Valle del Sol. That evening they dined on fresh calf's liver smothered with peppers, tomatoes and onions, salsaed corn and rice, and a rich wine from the small vineyard on the ranch. In the hours before darkness Timmy and Katherine had been given a guided tour on buckboard around the hacienda, where they visited the horse-breeding pastures, fighting-bull pens, vegetable fields, orchards, stables, barns, streams, and glades. This was conducted by Rodriguez, Buck Callahan's former assistant foreman, now promoted to Callahan's old position, who entertained the children with lavish stories of life at the ranch.

Next morning, the Colonel began assessing

the damage. More than five hundred head of cattle had been driven off by Villa's men in the raid. What was more, Villa had left behind a party who continued to rustle the ranch daily — or rather, nightly — and because of the size of the property there was little anyone could do about it.

"I won't put up with it!" declared Colonel Shaughnessy. "At this rate they'll bankrupt us. We're American citizens and deserve protection. If the Mexican government won't do it, the United States government should."

With this pronouncement ringing in the air, he sat down at a desk and began scribbling out telegrams to President Wilson, Secretary of State Bryan, the secretary of the army, and the American ambassador to Mexico, with copies to the other big American landholders in Mexico. Next he rang the telephone operator and told her to place a call to the White House in Washington and ring him back when she got them. When he finished, the Colonel called for a rider to take the telegrams to the wire office in Torreón and rose from his chair.

"C'mon, Arthur," he said, "let's have a look around."

The two of them rode alone in the cooling evening along the roads beside the fields of cattle and produce.

"That young Johnny Ollas is a fool," said the Colonel. "Can you imagine somebody going after a man like Villa with four men? I only hope he escapes with his life. He's a good boy — would have made a good matador, too, maybe."

"Well, he might come out all right."

"I don't know," the Colonel replied. "He's hotheaded like all these Mexicans."

They topped the rise of a hill and spread out before them was a sight that almost took Arthur's breath away. Across the horizon stretched thousands upon thousands of cattle, silhouetted against a blood-red setting sun. There was very little movement among them; it was almost as if he were looking at a cyclorama. They reined in their horses to take in the view.

"Poor ol' Buck Callahan," the Colonel said finally. "He didn't deserve what happened to him."

"Senseless," Arthur said. "A damned depraved act."

"One time," the Colonel went on, "Old Man Swift telegraphed Buck Callahan from Chicago saying that his company needed to buy forty-five thousand head of cattle and could we supply them. Know what Buck did?"

"Umm," Arthur said, shaking his head.

"Wired him back: *We can supply. What color do you want?*" The Colonel chuckled, then burst out laughing. "What color . . . !"

Arthur had to laugh, too. That was the

exactly the kind of story the Colonel loved;
the power, the sheer arrogance of it.

TWENTY-SIX

With the long-distance telephone lines temporarily repaired, at three in the afternoon the Valle del Sol telephone rang for the first time in nearly a month. It was answered by Señora Pardenas, who had been dusting paintings in the hallway and who let it ring nearly ten times, hoping that somebody else might pick it up.

"Bueno?" the señora said softly into the receiver.

"This is the White House calling," said the voice at the other end. "We are trying to reach Colonel Shaughnessy."

"The Colonel, he taking his siesta," Señora Pardenas replied.

"Yes, well, if you'll just tell him it is the White House calling . . ." said the voice.

"No, señor, the Colonel, he having his siesta now. Be one more hour." She then hung up the phone. Five minutes later it rang again.

"Sí?" Señora Pardenas answered, annoyed.

The phone, even when the lines were working, often didn't ring more than a few times a week — and now twice in a few minutes. She didn't like answering the phone anyway because she didn't trust it. Voices coming out of a little box; it seemed sacrilegious, or worse.

"This is the White House calling," said the voice, peevishly. "We need to speak to Colonel Shaughnessy, please."

"Señor, I already tell you, Colonel taking siesta. Colonel say nobody wake him up while he taking siesta."

"But madam," the voice pleaded, "this is important. You must tell Colonel Shaughnessy that this is the White House."

"Not matter to me, señor, *what color* house it is," Señora Pardenas answered. "Colonel no like be waked up from his siesta. *Buenas tardes.*" She hung up the receiver once again, and this time the phone did not ring anymore. Later that evening she reported the incident to Colonel Shaughnessy.

"Well, my word, woman," he exclaimed, "it's probably too late to call them back now. Somebody should have woke me up. It was the White House! The president of the United States!" he growled. "Don't you people understand anything? My word!"

"Yes, Señor Shaughnessy," Señora Pardenas replied. "We understand you not wish to be got up from your siesta."

273

Just then the phone rang again, and Shaughnessy answered it himself. Finally he got his conversation with Woodrow Wilson. He catalogued the list of depredations at Valle del Sol by Villa and his men: sabering to death his ranch manager, killing his prize fighting bull, brutally clubbing his young ward Johnny Ollas and kidnapping his wife.

"Not only that, Mr. President, but they are rustling off my cattle at night," the Colonel blustered. The president listened patiently but said nothing.

"Well, sir, we are American citizens. What do you intend to do about it?"

The thin voice of Woodrow Wilson finally replied to him through the miracle of the telephone. "Colonel Shaughnessy, you must understand this is a delicate situation. It involves more than your ranch and livestock. Mexico's a nation of twenty million people along our very borders in great turmoil. The interest of the United States government is to stabilize the situation, not add to it. Any suggestion of intervention on our part will undoubtedly make matters down there worse. The citizens of Mexico have suffered enough."

"Citizens of Mexico!" the Colonel fumed. "Hell with citizens of Mexico — I'm talking about United States property!"

"You have cattle belonging to the U.S. government?" the president inquired.

"No, of course not, but they are property of a U.S. citizen — me — and they feed other U.S. citizens and taxpayers, maybe even you, for all I know, and I can't see why the American government can't come down here and do something about Mr. Villa and his companions. What do we have an army for in the first place?"

"Colonel Shaughnessy, if you had chosen to raise your cattle in the United States or its territories, I assure you the government would protect you," the president said. "But we can't interfere with the internal affairs of a foreign power just because someone's stealing your livestock."

"Well, they're also molesting Mr. Harriman's railroads and Mr. Guggenheim's mineral mines and everything else. Why, sir, you invaded Veracruz just a year or so ago over a diplomatic insult. Why can't you do something now?"

"Because Mr. Bryan and I both feel that Mexico must be let alone for the time being. We are aware of Mr. Villa's activities, which is one reason we have chosen to recognize General Carranza as president. Another is that he seems to be winning now. When Carranza subdues Mr. Villa and his associate Mr. Zapata, peace will be restored to Mexico. That is our policy."

"*Mister?* Mr. President," the Colonel shouted, "these people are criminals! And your Secretary Bryan doesn't know his ass from live steam. Besides," he added as an afterthought, "he is some kind of religious nut!" After a grumbling a thanks-for-nothing good-bye, Shaughnessy put the phone down angrily and waved his hands in frustration. "This is what happens when you put damn Virginians in the White House." The Colonel had barely concluded his fulminating when Rodriguez, the new ranch manager, came through the door to report more cattle rustling the previous evening.

"Three or four hundred head this time, boss," said Rodriguez. "My people saw them but they're afraid to chase when those guys might have got machine guns."

"Yes, I can understand that," the Colonel said dejectedly. He sank back in a chair. "You sure this is Villa's doing?"

"No, sir," explained Rodriguez, who had gone to school in New Mexico and spoke English well. "There's several bandit bunches operating out in those hills."

"Hell," said the Colonel, slumping deeply into the chair.

After dinner that evening the Colonel announced his decision. The family was gathered around the huge formal Honduran mahogany table, being served grilled veal chops and asparagus fresh from Valle del Sol's vegetable garden. Mexicans still grew good food.

"The news is final," proclaimed Colonel Shaughnessy. "We are on our own. No help at all from the imbeciles in Washington."

"What does it mean, John?" asked Beatie, who had left the table but wandered back into the room after hearing loud voices, thinking coffee might be served.

"It means that if I'm going to lose this land I'll be damned if I'll sit around and lose everything on it as well. We've got a million and maybe more dollars of prime beef on the hoof that are going to be stolen away piecemeal unless I can get them up north and safely across the border. Those cows are worth ten times as much as I paid for this entire property. Furthermore, from all that's gone on here recently it is obvious this place is far too dangerous for you women and children to remain. I had no idea; I shouldn't have brought you." This was about as close as the Colonel ever came to an apology.

"You mean we can't stay?" Katherine asked.

"That's right, honey," said the Colonel. "I'm going to have to get you all up to Chihuahua City as soon as we can and put you on the first train back to El Paso."

"But Grandpapa, you said I could ride the horses we saw. You said . . . Please." She said it so softly, as she always did; the mere sound of her voice gave the Colonel pleasure.

277

"I know I did," replied Colonel Shaughnessy. "But Mr. Woodrow Wilson just told me we are on our own. And we know what Villa's capable of. I just can't risk it."

Arthur shot a glance at Xenia, who looked absolutely crestfallen, her eyes glistening as if about to tear. She didn't look at him, but stared straight down at the table as if she could see a thousand miles.

After dinner the Colonel summoned Arthur to his private study. Along the walls were photographs of his famous bulls, including Toro Malo, as well as the ears and tails of others that had been raised to be killed in the ring. Matadors, including Johnny Ollas, had presented them to him over the years.

"You'll be coming along on the drive, Arthur?" he asked, more as a statement than a question.

Arthur assumed that was why he'd been summoned. It made him cringe. This was the kind of thing for which he felt entirely ill suited. He could ride, of course, but this — some kind of screwy cattle drive over miles of desolate terrain . . . and with a madman like Pancho Villa on the loose . . . Arthur certainly wasn't a coward; at least he didn't think he was. But he was a businessman accustomed to fine suits, leather chairs, private cars, the telephone, and clubs and financial discourse. He was also a pilot, but that was different. Danger wasn't really a factor in a thing with so much passion. About the closest he came to enjoying the great outdoors was when he was out collecting his butterflies.

On the other hand, he was troubled by his father's recent behavior; the crazy trip to Ireland on the *Ajax,* the startling revelation of his personal financial decline, the impulsive insistence on a trip to Mexico in the midst of a war, and the baffling story Arthur had been told about the acquisition of a bear on the train at Memphis. Might be, Arthur thought, the Old Man needed looking after.

"Who's going to stay with Mother and Xenia and the children?" Arthur asked. "If they're going to Chihuahua to catch the train, they need a man along. And even if —"

"Of course they do," the Colonel interrupted, "and I'm going to send Bomba with them, as well as several of my best men. They'll be well taken care of."

Arthur had been trying to get a grasp of his father's scheme for moving the cattle. If the railroads had been running, of course, they could have simply herded them to the railheads and loaded them on the cars. But this was very different, to drive that many cows hundreds of miles across a desert. He could hardly imagine it. How many head would they lose? Arthur had checked the wholesale price of beef in Chicago before they left: it was low — $75 a head. And how would the arrival of this huge herd affect that price?

What could they hope to collect at the end of it, and how long could such a welcome infusion of cash affect the operation of the NE&P?

"What do you think we will make out of this?" Arthur asked his father.

Without blinking, the Old Man said, "Maybe two million dollars at best."

"Based on what price?" Arthur asked.

"Twelve cents a pound. That's been the usual price of beef lately."

"Well, when I left Chicago it was nine-point-eight," Arthur informed him. "And don't you think those cows are going to lose a lot of weight on this drive — let alone the ones that die or get lost? And have you considered what will happen to the price when that many cattle are flooded into the market? And have you calculated the expense of shipping them, and the auctioneers' fees, and the feedlot fees, and —"

"Dammit, Arthur," the Colonel cut in, "we have to get those cows out of here before Pancho Villa and his gang run off the whole herd, or we won't have any cents' worth."

"The way I'm figuring it," Arthur said, "you'll be lucky to get half of what you think." He ran his fingers through his hair. Whether or not moving the cattle across the border and selling them would keep the railroad afloat, he knew the Old Man needed him just now. In a way, it was almost flattering, and for chrissakes, somebody had to keep an eye on him.

"I'm thinking tomorrow," replied the Colonel. "We'll put the family in the cars, and we'll swing up north of Chihuahua, away from Villa's operations. The cattle will be safe enough with us as anyplace else. I'll have a good many men riding herd."

"I guess I'd best go and start packing," Arthur said.

"Oh, there's plenty of time for that," the Colonel replied merrily. "Why don't you stay and have a drink?"

Arthur didn't stay or go straight to bed, or pack. Instead, he went into the parlor and privately poured a large tumbler of whiskey while he fretted over Xenia and what might be happening to the two of them.

In the past few years she'd immersed herself in pursuit of art and intellectuals, while he drifted deeper into the task of saving the NE&P. Until her recent bout with melancholia, he'd watched impotently while Xenia grew more outgoing and ebullient and he wasn't feeling that way at all. It was like they were two comets whose orbits had matched for years but were now beginning to spin away in opposite directions.

A lot of it was his own fault. He didn't particularly enjoy Xenia's friends; this new crowd of thinkers and doers who talked a mile a minute, much of it in a language he didn't understand.

They spoke of transcendentalism and of the greed of the psalm-singing Chautauqua programs. They talked excitedly of Vachel Lindsay, Carl Sandburg, Edgar Lee Masters, and Amy Lowell, and smoked cigars and swooned over realist painters like George Bellows or abstractionists such as Stuart Davis.

Xenia's smart set spurned *Collier's* and the *Saturday Evening Post* for the *New Republic* and *Seven Arts,* and some spoke openly of socialism and free thought. On nights when Xenia held her salons, young men such as Walter Lippmann or Van Wyck Brooks might turn up, and the rooms would be animated and gay in a haze of alcohol and blue tobacco smoke, while Arthur often found himself standing in a corner, alone.

When he and Xenia were by themselves she often tried to draw him into conversations with which he felt uncomfortable, either from ignorance or the radicalism of the topic. Much of the talk was either against his upbringing or so silly he didn't want to expend the energy on something he couldn't agree with anyway. To avoid this he became taciturn and distant, but this seemed only to drive Xenia deeper into the fantastical world of her friends.

He even considered the old "If you can't lick 'em, join 'em" solution, but quickly discarded that as impractical. Arthur was a man of commerce and honestly didn't much care what most of those friends of hers were talking about; many of their ideas seemed weird, even dangerous.

Arthur disliked the notion of sending Xenia back to those people. He had begun to believe they had somehow corrupted her and were a part of whatever was causing her troubles. He wished he could take her to El Paso and the two of them could climb into *Grendel* and just fly west, and keep on flying.

TWENTY-SEVEN

Villa's whole army had moved out of Coahuila now, southwestward toward Chihuahua City. In the vanguard, journalist Reed rode next to a dark sour-looking aide to Butcher Fierro, a Lieutenant Crucia, who was wearing a charm necklace that Reed had trouble taking his eyes off of. There were dozens of blackened, dried fleshy objects strung on a piece of twine. They reminded Reed of noses.

"What are those on your necklace?" Reed inquired.

"Noses," Crucia replied.

Reed leaned over in his saddle and peered closer. He felt himself shudder. "Why noses?" he asked reflexively, and because he thought at least he ought to respond in some way.

"Perhaps the owners stuck them where they did not belong," Crucia said, his face suddenly cold and distant.

Reed pulled back on the reins imperceptibly, trying not to give the impression of drifting away from Lieutenant Crucia. He took an instinctive dislike to Crucia, whose eyes were narrow and slitty and who had a long a face with big ears. His head was shaped like a meat axe and, Reed suspected, contained about as much brains. But Reed justified his current position by telling himself that being on the righteous side of politics — such as glorious revolutions — often brought you strange allies. These were amazing people, Reed thought: perfect peasants, mostly Indians and Mestizos, subsistence farmers, but also former shopkeepers and tradesmen, mine workers, peaceful men in real life, salt of the earth, roused to such revolutionary fury they would collect other people's noses for souvenirs.

In the present world the masses were so thoroughly oppressed, reduced to poverty and powerlessness and hopelessness, Reed believed that without the great revolutionary struggle to throw off the yoke of the past they'd sooner or later devolve into an entire race of undignified animals — a separate and lower species entirely. But here was the beginning of this grand insurrection that would sweep the world and awaken the giant sleeping masses of czarist Russia and middle Europe, of India, China, and South America — yes, even the jaded and complacent United States of America.

Bierce rode up on a sleek black stallion Villa had lent him after the horse he'd bought from

Cowboy Bob turned up lame. It was typical of Pancho Villa: kill a man in one breath, give away a horse in another.

"Well, are you getting an eyeful, young fellow?" Bierce said.

"Do you suppose this . . . this attack . . . is very important?" Reed asked in reply.

"All attacks are important," said Bierce, "especially to those doing the attacking." For a while after Reed arrived, Bierce had kept his distance, worrying that even in his disguise Reed might identify him as who he was, and not as "Jack Robinson," but after a few days the young reporter still hadn't seemed to recognize him and Bierce let down his guard.

"I mean, is it critical?" Reed asked.

"Well, Carranza's Federals are in Chihuahua City, and whoever controls Chihuahua City generally controls Chihuahua." Bierce, who had risen to the rank of major in the Union Army, already fancied himself a strategist where the war in Northern Mexico was concerned. He had picked up just enough information among Villa's entourage to sound convincing.

"Chihuahua's right in the center of a state that's almost as large as England, France, and Germany put together," Bierce said authoritatively. "All lines of communication go through it. You ask me, I'd say it is damned crucial."

To Bierce's immense delight, Pancho Villa

had taken him on as sort of a staff confidant. The general had been impressed by Bierce's knowledge of tactics and engineering and was proud to have a former Union major from the great American Civil War to lend further legitimacy to his cause.

"General Villa believes there are about twenty thousand Federal troops in Chihuahua," Bierce continued. "But he doesn't see it as a problem, even if they outnumber him two-to-one, because he says they don't have the heart to fight. Of course, if the general had forty or fifty thousand men, like he did last year, instead of these ten thousand now, I'm sure he'd feel a little more comfortable. But his policy is to attack and not let the enemy have time to fortify. Besides, it's General Villa's studied opinion that the Federales in Chihuahua by now will have drunk up all the liquor in town and be nursing hangovers precisely at the moment of his assault."

"That's good thinking," Reed said. "But it seems like a strange way to fight a war."

"Not a war like this one," said Ambrose Bierce.

"Did you know one of General Fierro's men wears a necklace made of human noses?"

"That not surprising," Bierce replied. "They're savages."

"You're wrong," Reed said. "They're men caught up in savagery, but they aren't savages

287

themselves. The war's made it so, but when it's over, they'll go back to being men."

"So you say, Mr. Reed. But most of these soldiers are direct descendants of tribal Indians. Killing and maiming each other and even collecting people's ears and noses has been their natural condition since the dawn of their existence."

Reed was silent on this declaration, but Bierce certainly believed it was in their blood. The ancestors of these people, the Aztecs, before them the Toltecs, were the very same people who plucked out the still-beating hearts from their sacrifice victims' chests and ate them in front of God before they chucked the bodies down the sides of their temple steps. If that wasn't savagery, Bierce didn't know what was.

When Reed sent his first dispatch to New York, noses would not be mentioned, and this old fool wasn't going to convince him otherwise.

Next day, Villa's army arrived at the outskirts of Chihuahua City and camped behind a low ridge of hills that wound around the eastern part of the city, inside the mountain range that ringed it. The trains of Villa's men began converging, too, carrying the main body of troops, cannons, mortars, mounds of equipment, and the general's pride and joy, twenty-eight immaculate hospital cars (which he had liberated from the previous government) containing operating theaters lined with white porcelain tile and staffed by sixty trained doctors (whom he had also liberated).

Villa didn't really need to study the terrain; he knew it by heart. He usually planned a predawn attack, which had become something of his specialty, but this time he reconsidered for a peculiar reason.

A week earlier, about the time Reed and Bierce had joined his army, a motion picture crew from California had also arrived, with a request that they be allowed to film him in battle. One of Villa's favorite pastimes had been going to moving pictures. He especially enjoyed American cowboy films, newsreels, and the Keystone Cops.

The enthusiastic Hollywood crew persuaded Villa that a movie of him leading his army in battle would add vast political value to his cause in the United States, if not the entire world. So when he issued his final battle orders, General Villa set the time of attack at six-fifteen a.m., shortly after sunrise, hoping the day would be clear and the light good enough for the cameras to record his victorious assault. That, if nothing else, would certainly get the attention of the doubting Americans.

In the evening, he held a counsel of war, carefully giving instructions to his generals. First the presidio on the northeast side of town must be reduced. He would lead the attack himself, captured on film. As the battle progressed, other regiments of the Grand Army of the North would move in a vast sweep east to west against the city. There was a long sloping plain ending at the outskirts of town where Villa hoped for the main breakthrough. Federales would be manning positions in and around the rickety houses, and consequently speed was important — get into the city and let the fighting be in the streets. This would mitigate the Federales' artillery and manpower and throw them into confusion so he could bring up the reserves for the final coup.

Bierce was silent through it all.

It was a good plan, as far as he could tell, but he was dubious about how the army would fare against entrenched machine guns and barbed wire. Just one of those vicious little hornets would have been worth the firepower of an entire company of riflemen during his war. He'd suggested to Villa a siege instead, but the chief reminded him that the Federales were likely sending up reinforcements from the south even as they spoke. Bierce was sitting on an ammunition crate next to Reed when Villa pointed a finger at Butcher Fierro.

"And you, General, I must spare for something more important," Villa said.

Fierro, who had been absently throwing a

knife into the dirt, jerked his head up with a furrowed brow.

"We are going to need further provisions, however this fight comes out," Villa said. "Especially if it does not go our way. I never like to think of this possibility, but it remains, and if we are forced to withdraw, we will need beef — great quantities of it. Enough for ten thousand men for as long as, well, who knows? The few cows we were able to pick up in Coahuila are not nearly enough to feed this army. And the only place I can think to get such a herd is back at that stinking Shaughnessy place down near the San Paolo River. I want you to take a company — a regiment, if necessary — go there and liberate as many beefs as you think practical and have them back here as soon as you can."

"But General —" Fierro protested.

"Tonight," Villa said. "It's urgent."

Fierro began to protest again but Villa waved him off. "Enough. Get it done, General. Do you think I waste my generals on trivial things?"

Fierro spat on the ground and slouched away. Sometimes the chief really pissed him off, but even Fierro knew not to buck him. He'd not only seen the consequences of that, but in fact had often been the instrument of such consequences. His firing squad was considered one of the best in the army.

■ ■ ■ ■

Villa returned to his tent and lay down on a cot. He had a headache and felt apprehensive over what would happen tomorrow — above all because he thought he'd seen Sanchez's ghost again. The last time he'd had the vision was six months ago, and they'd lost a battle. Villa never saw Sanchez clearly, just a shadowy outrider on a horse who cast no shadow. Villa had suspected Sanchez of being a turncoat. The flimsy evidence later proved to be untrue, but at the time Villa had had him executed. "General Villa, at least shoot me like a soldier, *por favor,*" the old man had pleaded. "Do not hang me like a dog."

Villa had hanged him anyway.

Once Sanchez had stopped kicking, they all noticed his body seemed to cast no shadow on the ground.

Afterward, when the real traitor was caught red-handed in a telegraph office, Villa felt sorry about Sanchez; then he began to feel guilty, and finally afraid.

Ambrose Bierce noted an air of merriment in Villa's camp that night. Hundreds of fires blazed across the broad plain that swept up to the foothills, beyond which lay Chihuahua City and the Federal army. The sounds of singing wafted in the air and somewhere a mariachi band played "La Cucaracha"; the skies were clear and there seemed to be little in the mood to indicate that a great battle was to take place the following day. While he walked to another section of the bivouac, Bierce noticed the handsome dark-haired man he'd seen around Villa's staff doing tricks on a big palomino horse for a pretty brunette seated on a stump. She did not look happy but nodded in acknowledgment as the man made the horse paw the air, bow, and sit on the ground.

"That's a fine trick horse you got there," Bierce offered. "Ought to take him to a circus."

"He don't like crowds," the man replied.

"My name's Robinson," Bierce said. "Jack Robinson."

"Tom Mix," replied the cowboy, extending his hand.

About then, Reed also turned up, and Mix introduced himself to him, too.

"This lady here is Señora Donatella Ollas," Mix said politely. "She is accompanying us on our little expedition."

"I am your prisoner, you mean," Donita said acerbicly. She felt a shudder ripple through her shoulders.

Bierce and Reed introduced themselves and Reed asked Donita, "Do you have family with this army?"

"Of course not," Donita said, "I told you, I

am kidnapped. These people are bandits and scum. They are holding me for a ransom."

Bierce and Reed looked at Mix, who smiled and shook his head. "That's not exactly right, gentlemen. She is a hostage of sorts, though. She belongs on a big spread about forty miles from here that's owned by an American railroad tycoon."

"You take captives of women?" Bierce said disapprovingly.

"General Villa does now," Mix replied. "I ain't seen him do it but once before, male or female, and somebody killed that guy anyway — an Englishman, foreman of a big copper mine. They took him a few months ago after he mouthed off to one of the general's officers."

"Why was he killed?" Reed asked.

"Kept mouthing off, I guess."

"Hostage-taking is always barbaric," Bierce remarked, "but I guess customs have changed."

"What happens to her now?" Reed asked.

"Who knows?" said Mix. "Maybe the general will marry her."

"Marry her?" Reed said.

"I'd rather be dead," Donita spat.

"Ain't she already married?" Bierce asked. "You said she was Señora somebody . . ."

"Oh, the general — I don't think that would worry him. He just gets the marriage annulled. I've seen him do it."

"By the church?" asked Reed.

"It's easy," Donita said. "He puts a gun to the head of a priest. He's a real gentleman, this General Villa."

"If I was you, señora, I wouldn't talk that way if the general's around," Mix said. "You might catch him in a bad mood."

Suddenly the dark face of Butcher Fierro appeared in the firelight.

"Señor Mix," he said, "I need you to come with me tonight on a special mission for General Villa. We leave in an hour. Bring your company with you — especially anybody who's worked cattle. Two days' rations and outfitting."

Mix nodded. "I'll be ready."

After Fierro left, Mix said, "Wonder what that's all about."

"One thing I remember," Bierce said, "is that in war, somebody's always changing something every few minutes."

"I suppose," said Mix. "But I was ordered to take my cavalry against the west part of town. I'd thought we were crucial."

"Only time a soldier's crucial is at the moment somebody tells him he is," Bierce said.

Johnny Ollas and his cuadrilla had ridden all the way up to Creel to find out Villa not only wasn't there, but hadn't ever been there. Gourd Woman followed along, gathering straw from the plains and plucking branches from trees, weaving brooms by night and selling them at the little villages they passed along the way. Johnny was disgusted with her for misleading him but felt a grudging admiration for the woman. It felt good to have a woman along on the trip. It somehow made you think things might turn out all right.

"So, your bones said he was here, huh? We come all this way for nothing."

"Maybe I dropped them wrong," Gourd Woman said. "Can't always be right. Besides, I heard somewhere Villa's got a house here. I figured he might have come home for a spell."

Johnny looked off into the distance, shaking his head. At least in Creel they had gotten wind that Villa was presently on the outskirts of Chihuahua City, preparing for battle. Johnny hadn't seen a battle, but he thought that in the chaos there might be a chance to sneak in and get Donita.

"Are you going to Chihuahua City?" Gourd Woman asked.

"Yes," Johnny answered.

"Mind if I still come along? I know you're mad at me."

He shook his head. "Do what you want. But if you're coming, you better get ready. Soon as I buy some supplies, we're going to hit the trail."

They camped that night beside a rocky brook, where Gourd Woman even managed to spear several fish with a pointed stick she'd carved. They ate roasted fish and onions and beans with garlic and peppers. As the campfire embers dimmed, the men of Johnny's party slept peacefully in their serapes beneath the stars, faces covered with big sombreros. Johnny sat by the stream listening to its noises, the water shining effervescently white in the nighttime as it rushed between the rocks. He tried again to determine how he would deal with Villa when they got to Chihuahua City.

"You working on a plan?" Gourd Woman's voice came from behind him, almost disembodied.

Why, he wondered, does she always seem to be reading my thoughts?

"Maybe," he said.

"You gonna try to get in and sneak her out?"

"I don't know. Depends on the situation," he said. "Maybe I will have to fight him like I fight the bull."

"Well, he looks like a bull," Gourd Woman said. "I've seen pictures. He has a big, thick neck and powerful shoulders. He even has eyes like a bull."

"In the arena," Johnny mused, "the secret is to lure the bull out of his *terreno* — the territory between where he is and the center of the ring."

"How is that done?"

"In a bullfight, those men there do it first,"

Johnny said, pointing toward the sleeping cuadrilla. "First the picadors go in and madden him with the pics. Get him frustrated and correct his hookings. Then the banderilleros do their work from horseback. The banderilleros' knives are put into his neck, that big hump of muscle behind the bull's head, which causes him to lower his head. I can't kill him while his head is raised."

"Why not?"

"Because I can't reach that high," Johnny told her. "They're on horses." Her questions challenged him: to have to try to explain all this to a woman who didn't even like bullfighting and had never seen a fight; it was like trying to explain blue to a blind man.

"That doesn't sound good," Gourd Woman said.

"No, but it is also the time when the bull is most vulnerable," Johnny told her. He pictured it in his mind: the tired bull, the head lowered, would then go into its *querencia,* which was the place in the ring where it felt most comfortable, if that was the word for it. Where it felt safest. Usually it was by the gate he came in through. Even though he couldn't get out through the gate the bull remembered it. A familiar place. It was where he usually went in the end. How could he explain all this to her?

"I think that's sad for him," said Gourd Woman.

"Not for a brave bull," Johnny said. "A cowardly bull will want to get out, but a cowardly bull is only fit to be gelded and to pull carts. A brave bull thinks only of killing me. And here I must be very careful, because the most dangerous thing a matador can do is enter the bull's *querencia.*"

"Why's that?"

"Because by now the bull is no longer wild as he was at the beginning, but he's wary and defensive and I have to lure him out of his *querencia* with the cape. But once he comes out for that last charge, his head lowered, a little slower now, I put in the sword, just so, in the back of his neck. And then it's done."

"And you think Villa will behave that way?" she said.

"I don't know, but I don't know how else to fight him."

"But don't you need some more men? I mean, this man has an army, and you are only five."

"What do I need more men for?" Johnny replied. "I can't raise an army bigger than his; he has thousands. A fighting bull weighs five, ten times what I weigh. Am I going to do exercises to improve my strength against him? No, like I said, I have to do it with the cape work and the trick so that he finally doubles up on himself and I can get in the sword. All the greatest matadors can do this

perfectly, and I have only read about them,"
said Johnny Ollas.

TWENTY-EIGHT

At Valle del Sol, cowhands had worked all day and through the night, massing the steers into a single herd. From the manager's office, Colonel Shaughnessy had been issuing orders when a rider appeared with a message that General Villa had sent a wire, which arrived at the telegraph office in Parral, demanding money.

This document had made a circuitous route. Villa had sent it nearly a week ago — all the way to the Colonel's New York offices, then it was repeated and resent and wired back down through El Paso, and finally to Parral, after it was determined that for some reason the telegraph station at Chihuahua City was no longer accepting commercial traffic.

He looked at the telegram carefully, shaking his head in awe. "My God!" the Colonel exclaimed. "This maniac wants me to pay him fifty thousand dollars!"

Arthur had been studying an old wall map

of the state of Chihuahua, trying to understand a little of the route the cattle drive would take to El Paso. The map somehow reminded him of ancient mariners' charts that depicted the faces of the Four Winds blowing and made observations such as: "Beyond Here There Be Dragons . . ."

"Here, read it," snapped the Colonel.

Arthur accepted the telegram:

GENERAL PANCHO VILLA GRAND ARMY OF THE NORTH PLEASE TO INFORM YOU SEÑORA DONITA OLLAS WILL BE RETURNED UNHARMED FOR FIFTY THOUSAND AMERICAN DOLLARS WIRED TO TELEGRAPH STATION AT CREEL.

"That's simply outrageous," said Arthur, shaking his head.

Donatella is a very fine and upstanding woman," said the Colonel. "But this kind of blackmail only leads to more. If I give in to it, he'll just keep coming back and kidnapping my people until I'm bled dry."

"A young woman," Arthur said. "What kind of *general* would do that?"

"He's only a general because he says he is," Shaughnessy replied.

Just then his new foreman Rodriguez entered the room. "Colonel," he said, "I'm afraid there is a problem up in Chihuahua."

"What's that? No trains yet?" asked the

Colonel.

"Yes, and worse. There's a battle being fought there — or about to be. Villa arrived yesterday with his army. No telling what's going to happen."

"Christ!" said the Colonel.

"What about Mama and Xenia and the kids?" Arthur asked, alarmed.

"Not only that," Rodriguez continued, "but some of Villa's men are spread out north. One of my people said he spotted a party of them along the San Pietra, about twenty miles from here."

"Were they headed this way?" Arthur asked.

"I don't know," Rodriguez replied.

Colonel Shaughnessy turned and stared out the window, shaking his head. "Nothing goes like I want it to," he groused. "I had it all worked out . . ."

"So what now?" asked Arthur.

"Move fast," his father responded, regaining an appearance of self-confidence. "We have to get those cattle away from here before whatever happens in Chihuahua happens."

"And what happens to Mama and Xenia and the children? You can't still be thinking of taking them with us, can you?"

"Certainly not." The Colonel walked over to the wall map. "I suppose we could send them south," he said hesitantly. "There's not one decent road in this whole damn state that goes anywhere but north or south, and we certainly can't send them north. Of course, if we can get them over to Torreón, then they could head east to Monterrey and on up into Texas, but they'll have to cross the mountains. No, I think we'll have to send them south and then to the coast and they can pick up a ship.

Rodriguez cleared his throat and shuffled with his hat still in his hands. "Colonel," he said, "I don't think south is a good idea. Zapata's got his people all through there. He's attacking the Federal trains coming from Mexico City. Some people say he's worse than Villa."

Colonel Shaughnessy winced sharply as the magnitude of the situation began to sink in. Something in him seemed to sag. "So, then, we can't send them north and we can't send them south or east, and there aren't any roads going to the west coast. So what do we do?"

"Maybe we should all stay here," Arthur suggested.

"Out of the question," barked the Colonel. "Those cattle are going to be a magnet to Villa once he is done with his business at Chihuahua. Even if I armed all my men here to the teeth they'd be brushed aside like gnats, and then where would we be?"

Rodriguez spoke up again. "There's a lot of places on this property to hide," he said. "There's dozens of houses out there, and some of them aren't half bad. I'd say if you got the family away from the big house here, they'd be safe. Villa's not gonna go around searching a million acres of property looking for something he don't even know is there."

Not a great solution, but Arthur and his father looked at each other.

The Colonel felt shaky. He'd built an empire on planning and calculation, but now he'd managed to land his family right in the middle of a murderous war. If anybody else had done that, he'd have told them they were idiots.

Rodriguez broke the silence. "There's a nice place about fifteen miles west of here. A family named Gonzales; real decent people. He manages the orchards in your San Pietra River section. He'd be honored to have you."

Finally the Colonel spoke. "Well, that's it, I guess. Rod, will you see that everything's prepared for them? Luggage, fresh bed linens, lamps, books, whatever they need. Bomba will be going with them, and I want you to take a dozen or so of your best men. Have them posted as lookouts and guard the place, but don't make it look conspicuous. You understand?"

"Yes, sir." Rodriguez nodded and left the room.

Arthur glared in disgust at his father, but said nothing.

"Now, look, Arthur," said the Colonel, "what else can we do? There's no safe way to

305

get them out. We've happened to have come at a bad time. Whether Villa wins or loses, he won't stay in Chihuahua indefinitely. Carranza's got plenty more troops to send up here and drive him away. The best thing to do with the family is keep them put until this situation blows over and the trains start running again. As for us, we're going to get those cattle out of here. Come along if you wish."

That again. A challenge since the day he arrived on the Shaughnessy doorstep.

"Don't worry," Arthur said. "I'll be there."

Arthur went to Xenia shortly afterward and told her the plan. She seemed shaken by it — and Xenia was not often shaken.

"I know it sounds frightening," he said, "but you're safer staying here."

They were in her room at Valle del Sol; a breeze from the blue distant mountains fluttered the curtains, reminding Arthur of those afternoons in Paris when they'd first met. Through the big window, they could see the orchards spread out along a hillside crowned with the silhouetted dots of cattle walking slowly along the crest.

"Well, I said wanted an adventure," Xenia remarked.

"Something to tell our grandchildren." God, he thought, I'm beginning to sound exactly like Papa. "I wish Mick was here," Arthur said.

"Why do you say that?" she snapped.

There was something in her tone Arthur didn't understand. "He's a negotiator," Arthur replied. "I'll bet he could negotiate with Pancho Villa, if it came to that."

"I thought he was the lawyer for the gangs," she said. Arthur sensed discomfort in her voice.

"Did you know the government once hired him to arrange the release of one of its diplomats?"

She shook her head.

"Mick's a salesman. He sells ideas to people — puts ideas in their heads they thought they'd never have."

Xenia came to him for what he at first took for a hug of affection. He took her gently in his arms, not holding her tightly, but enough to feel the warm curves of her body, and ran his hands over her back, and then moved them down.

"Oh, Arthur . . ." she said.

He didn't answer, but continued touching her, until she suddenly pushed herself away and turned her back to him.

"There is something I need to tell you," Xenia said. As she sat on the bed facing him, noise from the courtyard below swelled up, *charros* flirting with señoritas. Then she let out a breath and began.

When Arthur was away in Chicago a couple

307

of months back and she had gone to Back Bay for a ladies' luncheon at the Copley House, Mick had spied her in the lobby as she was leaving.

"Well, now," Mick said jovially. "Where is our young Arthur? In Chicago, I'll bet, counting his money." Mick was dressed to the nines, his face tanned, his shirt collar starched and firm around his muscular neck. He'd removed his top hat and bowed.

"Yes, you have it right," Xenia said. "We've been wanting to have you to dinner, but Arthur is just so busy these days . . ."

"Not to worry, my dear, I understand. I'm just old Mick, a poor relation . . ." He began to scrape and tug at his forelock, an old joke between him and Arthur. It made Xenia laugh.

"So if the man himself is not available, why don't you come and join poor old Mick for a libation? You see, I just settled a rather large matter, and crave companionship."

Mick was already a drink or two in, but Xenia didn't want to seem rude, even if it *was* the height of impropriety to be seen in public with a man not her husband. And just at the moment Xenia didn't care. Seeing Mick always put her in a good humor, as it did for Arthur. Mick was full of smiles and stories and dash, and she found him handsome. Besides, she was a modern woman who'd just had an excruciating lunch with a hundred biddies whom she couldn't care about less. It had not been her avant-guarde literary set today, but the obligatory annual luncheon of the Back Bay Women's Society, which had devolved into a silly society of bluenoses partially interested in planting flowers in the city's parks.

"All right," Xenia said.

They sat at a table beside big palms growing in hammered brass urns. Mick ordered a whiskey and a bottle of white Bordeaux, which was brought to their table in a bucket. It was midafternoon and there were few patrons there, which made Xenia feel more comfortable. She sipped her wine and made small talk, then had another glass, which she drank a little faster. It was terribly unlike her, but by the end of an hour she'd drained two-thirds of the bottle.

"I'm going to Paris, France, at the end of the month," Mick was saying.

"Oh, wonderful," Xenia said. "That's where —"

"I know," he cut her off.

"There's a little pension, just off the Champs —"

"I know about that, too."

"I bet you'll meet a girl there," Xenia said. "Just the way Arthur and I —"

"Such luck." He sighed. He seemed to be cutting off all her thoughts.

"I wish Arthur and I could go back there."

"For a renewal?" Mick asked.

"Something like that. He's just so —"

"I know." He cut her off again.

Tears brimmed in her eyes. "Could I have another glass?" she said. "I'm worried about Arthur." She told him: Arthur worked too hard, was away so much of the time, and when he was home he didn't seem to enjoy the company of her friends. He either went flying or stayed up in his study with the butterflies or coins and stamps. He didn't even seem to have much time for the children.

Mick nodded and listened. He offered an opinion that Arthur actually didn't like her friends or enjoy her salon parties.

"But he's always encouraged me," she said. "He seemed to be having a good time, at first, anyway . . ." She nodded when the waiter offered to refill her wine glass.

Xenia still had trouble piecing together what happened next; it seemed like a long, odd blur. She remembered talking to Mick about Arthur, about their lives. She remembered at one point that he reached over and put his hand on top of hers. She didn't remove it, and then she recalled turning her hand over and taking his in hers, the fingers entwining. The sun seemed to be going down outside, casting bright slanted shadows on the palm fronds. Another bottle of wine arrived. People began to fill up the place. She remembered looking into Mick's eyes. Both of them were leaning toward each other across the table. The point she tried to make seemed important. Mick was terribly sympathetic, the most sympathetic person she'd ever met.

Then he looked up and said:

"Xenia, I think that's old Thomaston, from the bank. He'll have with him a party you'll know. I keep rooms here. Do you think we might be more comfortable up there?"

She didn't think. She nodded. Waiters came, chairs were moved. They were on an elevator, in a hallway, a door opened. She was in a large elegant suite. Wine was put to chill in a silver cooler. A glass. He pressed against her from behind. She could feel his breath, his excitement. She tried to move away, but he held her firmly and put his hands around her waist. She tried again, but he had her tightly, pressing harder and harder.

"No, Mick," she said, "no — what's this?" It seemed like something that was not actually happening and that her voice was incorporeal.

He turned her around and began to kiss her. She turned her head away, but he grabbed her hair and pulled her back. She tried to talk through his mouth on hers, telling him, "No, no . . ." But he held her arms tightly and pushed her onto a sofa. She kept saying, "No, no, Mick, please . . ." But he was too strong. She started to scream, but he put his hand over her mouth and with the other was fumbling under her dress. She remembered feeling fright, panic. Then he was on top of her, with his hand still over her mouth. She managed to get an arm free and raked his face hard with her nails, but he twisted it back and held it down. She kept struggling and crying, "No, no," but all that came out were muffled noises.

Afterward he'd gone into the bedroom and she lay there, finally staggering to the bathroom, where she threw up. She looked into the mirror: her makeup was smeared and there were black streaks on her cheeks where the mascara ran. She washed her face and straightened herself up as best she could. There was blood on her collar. When she came out of the bathroom, he was waiting for her.

Mick offered to escort her down to her car and she let him, stunned, shocked, and still under the influence of drink. No words were exchanged.

She woke up before dawn in her own bed, head splitting, and it took several minutes for her to remember, but it hit her like a blow to the stomach. Her mind was swimming and confused. She was still dressed and she began to tear at the clothing and throw it in all directions. This kind of thing doesn't happen, she kept repeating to herself.

Arthur's best friend! What if anybody found

out? Who would believe her? For a moment she decided it hadn't happened; only a monstrous dream. But no, no dream. She went into the bathroom and became sick again, then bathed, and that's when she noticed blood under her fingernails. At least she'd fought.

She sat on the edge of her bed as her mind raced hysterically. How could she explain to Arthur, or anyone, what she had been doing in Mick's hotel suite — drinking? It would be Mick's word against hers, and he was a skillful lawyer. Suppose no one believed her? Suppose . . .

That morning a spray of roses arrived. No card. She knew who they were from. An hour later the maid came to her room to announce a visitor. She knew who that was, too. Xenia came down in her dressing gown and robe. They sat in the parlor with the door closed.

"What have you done, to come here?" she demanded desperately.

"Not me — us."

"You rotten thing! You know exactly what . . ." There were deep ugly scratch marks on his right cheek. She was glad to see that; it was like the mark of Cain.

"I want to apologize," he said.

"You . . . raped me!" she spat between clenched teeth.

"Xenia, that's not so!" His voice was firm;

even. His opening argument clearly had not worked.

"I was drinking wine, Mick. I only wanted to tell you about Arthur."

"You didn't need to tell me a thing."

She remembered how he kept cutting her off, her thoughts truncated by this smooth-tongued killer of men.

"I want you to leave now," Xenia told him. She had to look away because she was confused by what she felt — other than sheer revulsion.

"Why? Because of something we've both known was bound to happen between us for the past ten years?"

"That's not true! *Nothing* was bound to happen! I was trying to talk to you, and you took advantage of me!"

"I *am* Arthur!" he burst out. "Arthur and I are as the same person, and we have been all our lives — since either of us can remember. I would do anything under the sun for him, or for you."

"You are insane! Get out!" she said, but Mick ignored the order.

Mick, too, had tried to make sense of it in his own desperate, impulsive way. He told her that the three of them could work it out — Arthur in Chicago four days a week and then . . .

"You're crazy!" Xenia said to him, appalled. "Do you have any idea what you did?"

Mick was not paying attention to her. She watched as he began to grovel. Yesterday he had forced her; today he fell to his knees. It would have been comical in a play, with her in the audience and not onstage. He began blubbering, "I am not a bad man. Believe me, I'll make it right."

"You're sick, you're crazy," Xenia told him. It was all she could do to keep from shouting, even from scratching his eyes. No, nothing could make it right. Mick, the man of action — but that's all he was, with none of Arthur's refinement or decency.

He began to weep inconsolably. She sat and watched him for a long time until he finally sobbed himself out.

Xenia made the decision. She would keep this thing to herself. Even if Arthur believed her, and she knew he probably would, the impact it would have upon them all could be devastating. And, worse, she decided it had been her fault, too. She'd had no business to go for drinks with him, let alone get talked into going up to his room. That was why there were rules, and she had broken them.

Finally, when Mick was reduced to quiet little choking noises and trying to struggle to his feet, Xenia shook her head sadly and spoke. "You have always been a friend to Arthur, Mick. And he cares for you. So he isn't going to hear of what happened from my lips, because it might well ruin all our lives, if it hasn't already. But I don't wish to ever see you again. I hope you understand that."

"I have always considered you and Arthur my family," he said.

"Arthur and I have our own family." There was a cold composure in her eyes.

Mick seemed finally to understand. He rose and took his hat and looked at her for a long moment. "I'm sorry," he said. "I think I'm beginning to see, and I'm very sorry."

She looked away until she heard the door close. I hate myself, she thought, as she heard his car start up and drive away. It's my fault, too, and I hate myself . . . She sat in the parlor, where the sun streamed in through the windows, for such a long time that the downstairs maid finally knocked on the door to see if she was all right. She wasn't. This was a scourge that would not wash away, at least not that she could foresee — it was an indelible stain on her whole being.

Arthur reacted with a steely anger that he'd never felt in his life. He'd tried to interrupt several times to clarify some point that Xenia had told him, but she had waved him off until she got the whole story out. There was so much to take in, Arthur could barely comprehend it, but two things above all were clear: his best friend had raped his wife and left her to bear his child.

He fought to control his outrage.

"Does he know?" he said finally.

"No, not about the baby," she replied.

"Do you . . . are you going to . . . ?"

"I can't see anything else," she said.

"Well, there are people who can do things . . . ?"

"I've considered that. It isn't right, I've thought about it long and hard."

"I'll agree to what you say," he told her, "but he must be dealt with, too. I will see to it."

"That's something I've also thought about," she told him, "and the best thing is to let it go."

"Leave it!" Arthur cried, rising, fists clenched. "He's a brute and a coward, and if it's the last thing I do on this earth I will make him pay for what he's done to you."

"I knew that's how you'd feel," she said, "but I think when you've had time to consider it, you will see it more my way."

"But what of this baby?" he said. "Every time we look at it, we'll think of this." He felt suddenly ashamed of saying that.

"No," Xenia told him. "We can't let that happen. It certainly was not the baby's fault. We can't put it in an orphanage."

"No, not that, never." Arthur's stomach was in knots and he felt light-headed and sickened, and had to sit down. He felt he must stay with Xenia now and not go on the Colonel's cattle drive, but how could he ever explain that to his father without the whole story? Xenia must have sensed what he was feeling, because she came to him and put her hands on his shoulders.

"So when do we go to this country place?" she asked.

"Today, in a little while," Arthur said. "They'll get your things together. Bomba will drive all of you there. He'll stay with you."

"Well, you, my darling, take care," Xenia said tenderly, "and come back soon and get us." She kissed him on his forehead. "Because you are truly the only love of my life." She meant it now, more than ever.

Twenty-Nine

Ambrose Bierce sat in the shade of a willow tree writing in a tablet of stationery, tired and a little cranky after a lunch of cold beans and tortillas — what he wouldn't have paid for a fresh ham sandwich on hot rye bread with mustard, Swiss cheese, and a glass of sweet milk. Instead he'd dutifully scooped up a portion of the beans from the pot in Villa's mess area and washed them down with a cup of stale, tepid coffee.

Villa's headquarters camp had become nearly deserted now except for some mess cooks and a few other flunkies. Everybody else was down where the fighting continued, and which Bierce could see fairly well from his position under the tree on the slope of a hill. The dull thud of artillery fire rumbled continuously back toward him and he could see soldiers moving in the smoky din, like ants whose hill had been disturbed. Bierce still could not get used to the constant staccato rattle of machine gun fire. If they had

had those things back in '63, he thought, well . . . what? The very notion of it made him shudder. There were also numerous loud booms he couldn't account for; it wasn't artillery; maybe they were using some kind of bomb.

The fighting had been going on for nearly seven hours, and from what Bierce could tell from his vantage point, the issue from Villa's point of view was in doubt:

You might not believe this *[Bierce wrote Miss Christian],* but General Pancho Villa postponed the Battle of Chihuahua City until after sunrise this morning in order to have himself filmed by an American moving picture crew, leading the charge. His army attacked the well-fortified presidio and from what I can see, with little success. They have continued attacking it all day with artillery and infantry charges and mortars. A few chunks have been blown away but the Federals seem to be no worse for wear. The enemy have constructed trenches and barbed wire like they do in the European War and the toll Villa is taking from their machine guns must be terrible. I can see dead horses scattered all over the battlefield.

The general opened the battle with what one of his lieutenants described variously as "the sombrero gambit," or "the Mexican hat trick." During the night he had thousands of his soldiers remove their sombreros and spread them on a hillside. From the city it would look to the enemy like thousands of Villa's troops were massed there for attack. From here, however, it looked like the hillside was full of toadstools. Unfortunately it did not work. Down below I saw several battalions who appeared to be re-forming for another assault but, in fact, they turned out to have been made prisoners.

He might be having more luck on the western side of town; you can hear heavy rifle fire from there and at least some of his soldiers seem to have gotten into the city streets. There has been a steady line of wounded, walking and otherwise, returning from the outskirts of the city. These are being attended at his hospital train. I went to it a while ago and was struck by the gore. Many men had arms and legs missing — horrible wounds. I was told the Federal troops are using some kind of explosives against them. I did not join in this attack as I feel I am too old for such things. Besides, I have a panoramic view of it from here.

As I write, a battery of artillery is being moved across my front toward the west, which seems like the best area to concentrate if Villa is to reduce the city. There is much activity all along the outskirts but difficult to tell exactly what is happening there.

I wish I had a pair of binoculars or a spy-glass.

Villa himself is somewhere down in the thing. I haven't seen him since dawn but he must be all right since an orderly rode up a while ago and rummaged in his tent for some cigars to take to him. A young reporter for the New York World named Reed is down there too. He's nice enough but just another dunderhead who believes all this is being done in the name of <u>humanity.</u>

Bierce stopped writing for a moment and put down his tablet. An entourage came riding up the slope toward him and he recognized the bull-like figure of Villa in the lead. Behind him were several officers plus the moving-picture crew. As they reached the field headquarters, Bierce stood up to greet them.

"Well, General, how is it going?" Bierce asked. Villa's khaki shirt was drenched in sweat and his face was grimy. He seemed weary, too.

"Tough fight, Señor Robinson," the general said. "I figured they'd run away, but so far they haven't." He went to a large *olla* filled with water and dipped out a ladelful. "Pepe," he said to one of the cooks, "fix me some lemonade."

"I thought I saw some of your people have gotten inside the town," Bierce said. "Any success?"

"A little. Those stinking Federales are throwing dynamite sticks at them." Villa took off his hat and plopped down in a folding camp chair. The film crew began setting up the camera to shoot more footage.

"When do you think the outcome will be known?" Bierce asked.

"Can't be too long," the general replied. "My army has to eat sometime and rest, too. I think if it ain't settled by tomorrow morning we better go off to fight again another day. It's been a long war."

"There's much truth in that," Bierce responded. "It's a wonder you keep on doing it." Bierce scratched himself, shifted his footing; he felt stiff and tired and old, suddenly wanting of a drink of whiskey.

"Oh, I know exactly why we keep on doing it," Villa said, squinting at Bierce quite deliberately. It gave the old columnist an uncomfortable feeling. "Our government treats my people like donkeys."

Bierce nodded, and the two men were locked in a somber gaze that might have been even more unsettling if Bierce had really known what Villa was thinking. In fact Villa was experiencing the onset of one of his famous rages. Some old gringo coming here and even hinting that they ought to give it up. He felt the rage well up, but took a breath and choked it back down. He liked the old man in spite of himself; otherwise he'd have killed him on the spot. He'd killed people for far less.

Villa remained civil; he went on: "I was born in this country, Señor Robinson. Far as I know, my people have lived here forever. But do you know who claims to own this state, a single state in Mexico, which is three times as big as Spain? Your Mr. Harrimans and Mr. Guggenheims, and Mr. Hearsts and Mr. Whitneys and Mr. Shaughnessys, and a lot of other rich gringos, as well as the stinking Spanish, that's who. Tell me, what right do they have to own Mexico? Just because the crooks in Mexico City sold it to them for a handful of pesos? What right do any foreigners have being here? Even those *gachupín*?" He felt the fury again but restrained it.

"I'll tell you how bad it is," Villa continued. "Last year a delegation of Japanese came to see me, all the way up at Juárez, because I had the biggest army in Mexico at that time. Know what they wanted? They wanted me to sell *them* the Baja. Can you imagine it? Bunch of beady-eyed Japanese in top hats and striped pants. Offered ten million, in gold!"

"The Japanese want to buy the Baja Peninsula?" Bierce said. "Whatever for?"

"To keep a fleet there, I suppose," Villa replied. "Set up a coaling station and resupply, or so they said. Does everybody in the world think this country is for sale?"

"Seems that way," Bierce said cautiously.

"Can you imagine what you could do with this country after the revolution is won?" Villa had it already pictured: irrigation ditches for hundreds of miles — endless hectares of crops, mounds of fertilizer, corn, peppers, melons, tomatoes, instead of dust and scrub.

"Why, we might even raise bananas," Villa suggested.

"Little dry for that, no?" Bierce noted, becoming more at ease.

Villa shrugged. He had it all laid out. "Our own prosperity, that's what we're fighting for, Señor Jack Robinson, and you Americanos would do well to understand it."

"General, that's nicely put," Bierce said. He meant it, too. After all, his own country had fought a revolution a hundred and forty years earlier for more or less the same reasons, and crushed a rebellion eighty years after that. But this war was so much more confused than that, with all the factions. Villa's people may have known what they were fighting for, but did they know who they were fighting? Friends became enemies, and enemies became friends, with such startling regularity that it was hard to keep straight.

"What if you lose this fight here, General?" Bierce asked. "Last year your army had over fifty thousand troops. Now you're down to ten thousand. What's next?"

"Do you know what the newspapers used to call me, Señor Robinson?" Villa said, ignoring the question and fixing him with a dark-eyed stare. He suddenly liked this old man for his courage.

"The Centaur. The Centaur of the North," Villa said magisterially. "Well, maybe I won't be a centaur anymore, huh? Maybe I'll just be a horsefly. But I tell you this, señor, I'll be the most annoying horsefly ever."

THIRTY

They had been on the move for nearly eighteen hours, but the last of the gigantic herd was probably just leaving Valle del Sol property, twenty miles back. Still, Shaughnessy was relieved because they were now beyond and to the west of Chihuahua City and were so far unmolested by Pancho Villa.

"Look at that!" the Colonel exclaimed. He was seated on a camp stool beside Arthur, next to the chuckwagon, where Ah Dong was boiling coffee and frying bacon and hotcakes in big pans over an open fire. While other crews of cowboys continued north with the herd, some had stopped to eat breakfast. In the east, the aurora of a new day's sun glowed golden behind the mountains, while all around were the grunts and lowings of tens of thousands of cattle. The Colonel had just remarked on a lone rider who was slowly approaching their front.

Even in the dim light, the Colonel made out that he was probably not a Mexican. He didn't dress like one, anyway. He was wearing a brown duster and a gray western hat creased in the middle.

"Wonder what he wants out here this time of day," the Colonel said suspiciously.

Arthur gave no reply. He still seethed from Xenia's revelations, yet despite the horrible story she'd told, he felt at least a slight relief that the disquietude she'd shown over the past couple of months was due to that, and not from any deeper problem she had with their marriage.

The horseman finally reached the camp of the Colonel's band of drovers. "Mornin'," he said.

"Mornin'," the Colonel responded. "Are you just out for an early ride?"

"You might put it that way. I been over to Chihuahua City, where it got a little hot, so I decided to move on."

"The fighting, you mean?" asked the Colonel, taking note that the man was dressed like a cowboy. He was about forty years old and rawboned, with a shock of blond hair, deep brown eyes, and a nose like a squash. Beneath the duster he had on a red flannel shirt with flaps that buttoned across his chest.

"Like I said, it got a little hot."

"Who's winning?"

"Couldn't tell. Villa got there two days ago and that's when I skedaddled — before the shooting started. You fixing to take them cows

up north?" he said, eyeing the seemingly endless stream of cattle.

"And who might you be, stranger?" the
Colonel asked, still wary of a lone rider way
out on the range.

"Name most people call me is Cowboy
Bob."

"Where you from?"

"Amarillo, originally. I hang around El Paso
now."

"Are you down here on vacation or something?" queried the Colonel.

Cowboy Bob eyed the breakfast hungrily.
"No, sir. You see, I'm kind of a guide. I
brought a man from El Paso that said he
wanted to meet Pancho Villa."

"You know Villa?" said the Colonel.

"Yep. Knowed him for years."

"You see a young woman with him? He
kidnapped the wife of one of my ranch
hands."

"Nope," said Cowboy Bob. "But I was only
there one night. I just delivered this old guy
to him and cut out. With Villa, it ain't smart
to hang around long. Somethin' unfortunate
might happen."

"This person you 'delivered' to Villa,"
Shaughnessy asked, "what of him?"

"Said his name was Jack Robinson, is all I
know," said Cowboy Bob. Talked about havin'
been in the Civil War. Prob'ly was, too. He
must've been seventy years old. Had a kind

329

of nasty wit about him, like he's mad at everything."

"You're a guide, you say? You know your way around this territory, do you?" asked the Colonel.

"Not nearly like I do Texas. I runned a lot a herds in Texas."

Arthur wondered about this cowboy. He was smooth enough that he might actually be working for Villa; after all, what would be more cagey than to send out a gringo scout? He kept his thoughts to himself, however.

"Tell you what," said the Colonel. "Why don't you get down and have some coffee and breakfast? If you're headed back to Texas, you can sign on with me, 'cause that's where I'm taking these cows."

"Thank you kindly," Cowboy Bob said, dismounting. "If you're going to Texas, you are headed in the right direction. That's a damn good-size herd, from what I can see here. How many head?"

"Don't know exactly," replied the Colonel, "but I expect it goes back fifteen, twenty miles or more."

"Huh?" said Cowboy Bob, "fifteen miles, that's —"

"Like I said," interrupted the Colonel, "we're taking these cows to El Paso, Texas."

They had been on the trail for seven days and Cowboy Bob had proven himself valu-

able to the expedition, scouting and recon-
noitering. The Colonel and Arthur found him
good company, as well. They had plotted a
route along the Santa Clara River as far as it
went, so as to water the cattle. To ensure
speed, the Colonel had decreed there was to
be no rounding up of single strays, but he
knew the pace of the drive would leave the
cows thirsty. By midmorning they ran out of
river and reached the outskirts of the Great
Chihuahuan Desert.

Along the river route, they had passed by
any number of villages. Arthur marveled that
despite their distressing poverty, practically
every one seemed to be holding or had
recently held some sort of fiesta.

"Any excuse to keep from work," the Colonel said when Arthur commented on this.

"I've never seen people so poor," Arthur
said. "It's enough to turn you into a socialist."

"Don't say that even in jest," reprimanded
the Colonel.

Arthur tried to let the matter drop. He
didn't want to get his father started on Roosevelt again, "the traitor to his class."

The Colonel, long ago, had decided that
the world had begun to unravel when Carne-
gie started giving away all his money. Now
just look at things: dynamite bombs set off
everywhere by labor unions; some Americans
actually voting for Marxists; anarchists killing

off the kings of Europe; then an unimaginable war in Europe, and even the Congress supporting an income tax.

"Your grandchildren will probably wind up in the poorhouse," the Colonel predicted, but Arthur didn't rise to the bait.

The sun had risen high, and his father wiped a bit of sweat from his brow. Arthur knew the Colonel had the perfect motto, if the Shaugnesseys had a family crest — which, being descended from bog Irish, of course they did not: *Fidas Non Virum.* Trust No Man.

Several days later they began entering the bleak scrub country: creosote bush, mesquite, crucifixion thorn, and all variety of cacti. In the distance to both east and west were the two chains of sierras, which were too far away to see even in the clear desert air.

On the edge of this vast wasteland, Cowboy Bob suggested that they reshape the drive into one huge and continuous line about ten miles across and two miles deep. This, he argued, would get them across the desert faster, which was important because, with the scantiness of water, thirst would become a problem. The Colonel liked the idea and began giving orders to his drovers.

As night fell on the fifteenth day, there came a sinister grumbling of thunder from the west. The sky turned gray and blotted out the stars. It was a surprise to everyone, as rain was rare on this high plateau, nearly a mile elevated.

Arthur was seated on a log somebody had drawn up to the fire, with a cup of Ah Dong's mutton stew in his lap. The Colonel had spied a Mexican desert sheep and dispatched it with his custom-made 30.06 rifle. Some of the cowboys were telling stories of the desert — of venomous reptiles; horses, cattle, and men going mad with thirst — but Arthur's thoughts were far away.

He'd said his good-byes to his mother, Xenia, and the children at the hacienda while Bomba was loading their luggage into one of the big Packard convertibles. It hadn't been a scary or awkward parting, but there was a sense of danger, of uneasiness in the air, at least for Arthur. The women and children trusted him, trusted the Colonel, that they were all doing the right thing, but shadowy premonitions had gnawed at Arthur ever since they'd left Valle del Sol.

He missed his beautiful blond Katherine, with her bright smile and sparkling blue eyes and merry laugh, and Timmy, who was growing into a perfect gentleman, kind, respected, and smart, even though the Colonel thought he was pampered and didn't hesitate to say so.

The appalling insult by Mick Martin came back to him all too often; whenever it did, Arthur shivered. He knew he was no match for Mick physically, but there were equalizers such as guns — or lead pipes, if it came to that. Xenia had been right about one thing: it would do no good to press charges. Courts required corroborating evidence in rape, and in this case there was none except, of course, the baby — but who could prove it, and the scandal would leave no one unstained. So the hate in Arthur simmered, pushing out other thoughts, and he sat on his log eating his stew meanly and trying to keep his emotions under control.

As a nightcap, right before he was about to turn in, Arthur had just polished off a tin cup of his father's brandy when the skies above suddenly began to light up with blinding flashes of lightning. The acute smell of ozone and a chill rose simultaneously in the desert air, and huge claps of rolling thunder exploded all around them. Some of the cowboys muttered apprehensively to each other that there was no place here to hide. Some went to their saddles for rain gear; others looked to their horses. There were restless sounds from the herd.

The first raindrops were tiny, stinging, then hail began to fall. By the light of the campfire Arthur saw hailstones the size of a golf balls bounce on the sandy ground. Then one the size of an orange landed directly in the fire, which exploded and hissed and sparked. Colonel Shaughnessy had turned in early in the back of his personal wagon, where they had set up a sort of bedroom cabin for him. He emerged from this only to be conked on the head by a baseball-sized hailstone that left a deep gash in his scalp.

Arthur dived under the chuckwagon along with a dozen other drovers; the rest were left to fend for themselves. Men knelt like ostriches, covering their heads, trying to expose as little of their bodies as possible.

One attempted to hide under his horse but was trampled when a hailstone hit the animal. Arthur saw some hailstones roll into view that were the size of actual grapefruits. Out in the darkness, the cattle were being struck, too, and frenzied shrieks and bellows rose up from the herd.

Then, quick as the storm fell, it ended. Only a light drizzle lingered, and bewildered men began to come out from what few hiding places they had found, or simply rose up from the ground where they had lain, pelted, covering their heads with their hands or saddles. People attended to the prostrate bodies of two cowboys in the dim recesses of the campfire light. Arthur was wondering about the cattle when the Colonel appeared, blood running down his face from the cut.

"Good God," he said. "What about the herd?" The ground as far as they could see was covered with thousands of hailstones; walking became nearly impossible — the hailstones had to be kicked out of the way. The canvas of the chuckwagon hung in tatters; the fire pit smoked and hissed with melting ice.

Cowboy Bob peered out from under one of the wagons, wild-eyed and wary-looking.

"Colonel, I didn't hear no stampede, but there was so much noise, who knows? We'll get a look soon as it lightens up a bit."

Ah Dong, who had protected himself in the chuckwagon beneath wooden boxes of onions and peppers, examined the Colonel's wound.

"You need salve," he said, and struggled back to the wagon, where the medicine chest was kept.

"I thought it wasn't supposed to rain in the desert this time of year," Arthur muttered.

"Me, too," the Colonel replied shakily.

From what they could tell, scores of cattle had been killed by the huge hailstones, and many more were stunned; in places where lightning had struck directly, dead cattle were bunched up on the ground. But at least it hadn't been a disaster. The whole thing had come and gone so swiftly that for some miraculous reason the cattle hadn't launched a stampede, and a report from drovers down the line indicated that the storm was relatively small in terms of area. Cowboys were moving the cattle north again when the morning dawned bright and clear.

Arthur rode alongside Cowboy Bob, whom he had come to admire. Bob was all the things Arthur wasn't: tough, terse, and self-assured in the wild and unpredictable outback.

"What's Villa like?" Arthur asked. His behind was raw with saddle sores, his hands chapped from the reins, and his nose peeling from sunburn.

"That ain't a easy question to answer," said Cowboy Bob. "Sometimes he's polite as can be, but you have to understand he's a killer."

Arthur asked about the other the people around Villa, and Bob described such characters as Fierro, Santo, and Tom Mix, the American.

"An American, huh?" Arthur said. "What's he doing there?"

"Well, I knew Mix back when he first came to El Paso. He's got him a trick horse, and for a while he did stunts at rodeos and little western shows around town. Used to throw a dime up in the air and shoot a hole in it with his pistol. Stuff like that. Told everybody one day he was going to Hollywood."

"That's a pretty good trick," Arthur offered.

"Yeah, except for one thing," Cowboy Bob continued. "He don't use bullets like everybody thinks. He loads his shells with rat-shot, so's if you aim anywhere within half a foot of the dime you're likely to hit it."

Arthur shook his head. "That's still pretty

good shooting, I'd say."

"Yup," said Cowboy Bob. He reached in his pocket, pulled out some change, and reined up his horse. "Here," he said, handing Arthur a dime. "Throw that up. Don't flip it, just toss it."

Arthur looked at the dime, then back to Cowboy Bob. "Where?"

"In the air. Anyplace."

"When?" He noticed Bob hadn't yet drawn his gun.

"You call it."

"Okay," Arthur said. "Now!" He tossed the dime straight up, underhanded.

Before his hand had even dropped, Cowboy Bob snatched his pistol from the holster and fired. Arthur, ears ringing, looked for the dime.

"What's left of it's over there, between them rocks," Bob said.

Arthur rode over and dismounted. "Little bit to your right," Bob told him. Sure enough, in the sand was a shiny piece of metal. Arthur picked it up. It was half a dime, hot in his hand.

"Tom Mix uses a .22 for his stunt, even if he does load rat-shot," said Bob, "but with this here .42 you got to hit the dime right on the edge. Otherwise, won't be nothin' left of it."

Arthur shook his head in amazement and brought the piece of dime back to Bob.

"Don't know what good half a dime'll do me," Bob said dryly. "Maybe they'll take it for half a cup of coffee back in El Paso."

"You could take that trick to New York City and make a lot of money," Arthur told him, still astonished. "Join up with Buffalo Bill's Wild West Show or something."

"Then I'd have to use rat-shot," Bob remarked. "And that makes it fake."

"Why? You just did it here with real ammunition."

" 'Cause with real ammunition I'd put holes in Buffalo Bill's circus tent. Rat-shot don't carry that far, but this here bullet does. After a while his tent'd look like a side of Swiss cheese."

"Even with rat-shot, it's a remarkable trick," Arthur said. "I know some people in the theater business who are friends with Buffalo Bill Cody. If you want, I could put you in touch."

"Nah," said Cowboy Bob. "Anyhow, you use it enough, rat-shot'll ruin the insides of your gun barrel."

THIRTY-ONE

The morning after Colonel Shaughnessy began the grand cattle drive to El Paso, General Fierro arrived at Valle del Sol to rustle his cows. He had taken only Tom Mix and a company of men with him. Not wanting any trouble with the Colonel's cowhands, the Butcher hurriedly swung wide around the property to do his stealing on the remote ranges miles from the hacienda. At first, Fierro was mystified when all he found were a few old cows and calves and a handful of mangy steers, and the farther they rode onto the Colonel's spread, the more perplexed Fierro became, until finally his confusion turned to rage.

"Mierda!" he spat. "The stinking gringo has moved his animals!"

"Seems so," said Mix. "Maybe he's moved them to another part of the ranch."

"Well, we haven't got all day," Fierro said. "We'd better send out some scouting parties. You can't hide that many beefs." Mix detailed four groups of five each to fan out in all directions and return by sundown. The rest of the company would wait by the river. Fierro's mood was becoming fouler by the moment. He was disgusted by being sent on what he considered subordinate duty, though he knew Villa had always been particular about assigning food as one of the army's highest priorities. But Fierro loved nothing better than battle, and the suspense over whatever was happening up at Chihuahua was eating at him. He hadn't shared Villa's notion that the Federales would run away. They outnumbered Villa's men two- or three-to-one, and if in the old days he wouldn't have considered these bad odds, these weren't the old days. In any case, he sat by the river drinking coffee and tequila, and all the while he stewed.

Just a few miles away, at the Gonzales home, Katherine Shaughnessy climbed aboard a beautiful black gelding that wore a saddle festooned in silver and turquoise. This was Señor Gonzales's favorite mount and for the occasion of the owner's daughter's visit he had strapped on the horse his prize possession, the exquisite hand-tooled saddle that was used only for fiesta parades and other distinguished events in Parral, Torreón, and Chihuahua City. Señor Gonzales had to let out the stirrups all the way, but even though she was only twelve years old she almost needed more for her long legs.

The Gonzaleses' hacienda was located at the head of a small valley on the edge of Shaughnessy's land, and Xenia, Beatie, Katherine, and Timmy had been accorded the royal treatment — at least so far as the Gonzaleses could bestow it; for the Shaughnessy family, however, it was an adventure more akin to roughing it. They had stayed up late that first night; the children playing Rook by lamplight. Xenia was reading *Of Human Bondage,* while Beatie crocheted a doily and the voice of Caruso rang out from a crank-up music box. Bomba sat in a chair by the fire, whittling toothpicks from a stick.

Next morning, Katherine was excited. She'd asked Timmy if he wanted to go riding but he'd declined, deciding instead to work on a jigsaw puzzle. Four ranch hands were detailed to ride with her for safety. The day was crisp and as they set out, the grass was dewy and the air filled with the smell of mown hay. They rode down the little valley and up a trail across rolling hills that led to the river. Katherine was trying to get used to the fancy Mexican saddle and was even beginning to like it. It was a distinctive ride in a gaudy sort of way, and she thought it even had a certain elegance to it. Katherine had only ridden English-style before and it took a while to get accustomed to the rocking motion, but she could see why such a saddle could be useful out on the plains.

She thought perhaps when they got back to Boston she might acquire one of these Mexican saddles. What a trump it would be on her riding companions! She might come back to Boston as "Cowgirl Kate," another Annie Oakley. This reverie of acquisitive dreams was quickly interrupted when Katherine saw the lead rider abruptly halt and raise his hand.

They had emerged from the hill trail onto a large open swale where, not a hundred yards away, another group of riders clad in what looked like military uniforms with rifles slung over their shoulders were bearing down straight at them. Katherine saw them at the same time as her guards. The distant men had paused on a knoll, looking, looking — and then they quickly wheeled and headed toward Katherine's party.

The head of Katherine's guard had already begun backing his horse into the line of trees but it was too late. A shot rang out from the military men and one of Katherine's guards dropped wordlessly from his horse. More shots were fired, and by the time Katherine had reached the forest the soldiers had fallen upon them. Her group scattered. She bolted up a hill, but one of the soldiers flew past and grabbed the bridle of her horse. Katherine found herself looking into a wild-eyed but smiling face of a young Mexican — perhaps no older than she — who waved his hand in front of her face.

"Basta!" he said.

Among the trees more shots were ringing out but she could see no one else. The Mexican lifted the reins of her horse over its head and began to tow her back down the trail, back across the swale, and then onto a level pasture that led to a river. Katherine was so scared she kept her eyes closed until they slowed and she heard voices. There was some sort of camp by the river. Smoke from a fire hung lazily in the air and scores of men sat or milled around, their horses tethered to cottonwood trees along the banks.

"So, little señorita," General Fierro said. "Suppose you tell me who you are?"

Katherine gaped at him while her mind raced but got nowhere. These were obviously the people who had attacked Valle del Sol, who hated her grandfather, who had come to steal their cattle. But what was she to do? Tell them — what? Fierro suddenly took hold of her wrist and squeezed it hard, smiling. It hurt. She cried out, "Let go of me!" The general did so but laughed cruelly.

"We want to take you back home," Fierro said with an ugly smile. "You must show us where."

"I can find my own way," Katherine told him.

"Oh, no, señorita, we can't let you do that. There are dangerous men out here. I want to see no harm comes to you."

"I want you to let me go," Katherine said shakily. "My grandfather owns this property. You've got no right to be on it." She knew her lip was quivering but also felt anger and hatred pushing through the fear.

Fierro broke into a big cruel grin. "Ohhh . . ." he intoned. "So you're one of the big-shot Americano's family, eh? Well, how about that?" Instantly Katherine regretted making her statement. She tried to control her trembling by closing her eyes for an instant. When she opened them, Fierro was still there with his turned-down sneer.

"And where is your grandfather, then?" Fierro said. "We will take you to him, I promise."

"He's away," she said.

"And his cattle, where are they?"

"I don't know."

Just then several riders stormed into the camp. With them they had two of the ranch hands who had been with Katherine. The ranch hands were seated glumly on their horses, hands tied behind their backs.

"These vaqueros were with the little girl," said one of the Villistas. "They come from a place in a little valley over those ridges there. We killed the other two. But there's a hacienda there. And there's a bunch of horses in the corral, but we saw a lot of men so we didn't go down there. There's a big fancy automobile there, too, General," he said.

"Ah," Fierro said sweetly, turning to Lieutenant Crucia. "So shall we all go visit the hacienda? Maybe they will give us some beans and bread, eh?"

He summoned Tom Mix. "Take this girl and make sure nothing happens to her, huh?" he told him. Mix looked at Katherine. She was gazing out across the river, as though willing herself away from the scene. He took her by the hand, but she jerked it away. Suddenly the young boy from the woods, the one who had captured her, appeared by her side from the group who stood around the fire.

"He's all right," the boy told her, almost in a whisper. "He's a good man. You go along with him, huh?"

Katherine turned to him, dumbfounded. She felt tears beginning to come but fought them back.

"I go along, too, okay? You'll be all right. Nobody hurts girls," he said. "We're not animals."

Katherine was too stunned to do anything but obey. She was helpless and knew it. If she ran afoot they would catch her; if she tried to jump on a horse and run she wouldn't stand a chance, either. Nobody had prepared her for this kind of situation. She could only do what she was told. All her life people had taken care of her; she could only pray they would now, too. Her mother always told her the same thing her own mother had told *her:* "Darling, in life, always ask yourself, where is this leading me?" Now she didn't have a choice.

THIRTY-TWO

Bomba saw the soldiers first. He had been hand-pumping water from a well to wash dust off the big Packard convertible when he noticed riders coming down the road to the hacienda. Bomba rushed inside and gathered the family, herding them toward the car. He immediately thought of Katherine, but there was nothing to do about her for the moment.

He quickly saw the problem: the only way out of the valley by car would take them directly into the path of the riders. The ranch hands were alerted now; rifles and pistols were drawn and ready, and the men took up various positions around the house and outbuildings. Bomba pulled the Packard into the barn, ushered the family into it, started the motor, and left it running. He went outside, quietly closing the big barn doors but not locking them. As the riders drew nearer, his fear was confirmed. They wore military uniforms.

There were only a dozen in Fierro's party,

about the same number as the ranch hands — at least that was in their favor. As the soldiers neared the house, Señor Gonzales walked out to meet them. He was visibly trembling, but tried to keep a smile on his face. Keen in his recollection was what he had heard that Villa had done to ranch manager Callahan.

"You people expecting thieves?" Fierro said to Gonzales, as he drew up in front of the man. He nodded toward the armed ranch hands ensconced behind hay bales and barn doors.

"No, señor," said Gonzales. "Well . . . yes, maybe." He took off his hat and held it in front of him. "We had some rustlers around lately. Can't be careful enough, you know?"

"You missing a girl off this place?" Fierro said. His teeth shone brightly behind his drooping mustache. Fierro had a way of squinting the eye with the drooping lid so that the other seemed huge and fierce.

"A girl?" Gonzales stammered.

"You see, we found a girl riding alone by the river. Does she belong here?"

"Why, yes, señor, she was out riding with some of my men. You say you found her?"

"Something like that," said Fierro. "But she says she's in the family of the big gringo that owns this *rancho*. She's pretty far from home, eh?"

"Well," Gonzales stumbled, "maybe so . . .

I guess, you see, she came out for a little ride. I let her use my saddle . . ."

"Yes, we found your saddle. It's a nice one. A real beauty."

"And she, well, she was with my men."

"We have found your men also," Fierro said, openly delighted to watch Gonzales squirm. "Two of your men objected to seeing us, however, and had to be punished. The other two are in our hands for safekeeping."

Bomba was peering out from the side of the barn but was too far away to tell what was going on. He considered getting the family out of the car and hustling them into the woods, but then they'd be afoot and helpless.

"You say you got the girl?" said Gonzales. "Did you bring her back to us? We were worried . . ."

"Yes, we got her," Fierro said. "She is perfectly safe. Say, my men tell me somebody's here with a fancy car. Who is that?"

"A car?" Gonzales choked. "What kind of car?"

"You own a car, señor?"

"No, señor."

" 'General,' " Fierro said.

"Yes, sure . . . General. No, I don't own a car."

"Then where is it — and whose is it?"

"It . . . belongs to the estancia," Gonzales said.

"So where is the car?"

"It's — I been in the house. Maybe they left."

"Who left?"

"Who?"

Fierro was bored now by toying with Gonzales. "Look, you dumb *cabrón,* I got no time for this. Tell those men of yours to put down their weapons and come out here."

"Put down . . . ?" Gonzales said. "They — they're really not my men . . . they belong to the estancia, too."

"So what are they doing here?" Fierro said with renewed interest.

"They brought out the girl. For horseback riding."

"Well, you go back and tell them to put down their guns and come out, okay?"

"I don't know if they listen to me, señor . . . ah, General . . . They are estancia men."

Fierro was through playing. He nodded, then waved an arm in the air, motioning. "Look there," he said, pointing to the low hills that formed the valley. Mix's soldiers slowly began to emerge from the trees and into the open so as to converge on the hacienda. Gonzales's heart sank. They were surrounded. The ranch hands saw this, too, and so did Bomba.

"Now," Fierro said, "you go back and tell them what I told you to."

"Yes, General," said Gonzales. He plodded back toward the house, hat still in hand.

Bomba felt panicky. He hoped Katherine would not return just now, and that she was safe out there across the hills. He also understood that there was no hiding in the woods anymore, and that the only options were either to wait for whatever was about to happen or to make a break for it. If he could get the car past the bunch blocking the road they'd never catch them. But what if they opened fire? He didn't know what had gone on between the soldiers and Gonzales, but it was a dangerous situation. Bomba made his decision. He raced to the car and motioned everybody to get down low in back.

"What's happening?" Beatie cried.

"Bomba . . ." Timmy said.

"No!" Xenia exclaimed. "Katherine! Where's Katherine?"

Bomba put the car in forward gear and gunned the engine; the big Packard shot out from the barn in a spray of dirt, scattering chickens, dogs, pigs, and ranch hands in every direction. Bomba roared through the gate, pedal to the floor and the Packard's horns blaring, heading straight for the startled Mexicans on their horses. He was only twenty or so yards distant and they scarcely had time to get out of the way. Their horses began to rear and plunge. Fierro and the Mexicans bolted off the road in a hail of profanity as Bomba and his precious cargo roared past them, the car swerving in the dirt from overgearing and acceleration.

Bomba didn't look back. As he sped past blurred fence posts he looked ahead and saw only the open plain and safety. That was when the rifle shot hit him. It tore through his right shoulder and violently wrenched his right arm. The automobile lurched out of control. He slammed on brakes but they were going too fast, spun sideways, and crashed into a ditch. Bomba's head struck the steering wheel and he blacked out from the impact.

When he regained his senses he heard shouts and horses' hooves rushing toward them. He tried to reach for the big pistol strapped around his waist, but the arm lay helplessly limp, like a broken wing on a bird; the bullet hadn't hit a bone — he knew that — but had paralyzed a muscle that probably saved his life. Bomba turned to the backseat and saw a pile of bodies with blood everywhere. The pursuing party had arrived, and one of them reached down from his horse, opened the car door, and jerked Bomba out by the collar. He fell on the ground. Fierro rode up and looked into the automobile.

"Seems like these here are not so good," Fierro said. Then he looked at Bomba, lying dazed in the dirt.

"Who is this big Negro? He sure don't belong around here."

By now others in his party had opened the rear doors and dragged Beatie and Xenia out onto some grass by the side of the road. Both were unconscious and bleeding profusely from their scalps. They had been smashed against the folding walnut dining trays built into the Packard's seat backs. Down on the floor, Timmy was still conscious but in shock. When someone hauled him out by the scruff of the neck he saw his mother and grandmother and began to scream. One soldier dismounted and dragged him away from the scene. Just then Mix rode up. He'd watched the whole thing while leading his company down the hill and was appalled by the sight of the women lying on the ground.

"They dead?" he asked unsteadily.

"Don't look to be," Fierro said. "I think they're just bunged up."

"The boy," Mix said. "One of them's his mother and the other's his grandmother — she's the wife of the owner of this spread. At least I think that's who they are."

"How do you know that?"

"The girl told us. I got to talking to her while we were waiting. Says her grandfather'll pay you a lot to leave them alone."

"Yeah," Fierro said, "I bet he will, and we're gonna find that out soon enough. Get some people to take these women back to the hacienda, and then put the boy on somebody's horse. He's coming with us, too."

"Is he hurt?" Mix asked.

"Nah, just scared. I'd take these women,

too, but they're hurt and they'll slow us down. I figure if we got the two kids there's gonna be a nice payday down the road. These stinking gringos have more money than the priests — then they come down here and buy up everything and turn our people into paupers. Well, it's time they pay up."

"Well . . . children, General . . ." Mix said. "I don't know . . ."

"It ain't for you to know, Capitán Mix. It's for you to do what General Villa wants. And for that matter, me, too," Butcher Fierro informed him.

"What about this one here?" said a soldier, indicating Bomba, who was now sitting up, holding his shoulder to stem the flow of blood running down his sleeve out onto the dirt road. The voice belonged to Lieutenant Crucia — in fact, Crucia seemed to be peering intently at Bomba's prominent flat nose. "You want us to put him out of his misery?"

"Nah," said the general. "He's just some dumb gringo's nigger. He's shot bad. He won't do us any harm."

■ ■ ■ ■

PART THREE:
THE SIERRAS

■ ■ ■ ■

THIRTY-THREE

Fierro's scouting parties returned with the annoying information that there were few cattle left on Valle del Sol. This vexed the general but he decided to round up what strays and castoffs he could lay hands on and return as quickly as possible to Villa at Chihuahua City. The most direct route would carry them past Colonel Shaughnessy's big hacienda — which Fierro decided would be easy pickings, since he now understood that most of the ranch hands were away on the cattle drive.

Tom Mix had swung the sobbing Timmy up on his own horse and tried to comfort him a little.

"They aren't dead, your mommy and grandma," Mix told the boy. "They probably aren't even hurt bad. You'll see. They'll be fine."

"Where are we going?" Timmy croaked.

"We're taking you to a safer place," Mix lied. "Where your sister is."

"Where is she? She went riding."

"I know," said Mix. "We're all going to meet a very great general of the Mexican army. His name is Pancho Villa. I'm sure you've heard of him."

"Grandpapa says he's a bandit and a murderer."

"No," Mix corrected him, "General Villa is a great man." But Tom Mix was beginning to wonder about this, too. He did not like kidnapping children. And he had seen brutality that disgusted him. In Mix's view, cowboys were supposed to be good fellows. But a Mexican army wasn't for good fellows, it was more for heartless brutes. He felt a pang when he thought of these two children. Mix could remember when he had been Timmy's age and had wandered into the far end of town where a bunch of bully-boys held sway. He could imagine how frightened and alone Timmy must feel.

"He killed Mr. Callahan, who was going to show me how to carve things."

"Who?" Mix asked.

"Mr. Callahan ran Grandpapa's ranch at Valle del Sol."

"Oh," said Mix. "Yeah, I heard about that. I don't think General Villa killed him, though. I think it was a mistake, maybe."

He was a little annoyed at himself. He didn't like lying to children any more than kidnapping them. Mix decided to keep

Timmy back in the line of march, for the time being away from Katherine, who had been sent ahead with one of her captors. He figured if the kids got together right now it might cause difficulty — especially when she found out what had happened to her mother and grandmother. From what he'd seen of the girl, she had spark, and she was already plenty unhappy with her circumstances. It must be bad enough for a boy to be captured by all these rough grown men, let alone a girl.

They came up over a big rolling hill and the full beauty of Valle del Sol spread out before them — huge fenced pastures, orchards, and vegetable fields, the vast hacienda itself. All that was missing were the cattle.

Fierro rode far ahead. After leaving a couple of men to watch over Katherine, he and most of his band entered the hacienda proper, startling and terrorizing the few workers who remained there. Fierro was both surprised and delighted to find a nice herd of cows in a large fenced pasture. With these and the strays his men had managed to collect, he might not disappoint the chief after all. He told Lieutenant Crucia to round them up.

"What are you doing?" asked the new ranch manager, Rod Rodriguez, as Fierro's men began opening the gate to the big pasture.

"Taking these beefs," said Crucia.

"Beefs!" cried Rodriguez disgustedly.

"Those aren't beefs in there, those are fighting bulls. This is the fighting bull pasture." He moved in front of the gate.

"Hell you say," replied the lieutenant. "I know a beef from a bull. Get out of the way."

"What you're seeing there is steers," said Rodriguez. "They control the bulls. The bulls are docile around the steers. But you get close to one of those bulls, and soon enough you'll find out something you don't want to know." He stalked off and climbed up on the fence a little distance away. He'd gotten a whiff of Crucia's nose necklace. He'd seen such things before and didn't want anything to do with this creature.

Crucia hesitated for a moment, peering out at the mass of animals. Indeed, he could then see some of them had the large humps and long horns of fighting bulls.

Just then Fierro rode up.

"What are you waiting for?" Fierro said. "Go get those beefs."

"There's fighting bulls out there, General," said Lieutenant Crucia.

"Where?"

"There, see them?"

Fierro stared out at the cattle. The man was right; Fierro, too, saw a few big humps and horns.

"Well, there's a lot of steers out there, too. Mostly steers, far as I can see. Go and get them."

"What about the bulls?" Crucia asked nervously.

"Well, you're a cavalryman," the general snapped. "You can ride, can't you? Take your chances." He wheeled and trotted away toward the main house.

Crucia nervously leaned down and unlatched the gate. He rode through it, followed tentatively by a dozen or so of his men. "You better get your rifles ready," he said, "in case some of those bulls get the idea you are matadors." The men began unlimbering their weapons.

"Please," pleaded Rodriguez, "don't shoot the bulls. Those bulls are the best in Chihuahua."

"I don't give a rat's ass if they're the best in the world," replied the lieutenant. "I got my orders, and I'm not going to get killed by some stinking bull."

Meantime, Fierro had arrived at the main house with more of his men. The first person he saw who looked halfway official was Señora Pardenas.

"Where do they keep the money?" Fierro asked.

"Who am I to know?" she replied.

"If you value your life, you'll take me to somebody who does," Fierro stated. He was in no mood for word-fencing.

"They all gone away," said the señora.

Just then Rodriguez turned up with unfortunate timing. He'd come to see if the phone was working. Rodriguez figured since the Colonel had been driving the herd around the clock for two days, he'd probably be about sixty or seventy miles north by now. He was wondering if he ought not send somebody to the telegraph station at Parral, which might get a message through to the Colonel that Villa's men had returned to Valle del Sol. After all, a herd that size wasn't hard to spot. In any case, it was worth a try, or so Rodriguez thought, until he stumbled upon the scene between Fierro and Señora Pardenas.

"What's your authority around here?" Fierro demanded.

With the fate of his predecessor freshly in mind, Rodriguez responded, "I just work here."

But Fierro had already noticed the notebooks sticking out of Rodriguez's shirt pockets and he observed that he was of Spanish, not Indian, descent, and didn't look or dress like an ordinary ranch hand.

"Where do they keep the money?" Fierro said coldly.

"How would I know that?" Rodriguez told him. It was an ill-starred reply, after Señora Pardenas's earlier demurral.

Without so much as a wince, Butcher Fierro drew his pistol and shot Rodriguez between the eyes. The bullet sent him sprawling in a grisly, bloody heap.

The general then got down from his horse and, brushing the horrified Señora Pardenas aside, strode into the great hall, where so many dances had been held. His men followed, fanning out into adjacent rooms. It wasn't long before one of the soldiers reappeared before Fierro with a pleased expression.

"General," he declared, "I think we found it." He led Fierro through a parlor into some kind of office, where along a wall was a huge safe adorned with elaborate engravings and gold leaf. It certainly looked important. The general tried the handle but of course the thing was locked, causing him to conclude that valuables must be inside.

"Bring me Chavez," Fierro barked. Chavez was one of the general's bootlickers who had made an abbreviated career of bank robbery before joining the revolution — abbreviated because on his second outing he was caught and thrown in jail, where he languished until Pancho Villa's troops liberated the prison and made soldiers out of the inmates.

"Somebody got any dynamite?" Chavez asked after examining the safe.

"I'm sure some of Mix's people got some," replied Fierro. He sent a man to find out. They used a lot of dynamite to blow up bridges and trestles, and many people in

Mix's command had come from the mines, where the use of explosives was common. Shortly the man returned with a canvas sack containing the dynamite. Fierro gave it to Chavez, who peered into the sack.

"Well?" the general said impatiently.

"I only used this once," Chavez said reluctantly. "Actually, the other guy was the one who used it. I just watched."

"Then you better have a good memory," Fierro told him, "because I'm going outside, and when I come back, I want to know what's in this safe. He strode out of the room. Chavez shrugged and began fiddling with the dynamite.

After a while Chavez appeared in the main doorway of Valle del Sol. "General," he said, "I have lit the fuse. It will be only a —"

Suddenly there was a gigantic, earthshaking explosion belching fire and smoke, followed by a rain of plaster, glass, and wood. A heavy wooden door landed in a fountain in the courtyard.

Chavez was shot through the air and landed facedown in a rose garden. General Fierro was knocked flat along with half a dozen of his men. Everybody's horses ran off. All the windows in the hacienda were shattered and the whole front part of the building seemed to sag.

"Are you crazy?" Fierro shouted at Chavez. "I didn't tell you to blow the house up!"

"I guess maybe I used more than necessary," replied Chavez, who had turned over and was sitting upright in the rose garden. "I figured you were in a hurry."

"Well," Fierro said, "let's go find out what happened." He stuck his head inside the house, which was still belching acrid gray smoke. They plowed their way through wrecked furniture and cracked beams and broken plaster until they got to the office, a scene of amazing devastation. Burned papers were strewn everywhere. A huge hole was blown in the rug and down through the floor. Draperies were on fire and the side of the building where the window had been was torn away. Desks and chairs were smashed and smoldering. Everything was ruined but the safe, which stood almost untouched. Fierro inspected it, then turned savagely on Chavez, who was cringing in a corner.

"You stinking imbecile!" he hissed. "Where did you place the dynamite?"

"On the floor, by the safe," Chavez told him.

"Floor!" the general shouted. "Why?"

"It's where the guy that was robbing the bank with me put it," Chavez replied.

"So how come it didn't it work?" Fierro demanded.

"It didn't work then, either," Chavez informed him. "That was when we got arrested."

Fierro lunged as if to strike Chavez, when Mix suddenly stuck his head through the door.

"Everything okay, General?" Mix asked. After hearing the explosion, he'd left Timmy with some of his men to investigate.

"Hell, no!" replied Fierro. "This idiot calls himself a bank robber and can't even blow a safe."

Mix looked at the safe, then went over and inspected it closely. "Well, if you want, I could give it a try," he said.

"You? You are a safecracker, too, I suppose?"

"Long time ago, when I was just a kid. Guy said he was called Black Bart come through town, said for a dollar he'd teach anybody who wanted to know how to pick a lock or open a safe. Couple of us boys scraped up some money and went to his exhibition. I used to do it as a stunt in Wild West shows — getting out of handcuffs and stuff, like that guy Houdini's doing now."

"Well, go ahead, then," Fierro told him. Mix bent down and put his ear to the safe right above the lock. It was still hot from the explosion. He turned the knob this way and that half a dozen times.

"I need a lot of quiet," Mix said. "See, when I turn this dial, at some spot in the rotation it's going to pass one of the tumblers and make a tiny little noise. That's part of the combination. It's a process of elimination and it takes a while. I might be able to get it open."

"Well, we'll leave you alone, then," Fierro said, scowling at Chavez, who was still hovering in his corner. "C'mon, you moron," the general said. "Let's leave this man to his work."

Meanwhile, Lieutenant Crucia's steer roundup was in progress, though not without difficulty. For one thing, the fighting bulls had killed several of the soldiers' horses, and in one case tossed a rider half a dozen feet into the air, then gored him to death on the ground. But finally the men either shot or separated most of the bulls from the steers and were herding the steers out the pasture gate. There was still at least one bull left among them, but no one could get at him or even shoot him without killing steers. He seemed tame enough for the moment, among the steers, and it was decided to move the herd with the fighting bull as part of it.

"General, I have opened your safe," Mix proudly announced from the hacienda doorway. They all marched inside and Fierro began rooting through the contents. Something in the very bottom caught his eye. In a bin were eight or ten oilcloth sacks. He picked one up and became excited. Its very weight told him something. The bag was tied with a leather string and Fierro opened it and looked inside.

"Eiyeeeee, caramba!" he cried. Each sack contained bars of solid gold stamped with the emblem of the mint in Mexico City. "There must be — who can tell? Three, four hundred pounds, maybe more!" Fierro ordered several men to remove the bags and he personally supervised loading it onto their horses. He also emptied into his own saddlebags several dozen of the gold bars. Certainly enough to keep a man wealthy for a while. He wondered why Villa hadn't thought to pillage the place on their last visit, but in any case he, Fierro, had done a thorough job of it this time, bringing to the army not only the beefs and two valuable hostages, but a hoard of solid gold. So far as the general was concerned, it had become a very good day.

THIRTY-FOUR

Señora Gonzales and her cooks tended to Xenia and Beatie. Both had nasty cuts and contusions on their heads.

Bomba appeared worse off. It took four of Gonzales's men to carry him into the house, where Gonzales put him on a bed and gave him a bottle of tequila, which Bomba declined. Then Gonzales inexpertly probed for the bullet in Bomba's shoulder. After a while he gave up. He walked out to the Packard and examined the dashboard, in which he found a big hole through the speedometer. It occurred to him that he could have spared Bomba a lot of torment if he had realized from the start that since there were holes in both the front and back of the shoulder, the bullet had obviously exited.

He returned to the house and examined Bomba again. The huge man's eyes were impassive; Gonzales couldn't understand why he didn't cry out. There wasn't too much bleeding, he noted, so at least an artery hadn't been cut. And when he moved the shoulder he couldn't feel any evidence of broken bone, either. Maybe it was a clean through-and-through. In any case, Gonzales swabbed the flesh with iodine and dressed it with bandages and gauze.

Xenia was beside herself when she was told about the children; a horror beyond nightmares. She tried to sort it out rationally but her mind raced so fast she couldn't think.

How had they let it happen?

She began to blame Arthur and the Colonel, but quickly decided that blame was just a way of avoiding the question of how to get the kids back. She suddenly wanted her father. He might be a dumb Pittsburgh Polack, but for the first time in her marriage — including the terrible business with Mick — Xenia felt completely alone and isolated.

Beatie was plenty distressed herself and could do little to comfort her. Nobody knew what to do. Here they were, in the middle of nowhere, and a bloodthirsty bandit had kidnapped her grandchildren while her husband and son were off on an insane cattle drive somewhere in the wilds of Mexico. What sleep either woman got that night was restive.

Only Bomba had a plan, such as it was.

The ranch hands determined that Fierro's bunch had headed east toward Valle del Sol, probably for the big hacienda, but didn't see any sense in giving chase, since they were outnumbered ten-to-one. Bomba had stayed up much of the night, and as the shock of the wound wore off he decided to get in the Packard and head for Valle del Sol himself. He could make a lot better time than men on horseback. Once he got there, he didn't have a plan at all, but hoped one would evolve. He felt feverish, but was able to move his arm a little.

At daybreak, Bomba put on a pair of jodhpurs and a khaki sweater and set out for Valle del Sol, where he arrived an hour or so later. The household staff greeted him with tears and hand-wringing, all of them vying to tell him what had happened. He couldn't understand much, but could see some of it for himself: part of the house was destroyed and still smoldering. Rodrigez's corpse was laid out on a table on the veranda, a bullet through his head. From what Bomba apprehended, the soldiers had taken off less than eight hours earlier, headed toward Chihuahua City, driving steers before them. The tracks led across fields toward a distant woods. The Packard would be of no use to him now.

He went to the barn and indicated to a cowhand he wanted a horse. The cowhand saddled up a big bay. Bomba stepped up to the animal to mount it but the horse tossed its head and sidestepped away.

"No, no," shouted the cowboy. "You're on the wrong side. You got to get up on his left side."

Bomba looked at the man, puzzled. He'd never ridden a horse, but figured there couldn't be that much to it. The cowhand took the horse by the reins and indicated for Bomba to board on the horse's left. Bomba tried again but this time put the wrong foot in the stirrup, a mistake he quickly realized even before he hoisted himself off the ground.

"Look here," said the cowhand. The reins in his left hand, he put his left foot in the stirrup and mounted the horse. Then he got down and handed the reins to Bomba, who nodded back in recognition. This time he got it right. He shook the reins and the horse walked slowly out of the barn and into the road. Bomba's injured right arm hung limply by his side but he was able to guide the horse with his left. Everything he had become was now lost: his charges, the children, gone away with murderers. All these years he'd been immensely proud that no harm had come to anyone in the Shaughnessy family. But now Bomba felt deeply ashamed and personally humiliated. He looked north, where he could see the tracks of many cattle. Then, as he'd watched the Colonel do many times, he kicked his horse in its flanks. The animal, straining under Bomba's enormous bulk, reared slightly, then flew into a wild gallop in the direction of Chihuahua City, with Bomba hanging on for whatever he was worth.

THIRTY-FIVE

That same day, Johnny Ollas's party had seen dust from several miles away, which they mistook for Villa's army. Johnny sent Julio to investigate but he returned to report it was just somebody moving a lot of cows. Julio hadn't gotten a look at the whole herd; he'd just topped a ridge when he saw part of the drove in the distance. In any case, Johnny kept on the route to Chihuahua City. By early afternoon they were still about twenty miles away, when they encountered the first of Villa's retreating troops.

Villa had ordered the withdrawal early that morning when the stubborn Federales refused to budge from Chihuahua City. Indeed, the expedition was a disaster; he'd lost more than half of his remaining army killed, wounded, and captured, and the rest were exhausted and demoralized.

Villa had little to be cheerful about, with the exception of Fierro's triumphant return to his camp. The gold the Butcher had brought back could be turned into American dollars for soldiers' pay and supplies.

Villa sent away most of the cattle Fierro had stolen from Valle del Sol with the main body of troops headed for the state of Coahuila, retaining only a small herd for himself. He was going to the mountains for safety with his headquarters staff and several companies of cavalry until his next plan of action became clear. He was also pleased with the arrival of the Shaughnessy children. Compared with them, the ransom value of Señora Donatella Ollas paled. Villa placed the children in the custody of Tom Mix. As soon as he got a chance, he would compose another note to that stinking old gringo.

At the head of the caravan of Villa's army rode a young lieutenant, who was the first to encounter Johnny Ollas's strange party.

"Is this the army of General Villa?" Johnny asked.

"What's left of it," replied the lieutenant. Johnny noticed that he was wearing a peculiar necklace. He could not make out what exactly it was made of, but he thought he detected a faint reek in the air.

"Well, we came to join up."

"You picked a fine time," said the officer. "What are your skills?"

"We ride. I guess we can shoot, too."

"Why do you want to join us now?"

"For the glorious revolution," Johnny Ollas

answered. He felt like holding his nose. Johnny was operating on gut instinct now. Joining this army might well be his death warrant, and his brothers' also. But he couldn't think of any better way to get close to Donita. Certainly he ran the risk of being recognized, but chances had to be taken. He knew that from the bullring.

"All right," the lieutenant said. He turned to a sergeant beside him. "See that they are properly enlisted and equipped. Then take them to General Santo's adjutant. He'll have to figure out what to do with them."

The sergeant motioned for Johnny and the others to go with him toward the rear of the column. Gourd Woman hobbled along behind.

"What's with her?" the sergeant asked.

"We ran into her a few weeks ago out on the llanos," Johnny told him. "People were saying she's a witch, but she's okay. She just makes brooms and peddles them for a living."

"Why is she following us?" asked the sergeant.

"I don't know. Why don't you ask her?"

"Hey," the soldier said, "where do you think you're going?"

"I been with these guys all over the territory," Gourd Woman replied. "I guess I can join up in the army with them. They been nice to me. Nobody else is."

"Well, there's no law against it," the sergeant said. "We got some women in this army — but you're limping. What's wrong with you?"

"My foot hurts, but I can get around. I came with these men probably two hundred miles, didn't I?"

"That's right," Johnny said. "She did."

"What are your skills?" the sergeant asked.

"I make brooms and I can cook."

"Cook?" the soldier said. "Well, maybe you can make yourself useful. This army needs all the men it can get right now."

John Reed was furious. He had been down among the fighting for two days and felt a tinge of neurasthenia. He was covered with the stains of battle: dirt, sweat, grime. He'd gone in with the troops who'd attacked the day before, and watched as Villa's men fell back against the resistance of the Federales, who fought house-to-house from windows, corners of houses, rooftops, and doorways, often tossing sticks of dynamite at the revolutionaries, who'd had nothing of the sort to reply with.

"They fought magnificently," Reed told Bierce, "but were overcome with unfair tactics."

"Unfair?" Bierce said to him from his perch, in the twilight, atop an empty keg of gunpowder. They were sitting around the campfire of Villa's headquarters, where they'd yet again finished a dinner of unsatisfying beans and rice. "What kind of tactic was that?"

Reed described the dynamite. "They exploded innocent people's homes."

"Well, welcome to war, young man," Bierce told him. His mind raced back through the years, to the desperate slaughter at Shiloh and Chickamauga, where men ran bayonets through other men's hearts and heads and thought little or nothing of it. To the ravine full of dead from his own regiment at Shiloh, later eaten by feral pigs, so that their corpses were unrecognizable; and to the body-strewn landscape at Franklin, piled waist-high with the dead, and. . . .

"Yes, well, you tell that to the people who are homeless and starving tonight, Mr. Robinson, that are dead," Reed countered. "I tell you, it was brutal."

"But don't you think if General Villa's troops had dynamite sticks themselves," Bierce said, "they would have done the same thing?"

"No, in fact I don't. These men are fighting *for* the people, not to destroy their homes and families. There were also women and children inside those houses. Some came running out set on fire. It was sheer cruelty."

"Ask the people of the American South what General Sherman told them," Bierce answered.

"Sherman didn't dynamite them out of their residences."

"No, we merely set fire to their residences," the old man said serenely. "Believe it or not, they came out all by themselves."

"At least they were given the chance to escape. These people were burned and exploded alive, I tell you, those were humans, ablaze!"

"It's a new century," Bierce answered, "and a new kind of war."

"If that's so," said Reed, "God help us all." He paused and looked at Bierce with a cold eye. "And God help you for thinking such a thing."

Bierce disliked this naive young reporter, John Reed — too full of himself and his school-bought notions. Bierce was a pragmatist of the first order. He did not believe in God or people. And he did not believe in fate. So there wasn't much left, except for himself, and even that was a facade.

For Reed's part, he didn't exactly know what to make of this fellow Jack Robinson, except for a vague feeling that he had seen the old coot before. That old men like him couldn't or wouldn't understand the notion of civil revolution was a source of constant astonishment and irritation to John Reed, but possibly an object of conversation — maybe even a chance for converting the old man to

Marxism.

Just then Villa, Santos, Fierro, and others emerged from the commander's tent, where they had been conferring. They were all smoking cigars and joined Reed and Bierce around the campfire. The late afternoon sky had turned a sickly yellow gray that faintly stank of gun smoke.

"You fellows get enough to eat?" Villa asked. "I'm sorry we didn't have time to butcher one of those beefs. But tomorrow we ought to be far enough away from here to have a little rest, huh?"

"Your soldiers fought gallantly," Reed told the general. "I was there. The brutality of your enemy is appalling."

"Yes, I know," replied the general. "I just wish I had thought to supply our people with a lot of dynamite sticks." He sounded remarkably nonchalant about losing the battle.

Reed looked startled. Okay, so what if Villa would have used the dynamite, too? Reed reasoned. It was used against *him*, wasn't it? Revolution was revolution, and once you were into it, no cost came too high, he rationalized, since the revolutionaries, if defeated and caught, would be put to death.

"So, General," Reed asked, "where do you fight again?"

"We've just been talking about that," Villa said. "But I'm afraid if I tell you my plans,

I'll have to keep you here with me for a while."

"That's okay with me," Reed said. "I'd rather file a good story late than file something that doesn't say anything."

"And you, Señor Robinson?" Villa said. "You told me you had been a writer, too, at some point."

"I'm just writing letters to a friend, and so far I ain't even found anyplace to post them." This was about true, too. Bierce had quit writing professionally several years before, following the horrendous reception of his *Collected Works*. The critics, waiting with their shovels, had buried him, as he had buried them and ten score of other writers. They had actually made a carnival of it, a unanimous humiliation, prompting Bierce to say to one of his few friends who was still alive and still speaking to him, "My work is finished, and so am I."

"I'm not filing any stories," Bierce told Villa.

"Good," the general said. "Let's keep it that way. I wouldn't want to feel I got spies in my camp."

"So, where from here?" Reed asked, his voice bright and eager.

"The mountains," Villa replied. "We all need a little rest. Ain't nobody going to follow us into there — not where I go. Then I'm going to make up a plan to get at one of the Federales' positions I think I can lick. There

383

are several garrisons up by the border. I'm not going to fight any more big battles unless I have the strength to win them. But I can sure pester a lot of outposts and keep those traitors down in Mexico City guessing where I'm gonna turn up next. I'll be like a ghost."

"Yes, that's it!" Reed said. "I can see that clearly: 'The Ghost Revolution.' It's a wonderful headline."

"Just make sure nobody sees it before I tell you," Villa said. "Besides," he added, "I think I may be more like a horsefly than a ghost — a pesky horsefly that never leaves you alone."

Bierce sat staring into the low campfire, contemplating Villa's new strategy and watching the sparks waft up into the yellow-gray sky. He felt his seventy years but took pains not to show it, even though he'd come to Mexico not expecting to return. His two sons were gone, one a suicide, the other from pneumonia, and his wife as well. He'd lost so many friends between death and arguments that he'd thrown his address book away years ago. He sent everything to Miss Christiansen and had her forward letters if necessary.

Bierce, at length, had decided there wasn't a place for him in America anymore, and ever since the war he'd been living on borrowed time. In his *Devil's Dictionary,* under the letter *S,* Bierce had offered a definition of suicide: "An excellent solution, too seldom used," he'd written — and then, years later, his son had broken his heart by killing himself. In any case Bierce himself wasn't ready to die quite yet; there was interesting stuff happening and he wanted to stay around awhile and see how things turned out.

Tom Mix was at a separate campfire half a mile away with the hostages. At first he'd been worried about bringing them together lest they conspire to escape, but when he weighed this against the difficulties of trying to keep them apart, he changed his mind. Besides, the children would need a woman of some sort to look after them, and that would give Señora Ollas something to do.

Katherine was shocked and frightened when Timmy told her about their mother and Beatie, but Mix assured her they were all right.

"How do you know?" Katherine demanded.

"I saw them," Mix said. "They were hurt a little in the car wreck, but they're fine now."

"What about Bomba?" Katherine asked.

"That big darkie? The driver? Just winged. He's all right, too, I guess. But he tried to run down General Fierro and his men with a car."

Actually, Mix wasn't sure of anything he was telling them, but justified it on the grounds it was better to keep them happy.

"Why can't we go home?" Timmy asked.

"Because first General Villa is going to

communicate with your grandfather. Shouldn't take long."

"It means we're kidnapped," Katherine said with raw hostility.

"Kidnapped, yes! That's exactly what it means," Donita interjected. "These people are sadists and murderers and kidnappers." For some reason she felt she could get away with saying such things in the presence of Mix.

"Have we treated you badly?" Mix said.

"No, but it doesn't mean you won't. What kind of people kidnap women and children?" Donita demanded.

"Actually, it ain't my preference," Mix said uncomfortably, "But right now I just do what I'm told."

The next day, Villa selected a vanguard for his party, and a wagon train was formed for the trip to the Sierra Madre. Villa himself and a dozen bodyguards were at the head of the column. Fierro and some of the other high-ranking officers were behind. Next was a column of fifty men riding side by side, and following that were the commissary and cooking wagons. Behind them was a medical wagon with a doctor; then came Mix, ambling along on his horse beside a wagon containing the children and Señora Ollas, driven by a bored-looking peon. Following that were the ammunition wagons and a few pieces of light artillery, and bringing up the rear were the cattle.

After nightfall, at the tail end of the caravan, Johnny Ollas, with his cuadrilla and Gourd Woman, had just finished a supper of beans and cow's liver. After they were enlisted, they had been given army rifles and ammunition, and taken to Villa's adjutant, who, when he learned they had punched cattle, assigned them to the remainder of the herd of cattle Fierro had rustled from Valle del Sol.

"You're not gonna believe this," Julio said to Johnny. "Look there in the middle of the herd." Johnny's brother Julio was a picador in the cuadrilla.

They were standing on the side of a low hill next to a draw where the cattle could be hemmed in. Johnny gazed out over the herd and actually did a double-take. There, amid the steers, he saw a pair of big horns and a huge hump on a reddish-colored fighting bull.

"It's Casa Grande," Johnny replied.

It was unmistakable. Casa Grande was a grandson of the late Toro Malo, just this year turned fighting age, and further recognizable by the flash of white on his throat.

"Then they must have stolen this herd from Valle del Sol," Johnny said. "From —"

"Yeah, from the bull pasture, too," Julio finished the statement for him.

Johnny shrugged. "But why go into the bull pasture for cattle?" he asked, "Jesucristo, there's cattle all over the place out there."

"I don't know," Julio said, "but unless Casa Grande just got loose somehow, that's what they did. It's a lucky thing, too, because they must've taken some of our herding steers along. Lucky they're staying with him, too."

Julio was right about the steers. Steers kept the bulls manageable because the bull's herding instinct takes over. But the moment it was left alone, the bull would become a killing machine, charging and goring man, horse, wagons, cars — anything that moved and some that didn't, such as trees and houses.

"You think they don't know he's in there?" Johnny inquired.

"These people are weird," Julio responded. "They do weird things."

Bomba had managed to stay on the horse, and even learned how to control him somewhat. He didn't know the way to Chihuahua City, but the cattle Fierro had rustled left such a distinctive trail that Bomba had no trouble following it. After a while, however, Bomba realized there were too many tracks for them to be from the same cattle that Fierro's band had stolen. He doubled back until he found what appeared to be fresher hoofprints and followed their trail.

He rode all morning with the single-minded purpose of bringing back the children but without the faintest notion of how to accomplish it. One thing he knew was that, dressed as he was, in jodhpurs, jacket, and English riding boots, he stood out like a sore thumb. So when he reached the banks of a stream and the horse bent down to water, Bomba dismounted and removed his shirt and jacket. Then he got down in the mud and rolled around. When it dried, he was in effect camouflaged. He kept his khaki shirt — now slung around the saddle horn — to carry his collection of throwing knives.

As late afternoon approached, Bomba noticed that at a fork in the road some cow tracks veered off east, and on a hunch he followed this trail. During the course of the morning he'd discovered his horse's various gaits, which he compared to the gears on an automobile. He concluded that a canter was the best speed to run the horse with some hope of catching up and yet not wear the animal out. The animal also needed rest and a place to graze for food.

At last the road topped a rise and Bomba saw the stolen cattle, herded only by a handful of men. Villa's drovers were moving slowly across a little valley marked by stands of small trees and scrub and knee-high grass. The brush stands would provide Bomba with a cover but he'd have to swing wide through woods to keep from being spotted in the open. He turned the horse and headed quickly for the trees, whose branches slapped him in the head.

When he emerged, he was abreast of the herd and screened by stands of brush. He could see the drovers plainly, especially the one riding drag, atop a horse with the fancy silver and turquoise saddle that had belonged to Señor Gonzales.

Bomba saw no signs of the children. For a while he shadowed the herders, ducking behind brush until he came up just on the other side of some blackjack pines not a stone's throw from the rider with the horse and silver saddle he'd seen Katherine get on two days earlier.

He dismounted and tied the reins around a small pine, took three knives with him. They were as flat and balanced as the one he'd originally brought with him from Samoa. A year later, as a Christmas present, the Colonel took him to a cutlery manufacturer and, using his Samoan knife as the basis, Bomba began to design throwing knives, each for a different purpose. He wished he had them all now, but would have to make do with what he'd brought.

Bomba crept to within a few yards of the rider. He flung one of the knives, a short thick one, in a way that the hilt, not the blade, struck the rider in the back of the neck.

The man lurched forward and slumped in the fancy saddle, his fingers twitching reflexively. Bomba rushed out and pulled him to the ground. He grabbed the horse's reins and led the animal into the brush, dragging the rider behind him by the collar of his shirt. In the quiet of the little grove, Bomba knelt over the man and pinched his cheeks to bring him around. When the man opened his eyes, Bomba put on his fiercest expression and held a blade to the soldier's throat so it barely pierced the skin.

"Where?" he said.

"Huh? Who?"

"Children."

Bomba struggled to make himself understood.

"Huh?"

"Where?"

Bomba pressed the knife in harder, pushing the man's neck skin so far back it not only cut him more but was strangling him.

"Where?"

The soldier gurgled, and Bomba relieved the pressure a little so he could talk.

"They all gone ahead," the rider said. "With the general. They just told us to bring along these beefs."

Bomba looked into the man's eyes. They were terrified, wild, and with good reason. He put a huge hand over the man's mouth and plunged the knife all the way through his neck till it not only went through his Adam's apple but ruptured the spinal cord in back.

The man's hands twitched violently before falling still.

Bomba stuck the knife into the dirt to clean it, then went to the horse stolen from Señor Gonzales and got aboard the fancy silver saddle. Even Bomba could tell this was a much better animal than the one he'd been riding. Without so much as a glance at the dead man, he continued shadowing the drovers, leaving the bay horse standing among the blackjack pines.

He began to experience a new kind exhilaration. He felt invisible, like a stick insect, among the trees and rocks and men.

THIRTY-SIX

Colonel Shaughnessy was in high spirits. He'd driven the priceless herd nearly two hundred miles in just over three weeks, surely a record of some kind.

Along with a dozen drovers, the Colonel, Arthur, Cowboy Bob, and Ah Dong in the chuckwagon were riding out ahead of the drive when some of the horses began acting up, tossing their heads and straining at the bits. The horses, it turned out, had smelled something.

To everyone's surprise, they soon came upon a strange desert oasis, a long rift in the parched and scrubby soil filled with azure-colored water. No trees grew here, but the flora around the lake grew luxuriously. There were ferns, and creeping vines festooned the surrounding rocks with yellow and purple flowers. The Colonel and his party led the horses down to drink. The lake was shallow and crystal-clear but there didn't seem to be any wildlife of any sort around, except for insects on the flowers.

"I used to hear about a place like this," said Cowboy Bob. "I mean, some big lake right out in the middle of the desert. I always thought it was just a old wives' tale."

"It's limestone," Arthur said, studying the rock. "Must be a spring or artesian well somewhere." He got off his horse and went to the water's edge and scooped up a handful.

"Gosh, it's cold. It's like ice," Arthur continued. He started to take a swallow, then flung the water on the ground. "It's not sulfurous, but it but it tastes sort of like dishwater."

"Glad you took it on yourself to check that out," Cowboy Bob said. "Rumor was this here water is deadly poison."

"What!" Arthur exclaimed.

"Just kidding," Bob said. "Matter of fact, I think I might just jump in and wash some a this desert off me before they get the herd turned this way and foul the water all up. This'll likely be the last water them cows drink before we get to El Paso." He got down and began stripping his clothes off. A number of riders joined him.

"Ah Dong," said the Colonel, "this place looks like a good spot to have lunch, huh?"

The cook nodded, and with his mess boys began unloading gear. Arthur went walking along the lake, hunting for butterflies in the flowers. He didn't have a net but saw some interesting-looking specimens, in fact some he'd never even read about before. It took his mind off the pressing problems. Here was an opportunity, Arthur hoped — maybe he'd even find an entirely new type of species.

Arthur was a hundred or so yards away from the Colonel's party, and frustrated because he couldn't catch any of the butterflies without a net. They would let him come right up and then flit away. After a while he gave up and began walking back, when he came across what seemed to be an old rusting piece of metal, half buried in the sand.

He nudged it with his foot, then bent over and worked it loose. The metal was queerly shaped and some of it rusted away entirely. Then he saw what seemed to be a helmet lying in the same hole he'd made when he worked the first piece loose. He picked it up and examined what certainly looked, for all its wear and tear, like one of those old armored helmets the conquistadores wore. Quickly he went back to the other object. Now he saw that it looked something like a breastplate — at least half a breastplate. He was stunned. A party of the conquistadores must have come this way, found this lake . . . three, four hundred years ago — and here in his hands was historical evidence. He took the relic back and threw it in Ah Dong's chuckwagon, thinking when it got shined up it would look good on his office wall.

The Colonel was well pleased with the progress of the drive. They had not lost many of the herd and he felt confident that not only would the railroad be running by the time they crossed the border, but Pancho Villa and his band would be long gone from Chihuahua City and the environs of Valle del Sol.

It was a fine compliment to the drovers that they kept the drive headed north toward El Paso. Though the herd was still two days out, the residents of the city were astonished to see the gigantic cloud of dust it raised, coming toward them, and mistook it for a great desert sandstorm.

THIRTY-SEVEN

The news of Villa's defeat at the Battle of Chihuahua City had been on everyone's tongue when the Colonel and his party arrived in El Paso. It began as a good day. The herd, in spite of setbacks from the hail and lightning storm and attrition from thirst and weakness, survived mostly intact, though a good bit lighter in weight. Problem was, what to do with them. There were now ten times as many cattle in El Paso as there were citizens. The Colonel had spent the day handling the enormous logistics of arranging for the cows to be put on railcars bound for the Chicago slaughterhouses.

Meanwhile, time and again Cowboy Bob had proved a godsend. He spent his time arranging for places to keep the cattle while they awaited final disposition, which was no small task, since nobody around El Paso kept enough fodder for a herd like this and the largest single source of water available to them was the Rio Grande — which residents swam in, washed in, and drank from as it flowed through town. But Bob knew cattle and he knew El Paso, so he parceled out the herd by sections, spreading the Colonel's money around the countryside leasing land, and in the process making himself a very popular fellow.

What exactly had become of Villa and his army was not fully understood in El Paso. Press reports were conflicting. Some said Villa was marching on Juárez City just across the river. This rumor may have had to do with the great dust cloud stirred up by the Colonel's cattle as they neared the Texas border. Others said Villa was headed for the Sierra Madre, but yet other stories asserted he retired to Coahuila and from there was preparing to launch an attack against the oil facilities over on the Gulf of Mexico near Veracruz. One thing for sure was that the citizens of El Paso were in the dark about Villa's whereabouts; another was that for the time being they were up to their asses in cows.

The first thing Arthur did when they reached town was go to the telegraph depot and wire his office about the affairs of the NE&P. An hour later he received a long communication from one of the vice presidents overseeing freight and payroll that everything was running smoothly based on the infusion of money from the loan Arthur had secured on the *Ajax*. Paid miles were up slightly and there was even encouraging news about the possibility of one of the lucrative government munitions contracts. On the other hand, the railroad was hanging on by a fingernail, the official hinted, which would have to be dealt with when Arthur returned. But for now, with the sale of the cattle, Arthur hoped he could get the company out of the clutches of its creditors. All in all, things seemed to be looking positive.

After nearly a month on the trail, Colonel Shaughnessy and his top hands were having their first drink of whiskey at the polished mahogany bar of the Toltec Hotel, when a motorcyclist from the telegraph depot found him and handed him a personal message from the home office. It rendered the Colonel momentarily speechless; he flipped the paper to Arthur, then downed his drink in a single gulp.

Arthur felt his face flush as he read the message again.

"What is it?" Cowboy Bob asked.

"They have kidnapped my children," Arthur said in blank disbelief.

"Who?" said Bob.

"Villa." He handed him the telegram.

Cowboy Bob examined the document. "Well, I heard he's taken people hostage before, but it was never kids."

Señor Gonzales had sent the message from

the telegraph office at Parral. It told of Fierro's arrival, the capture of Katherine, Bomba's attempted escape, the injuries to Beatie and Xenia, and, finally, the kidnapping of Timmy.

YOUR WIFE AND DAUGHTER IN LAW WELL NOW REMAIN WITH ME STOP UNDERSTAND YOUR NEGRO SERVANT GONE AFTER VILLA'S ARMY STOP TELEPHONE STILL DOWN STOP ALL QUIET HERE FOR NOW STOP VILLA'S SOLDIERS RAIDED VALLE DEL SOL BLEW UP HOUSE KILLED RODRIGUEZ AND FIGHTING BULLS STOP SAFE IN YOUR OFFICE BROKEN INTO AND LOOTED STOP WHAT DO I DO NEXT STOP REGRET EVERYTHING GONZALES.

Arthur pushed his drink away. A shaft of pain exploded from his stomach upward, and at the same time a paralyzing weakness caused his legs and arms to tremble. This sort of thing was unheard-of in Boston or Chicago. For a moment, speech would not come to his lips. His mind seemed frozen in time. Then he managed to say, "My God." That was all, for the moment.

Arthur, Bob, and the Colonel stood at the Toltec bar gaping at each other in disbelief.

Arthur began to shake off the numbness, and his first thought was that they must raise ransom money for Villa as soon as he demanded it. His second was, where on earth would they get it?

The Colonel felt the rebuke in Arthur's face and for a moment tried to rationalize the situation. Suppose he'd taken all the family on the cattle drive and been attacked by Villa's people? Same thing or worse may have happened. Suppose he hadn't had a cattle drive in the first place and they'd all stayed at Valle del Sol? Wouldn't the same thing have happened there, too? He never got around to asking himself what if he hadn't brought the family down into Mexico at all, because he already knew the answer to that. Instead, trying to deflect attention from himself, he said, mostly for Cowboy Bob's benefit, "I don't give a damn about the house and the bulls, but Rodriguez was a fine manager. Cheerful man, good stock, like Callahan before him. It's been a bad year for ranch managers."

For the first time in his life, Arthur read fear and confusion in the Old Man's eyes. The Colonel knew that if the safe in his office had been looted, then his last readily available cash had vanished. There had been upward of $200,000 worth of gold bars in that safe — money he'd counted on to keep Valle del Sol running and also as a stash that he might draw on if he really needed it. No need to tell anyone, especially Arthur; no need to add misery to poverty.

"The only good thing is that Villa's been defeated," the Colonel finally responded, "which probably means the trains will be running again. We need the women on American soil as quickly as possible. In the morning we'll go to the telegraph office and the rail depot and find out what we can. Villa wouldn't dare hurt them." The Colonel put an arm on Arthur's shoulder. "We'll just have to figure something out, son. Believe me, we will."

John Shaughnessy got a further shock first thing next morning when a second messenger from Western Union showed up at his hotel room door. The telegraph from Villa demanding ransom money for the children had finally caught up with him. The Colonel burst into Arthur's adjoining room and thrust the offensive paper at him.

"A million dollars! I don't *have* a million dollars!" the Colonel said, shaking his head. "I may have a million dollars' worth of *things* here and there, but it wouldn't do us any good. Why must I deal with this monstrous heathen?"

"Maybe he'll negotiate," Arthur said, without really believing it.

"Negotiate with a bloodthirsty greaser?"

"I have some money of my own. These are my children. I think by selling my securities and taking a note on my property I could come up with fifty, maybe a hundred thousand."

"Yes, and how long do you think that would take? Besides, what guarantees do you have? Deliver such money to a madman and simply hope and pray the children are returned? Villa will laugh at fifty thousand dollars. He has overestimated me. He expects real money."

"So what in hell can we do?" Arthur said.

"First, we need to get Beatie and Xenia out of there before something like this happens to them," said the Colonel. "Trains ought to be running the next day or so, and if we find out it's safe for them to return, that's the first order of business. Then, what we need most is intelligence. Right now we don't even know where to locate the son of a bitch to give him any ransom even if we had it."

"We need information," Arthur said starkly. "We will find it right here," he said. "Here in El Paso. You can find out anything in El Paso, isn't that what you said, Father?"

In that, Arthur was correct, but the problem was how to identify phony information from the real thing. He turned to Cowboy Bob.

Bob had an old compadre called Death Valley Slim, who'd been a cavalryman and later a mineral prospector down in Chihuahua, and who was not only familiar with Villa himself but also with his elaborate network of spies hanging around El Paso picking up information and intelligence. When Cowboy Bob explained the situation to him, Slim said he'd return in an hour with solid news.

Meantime, Colonel Shaughnessy got on the phone and rang up the White House again. President Woodrow Wilson was having his breakfast when he took the Colonel's call.

"I believe I explained the situation to you before," the president said after listening to the Colonel's tale. "I am very sorry about your family, Shaughnessy, but we can't just go changing American foreign policy and possibly start a war over a man like Pancho Villa."

The Colonel fumed. "Roosevelt did it! Remember: 'Perdicaris alive or Raisuli dead!' " he said, referring to an incident in Morocco some years earlier when a Berber bandit named Raisuli kidnapped and held for ransom an American named Perdicaris. Roosevelt had sent in the Marines.

"Well, that was President Roosevelt's way of dealing with things," Wilson said regally.

"Yes, and he said something else, too: 'Speak softly and carry a big stick,' " the Colonel reminded him.

"It wasn't Roosevelt said that," Wilson corrected him. "It was his secretary of state John Hay."

"Whatever," snapped Colonel Shaughnessy. "How about you, Mr. President? Where is your 'big stick'?"

"I have one, Colonel Shaughnessy, but must use it wisely," the president said. "However," he concluded in the barest whisper, "I do believe I speak softly."

Furious, the Colonel hung up. "That man is an ass," he said to himself, wishing, despite everything, that he'd supported Roosevelt.

By midmorning, Death Valley Slim found Arthur and the Colonel standing in the lobby of the Toltec.

"What's left of his army's back over in Coahuila lickin' their wounds," Slim said, "but ol' Pancho, he's took to the hills."

"What hills?" Arthur asked. He moved them all to a table.

"Well, they're not hills, exactly," said Slim. "He's gone to hide out in the Sierra Madre. That's where he usually goes when he needs some time to regroup."

"How many men does he have with him?" demanded the Colonel.

"Regiment — maybe less," Slim answered. "It's tough travelin' in them mountains with anything more'n that. Tough enough travelin' in there anyway," he added.

"A regiment," said the Colonel. "Well, now, that's all he's got?"

"All he took," Slim said.

"Why, hell, I can raise a regiment!" the Colonel declared.

"What are you talking about?" said Arthur.

"Look, if Villa's separated himself from most of his army, then why don't we just raise us an army here in El Paso and go after him, before he pulls himself together and reunites himself with his band?"

"How are you going to raise an army?" Arthur said, trying to hide his astonishment at such a crackpot notion.

"Son, in case you forgot, I raised one right there in Boston back in '98 and took it up San Juan Hill with T.R. I'm not exactly unaccustomed to fighting these beaners."

"Yes, but — look, we need to be realistic here. For Katherine and Timmy."

The Colonel rose up from the table and motioned for Arthur to come with him. They went to a quiet spot in a corner of the lobby.

"Listen, Arthur, you asked me yesterday what I suggested we do. First, Wilson isn't going to do anything, so any help from our government is out. He offered to have our ambassador in Mexico City contact the Carranza government, but what in hell good would that do? Carranza can't even find Villa himself."

Arthur listened.

"Second, we don't have the money to pay the ransom, and every minute we wait, Villa's going to be harder to catch up with, and every minute the children remain in danger. So the choice is either to sit on our hands here in El Paso and hope something happens or take action."

"Action . . . ?"

"Yes, action! At the best, we might have a chance to sneak in and bring the kids out, because I imagine that's the last thing he'll be expecting. The other possibility is that if we do catch up with him and a rescue isn't possible, at least we might be able to negotiate, like you say."

Arthur closed his eyes and shook his head and ran his fingers through his hair.

"Suppose we try to rescue them and fail?" The bright faces of Katherine and Timmy kept flashing in Arthur's mind.

"You know Villa pretty well," Arthur said to Death Valley Slim after he and his father rejoined the group. "Do you think he'll harm those children?"

"Let me put it this way: I wouldn't put nothin' past him."

"I say since we know where he is we ought to at least give it a try," Colonel Shaughnessy said. "I'm not an unreasonable man. I think once we smoke him out, I'll just let him know it's not him we're after, but those children, and if he releases them, he'll not be molested any further by me."

"Father, that's . . ." Arthur's voice trailed off. He could not remember a time in his life when he felt real fear, real panic, at least not for any length of time. But now he felt frightened in himself, unsure of whatever

407

decision he made, yet he knew he would ultimately have to be the one to decide.

"Excuse me, Colonel," Death Valley Slim put in, "you said 'since we know where he is.' Now, that's not exactly what I said. I said he's gone to the mountains. That ain't like saying he's down the street at Mr. Foote's Saloon. Do you understand how large them mountains are? I mean, just in area, if you could scoop 'em all up together they'd prob'ly fill up the entire state of Texas — and Texas is big enough being flat. You got to appreciate what kind of mountains these is, Colonel," Slim continued. "You know the Rockies, and the Sierras up in California . . . well, these ain't like them. Those got civilization — roads, towns. These mountains here ain't got nothing like that. All that lives up there is a handful of Indians that came down from the Toltecs. Everything else is, well, just wild. There ain't even maps for most of it."

"So how does Villa get around there?" the Colonel asked, now annoyed.

"He knows the place," Slim said. "He's been in there a lot — ever since he was just a kid — and he's also got a few of those Indians — they call themselves Rarámuris — anyhow, they go with him. They know their way around."

"You been there yourself?" the Colonel said.

"Lots of times," Slim said. "But that don't mean I know where Pancho is. Like I told you, that place is thousands of square miles and a maze of canyons. And there's lots of dangers besides Pancho Villa."

"But you might have some notion of where he is, though? What part he might have located himself in?"

"I might," Slim said. "But it's no guarantee."

"Good," said the Colonel. "You're hired."

"For what?"

"To join our expedition against Mr. Villa and redeem my grandchildren."

"I didn't mean it that way, sir," Slim said. "I meant, what's the pay?"

Arthur said, "You name it."

THIRTY-EIGHT

Arthur thought it might be the screwiest scheme he'd ever heard of, but what choice did they have? It turned out raising an army was not so easy as the Colonel had predicted. On the cattle drive they'd had more than seventy-five Mexican drovers from Valle del Sol, but almost to a man they declined the Colonel's offer to go after Pancho Villa.

That afternoon Colonel Shaughnessy dispatched Cowboy Bob and Death Valley Slim with rolls of ten-dollar bills in their pockets. They went to dragoon the bars, whorehouses, stockyards, saloons, and flophouses of El Paso, offering a twenty-dollar sign-up bonus and ten dollars a day for any man willing to enlist in "Shaughnessy's Partisan Rangers," the name by which he had styled his expedition. If they were successful, the cost would be cheap at a thousand times the price.

Unfortunately, what turned up next morning was unsatisfactory soldier material, to say the least. Bob and Slim managed to enlist more than a hundred men, but less than half that number showed up, and of these, most were too drunk, too old, or a combination of both. Many had even lied about whether they owned horses and, for that matter, their own rifles or sidearms. There had been a lot of saloon talk during the enlisting process the previous evening, but in the light of a new day, as Cowboy Bob was fond of saying, "What we got here is a bunch of 'big hats, no cattle.' "

The Colonel was furious and tried to hold Bob accountable.

"You've always stepped up and done your duty," he told Bob, "but this time you've failed me."

"Well, last night they sure looked better than now, I give you that," Bob said defensively. "But, hell, Colonel, it was dark in them places. They was most of 'em makin' sense like a drunk'll do till he gets too drunk to stand up. Besides, where else was I s'posed to go? There ain't but ten or fifteen thousand people in this city. You expect to find a soldier for this kind of thing by visiting people's homes at night or canvassing the churches? I doubt it, sir. Slim and I did the best we could."

Death Valley Slim was standing beside Cowboy Bob and agreed.

"Colonel," Slim said, "I tell you what. While y'all been talking, I been lookin' over this crowd. You might be tarring them all with the same brush — some of 'em ain't as bad as they look." He took the Colonel aside.

"I know you was a big military man in the Spanish War an' all," Slim said, "but if I was you, I wouldn't want all these people with me anyway — even if they was perfect soldiers. What I'd do, I was you, is start whittling down. You know what I mean?"

"No, I don't," the Colonel said. He looked peevish and highly annoyed.

"Well, sir, here's the way I see it. What you're gonna come up against in them mountains, I don't know if you understand it quite yet, Colonel. Them mountains, they're not some joking matter. It was me, I'd take men with me who ever' one of 'em knowed pretty much what he was doin'. Even if I didn't take but fifteen or twenty. With that terrain in there, likely in a fight you couldn't engage that many at one time anyhow. And you could travel faster and lighter that way. Havin' a lot of people slows you down, you know?"

"Do you have some kind of military experience yourself?" the Colonel asked sarcastically.

"Matter of fact, sir, I have. I was with the Second Cavalry for seven years. We was the ones that captured Geronimo."

"I'll be damned," said the Colonel.

"Yessir, not too far from where I expect Villa's headed to hole up right now. In fact, I was a first sergeant. We chased that ol' bastid day and night for three years."

Arthur said, "You ought to listen to this man, Papa, he knows his way around."

They were still standing in the Toltec Hotel lobby, and somehow Arthur began to feel better about the expedition. Between Cowboy Bob and Slim and the Colonel, maybe they could do something after all.

In an open plot between buildings off of El Paso's main street, Colonel Shaughnessy, Bob, Slim, and Arthur began to check out the motley would-be "Partisan Rangers." Some could barely stand and a few actually fell down in the dust. Some still had bottles they were drinking from, bought with the Colonel's enlistment bonus. The Colonel and his party moved from man to man. If the man looked sober, they sometimes asked questions. If he looked too old or infirm, they moved on. But just as Slim had suggested, they found a number of the prospects who looked rigorous and in remarkably good shape.

One character the Colonel put on the roster was a daredevil stuntman and aviator called "Crosswinds" Charlie Blake, who'd been left behind by a flying circus after he fell off a barstool and fractured his arm. At least the man was sober, clean-cut, and well spoken, unlike so much of the other drunken riffraff that morning. He was short and slender, with short dark hair, gunmetal-blue eyes, and a rather long nose and prominent ears. He looked rather ratlike, in fact, but was as distinctive as he was unattractive. Arthur was impressed as soon as he learned he was a flier.

By noon, Colonel Shaughnessy had enlisted twenty-nine handpicked men and, that being accomplished, the Colonel interviewed Cowboy Bob about his progress in outfitting the bunch. Bob and Death Valley Slim had spent the morning acquiring the best rifles, pistols, ammunition, pack animals, dusters, wagons, field glasses, blankets, ropes and harnesses, and other hard supplies and extra equipment that could be had in El Paso. But that was when trouble appeared.

They were standing in the street talking when two U.S. Army officers walked up. Both were dressed in starched cavalry twill trousers, blouses, Sam Brown belts, and polished puttees. One was wearing the gold stars of a general.

"Sir, I am General John Pershing, commander of this military district," said the older man. "Lieutenant George S. Patton here is my aide."

"Pleased to meet you," the Colonel replied nicely.

"And I take it, then, that you are the Mr. Shaughnessy who is trying to raise some kind of military force?"

"I am Shaughnessy. This is my son, Arthur." He also introduced Bob and Slim. Patton seemed to be eyeing Arthur suspiciously.

"May I ask what the purpose of your endeavor is?" Pershing said.

"We have property down in Mexico that needs to be rescued," the Colonel replied evasively.

"From what?" Pershing inquired.

"From the Mexicans," said the Colonel, "who are lawless."

Pershing twitched his mouth and stroked his mustache with his thumb. "My people tell me you are signing on an organized force. Do you intend to represent the United States government?"

"Hell, no, General," said Shaughnessy. "I'm just gathering some men to help me protect my interests."

"Well, in that case I can't stop you," Pershing said, "but I warn you that Mexico is in turmoil right now and under our present orders we cannot protect you against harm."

"I know that already," Shaughnessy said. "I just got back from there. And as far as protecting us, I already talked to that namby-pamby in the White House and got back the answer."

"Might I ask what property it is you're trying to protect or rescue?" Patton asked. He couldn't help noticing that the streets were packed with the Colonel's cattle.

"You may not," Shaughnessy told him, "unless you want to come with us."

"Our situation vis-à-vis the government of Mexico is highly delicate," Pershing said. "We are not to cross the border unless attacked."

"Yes, that's been conveyed to us," Arthur broke in. "Say, you wouldn't have any idea of the whereabouts of Pancho Villa right now, would you?"

"He just fought a big battle in Chihuahua City and got licked," Pershing said. "We heard he's split his army up and is probably headed for Coahuila."

"Thank you," Arthur replied. "I read that in the newspapers."

"Well, I appreciate your time, Mr. Shaughnessy," Pershing said. "I hope you won't do anything you'll regret."

"That's the army for you," snorted the Colonel when the two officers were out of earshot. "Not only won't help, but try to discourage those who do. Those two men will never amount to anything."

The Colonel and his party repaired to the Toltec Hotel bar to plot their strategy, and there received some good news at last. The trains would be running again first thing in the morning. The Colonel instructed Cowboy Bob to hurry over to the rail depot and make sure they all had passage, including the horses, donkeys, and equipment. Then he went the hotel desk and wrote out a telegraph for the ranch, telling them to get Xenia and Beatie out of Valle del Sol quickly as possible and take the first train to El Paso. As he finished writing, a familiar voice addressed Colonel Shaughnessy from behind.

"Ah, my friend, so you, too, have returned to America — or did you ever leave?"

The voice belonged to the German, Strucker. He had just come back from Mexico City, where he claimed to have met with President Carranza about buying oil leases.

In fact, Strucker had done his best in Mexico City to persuade Carranza to nationalize the vast U.S. oil holdings around Tampico and Veracruz, hoping that would provoke a Mexican-American war. Unsuccessful in this, and because rail communications in central Mexico were then still cut, the German caught a steamer to San Diego, where he took a train back to El Paso. All along the way, Strucker smoked cigarettes, cigars, and drank brandy, considering what to do next. With no help from the Carranza government, his only option now was trying the idea out on Villa. Problem was, since Villa's defeat at Chihuahua City, he wasn't as formidable as he'd once been.

After Shaughnessy explained his own dire situation to Strucker and said what he intended to do about it, the German thought what an idiot the man was, to have put the children in such danger. He liked those children. But of course he mainly sniffed an opportunity here. It might not be the ideal way to get to Villa, but at the moment it seemed the only one. Strucker immediately signed on with the Colonel's little army.

That evening after dinner, the Colonel, Strucker, and Death Valley Slim went to their rooms, and Cowboy Bob was about to say his good nights, too, when Arthur asked him to stay for a nightcap. A fire burned low in the Toltec's lobby fireplace. Arthur had something on his mind that surprised Bob.

"I wonder if I can impose on you for a favor."

"What's that?" Bob said.

"Your experience, your skills — I need them, and there's not much time."

"I ain't sure what you mean," said Cowboy Bob.

"Let me put it this way," Arthur told him. "We're headed out against a dangerous band of criminals that are holding my two children. We're going into a savage territory, and I found it pretty awkward just going on the cattle drive. The fact is, I wasn't cut out for this sort of thing."

"I thought you done okay," Bob said. But Arthur went on.

"I don't know how to shoot a pistol at all. I know something about shotguns, but I've only fired a rifle a few times in my life. I don't know much about anything else. But you grew up with it. So I need you to help me learn, because if it ever comes down to it, if I ever have to fight this Villa or anybody else, I'd like to be up to it."

"So, you still fancy yourself some kind of tenderfoot, huh, even after all that on the trail?"

"Yeah, that's what you'd call it, I guess."

"And you want to ride, shoot, be a tough guy, is it?" Bob chuckled. Bob had come to like Arthur, appreciated his company, but until now figured him as pretty much a poobah of the big American rich — come down here and think they just picked it all up in a week or two, then go back to their yachts and lawn parties and tell everybody they'd been a cowboy. He'd been impressed, however, at Arthur's adaptation to life on the cattle drive. Arthur had pulled his weight, learned, ate beef and beans, asked questions when he didn't know the answers. As Bob glanced down at the flaked, sunburned skin on his own big hands, he thought of all the broken ribs and arms and the smashed nose and the times he almost died from frostbite and sunstroke and starvation and a prairie fire, even suffered a bullet or two in his body, but he kept those thoughts to himself.

"Something like that," Arthur said. "I know it doesn't sound likely, does it?" He was smiling what Bob thought was a strange smile.

Bob studied his drink for a moment. "Tell you what, compadre, just stick close with ol' Cowboy Bob, an' every spare minute I got, I'll do my best."

Bob suddenly got an uneasy feeling about what he was hearing, because there was something in the tone of how Arthur said it, and the sheepish look in his eyes. Bob had seen it before, where a perfectly normal guy gets a bee up his ass, and suddenly you got a crazy would-be killer on your hands. He had a feeling there were other things going on there besides what Arthur had told him. It made Bob a little uncomfortable.

"I appreciate that very much," Arthur said quietly.

"Not a'tall," Bob replied.

■ ■ ■ ■ ■

PART FOUR:
THE BARRANCAS

■ ■ ■ ■ ■

THIRTY-NINE

Pancho Villa was on the move for a week before he reached the foothills of the Sierra Madre. But he still had more distance to cover before reaching his refuge, the barrancas, which lay within the mountains. The previous evening, Villa turned up at the campfire of Tom Mix and his captives, Katherine, Timmy, and Donita Ollas. Villa's face was freshly scrubbed; he wore a new suit of clothes and smelled of perfume. He held something in his hands and smiled wolfishly, licking his lips with his thick tongue, like a man with something important on his mind.

Katherine and Timmy shrank back. They'd been seated on a log by the fire after a meager supper of stewed beef and beans. The weather was turning colder and they'd drawn themselves closer to the fires in the last few days. Villa had visited their camp several times since they were captured, but the children remained fearful of him. So far he hadn't spoken to them, but instead just stared at them while he talked to Mix or his aides. But tonight when Villa entered the little clearing he seated himself on the opposite end of the log Katherine and Timmy were sitting on.

Donita Ollas, who'd also been seated on the log, rose huffily and moved to a log of her own. She was perturbed of spirit and light-headed from lack of sleep and worse, in pain from a rash on her bottom from endless days in the wagon. But she'd be damned if she'd let anyone in Villa's party know that, and still winced whenever Villa came into her sight. Why, he's licking his chops, she thought — he's standing there looking at me and licking his chops!

"So, Señor Mix, have these two muchachos been behaving themselves?" Villa asked pleasantly. Shadows from the firelight flickered gently on his face.

"Yes, sir, General," Mix replied. "They been proper little troopers so far."

Katherine had taken Timmy's hand. His mouth was dropped open and his eyes large and apprehensive. Villa turned and fixed them both with a benign look. He handed an object to each of them, something he'd been holding. They were little wooden animals about two inches high and had been carved out of fresh pine, and the aroma of the pine was still with them. Timmy got a dog, Katherine a cat. The children examined them in the firelight, unsure how to react. Villa broke the silence.

"I would have made one of these for you, too, Señora Ollas, but you so ugly to me, I don't think it would do any good. Maybe I will have to give you jewelry, eh?"

"You can give me my freedom," Donita snapped. "And while you're at it, turn these kids loose, too."

"All in good time, señora," the general replied. "We got lots of time. It's boring in the saddle all day. I amuse myself with my little knife on these trinkets. Do you think these kids like them?"

"What do you say?" Tom Mix nodded at the children.

"Thank you," Katherine said flatly.

"Thank you, 'General,' " Mix reminded her.

"Thank you, General," Timmy said. He didn't know what to make of the gift. In a way, he was flattered that the powerful man had given it — had even taken the time to carve it himself. But what did it mean — that he wanted to be *friends* after all he'd done? Anyway, Timmy felt he was too old for this kind of toy.

"I give you the cat, little señorita, because it's feminine," Villa went on. "And the dog for the boy because the dog is masculine. Do you have a dog at home, boy?"

"No."

"No, 'General,' " Mix corrected him.

"My father won't let us have dogs, General," Timmy said. He was wondering why, if Villa had kidnapped him, he would care one way or the other if he owned a dog.

"Why not?" Villa said with surprise.

"We used to have one, but a car hit it," Katherine said. "We were all so upset, Papa said he didn't think we ought to get another pet."

"Why, that doesn't make sense," Villa said. "I think he should have got you another dog right away. You soon forget the old one."

"Oh, no," Katherine said, "not Ranger. We loved Ranger too much."

"Then did your father shoot the driver of the car that killed him?"

The children were dumbfounded and looked at one another and back to Villa, and then to Mix. Timmy thought it was a bizarre question to ask, though at the time of the accident he'd felt so much hurt and anger that he would have been glad to see the driver injured, too.

"I guess not," the general said. "Americanos have no sense of honor."

"Why should he shoot him?" Timmy blurted out.

"Well, for one reason, then he would never do it again. And for another, you would feel avenged."

"We didn't feel venged in the first place," Katherine said. "We were just sad." She felt somehow emboldened that the great general of the army was sitting there talking to them and treating them with civility. She felt the little carved cat in her hand. It was the first nice gesture she and her brother had received since they'd arrived. Actually, that wasn't so, she realized. Tom Mix, too, had been kind, in his way. Katherine found him terribly handsome and dashing but at the same time detested him for holding them prisoner.

"Yes, well, you are good kids, I guess," Villa said, rising. He reached out and gave a quick playful pinch of Katherine's cheek between his thumb and forefinger, but she instinctively recoiled. Villa turned to Mix. "Señor, I think from now on you should move your camp to my headquarters. I want to personally keep an eye on these kids because they are so nice. It's good to have children around — makes you feel young, you know? And tomorrow we come to a big river, so finally everyone gets a good bath, eh?"

The very word struck music to Katherine's ears, till she wondered how, with all these men . . .

"*Buenas tardes,* everyone," Villa said.

After he'd gone, Katherine lay under her blanket by the fire, gazing at the cold, hard stars. Villa had looked at her in a way she'd only begun to notice but didn't understand. She did, however, understand that he'd looked, that he'd fixed her with a stare, or tried to, anyway. She'd noted the fresh suit, the scrubbed face, the combed hair, even smelled the cheap perfume, and it had somehow made him more human to her, less the brute. She was not attracted to him, of course, but she felt his attraction. Things were changing more quickly in her life than she could often make sense of. Katherine fell asleep in a reverie of confused dreams and musings of cool green New England autumns on horseback as leaves were beginning to turn. As she drifted to sleep, she clutched the little carved cat Villa had whittled for her; but it meant nothing, meant nothing — it was just something to hold on to.

Luckily, the cattle herd was far back from the main body of Villa's troops, even though it was also a long ways from Donita. Johnny Ollas and his brothers were enemies in the midst of the enemy camp, and the fact that they were isolated and less subject to discovery was a good thing. Every day Villa's soldiers would arrive and cut out a couple of cows they were going to butcher. From subtle conversations, Johnny learned that Donita — or at least a woman — was still with Villa's headquarters.

But he had wracked his brain and still hadn't come up with a plan to rescue her and deal with Villa at the same time. He figured there probably would be just one chance —

if that. For the time being, however, he and the cuadrilla were walking very close to the precipice.

Johnny Ollas had so far acted with extreme caution. But one evening Johnny's brother Rigaz did not return to Johnny's camp. He'd been away since morning at the drag end of the cattle drive and hadn't returned for lunch, which wasn't so unusual, because the men often took a little something to eat with them on the trail; but when Rigaz didn't come in at dark, Johnny began to worry. He took Julio and went looking for him. Nothing. Not a trace. They backtracked, but in the dark their search was almost impossible, even with the moon: too many hoofprints from the herd. Johnny came back to the camp, where Gourd Woman had a pot of beans going over the fire and a rack of beef ribs cooking on a spit.

"It's like he just vanished," Johnny said.

"People don't vanish," Gourd Woman replied, "unless they're ghosts."

"I can't believe he'd desert us," Johnny said.

"Maybe, I don't know," said Luis. "Could be he got scared. Being this close to Pancho Villa is a dangerous business."

"You shut up," Julio snarled. "Rigaz ain't scared of nothin'."

"Okay, okay," Johnny said. "Maybe he'll turn up before morning."

"But unless he's a ghost," Gourd Woman

repeated, "he don't just vanish."

At sunrise, Rigaz was still missing. Johnny was apprehensive about getting help, but he did it anyway. The search party Johnny led was composed of a dozen men from Villa's main group. They began working backward, fanning out from the cattle trail on both sides, until about noontime a cry went out and they rode over to find Rigaz's horse grazing alone among some trees. They fanned out again and an hour later found Rigaz. His body was wedged in the crook of a tree, his neck had been broken, and he'd been eviscerated. Johnny felt sick, felt faint, as they moved Rigaz from the tree and laid him on the ground.

Nothing had been taken from Rigaz — not his rifle or pistol or his belt or his watch or his saddle, or his innards, and there was still money in his pockets. This meant it was just plain murder. But who would do this, and why? Johnny and his little group sadly buried their brother, while the others rode back to report the incident. Some took out their weapons and had them at the ready.

Half an hour later Pancho Villa himself appeared on the scene. He wanted to be taken to the site of the killing. Villa seemed highly agitated. In fact, ever since the news was brought to him he'd been thinking of Sanchez's ghost. He got off his horse and studied the ground around the tree where Rigaz had been found. There were no hoofprints, foot-prints, nothing. No clues at all. This worried him further. He solemnly ordered a detachment of soldiers to be sent to flank the herd day and night. Villa wasn't sure what good this would do, but at least it made him feel better. As they rode back past the herd, Villa suddenly jerked his horse up short.

A bunch of steers were standing in an open space by the trail. "What the hell is that?" Villa shouted. He was pointing toward them. In their midst was Casa Grande, with the big set of horns and a great hump on his shoulders, looking at him.

"That is a fighting bull," Villa continued, answering his own question.

"Yes, General, it is," Johnny said darkly. He had his sombrero pulled down over his forehead, petrified that Villa might recognize him from back at Valle del Sol.

"Well, how did he get here?" Villa asked, dumbfounded.

"He was here when we arrived, General," Johnny told him. "He's pretty calm. He's in with those steers. I figured we'd just bring him along with us."

Villa peered at Casa Grande again. "He's a big one, ain't he? That's a fine-looking bull."

"Yes, General, he is," Johnny agreed.

"Well," said Villa, "you take care of him, huh? But don't let no people get near that animal. Do you have any idea of what something like that can do to a man?"

"Yes, General. I told my people to keep clear of him. But he's all right. He's pretty docile around the steers."

Villa snorted and shook his head. It was eerie to him: first a mysterious killing of one of his men, and then to find a fighting bull among his herd. It was like going into a henhouse and finding a wolf. An image of Sanchez swinging from his rope and casting no shadow again came to him. He'd heard strange stories, of dead people changing forms, turning themselves into cats or snakes or birds or fish. Villa was eyeing Casa Grande again when something in the trees on the side of a hill caught his attention. Maybe it was nothing, but it seemed to Villa he'd seen a man on a horse. A large dark man and just a glimpse of a silver saddle. Was this one of his men?

"Are you all right, General?" Johnny asked.

"All right . . . yes. I thought I saw something."

"You want us to go have a look?" Johnny offered. If whatever Villa had seen had anything to do with Rigaz's death, he was ready.

"No — I think it was nothing."

"Well, you want us to keep an eye out — but what for?" Johnny asked.

Villa shook his head wearily and looked up toward the sky. He regretted hanging Sanchez more than ever now. "I don't know," Villa said, "but if you see an old man out there, and old man with a white beard, riding a gray horse . . . you come and tell me at once."

"Yes, General," Johnny said quickly. "Right away."

"On second thought," Villa said, "you better go up there and have a look around now." The sky had turned an ashen gray, through which the sun peered somberly and cast unsettling shadows for an afternoon.

"For the old man on the horse?" Johnny said.

"Yes," replied the general. "If you see him, shoot him."

Johnny rode off toward the hillside, wondering what in hell that was all about. An old man with a beard and a gray horse. Who knew anything out here?

In camp and around the fire, Rigaz's death lay heavily upon them, and they ate their supper without relish. Johnny said, "Listen. I want you to know that from now on I release you from any pledge to go along with this. You want to leave, go home — do it. I understand. I'll tell the sergeant you just went away."

"No," Julio said. "We're here. We're staying." The other two nodded.

"Well, I appreciate it," Johnny said.

"Something evil is out there," Gourd

Woman said. She had been sitting in the shadows, throwing her bones in the dirt.

"What's that supposed to mean?" Johnny said.

"Something is out there. It will return. Bones tell me."

"Bullshit," said Johnny. "Those same bones told you Pancho Villa was in Creel, too — didn't they?"

"Like I said, maybe I didn't throw them right that time."

"So what makes you think you're throwing them right now?"

"I don't know; I got a bad feeling."

When Villa got back to his headquarters, he found more turmoil. At the river crossing, Donita had taken Katherine and Timmy down to the banks. Mix and a couple of his men followed. It was a clear refreshing stream that began in the mountains and was about a hundred yards wide and shallow, with the water gurgling around big rocks. On the sandy banks, they knelt to scoop up handfuls of water to drink, and it was sweet, tasting a little of autumn leaves. Donita and Katherine ached to wade in and scrub themselves clean of trail grime — but how to do it with these people here — or must they bathe in their clothing?

"Okay," said Mix. "We'll ride over behind that little knob there. But remember, you run off now, we're gonna catch you, and there won't be any more bathing or anything. General Villa, he might put all of you in a cage."

Donita and Katherine removed most of their clothes and waded into the stream. Even though there was a chill in the air and the water was icy, it felt wonderful. They passed a bar of soap between them and luxuriated in the bath. Timmy had walked away upstream so as to have his privacy, too, and he sat down in the river and washed himself, then toweled off with his shirt. He sat on the bank for a while, watching the water and wondering what would become of them. He was frightened for his mother and his grandmother; last time he had seen them, they had looked so bad, but Mix continued to reassure him. He wondered about Bomba, too — was he dead? Mix didn't actually know anything about that. And he wondered about Grandpapa and his father and what they were doing to save them. He knew they would do something. They wouldn't just leave them here; in fact, Timmy would not have been surprised to see his father and the Colonel riding up right now to take them home.

Enveloped in these thoughts, Timmy got up and began walking along the riverbank, when he noticed a hole about a foot wide in the dirt. For an instant, when he peered into it, he saw something glimmer in the darkness of the hole, like a jewel. He reached inside to pick it up.

Katherine and Donita finally came out of the water. They would have stayed in longer if it hadn't been so chilly. They dried themselves off with their clothes, dressed, and walked up the bank to sit down when an unearthly shriek split the air.

Mix and his people heard it, too, and came galloping over the rise. Timmy was out of sight and around a bend, but he was screaming so loudly it echoed down the river and across the nearby meadow. Donita and Katherine scrambled up and rushed toward the commotion. Mix had arrived before them and leaped off his horse to grab Timmy, who had been seized on the wrist by a gila monster that had been looking out at him from inside its lair. The gleaming eye had, for an instant, looked like a jewel. Timmy flailed his arm wildly, but the thick coral-and-black-tinted reptile wouldn't let go. Mix grabbed Timmy by the shoulders and dragged him into the water, pressing the arm down so the gila monster would go under. It still wouldn't turn loose.

"Get me a stick!" Mix hollered. Other members of the party had rushed to the riverbank. Someone produced a stick. Mix jerked Timmy's arm out of the water and began beating the creature. It still would not let go. He pried at the gila monster's mouth. Timmy was still screaming awfully, and his eyes were wide with fright and horror. Mix continued to pry. When Donita and Katherine ran up and saw what had happened, Donita put her hands to her mouth and Katherine rushed into the water to help.

Finally Mix managed to get the stick between Timmy's wrist and the jaws of the thing, and when it moved its mouth momentarily to improve its grip he jerked Timmy's wrist from the creature's grasp. The gila monster plopped into the water and drifted away downstream. Several of the men fired at it but missed. Mix carried Timmy to shore; his arm was a bloody mess from the sharp teeth and claws of the monster.

"We've got to get him back to the doctor, now," Mix said. He slung Timmy on his horse and took off at a gallop. Katherine wanted to go, but others restrained her.

"What, what was that?" she cried.

"Gila monster, missy," one of the men said, "least that's what they call 'em over in Sonora. I seen one before."

"He's badly hurt?" Katherine said.

"Yes, miss. That thing's got poison. But Doc'll take care of it, I guess."

"See what you've done?" Katherine growled, losing control. "My little brother might die!" She wasn't just scared, she was furious. They didn't belong here, and it was

437

outlandish, kidnapping people and putting them in situations they didn't know how to cope with. They should be home and going to school and dances . . .

"Doc takes care of a lot of snakebites and such, miss," said the man, "but he's gonna be one sick little boy."

Tears of frustration came to her eyes. Katherine began to sob and turned away.

Bomba had not intended to kill the man from Villa's cattle party, but in his intensity to learn information he'd gone too far. He had shadowed the herd ever since intercepting the soldier who'd been riding Señor Gonzales's horse. Several times he'd tried to catch one of the drovers riding drag off guard, but something always seemed to work against him. For one thing, they had entered the *lomas,* the plains, and he'd had to conceal himself far away behind swales in the landscape or lag far behind, catching up when night fell.

At one point near a stream he saw a canebrake and cut off a long hollow cane stem, which he whittled into a blowgun. Bomba had noticed a few poison frogs along the way, and next time he came upon one, he caught it in a big leaf and scraped off a little of the skin from its back, which was deadly toxic in anything other than tiny doses. As Bomba hung back and shadowed Villa's band, he whittled darts from branches of a hickory tree and later made a paste of water, clay, and a little of the poison, which he put on the tip of the darts. It would be cleaner and quieter than trying to knock somebody off a horse with a knife.

One afternoon another chance presented itself. A man from the cattle party, at the back of the herd, had gotten off his horse to urinate. He seemed to be alone, and Bomba moved stealthily on foot and from about fifty feet, with the man's back to him, put the blowgun to his lips and blew out a dart, which hit the man in the shoulder. The man swatted at the sting, probably thinking it was a bee or wasp.

When he went down face-first in the grass, Bomba dragged him back into the woods. He shook the man and pinched his cheeks to bring him to, and when the man's eyes opened he bent close to him.

"Where the children?" Bomba demanded.

The man blinked. "Huh?"

"Where? Kids?" Bomba said.

Suddenly the man began to struggle and yell. Bomba clapped a hand over his mouth and held him down.

"Where?" he repeated. When he continued to struggle, Bomba lifted him off the ground and wedged him into the fork of a tree. He stood in front of him and demanded again, "Where children?"

When the man still fought back, Bomba grabbed him by the head and jerked it back. It was meant only to make him answer, but to his surprise Bomba heard a loud crack as a vertebra snapped and the man went limp. Bomba lifted the head and stared into his lifeless eyes. The man took a few more breaths, then stopped breathing. Bomba stepped back, angry at himself. He might have learned something from this man. The cattle herd had moved on, so just the two of them were in the quiet of the woods. No birds sang, no breeze blew. He walked around the tree where the man's body was wedged. Then he lifted up the man's uniform shirt. The skin was beginning to pale and turn gray.

Bomba took out his knife and made a quick incision in the side. He peeled back the skin and continued to cut until he saw the liver. It had been the custom of his people that eating the liver of your enemy made you invincible. Bomba had been living in civilization now for twenty-five years, and he knew better, but these were desperate times that called for desperate measures. He looked at the liver and was within an inch of cutting it out, but something stopped him. Here he was, a grown man, actually thinking about eating the liver of a man he'd just killed. He was suddenly horrified, and backed away from the dead body. He could never look the Colonel in the eye again, or Mrs. Shaughnessy, or Arthur or Xenia, or any of them, including the children, if he had done that. He felt ashamed. Meanwhile, the wound in his shoulder continued to fester.

FORTY

The train in which the Colonel and his party rode south was halfway to Chihuahua City when they encountered a dreadful spectacle. Rounding a curve, they could see ahead of them a black spot far down the tracks that slowly turned into the scorched hulks of a locomotive and many railcars lying in a ditch. As they got nearer, they saw objects dangling from the telegraph poles beside the tracks.

These turned out to be the bodies of soldiers, hanged, wearing the plain white peasant uniforms of Villa's army, three or four bodies to a pole. The train slowed while everybody looked out the windows in revulsion. The bodies were perfectly mummified in the rarefied air of the desert plateau. Vultures flapped up as the train rolled by and resettled after it passed. There were bodies as far as the eye could see.

"Good God," croaked the Colonel; his stomach turned. Never, even in war, had the Colonel encountered such a sight. Many in the train drew away from the windows and sat in silence. Finally, Cowboy Bob said, "Well, the Federales don't give no quarter, Colonel. I expect them people was prisoners taken at the battle, or maybe the Federales captured their train."

"Sheer barbarism," Shaughnessy muttered.

"They all do it," said Death Valley Slim. "Don't think no more about it than squashing a cockroach."

Strucker for once seemed subdued, and chewed on the nail of his thumb. He was dressed in a riding jacket and highly polished black boots. Before he left El Paso he'd spied a blooming camellia bush outside the Toltec, and had plucked a lush red blossom for his boutonniere.

"You still want to do business with these people?" Arthur asked. They were seated next to each other on the train, an arrangement that had not made Arthur particularly happy; he'd wanted to be alone, with so many things on his mind.

"Their cruelty is studied, reminiscent of Golgotha," Strucker declared in his guttural Prussian accent. "Staggering, isn't it, to believe that the same civilized and cultured people I met with in Mexico City two weeks ago are capable of this? Their mannerly airs must all be a facade."

Arthur barely paid attention to what the German was saying; he was thinking that

443

since the trains were running again, Xenia and his mother would also pass by this grisly scene on their way up to El Paso from Valle del Sol, and he wished for God's sake someone would come and take these bodies down.

When the sun began to sink a few hours later, Death Valley Slim told the Colonel they had reached the closest point to the mountains where he thought Villa would be hiding. When the train stopped, they stepped out onto a forlorn waste; not a house or living thing was to be seen. The unloading of the horses, wagons, and equipment took half an hour; then the train pulled away, leaving them all standing in a desert dotted with scrub. There was still a little daylight left and the Colonel, anxious to get someplace other than this, directed them to move out — thirty-four men on horseback, thirty-one pack animals, one large and three small wagons.

As Shaughnessy's Partisan Rangers began to move westward, someone looked into the blue and cloudless sky.

"Hey, look there!"

Everyone near him looked up.

"What is that?"

"I'm a son-of-a-gun," cried Cowboy Bob. "It's pelicans."

"Pelicans — impossible," said the Colonel.

They were three hundred miles from the nearest large body of water, but a flight of a dozen or so white pelicans soared low above them.

"What could they be doing here?" the Colonel wondered.

"Maybe they got lost," Bob offered.

The flock of pelicans swooped overhead, then turned gracefully to the north against the deep blue sky so that the sun shone golden off their white feathers and yellowish legs.

Slim figured the pelicans were an omen but didn't know what kind. Some others of the party talked about it that night over their campfires. Strucker didn't believe in that sort of thing, but he didn't like what he had seen so far. The hanging bodies had unnerved him.

Arthur felt the powerful rib muscles of the horse between his legs and ignored last night's talk about the pelicans. In spite of everything, he was anxious to get going, too, closer to his children with every step of the animal. All day a fury had been building in him, against Villa, against Mick Martin, against his father, too, for getting them into this mess. His anger was not frustrating, however, but somehow made him feel stronger, and he suddenly thought of a line he'd learned long ago in school: "If the sun insults me I will strike it down." Bold words, perhaps, here in the Mexican desert thousands of miles from anyplace, but the fury swooped down on him like an evil genie that would not let him be.

By the following evening, the desert country turned into rolling plains, which were covered with tall grasses that swayed easily in the light breeze. Then they came to an abandoned apple orchard where a dilapidated adobe house lay in ruins and the trees were overgrown and moldy. Far in the distance loomed the Sierra Madre, some peaks already snow-capped in the late autumn. Arthur made a point of sticking close to Bob and Slim, who were riding out ahead. Bob carried a large sinister-looking bullwhip on his saddle and Arthur asked him about it.

"It's something I learned when I was a kid," Bob said. "You know how it is, you're young and you're bored and so you just take something up." He unlimbered the black leather whip and snapped it two or three times. "I learned to plait my own out of hides."

"See that over there?" Bob said. He nodded to a tree about fifteen feet away with a dozen or so overripe apples on it. "Name one."

"Name one what?" Arthur asked.

"Apple. Which one you got in mind?"

Arthur looked puzzled. "I don't understand."

"Pick a apple," Bob told him, "on that there tree."

"All right, the one on the top, at the left."

Bob swung the whip in two or three long swaths to get it fully uncoiled and under control, then lashed out with a startling crack and the apple Arthur had named simply disintegrated.

"Damn!" Arthur yelped.

Cowboy Bob smiled and re-coiled his whip. "I used to snap off cigarettes from a guy's mouth at rodeos," he said. "Had to make a deal with him, though — he got two-thirds of the take and I got one. Seemed fair enough."

"Think you could teach me to do that?" Arthur asked. Before they left El Paso, Cowboy Bob had already begun giving Arthur shooting lessons and teaching him the fast draw.

"I reckon so," Bob said, "provided you apply yourself."

Bob was still wearing his red flannel buttondown cowboy shirt and Arthur asked him, "Aren't you worried that shirt stands out too much? You might get shot."

"I already was," Bob told him. "Not in this shirt, but another red one. Since it didn't kill me, I figure it brings me good luck."

One afternoon as they passed alongside a lake, the Colonel took his fancy Purdey shotgun and killed a number of ducks for dinner. As he was watching Ah Dong roast the ducks, the Colonel inveighed against the British notion of sportsmanship.

"The English build the world's finest shot-guns but they're vulgar in the use of them," Colonel Shaughnessy announced. "Not in their own country, mind you, but when they travel to somebody else's they'll go out with five cheap guns apiece and shoot fowl until the barrels get too hot to handle — then just leave the birds lying on the ground for crow's bait and ants."

"We did the same thing to the passenger pigeons in our country a while back," Arthur reminded him.

"Yes," said the Colonel, "but at least we learned our lesson. When we kill something now, we eat it."

"You didn't eat that elephant you shot, did you, Papa?" said Arthur, unable to resist.

"Somebody did," the Colonel retorted. "I took the head back to be stuffed, and the rest fed an entire native village for a month, I expect."

"What's it like, Colonel, shootin' a elephant?" Bob asked.

"About like shooting a cow, I guess, except it's about ten times as big and can stomp you to mush."

Colonel Shaughnessy respected this rough cowboy but also knew the man had never dealt with anything like a bull elephant in the wild. There were various forms of courage, but he, in fact, had faced down such a beast and conquered it — which was not something to be sniffed at. Something in Bob's tone made the Colonel wonder if Cowboy Bob was trying to make fun of him.

"Hummmm," Bob replied, "I don't much fancy hunting things that can hunt me back."

The old guy was tough, Bob thought, he'd give him that, but he still couldn't see how killing a big old elephant with a high-powered rifle made you a hero. People like the Colonel lived in a different world. But what was going to transpire over the next few days, or weeks, or months, now, that was going to be the test of the thing. That thought sobered Bob and made him wonder what he was doing here, except for the good wages, which he couldn't spend anyway if he ended up like one of those devils swinging from the telegraph poles.

"Well, what do you think we're doing *here*?" Arthur asked Bob in the awkward silence. "We're certainly hunting something that can hunt us back."

"It's different," interjected the Colonel. "This is a manhunt."

There was a bemused aspect in Slim's snaggletoothed grin. "Colonel, we kill ol' Pancho Villa, you gonna eat *him*?" he asked tentatively.

"I might," the Colonel grunted. "He ate my bull, didn't he?"

FORTY-ONE

Days later the Colonel's party was on the high plains and the cold had firmly set in. The mountains were more ominous now and loomed much higher as the travelers came near. Sometimes there were tall stands of ponderosa pine or groves of scrub oak, but mostly the plains were an endless stretch of desolation, with occasional wagon tracks leading nowhere in the dusty soil. During the day, Bob worked with Arthur on his pistol handling, and he was impressed; Arthur was becoming a highly competent fast-draw man, although in these days and times, the use, and art, of the fast-draw had almost vanished, except for Wild West shows.

Rifles were aimed using one eye, but with shotguns and pistols the weapon was simply "pointed" with both eyes open. Bob's trick, which he taught to Arthur, was making it all-important to take your time and set your body and your mind right, before firing. No jiggling, no waving the pistol, a firm wrist and steady hand. It didn't matter how fast you could get the pistol out of its holster if your shots went wild.

Arthur was a quick learner and, to Bob's surprise, actually seemed to enjoy learning this skill, though Bob understood too well that Arthur wasn't in this for the sheer sport of it. At one place Bob had collected a heap of dried wild sheep dung the size of small pancakes, which he kept in a sack slung around his saddle horn. From time to time he'd lag behind, then cry out, "Watch it!" and sail one of the turds into the air. Arthur had gotten quite good at hitting them.

Bob also taught Arthur the art of roping and how to keep his knife honed to a razor's sharpness. They worked with the bullwhip, too. Bob had some spare whips in his baggage, and for hours on end, as they plodded along, Arthur would sit in the saddle snapping the whip at objects along the trail, exploding leaves and knocking small stones sky-high. Arthur said, "You ready to put a cigarette in your mouth and let me cut it in two?"

"I don't smoke," Bob told him.

"Well, how about a stick?"

"I don't put sticks in my mouth, either," Bob said casually. "Birds shit on 'em."

"Then how am I going to find out if I'm really good?" Arthur joked.

"I'll let you know," Bob said, "trust me."

At night by the campfire Slim would bring out an old guitar and sing and, to everyone's surprise, he had a nice tenor voice. He'd belt out cowboy songs and love songs and songs about railroads and the olden days. The Colonel was delighted.

"You ought to form a dance band," he said. "You've got a grand voice."

"Takes money, and I ain't got any," Slim replied. But in fact a band was always a dream he'd had. Prospecting, cattle punching, doing odd jobs was all he'd known except for the army, and he was too old for that now anyway. He'd worked on a notion for years — to get a little band together and play the towns from El Paso to Deeming, New Mexico, to Las Cruces. He didn't want much and had never featured playing in cities like Dallas or Houston or San Antone, but there along the west Texas border he figured the cowboys and soldiers might come to places to hear a little music as well as get drunk, play cards, fight, and spend money on women. And if that was so, the proprietors might pay him a nice little fee to perform.

Slim knew just what kind of band he wanted, too: piano, fiddle, dobro, and himself on guitar, and he had the perfect name: Death Valley Slim and the Ghost Riders. But like everything else, this had always been beyond his reach. Years ago he'd been in love, but she actually laughed at him and his soldier's pay. So he quit the army and went prospecting in the Sierra Madre, but by then the American mining companies had sewn up all the ore prospects in Mexico. After eight years Slim turned up back in El Paso, busted out like a pinpricked balloon.

Singing and playing was the one thing Slim did well; he even liked to make up his own songs, which he sang by memory on dismal nights in the mountains or alone in his cheap El Paso flophouse; he enjoyed his own voice and the thoughts he put into his music but it didn't put any money in his pocket. So for Slim, at least, this ridiculous excursion was a matter of necessity, since he was dead broke again.

As Slim's music filled the sweet air, Strucker was resting full-length on the ground with his head propped up by his saddle, and was drinking from one of the bottles of expensive gin he'd brought along. He had no intention of lowering himself to anything as vile as tequila, mescal, or, God forbid, pulque.

"Maybe Colonel Shaughnessy can set you up when this is over," Strucker told Slim. "You could entertain at his fashionable parties." The German had stuck close by the Colonel since they had left the train. Riding together, they would talk about yachting, shooting, horse racing, and the latest polar expeditions. Rarely did the European war enter the conversation, and Strucker was grateful the Colonel didn't bring it up, because he hated having to prevaricate and apologize for his country and his kaiser. Americans, it seemed, were invariably on the side of the British and French.

"I might just set Slim up, at that," the Colonel said effusively, "provided he can learn to play waltzes."

Slim got up and walked from the fire to the edge of the darkness to relieve himself. He'd listened to these two big shots talk about him, and for a moment it seemed like something real. Then he came to his senses. I can play waltzes; I can play damn good waltzes you two old goat-ropers would have trouble dancin' to. That was what he thought.

Earlier, the Colonel had made a remark Strucker found interesting. The talk had turned to the general situation of Villa and the children, when the Colonel recounted his conversation with the president.

"He's afraid of starting a war down here," the Colonel announced contemptuously, "and so he lets murderers and bandits abduct innocent Americans while our own army squats at the border drinking whiskey and visiting prostitutes. I gave that man twenty-five thousand to ensure Roosevelt's defeat, and this is my reward? I wish I had that money back."

"Then what if Mexico should attack

America?" Strucker suddenly asked. The idea came to him seemingly from the thinness of the air around them. His theory so far had been to work Mexico into a position where it might provoke the United States into attacking *Mexico.* But here he saw the reverse; a novel plot.

"They wouldn't dare," Shaughnessy said. "They're content attacking defenseless U.S. citizens right here in their own country."

Arthur thought the conversation was something of a joke; there was no diplomacy associated with kidnapping the children. It was sheer thuggery, and the worst kind of cruelty for the parents.

"Yes, but what if they did?" Strucker went on. "What if for some reason Pancho Villa decided to attack American positions at the border? Wouldn't your President Wilson then commit to an act of war?"

Arthur looked closely at the German. He could almost see his mind racing, ticking, drawing conclusions — if this happened, thus and so would follow. He could tell a plan of some sort was forming. Strucker was devious, and might even be dangerous, of that Arthur was sure.

"I don't see how he could help it," the Colonel replied. "But I don't think Villa's fool enough to do that."

"Maybe, maybe not," Strucker said. "When I was on the train from California I read a news story that quoted Villa as saying the Americans were now his enemies. That he was going to confiscate their properties, that he would brook no interference from them."

"So what? He's been saying that for a while."

"Suppose somebody could get to him? Persuade him that he must also attack the Americans in America, because if he does, and the American army enters Mexico, the Mexican government would feel compelled to fight them. And that this would be an impeccable stroke of luck for Villa because his enemies would then be fighting the Americans and not fighting him, correct?"

"I suppose so," agreed the Colonel.

Arthur could scarcely believe his ears. The German was actually forming a scheme to draw the United States into a war with Mexico.

"And for you, too, perhaps a stroke of luck," the German continued, "because it would then get the American army down here in Mexico, and if they find Villa, they would probably also find your grandchildren."

"Theoretically," said the Colonel, slightly confused. "But who could convince him of such a thing?"

"Me, perhaps," Strucker replied.

"You? Why you?"

"Because I am a disinterested party," the German replied. "He would have no reason to distrust me. I also have, let us say, some resources which I could put at Villa's disposal. That might tip the scales."

Arthur somehow doubted the German's veracity.

"Well, I don't know," the Colonel said hesitantly. It sounded like a complicated — almost crackpot — scheme and difficult to comprehend.

"It may be you're on to something, Strucker," the Colonel said, "but we need to try to find the bastard first."

Next day around dusk, the Colonel's party came upon a small village of widows and orphans. Some of Pancho Villa's soldiers had swung through it days earlier and the villagers, thinking they were bandits, made the mistake of firing shots at them at first. For this they paid a high price. Almost all the men and some of the women had been ridden down, captured, and killed in the typical mayhem: flayed alive, hung, shot, stabbed, sworded, burned, dragged through the streets behind horses, thrown headfirst into wells. The Apaches did as much a generation or two earlier and Villa's Chihuahua Mexicans had merely refined their techniques.

Many of the bodies remained unburied and the stench hovered as an unholy fog. Even so, they all noticed that this village seemed fairly prosperous compared with others they'd seen: the roofs of the houses were made of corrugated zinc instead of straw and the foundations were sturdier. There were large livestock pens — empty now thanks to Villa's band — which had obviously held sheep, pigs, cattle, and horses. The reason for such affluence, they soon learned, was that a large mining smelter was located nearby, where the men once worked for good wages, but Villa had shut this down, too, and run off all the American engineers.

Even after the horrors he'd witnessed on the train trip, Arthur was appalled by what he saw in the village.

"It's worse than the French Revolution," the Colonel gasped. "These people kill everybody, not just the rich or landed. They murder their prisoners, then they go for the poor. At least in America we knew how to throw a revolution. We were never savages."

"Nothing I've seen in Europe remotely compares with this," Strucker agreed, breaking his rule of silence on the European war. "It's odd, isn't it, that all these Mexicans claim to be fighting for a republic?"

The Colonel wiped his nose with his bandanna. The stench hung so heavily he could almost grab it with his hands. He was tired but this also made him sick. Not only that, the scene struck a new dagger of fear in him for the fate of his grandchildren and made him feel guiltier. Back along the train tracks, he'd borne witness to what the Federals would do to soldiers, but if Pancho Villa would condone this grossness with civilians, then he was madman as well.

The Colonel shook his head and said to Strucker, "If these people can ever govern themselves, then our whole theory of democracy must be wrong."

As Arthur reflected on this, a small dirty girl came up beside his horse — little more than a rag, a bone, and a hank of hair, her eyes brimming with tears. She looked up at Arthur and began talking, and there was something so pathetically earnest in her expression that he motioned for Cowboy Bob to come over, since he savvied Mexican as well or even better than Slim did.

"What's she saying?" Arthur asked.

Bob leaned down to the girl and said, *"Qué dice, señorita?"*

She responded in a bewildered, sorrowful tone. Bob nodded and turned to Arthur. "She says, 'Why don't I have a ma?' "

Arthur let out a breath and looked away toward the darkening distant mountains. The girls words stung him like a hot needle; he felt an instinct to get down and take her up into his arms and hug her; tell her it was going to be all right, even though he knew it wasn't, and never would be. Instead, he reached into his pocket and pulled out a five-dollar gold piece and handed it down to the child. As if that would do any good. She looked at it, then back at Arthur.

"Gracias," she said, clutching the coin against her breast.

He gave a little wave and eased his horse away, feeling, with everything else that was upon him, as if he were trapped in some lurid nightmare. He turned in the saddle; she was examining the gold piece, which was American, and, Arthur thought, she probably didn't even know what it was.

They rode out of the village soon afterward. Arthur, Bob, Slim, and Crosswinds Charlie set out to find a suitable spot for the Colonel's main party to camp for the night, away from this charnel place. They had gone a short distance along a road out of town when they began to smell a foul aroma. Presently they came upon a band of Mexican men camped in the woods, afraid to return to the village.

These men had found half of a rusty oil drum to use for a cauldron, placed it on some rocks, and lit a fire beneath it. The fire consisted of anything that would burn: old shoes, leaves, sticks, corncobs, tattered and bloody clothes, empty cartridge boxes, along with cow, sheep, and goat patties and what looked like the dismembered parts of a corpse — all of which they kept in a nearby pile to keep the blaze going.

Crosswinds Charlie rode over and peered

into the cauldron. The dull, compliant, and utterly wretched Mexicans gaped up at him, their dirt-streaked faces flickering with the orange glow of the fire. He looked closer and saw a filthy brown liquid was boiling. Every so often Charlie saw what he took for a root or part of an onion or pepper; then, to his revulsion, the cauldron's main ingredient boiled to the surface.

By then Arthur and Cowboy Bob had ridden over and were staring into the cauldron as well. The Mexicans had apparently caught for their supper a large armadillo. Bob saw the fleshy reddish claws and tail and scaly shell as the thing bobbed slowly to the surface, sank, then boiled back up again, roiling slowly in the liquid before it disappeared yet once more. They had apparently boiled it alive.

Wanting to be polite, Bob asked the men in Spanish, "What are you fellows having for dinner?"

"Stew," one of them replied sullenly.

"What *is* that thing?" Charlie asked.

"Armadillo," Death Valley Slim answered him. "It lives in holes with owls and snakes."

"They mean to eat it?"

"Or starve," offered Bob.

They rode on. Arthur felt his stomach turn once more. To him it seemed like they had somehow stepped out of the bounds of civilization. He pulled his hat down lower on

461

his forehead. So this is what comes of glorious revolutions, he thought. He looked back. One of the Mexicans seemed to be giving him a dirty gesture.

Several days later, all the while climbing higher through the foothills, Shaughnessy's Partisan Rangers finally reached the mountains. They had entered a broad and deserted valley sandwiched between towering peaks covered with pines and firs, while at the lower altitudes there were aspens and birches that still had a few orange and gold leaves clinging on.

A pretty little brook meandered down the center, babbling between rocks. It looked like it might contain trout. The valley floor consisted of a golden brown sedgelike grass reminiscent to the Colonel of quail hunting plantations in southern Georgia. None of it reminded him much of Mexico at all. It was more like Wyoming or Montana in autumn, or, for that matter, southern Georgia in February, without the mountains.

He saw deer darting at the edges of the trees, and flocks of doves flushed skyward as his men passed by in columns of twos and threes down a wide dirt path in the center of the valley. The path seemed to lead directly into the mountains, now unfolded as sinister peaks grasping up toward a darkening blue

462

sky; at their base, several miles distant, were enormous rock piles of boulders from long-ago slides that, from a distance, took on the appearance of shattered teeth.

"Let me ask you something, Arthur," Bob said. "What's it like growing up rich?"

"Beats me," Arthur told him. They were riding side by side in the lovely valley. There was not a cloud in the sky and the place seemed almost enchanted.

"C'mon, I'm curious. I mean, did you go on big steamship trips and have a private railroad car and everything?"

"I'd rather hear about you," Arthur said. "We can talk about me later. Where'd you grow up?" Arthur didn't feel much like talking about himself. He'd been so preoccupied with his worries about the children and Xenia that talking about almost anything was a chore. He'd rather just ask questions and listen.

"Amarillo," said Bob. "It was just an ol' cow town; still is."

"What did your father do?"

"Punched cows till he got killed by a wild horse he was tryin' to break. He would've lived, except it throwed him over the fence and he landed headfirst on the only rock within a hundred feet of the corral. It was buried pretty deep in the ground and I guess they decided it was too much trouble to move. After Pa got killed, they moved it, though."

"That must have been hard." At least he had never had to face the death of a parent.

"I was just six, so I don't much remember him. Mama said he'd gone to God. It was a comfort at the time."

"What about your mother?"

"She didn't do well after that. Took in washing and did some piecework. We had to move in with my grandma. Then she got sick with consumption. Died when I was nine. That's when I went to work."

Arthur felt himself wince. "Doing what?" They were crossing the little stream that meandered back and forth across the valley floor. Arthur and Bob stopped in the middle to let their horses drink.

"Cleaning out stalls and livestock pens. I imagine I've shoveled more shit in my day than most."

"Did you go to school?"

"Up till then I did. Afterward, there wadn't no time, I guess."

"Well," Arthur said, "I've always noticed you reading when we get to camp. You must have been taught pretty well."

"Yeah, I read all the time. Trouble is, it's the same ol' books. I ain't got but four. Mostly I read 'em over and over. I'm partial to that one called *The Virginian,* but when you think about it, it's mostly a lot of crap."

"Why's that?"

"Well, for one thing, it skips over the rough parts of a cowhand's life. But that's okay, a cowhand don't need to be reminded of most of it anyway, I guess. Sort of makes it seem glamorous, even."

"It's probably a lot more glamorous than growing up rich," Arthur said.

"I wouldn't know. Say, you still ain't told me about that."

"What?"

"Growin' up rich. How was it?"

"I wouldn't know, either," Arthur said. "I grew up in an orphanage."

"You what?"

"That's right. Until I was nine; then the Colonel and his wife came and got me."

"Well, if that don't beat everything! Same age as I was made a orphan, you got yourself a family!"

Riding alongside Strucker, the Colonel returned to the subject of an American war with Mexico, about which he had some notions of his own. Before leaving El Paso, he'd sent a confidential wire to William Randolph Hearst telling him the situation in hopes the Hearst newspapers would kindle a fire under President Wilson to intervene. He had not, however, told Hearst of the kidnappings or of his plan to go after Villa personally, since for obvious reasons he didn't wish that news to become public. Instead he relied on Hearst's sense of greed, telling him he was in danger of losing his own vast Mexican holdings.

"Hearst got us Cuba," the Colonel continued. "Now let's see if he can get us Mexico, too."

"I didn't know a man could be so powerful who just published newspapers," the German remarked. "It's not that way in my country."

"Well, he is, the old parvenu," the Colonel responded disingenuously. "Why, my father was a United States senator when his family were digging up worms to sell." In fact, the Colonel's father had made his fortune not much earlier than the Hearsts, but it made him feel better telling it his way. "Still," Shaughnessy said, "I give it to him, he's built an empire on gossip and slander and the fear of the people."

Strucker was taken aback by the Colonel's contempt of the famous publisher, but tried not to show it. "Is he not an honest man?"

"Oh, yes, he has integrity, of course. He's actually a decent sort, too, but pompous. He believes his own bullshit and when he doesn't get his way he throws a tantrum like a child, except that in his case he throws it in front of twenty million readers."

Integrity or not, Hearst had broken Colonel Shaughnessy's confidentiality request immediately after getting his telegram. He sent one of his reporters to El Paso to find out more, and when the reporter informed Hearst that the Colonel had gone after Villa's band because they'd kidnapped his grandchildren, Hearst correctly smelled a sensational story.

They rode on in silence for a while and the Colonel became preoccupied with thoughts of long ago. This valley was a place such as he would have liked to take a girl; Beatie in the old days. She was lovely and smiling then, adventurous, too; now she'd become tiresome and a scold. He wondered how that had happened. He figured it had somehow started when she stopped going to baseball games with him. He didn't think he'd changed much himself, except to get a little wiser and a lot richer. Yes, he'd had other women, including the showgirl Beatie had found him out on, but it had meant nothing — a fling. He wished he could bring Beatie back to her old self. He didn't need beauty anymore; at his age he'd settle for real companionship.

Arthur's thoughts, too, were influenced by the pastoral wilds of the place. He regretted not having more time with Xenia before all these troubles began. He hadn't been a very good husband, being so much in Chicago, and he knew he had sulked around her salon to the point of peevishness.

He determined to change that, once this was over and he had settled with Mick. He looked back at the column of men and horses winding along behind them, which suddenly reminded him of a host of pilgrims, even crusaders on a sacred quest: the most vigorous cowboys, rovers, and mountain men available in El Paso, plus a few oddities like Crosswinds Charlie and Ah Dong. But all in all, Arthur thought, they were a sturdy bunch, men who rode tall in the saddle; men to be proud of. Armed and dangerous.

As the afternoon wore on, a strange black storm cloud rose without warning over the mountains to the west and lowered on the valley ahead with distant bolts of lightning and thunder. Arthur pointed it out to his father, who'd been riding behind them.

He cast his eyes upward and intoned, "Deliver us, please, from immoderate weather!"

The sky directly above remained clear as the storm from the west bore down, and the riders picked up their pace to a trot. Then dark thunderheads began to build to the east as well, towering high over the mountain peaks, and it wasn't long before these, too, began boiling into the little valley so as to converge with the tempest racing toward them from the west. Stranger still, the sky overhead was bright and blue as the tempests closed in on them from opposite directions. Soon they became bathed in a strange orange glow.

Bob said to Arthur, "I don't like the looks

of this. Never seen nothin' like it, but they say anything can happen in these mountains." He began motioning for everyone to hurry up. "Big storm comin'! Run, now!" Cowboy Bob yelled, pointing to a narrow gap in the boulders ahead.

Just then the two storms collided and mingled overhead with tremendous fury. Lightning lit up the sky while thunder crashed and echoed up and down the mountain walls. Breathtaking bursts of frigid air and electricity raised the hairs on men's necks.

Horses began to rear and plunge and the men had trouble controlling them. The pack burros balked and screamed. One of the wagons overturned. Then huge flakes of wet snow and bites of hail burst down upon them, too. Arthur thought it was like entering the maw of a netherworld. He looked behind for a moment, back to where they had come from. The storm was closing in fast there as well, but the sun was still shining, and to his amazement a big rainbow arced across the valley floor.

If this was an omen, Arthur didn't know what to make of it, but he wasn't a man of omens anyway. One thing he'd learned so far, though — in this land, peace and beauty could vanish as soon as they appeared.

FORTY-TWO

Timmy's gila monster bite was worse than they'd feared. It wasn't just a fang bite that a snake might make; instead, while injecting its venom, the monster had gnawed and chewed Timmy's arm, leaving deep gashes and a septic wound. Villa's doctor abraded the lacerations, pared away the torn flesh, and administered some kind of antiseptic powder, plus a native remedy extracted from a cactus plant. The doctor poured some ether on a cloth and placed it over Timmy's face during the procedure, and when he woke up he was both nauseated from the anesthetic and in pain from the bite.

Villa had Timmy placed in one of the little ammunition wagons and told the doctor to ride with him. Katherine was in the wagon, too, and Tom Mix rode behind. As Villa's troop wound its way through tall forests of pines and upward across rolling meadows and steep ravines, Timmy developed a fever, and after a few days his swollen arm had turned from pink, to red, to grayish purple. The doctor periodically pared away more flesh when he changed the bandages, so much so that finally he was forced to loosely stitch up the wounds.

Katherine held Timmy's good hand and wiped his tears and perspiration and clenched her teeth. The doctor was a young Mexican of Spanish extraction and had graduated from medical school in Mexico City only two years earlier. He was sympathetic toward Katherine and devoted all his energies ministering to Tim, but Katherine was not placated. She had begun for the first time to think that Timmy might actually die and, for that matter, herself, too. All this time she had remained convinced that any day her father and grandfather would come to their rescue, but as time went by this hope faded. She said her "Now I lay me down to sleep" prayer every night and the words began to take on a new but hollow meaning. At one point the doctor said, "He may have to lose that arm, you know."

Katherine merely stared at him with a steely look in her eyes. At night, when they camped, Mix and Villa spent time with Timmy, and so did Reed and Bierce.

"He needs to be got to a proper hospital," Bierce said one evening.

"Well, there's not any around here," Villa replied, "but he's in good hands."

"He's out in the open air," Bierce responded. "That's bad enough in itself. How far is the closest hospital?"

Villa was gazing upward at the tall purplish brown mountains that had darkened in the gathering gloom of night. He shook his head. "He's better off here with us. It's too far."

"Well, where is it?" Bierce persisted.

"Up over the border, in the United States. El Paso is the closest that I know of with a hospital."

"Well, can't somebody take him down to where there's a train? He might die."

"We're headed that way. He'll come with us. Doc'll see to him. He knows about these things." Villa had his back to Bierce and there was a tone in the general's voice that indicated he was not in a mood for discussion.

"What does the doctor say about it?" Bierce continued.

"Nothing," Villa replied, walking off toward his tent.

Tom Mix had told the cook to make up some sort of beef broth and he brought a bowl of it to Katherine to give to Tim.

"I'm sorry about this," he said. "It's one of those things out here. He'll be okay. Doc knows what he's doing."

"He'll die, or lose his arm," Katherine said icily. She had lifted Timmy's head a bit and was able to force a little of the broth between his lips. She was exhausted and had only slept a few hours at a time since the incident. It seemed like years since their capture; she'd made a calendar and kept notes in it. It was just a few weeks till her thirteenth birthday. Her parents had promised her a big party. And now here she was, almost getting used to things, bad as they were.

"Look, the general isn't going to let anything happen to your brother. I promise you," Mix said.

"How do you know that? You said you just do what you're told. If you were a real man, you would set us free."

Mix had no answer for this. Something in him told him she was in the right. For the past several weeks Mix had begun to feel he had taken a wrong turn when he joined Villa, and had begun to think of getting away.

Reed and Bierce had been seated on a log by the fire, listening to the conversation. Bierce started to interrupt but decided against it. He understood that the girl was upset, and there was no good reason to make it worse. He got up and went to his place at another campfire. Reed followed him. This was a miserable situation and he thought the old man might have an idea.

"Here," Katherine said, handing Mix back the bowl of broth. Timmy had gotten down all he could.

"Like I said, it's going to be all right."

Katherine lay down next to Timmy and

pulled her blanket over herself, turning away from the fire, but not to sleep. With her eyes shut, she could hear the horses snorting, tethered in the woods. Her heart felt gripped and she wanted to cry but forced herself not to.

"You know, Robinson, if I were you, I'd be a little careful how you speak with Villa. He's known to have a temper," Reed said when they were out of earshot of the camp.

"So I've heard," Bierce replied.

"Well, sometimes you seem to be trying to provoke him," Reed continued. They had sat down on some rocks in the darkness. The wind had come up again, a little chilly. Bierce adjusted his hat to keep his head warm. He knew from experience that when your head gets cold, everything in your body gets cold. He hadn't expected cold in Mexico.

"How's that?"

"Arguing with him. I think there's a point when he might explode. He's got a lot on his mind."

"Obviously it's not about that boy," Bierce shot back. "That boy's in trouble, and you damn well know it."

"Sure I do, but there's nothing we can do about it."

"Not while Villa is holding him for ransom," Bierce said.

"What makes you say that?" said Reed.

"You know good and well that's what he's doing. He doesn't have those kids along for their safety — I don't care what he says. He's famous for kidnapping people, and from what I understand of it, their family's got a hay load of money."

"Yes, the Shaughnessys," Reed said patronizingly, "they own railroads."

"Exactly," said Bierce.

"And from what the girl says," Reed continued, "they own a huge chunk of Mexico, too, which I expect they got for practically nothing and enslave the peons on it."

"There's no slavery in Mexico," Bierce reminded him.

"There's about the same thing when you have an entire class of people dependent on one big landholder."

"Why, Mr. Reed, you sound like a socialist."

"I am," Reed said proudly as he stood up and dusted the seat of his trousers.

Way back at the tail end of the caravan, Johnny Ollas and his people huddled around their fire, too. A cold wind was whipping in from the northeast and they were camped in an unsheltered meadow with the herd. Clouds had moved across the sky, blotting the tops of the mountain peaks, and gauzy mists began to descend. A pall of despondence had hung over them since the death of

Rigaz, and Johnny knew the deeper they went into the Sierra Madre wastelands, the harder it would be to rescue Donita.

"I've got to make his ear twitch," Johnny said glumly. Julio, Luis, and Rafael knew what he meant, but Gourd Woman didn't.

"I bet his ears would twitch to hear you talking now," she said.

"Just get him in his *querencia*," Johnny continued. "I can't kill him now, I know that. It would probably be too difficult. But I think I saw something that day when Rigaz died, when he came up and found out about that fighting bull. It was a look in his eyes; the way Villa was looking around at everything, talking about an old man on a horse, like deep down he's scared of something."

"Like he seen a ghost maybe," Julio said.

"He ain't expecting it from the inside," Johnny said. "I imagine he's always expecting it from the outside. And I sure don't think he's expecting it from us. So I think maybe we give it to him both ways. It has to be a perfect thing."

"You got an idea, then, boss?" Rafael asked.

"Not exactly, but soon," Johnny replied. "May be anytime."

"So you gonna fight him like in a bullring or something, then?" said Gourd Woman.

"Yeah, like I told you, it's the only way I know how." It would have to be a neat trick, Johnny knew, but if he could taunt Villa, drive him crazy, then the general might become so enraged that he would charge straight and blind like he was in traces. That's when the chance would come.

For the next week Villa's troops climbed upward until they were in the high sierras where the air was thin and the pines and firs sparser, and a few times it began to snow. Several times they spotted bear sign, and once someone reported a mountain lion. Surprisingly, Timmy's arm began to improve. It might have been the clear, thin air, or the drugs and potions the doctor was administering, or perhaps the venom had simply run its course, but finally he was able to sit up and take food, and his spirits improved; and so, likewise, did Katherine's. Villa had brought along with his caravan half a dozen of his fighting cocks, which rode in cages in the back of one of the ammunition wagons. He'd also brought along a cage of hens to keep the cocks happy, and each morning he made sure that eggs from these were sent to Mix so that Katherine, Timmy, and Donita could have them at breakfast.

In the evenings after they camped Villa paid visits to Timmy to check on his condition, and by the week's end he and Timmy were playing checkers together. Villa was an excellent checkers player and never lost, which, considering he was a grown man playing against an injured nine-year-old boy, made Katherine angry. She'd watched Tom Mix also play checkers with Timmy and noted that he always managed to lose about half the time. Finally, one evening she said to the general:

"Anybody can play checkers, but chess takes real skill and brains."

If this brazen declaration had any effect on Villa he did not show it, but merely replied, "Yes, I have seen them play chess. It looks interesting — perhaps you can teach me?"

Katherine was secretly glad, because her father had taught her to play chess from the age of seven and she was quite good at the game. Might be, she thought, that somehow she could get Villa to bet with her and, if she played her board right, maybe even win their freedom. At least it was something to hang on to.

Afterward, every evening Villa would appear at their fireside, reeking of perfume and often in clothes scrubbed fresh in a mountain stream, his face shiny and shaven clean except for the big bushy mustache. He'd had one of his crew make a chessboard and ordered him to carve out wooden chessmen based on drawings Katherine had made. But for the time being they played with tree leaves that Katherine had cut up for players. Villa was having trouble remembering all the moves of the different chessmen, so Katherine drew a board out on a piece of paper and drew the players in, writing notations on how they functioned. Villa glanced at it, folded it once, smiled embarrassedly, and put it in his pocket.

"I think I do better if you just show me," he said.

Finally, after a few days of Katherine explaining the rules and moves, they were ready for the first match. Naturally, it was not much of a contest; Villa still didn't understand the movement of the knights and often let his castles and bishops be taken. Katherine checkmated him five times both before and after supper. But Villa was good-natured about it all and, uncharacteristically to anyone who had known him for long, even seemed to delight in losing.

"Beautiful little señorita," he would bellow, "you are too smart for me, I think!"

Despite herself, Katherine enjoyed the games, not only because she won, but because she sensed it somehow gave her leverage against Villa. But there was something else, too, that both agitated and startled her — she began to sense that Villa was overly interested in her, but she had no idea what to make of that.

But she did have an idea about the chess. One day she let herself be checkmated. Villa was happy as a child and whooped and hollered and called for all those within earshot to come and look at how he had beaten the smart, beautiful señorita. Shrewdly, Katherine won the next three games, but each time allowed Villa to take a few more pieces before losing.

Finally, she said, "General, why not place a bet on the game? My father and I would do that."

Villa looked surprised. "And what would you and your father bet?"

"We started at five cents a game — up to a quarter a match."

His eyes widened. "Why, señorita, that's gambling!" he said with mock piety.

"It was only between Papa and me," Katherine replied.

"Well, do you have a quarter?" Villa asked.

"No," said Katherine, "but there are other things."

Villa's eyes widened further. "Yes?"

"Clothes," she said. "I need a new set of riding breeches. And it's cold now and Timmy and I both need clothes for that. Not just those castoffs you have given us."

"What? A tailor is what you want?"

"Well, if I win — something like that."

"And if *I* win?"

"I will sing and play for you, as soon as you can find a piano," Katherine said slyly. She had thought the thing out for several days. The notion of a piano might bring them closer to civilization.

"A piano!" cried the general. "Now, where would I find such a thing in these mountains?"

"Well, can't we go to a city? Or if not, I'll sing anyway. People say I have a pleasing voice."

Pancho Villa rose from the chessboard and dusted his pants. "You will sing for me, huh? Maybe I like that. It would be nice. Nobody sings for me much anymore. Do you know 'La Cucaracha'?"

"No," she said, "but I know some Victor Herbert tunes. Mama and Papa won't let me sing them at home, but I learned them at school."

"I don't know this Victor," said Pancho Villa, "but we will see."

"Only if you win," Katherine replied.

One day they came to an Indian village high in the mountains. It was located at the edge of a meadow, and smoke wafted up from a dozen fires. It being evening, Villa ordered his camp set up not too far away, and after the fires were started Tom Mix asked Timmy if he'd like to go over and see what the Indians were like. Mix asked Katherine, too, but she had her nightly chess match with Villa, and besides, she wasn't much interested anyway. So far she had secured for them several sets of riding clothes and even some for Donita Ollas, who had pretty much worn out hers. As a sop to Villa, Katherine only had to sing to him once — a piece from *Naughty Marietta* — and while she sensed that he didn't entirely appreciate the song, at least he'd been polite enough to listen and applaud and suggested that the next time he would send a few of his guitar players around to back her up. How a Victor Herbert operetta would sound on guitars Katherine did not know, but at least her scheme was moving along.

Mix led an entourage to the Indian village consisting of Timmy, Reed, Bierce, and Lieutenant Crucia, of the nose necklace. General Fierro decided to tag along also, accompanied by several of his aides, and at the last moment the Hollywood movie people who had shot film of Villa's attack at Chihuahua City also decided to join the party, but they left most of their cameras behind because of the lack of light.

The village belonged the Rarámuri people, a tribe of mountain runners thought to be descended from Aztecs, but nobody, including the Rarámuri, could prove it. They had established themselves in caves along a ridge that rimmed a large open meadow surrounded by oaks and ponderosa pines. When Mix's group showed up, the Rarámuri were in the middle of a footrace, which they ran every evening after working their cornfields or tending flocks of goats and sheep. The women had finished their race and the men were now just beginning to return — each running a ten-mile lap down the canyons and back up to the meadow, kicking before him a carved wooden ball. It was said that in ancient times the Indians once formed part of a vast network of messengers carrying news and orders for hundreds of miles through the mountains. It was also said that in olden times the Rarámuri used a human skull for the ball they were kicking. The Rarámuri were friendly enough when Mix and his people walked into their camp.

"We'd like to buy something for supper," Mix told a man in Spanish, but the Indian didn't seem to understand. Lieutenant Crucia tried in some Indian tongue and the man appeared to comprehend this better, but Crucia did not understand the man back. Soon they settled on a mixture of Spanish and whatever language Crucia was using. Presently a woman appeared with a large basket of hot corn cakes, about the size of pancakes, and these were offered to the group. They were tasty, though without salt; water was also offered from a gourd.

Fierro told Crucia to ask if they could buy some sheep and goats from the village because his men were tired of beef. The Indian looked pained at this, and said that they needed the sheep and goats for their manure to fertilize their fields. This answer displeased Fierro and he told Crucia to make the man an offer. Crucia did so, but the Indian shook his head.

"What's he say?" Fierro inquired.

"Says they can't get any more sheeps and goats up here," Crucia said.

"Tell him we'll pay him well," said the Butcher.

Crucia translated, and the old Indian looked baffled.

Fierro produced a wallet and displayed dozens of one-hundred-peso notes.

The Indian examined them and began to laugh.

"I don't think these people understand the concept of money," Crucia said hesitantly.

"Tell him we are the army of General Pancho Villa and are authorized to requisition whatever we need from the people, including livestock."

Crucia relayed this to the man and received his reply.

"He says he doesn't understand any of that," the lieutenant told Fierro.

"Then tell him we'll swap him some of our beefs for some of his sheep and goats," Fierro offered. But the old Indian shook his head and replied that cattle didn't live very long at this altitude.

Fierro glared with his hooded falcon eyes at the Indian, and it must have gone through the minds of Mix and anybody else who knew the Butcher what was probably going to happen next, but just then Villa came striding out of the gathering darkness.

"Well, General," he said to Fierro, "are you people having a nice chat?"

"He won't sell us any sheep or goats," Fierro said sourly. "I told him we would take them anyway."

"That's not very hospitable, especially since you are a guest in this man's village," Villa replied. "I am not going to touch a hair on the head or lay a finger on the property of anybody else in Mexico except the stinking gringos. They've stolen everything we need, and it was ours in the first place."

"Not up here in this wilderness," Fierro replied. "My men are sick of eating beefs."

"I remember when they were sick of eating beans," Villa reminded him. As if on cue, a woman appeared with a large *olla* containing a stew of beans, mutton, and prickly pear pads, and a plate of corn tortillas. Timmy thought the stew was as good a thing as he'd ever eaten. Fierro sulkily put his hands on his hips and wandered off back toward camp. Villa sat down on a stump and tasted his bowl of stew, pronouncing it *muy bueno*.

Reed, meanwhile, seemed fascinated by the Indians. He had walked to their caves and inspected them and all their furnishings and especially the Indians themselves, peering at their blankets and the crude vines with which they wrapped their feet, and was having a grand time taking everything in.

He wondered to Lieutenant Crucia if he would ask the Indian how long his tribe had lived here.

Crucia nodded at the old Indian's reply and said, "He doesn't know. A long time, but there were others that lived here before him. They were giants and they ate the Rarámuri children and raped their women until the people tricked them into taking poison."

"*Gigantes?*" Villa said, amused. The Indian spoke again.

While the Indian was talking, Bierce, who had also been observing things, remarked cynically, "These people live like they were already dead."

"Don't count 'em out yet, Señor Robinson," Villa replied. "They were here while your ancestors were still spearing rats in Europe." To Mix and the others, there still seemed to be a perceptible antagonism growing between Villa and Robinson. Where this might lead, those who had been around Villa long enough would not venture a guess, aloud or even to themselves.

Finally, Crucia translated: "Yes, he says that in the caves they have found some very big human bones — some the size of pine trees. And they found a head — a skull — size of a large *olla*. It was full of snakes."

"Well, in that case, I'm getting the hell out of here," Villa said, standing. He put his bowl of stew on the stump and nodded politely to the man and women and others of the tribe who had gathered around accompanied by a large variety of dogs and a turkey or two; then, like Fierro, he turned and disappeared into the gathering gloom.

As Villa crossed the meadow toward his own campfires, he thought he heard a noise and stopped. Everything was quiet except for distant singing from some of his soldiers. He took another step and heard it again; whirled, but nothing was there. The talk of giants in the mountains had made him jittery, even if they were long dead. Then he heard the neigh of a horse. It seemed to come from behind him. He turned again but saw nothing, so kept on walking, faster, stumbling over rocks and depressions. He couldn't keep from imagining Sanchez's ghost was somewhere out there, lurking at the edges of the ponderosas. He broke into a trot, and then a run, until he arrived slightly out of breath at the edge of his own encampment, where he met a member of his personal bodyguard.

"Are you all right, General?" the soldier asked.

"I don't much like this place. It's too high up in the air."

Meantime, Timmy had been playing with a skinny little Chihuahua dog that belonged to

487

the Indians. It hovered around his feet and scratched up at him with tiny claws. He picked the dog up and cradled it in his lap while it licked his fingers.

"He's just a little puppy," Timmy told Mix, who replied, "Nope, that's all as big as he's gonna get. Those dogs was brought here by the Chinamen a long time ago."

"You think I could buy him?" Timmy asked hopefully. He was remembering Ranger and the day he was killed by the car; the inexpressible sadness and loneliness when Ranger wasn't there to walk him to school in the mornings.

Mix frowned. "Nah, I wouldn't try to do that. You ain't got any money anyhow, and besides, General Villa don't like those little lapdogs. They yap too much and he's apt to shoot it. He don't like things to do with Chinamen, anyhow."

Timmy put the Chihuahua back on the ground. It stood on its hind legs and pawed at him pitifully with big bulging eyes. Mix felt a pang of guilt; he knew the boy missed his folks and was scared and seemed to crave an act of human kindness.

"Well," Mix said, "I guess we best be getting on back." As they walked toward their own campfires, a melon moon came riding slowly on a clear, starlit sky and bathed the meadow in a silver glow. Mix was feeling guiltier and guiltier about Timmy and the dog — and other things, too. He'd never had anybody to look after before, and had never really been looked after himself, even as a boy. He'd agreed with Robinson back when Timmy was really sick, that Timmy should have been gotten to a hospital. But Mix had not spoken up and he was ashamed that he hadn't.

By the time they got back to camp, Mix was miserable. No one else was feeling rosy, either. Katherine had thrown another chess match to Villa and had to sing for him again. It had put her in a melancholy spirit. Timmy went immediately to his blanket and curled up, staring at the fire. Donita Ollas, too, was glum and uncomfortable, owing to ant bites she had suffered when she'd stepped into a bed of them getting off her horse that morning. All in all, nobody had much to say.

Mix went to his saddlebag and took out a bottle of whiskey, which he rarely used. He marched off into the darkness of the pines and slugged down a long shot and stood there taking long, deep breaths of the thin air. The moonlight filtered through the tall pines, and in the distance the snowy peaks of the very highest mountains suddenly reminded him of an endless row of sharp and broken teeth, topped by a ghastly nose in the form of the moon. As he had more and more lately, Mix began to question what he was doing there. He might be able to just sneak away, but then he'd be deserting those kids. Seemed like he couldn't do right for doing wrong.

Next morning, Mix eased out of camp before anybody else was awake and returned while the cooks were preparing breakfast over a restoked fire. Slung over his saddle was some kind of animal, and Mix dismounted with it in his arms. It was not the Chihuahua, but one of the strangest-looking dogs Timmy and Katherine had ever seen. It looked more like a dark brown kangaroo with long front legs and no hair. The nearest Timmy and Katherine could imagine to such a creature was a naked Doberman pinscher with a long tail and big upright ears like a bat's. Mix put the dog on the ground and led it with a little braided leash over to Timmy.

"You wanted a dog and I found you one," he said. "It's a lot better than one of them Chihuahuas that yaps."

"What is it?" Timmy asked, stunned. The dog was sniffing him over.

"Mexican hairless, is what we've always called it. But they got another name for it down here I can't pronounce."

"He's so . . . so . . ."

"I know," Mix said. "Ain't got no hair, does he? That's why they call him a Mexican hairless."

"Where did he come from?" Katherine

asked. The dog began to prance around and sniff.

"Them Indians," Mix replied. "I saw him when we was there last night. They had two or three, but this one seemed like the best. Can't be more than a year old."

"Why hasn't he any hair?" Timmy asked, squatting down. The dog began rubbing itself all over him, nosing his arms and chest and face.

"That's the beauty of it," Tom Mix said. "See, these dogs go back to prehistoric times in Mexico. The old Aztecs used to eat them for food — real tasty, so the story goes. But later they decided they was sort of godlike and they buried them with their masters." Mix was warming to his subject and for the first time since last night he felt good, seeing the look on Timmy's face. He had traded three eating forks and three knives to the Indians for the Mexican hairless, but he could replace those at the chuckwagon.

"See," Mix continued, "since he ain't got no hair, his temperature's a lot higher than yours, so's he don't freeze. And what the Mexicans do, see, is they use them as a kind of hot-water bottle. Sleep with him, you know — keep you warm all night. And they also say they're good for cures for things like sore backs or rheumatism or bruises — just put him close to you and he heats you all up."

"What's his name?" Timmy asked.

"Well," Mix said triumphantly, "he's yours — you name him."

"He is?"

"It's why I got him." Mix chuckled. "I figured we got some cold weather coming. You might need him, nights."

"We could share him, too," Timmy said. He felt elation welling up; a dog, something of his own out here where he owned nothing but the clothes on his back; something to love him, something he could love and look after.

"We could at that," Mix said. "We sure could."

"So, what are you going to call him?" Katherine asked. The dog had now moved to her lap, nuzzling and licking, and she liked the way it was so friendly. It seemed remarkably clean, compared to most dogs she'd seen in Mexico.

"How about Pluto?" Timmy said.

"Pluto's the Greek god of the underworld," Katherine informed him.

"Whatever," said Mix. "Then Pluto it is."

About that time one of the Hollywood movie guys showed up in Mix's camp.

"We're getting ready to leave," one of them told Mix, "get all this film back to California. But my boss wanted me to take some film of you Americans that are traveling with Villa's army. Make a nice play in the newsreels," he said.

Mix had tried everything under the sun — except asking directly — to get the movie people to take pictures of him from the day they'd arrived. He'd done horse tricks, pistol tricks, and rope tricks, and flashed his eyes and his smile, but they'd only clapped and nodded, and nobody took any moving pictures. Finally, here was the chance. He could see the other movie people bringing their cameras toward him.

"You want me to get my horse?" Mix asked, trying to sound nonchalant.

"Yeah, why not?" said the movie man. "Might be a nice touch."

Mix had to stop himself from bounding off to the horse tethers.

"Please tell everybody that we are being kidnapped," Katherine said to the movie man. "Tell the president and everybody."

"General Villa says he is just escorting you out of possible danger," the man replied.

"That's bullshit," said Donita Ollas. "He killed the manager of these children's grandfather's ranch and kidnapped me. Then he attacked their mother and grandmother and took them, too."

"It's not the way he sees it, ma'am," said the movie man.

"Well, you put me in the movie and I'll tell them the truth," Donita said. Staggered by the long weeks on the trail, sunk in a fury of frustration, as if the end of this would never come, she felt a clap of doom, and at the same time the notion that she just didn't care anymore.

The movie man looked puzzled. "Do whatever you want," he said.

Mix had returned with his horse and somebody ordered the cameras to roll. He got his horse to rear up and waved his hat. He made the horse lie down so he could dismount. He got the horse to nudge him in the back across the campsite. He flashed teeth and eyes and fired his pistol in the air a few times, frightening the Mexican hairless dog. Presently Bierce, Reed, and Villa wandered into the scene.

"Just to get it straight," the movie man said, "your name is Reed, Jack Reed — is that a nickname for John?"

"It is," Reed replied.

"And you are a reporter for the *New York Telegram*?"

"No, the *New York World* — and I'm also covering this for the *Metropolitan.*"

The man squinted for a moment. "Ain't that one of those socialist magazines?"

"Well, progressive," Reed equivocated, "if that's what you mean."

"All right," said the man, eyeing Reed suspiciously. "S'pose we get a shot of you talking to the general here. You be writing in a notepad or somethin', like you're getting an interview."

Reed pulled out a pad and began to act. Next the man turned to Bierce.

"And your name's Jack Robinson — that stand for John, too?"

"No, just Jack," Bierce said. The cameras continued to roll.

"You a reporter, too?"

"No," Bierce answered. He shied away from the camera.

"Look over that way," the man said. "You don't want your back to be in the movies, do you?"

"I'd prefer it," Bierce told him. "I don't want my family to know where I am."

"You look old enough to me to make your own decisions," the man said testily.

"I am, and I don't want to be in the movies."

Before letting them film, Villa had instructed the movie people not to take pictures of the children or Donita Ollas because, he said, it might upset their relatives. He had declared he was going to turn them all over to the proper authorities, when he found some. But for now, he, Villa, was the proper authority. However, while Reed "interviewed" Pancho Villa, one of the cameramen accidentally swung his lens onto Timmy, Katherine, and Donita, who were standing at the edge of the campfire. He didn't shoot them long, but it was enough.

When the movie people had finished and

were packing up their cameras and equipment, Mix asked the man where and when the films could be seen. He especially wanted to know if they would be shown in Hollywood.

"Hell, feller, we're with Black's Movie News of the World. These pictures'll be shown in movie houses all over the planet — probably in a couple of weeks, providing we can get our asses to where we can catch us a train out of this hellhole."

Mix's heart jumped. He didn't know what Villa had in mind for them next, but he hoped to high heaven it included someplace with a movie theater.

"And you," the man asked, poised with a pencil and pad, "does Tom stand for Thomas?"

"No," Mix said, "it stands for Tom."

FORTY-THREE

The days seemed to spin endlessly by as Villa's troop ascended higher into the mountains, where the air was fragrant and sweet. They rode slowly through giant pine forests and down steep trails into valleys where often there was a rushing river, then up again to the canyon rims, where they could see for miles across the reddish brown ceilings and monstrous escarpments. Days earlier they'd turned northward, and kept in that direction until Reed figured they must be as close to the United States border as they were to Chihuahua City. Late one afternoon, as they reached the rim of one canyon, they saw what they took for an Indian seated on a large rock, a black silhouette against the setting sun. He sat scratching himself and looking around the valley like a thoroughly satisfied owner.

Bierce and Reed had been riding with Villa and Fierro, and Fierro saw the man first.

"That's strange," Fierro remarked. "These

people usually don't go around up here alone."

"He ain't alone anymore," Bierce remarked. "Now he's got *us* to contend with."

Fierro cut Bierce a slit-eyed glance. This meddlesome old goat was beginning to get on Fierro's nerves, too.

"An outcast, maybe," Reed offered. "I read up on these people a little before I left New York. Sometimes they'll kick one of their own out of the tribe if he doesn't do right."

Just then the man rose and climbed off the rock, and to their surprise they saw two other men emerge from behind the rock, leading pack animals. They headed along a thin rocky trail at the rim of the canyon, a trail that would take them straight to Villa's party if they kept on it. Fierro pulled out a pair of field glasses and studied the men as they plodded along.

"They're not Indians — not by a stretch," he announced, his eyes still glued to the binoculars.

"Maybe they're tourists," Bierce offered. "Hell of a view from up here. It's better than the Grand Canyon."

Fierro put the glasses down and looked at Bierce sourly.

"Señor," he said, "we have to be suspicious. Whoever they are, if they see us here, they might report it."

"So what?" Villa interjected. "Report to

who? What's anybody gonna do about it, anyway?"

By this time the man who had been out on the rock had climbed aboard his animal and taken a good lead on the others. Villa might have moved his party along, but he didn't. He waited patiently until the man was within speaking distance. The man was dressed in soiled white cotton peon's clothes and arrived on a filthy mule.

"Afternoon," the man said politely.

"Buenas tardes," Villa replied, noting that he was a gringo. "Are you lost or something?"

"Hardly," said the man. "My friends and I are making our way back to civilization."

"And from where did you come?" Villa asked.

"From over there." He swept his arm to indicate the endless maze of canyons to the west.

"Sounds like you came from over in Sonora," Villa said. "Those barrancas are a pretty good place to get lost in."

"Tell me about it," the man said. By now he had dismounted and was standing in front of Villa's party. "We got lost several times, but, well, now you have found us."

"And what am I to do with you?" Villa asked.

"We been eating nothing but beans for three weeks. Maybe you got a change of diet," he said hopefully.

"You see many Federales over in Sonora?" Villa asked.

"Well, Hermosillo's the only big town we went through, and we ain't been there for six months. But there was Federales there then."

"How many?"

"Thousands, I guess. We didn't count 'em all."

"Guns?"

"Yeah, they had a lot parked around town."

Villa grunted. The other two in the man's party had arrived by now. One was a grime-faced American and the other was an old white-haired mestizo. They halted some steps away from the man and stood holding their burros and shuffling their feet.

"Well, I guess you need some dinner and we need to make a camp. This looks like as good a place as any," Villa said finally.

"*Gracias*," said the man.

"*De nada*," Villa replied.

They sat around Villa's campfire as the sun beamed its last pink rays over the measureless expanse of canyons and mountains. The three newcomers greedily devoured freshly cut steaks and, in the firelight, their chins dripping grease, explained why they were there.

"El Dorado," the man said. He was small in stature, yellowed by what appeared to be jaundice, and had a head bald as a split pea.

500

"The lost gold mine?" Fierro asked.

"No less," said the man. He told them how he and his friend had worked their way down to Tampico on a steamer laden with oil-drilling gear, then got a job in the oil fields, and when that played out they bummed around for a while and he'd even wound up writing for an English-language newspaper in Mexico City. There they had met the old mestizo who talked all the time about this lost gold mine of El Dorado in the mountains, and the mestizo claimed to know an Indian whose tribe had worked it way back in the old days a hundred or more years before.

Priests found the Indians mining the gold, the man said, and, after converting them, made them slave in the mine for half a century to bring out gold for the Church. Then one day a party of soldiers were headed up the trail toward the mine and the priests were afraid they would report it and the government would confiscate the gold, and so they made the Indians fill in the mine and smooth out all traces of it, including planting cacti and other things around it, until nobody could ever find it again except them. Then they murdered all the Indians who had worked on it so they couldn't tell anybody. Before they died, the Indians put a curse on the mine.

The mestizo in Mexico City said he could produce the Indian who was the son of the lone survivor of the killings and knew where the mine was. And since the revolution was starting to heat up again in Mexico City, the four of them, the man, his friend, the mestizo, and the Indian, figured there was nothing to lose and set out from Hermosillo to find the lost gold of El Dorado.

"And did you find it?" Reed asked enthusiastically.

"Hell, no," the man replied. "We wandered all over those mountains and canyons nearly half a year, and all we found was rocks and bandits and snakes. It was probably all a bunch of horseshit."

"Might have been the curse," Bierce remarked. He believed in curses — sometimes.

"And what about the Indian?" Villa asked.

"Dead," said the man. "He was about to go crazy up there anyway, but one time he got in one of our packs and found a quart of whiskey. Got drunk on it and fell off a cliff."

"Too bad," Bierce remarked.

"Yes," said the man.

"I mean about the whiskey. I imagine you could have put it to better use."

"And so where are you headed now?" Villa inquired.

"Back to Tampico or Veracruz, I reckon. Maybe the oil fields have opened up again. Otherwise I guess I'll go to El Paso and then get on home."

"That's a hell of a good tale," Reed interjected. "You said you had been a reporter; maybe you could write a book about it."

"The hell with it," said the man, wiping steak grease from his chin with his sleeve. "We didn't find anything, did we?"

Ever since they had left the Rarámuri Indian village, a plan had begun to take shape in Johnny Ollas's mind. One thing he knew for sure was that with every passing day the time for action was getting short. So tonight, while Villa and the others were dining with the treasure hunters, Johnny laid out his scheme for the rescue of his wife. It's said the best-laid plans always have the beauty of simplicity, but Johnny's plan was about as complicated as the inner workings of a pocket watch.

"There is something he is afraid of," Johnny reminded them again. "That day Rigaz was killed he said something very strange about an old man on a gray horse, with a white beard and a rifle. He said this man was trying to kill him."

"To kill the general?" Julio asked.

"Yes, it was very strange, like he'd had a vision, maybe."

"Visions often come true," Gourd Woman offered.

Luis and Rafael sat on a log eating beans and beef spiced with peppers and onions. The campfire flickered in their faces.

"Well, I can't wait around for that," Johnny

said. "I've been working on something and maybe pretty soon we can pull it off. Now, one of these riders who came back today for some beefs told me we are gonna start down into the canyons tomorrow. That might be our chance, because what I have in mind wouldn't work up here on the canyon rims — its too close for visibility, and you can't jump over canyons. But down there, just maybe . . . and this thing he has about the old man with a rifle, that, too . . ." Johnny understood as a matador the advantage in knowing your opponent. Before a bullfight he often spent hours on the rails of the bullpens, watching and studying the animal he was to fight.

"What you have in mind?" Luis asked.

"Like I said before," Johnny continued, "I've got to make his ear twitch, make him nervous, see which way he hooks, then we know what he's gonna do. And when we get him jumpy, he'll go into his *querencia,* scared, confused, and only looking for one thing, and he will not be expecting us. But we can only stick him a couple of times, you know, 'cause anything more, he'll catch on."

Julio, Luis, and Rafael nodded obediently, just as they did before the bull-fights, absorbing each detail Johnny gave them, since they knew all their lives depended on it, then as now.

"First we need two things we don't have,"

Johnny said. "And we are going to steal them." The eyes of the cuadrilla widened.

Johnny said, "I noticed there are two small wagons at the very end of the ammunition train. I just got a glimpse, but in one of them are some rifle cases made out of leather that hold rifles with telescope sights. They are marked. We need to steal one of these. And in the other wagon there are electric torches. We need to steal two of those — maybe three, if it's possible."

"Stealing is immoral," Gourd Woman declared. The others looked at her like she was crazy.

"What, are you a priest now, too?" asked Julio.

"No, but I think it will be a bad omen to begin by stealing." Her hands were in the pocket of her dress, fooling with the bones.

"We are dealing with murderers and kidnappers," Johnny said. "Stealing is hardly a mortal sin in the face of that."

"The bones tell me it's the wrong way to go about it."

"Same bones that told you Villa was in Creel?" said Luis. "Don't make me laugh."

"Same ones," she said. "Laugh if you want."

After dark, Luis and Rafael made their way through the long encampment up to the ammunition train and, just as Johnny had described, the two smaller wagons were there.

Luis stepped into the firelight and asked if anyone had a cigarillo, while Rafael sneaked around between the wagons and managed to locate the flashlights in one of them. He put two into his jacket and stepped into the dark of the tall trees. Next evening they reversed the scam, Rafael stepping into the camp of the teamsters to ask for a tin of salt, while Luis slipped one of the cases with a telescoped rifle out of the wagon. The ploy almost blew up in their faces when Luis disturbed the fighting cocks and hens and they set up a squawk in their cages, but nobody paid much attention and he vanished into the woods with the gun.

Next morning, Villa's detachment began the long and perilous descent into the canyons. The descent came not a moment too soon, Johnny thought, because as dawn broke it began to snow, and this time it was heavy: big wet flakes at first, then smaller ones that swirled in the air and sometimes reduced vision down to a few yards. Within half an hour everything at the top of the mountain was covered in powder. The wagons creaked and groaned and sometimes skidded on the mushy gravel and dirt down the prolonged trail that wound to the floor of the canyon.

By midmorning, Katherine's party was below the snow and the leaden sky was now filled with rain. Winds whipped through the canyon, sometimes with such ferocity that it threatened to knock the wagons off the cliff-side. It was a slow struggle and those riding on animals, Katherine included, often closed their eyes and trusted the horses or mules or donkeys to pick their way down the steep rocky trail. To look down into a canyon bottom more than a mile below would fill all but the boldest, or craziest, with sheer, icy terror.

It didn't help that they saw a team of mules slip off the edge. Something had made one of the animals balk or shy and the others pulled the wagon around so it slid partially over the precipice. The teamster was walking in front of the mules, leading them, and he jerked at their harness and tried to get the wagon pulled back on the trail, but the wheels stuck and the mules panicked. They backed up to get better purchase, but the whole wagon slipped off, pulling the mules right along with them, into the rocky gorge without a sound, at least not one that could be heard in the back of the caravan. The mules went down as they had pulled, in the harness traces, but on their backs and with their legs straight up in the air and not kicking at all, as though they were lifeless already before they hit bottom.

FORTY-FOUR

Arthur Shaughnessy was riding at the front of his party with Cowboy Bob, Crosswinds Charlie, the Colonel, and Strucker when Death Valley Slim came cantering back toward them over a rise in the high mountain plain.

"There's Indians just over that hill there!" said Slim, pulling up on a lathered horse.

"Wild Indians!" the Colonel exclaimed.

"Well, I wouldn't exactly say that. It's Tarahumaras — or Rarámuris, is what they call themselves — them's ridge-running Indians. And they said Villa and his bunch passed through there not two days ago."

"Were the children with them?" Arthur asked anxiously.

"Villa camped his people a ways from the village. But they did see a little boy about nine or ten that came to their camp about dark. Way they described him, it sure must be your boy."

"Thank God," Arthur said. The rush of

relief and elation brought chills to his body. They weren't going on a wild goose chase after all, and Timmy — and in Arthur's mind it stood to reason Katherine, too — was unharmed for the moment.

"There!" cried the Colonel. "That's fine news!" He slapped his saddle with his hand.

Arthur suddenly had a renewed respect for the Old Man; somehow, of course with Bob and Slim's help, he had put them hot on the trail. Just being closer, and knowing it, was enough, for the moment.

"What's more," Slim said, "I think I know where they went. Before they left, they hired on a couple of Indians as guides to lead them down into the canyons — which figures, 'cause it's gonna start to get pretty cold up here."

"So you think we can find them?" Arthur asked tentatively.

"Yeah, I think so. I expect we ought to hire a couple of Indians ourselves. They know these canyons pretty good."

"And what, when we do find them?" asked Cowboy Bob, as if he'd been reading Arthur's mind. Bob had been silent and even distant most of the last couple of days. He had no illusions about their chances against a reinforced military detachment led by Pancho Villa.

"We'll cross that river when we come to it,"

said the Colonel. "The main thing is we're close."

Yes, but . . . Arthur thought. Until now they'd been tracking Villa's progress only by signs of a large party moving through the mountains — cigar and cigarette butts, cast-off food tins, what passed for toilet paper — and were never positive it was him. Now that they knew it was, what could, or should, they do? Arthur had tried to formulate plans ever since they had left El Paso. He could offer Villa the meager ransom he might be able to raise; they could somehow swoop down on the unsuspecting Mexicans and rescue the children; they might even abduct Villa himself and hold him for a reverse ransom. All of this seemed improbable, but Arthur felt he had to keep the wheels turning, even if he was wrong.

They followed Death Valley Slim to the village of the Rarámuris, who were waiting for them. Because it was getting dark, the Colonel encamped just outside the village, much closer than Villa had. The old Indian who had spoken earlier with Lieutenant Crucia greeted them with a pleasant nod, but Slim didn't know enough Indian language to communicate with him as Crucia had. To solve this, they both squatted down in the dirt and made themselves known in a language drawn on the ground with sticks. The Indian indicated he hadn't seen a girl; only the boy. He said that Villa's party needed goats and sheep but that he did not part with any. He said that one man had bought a dog from them, which, along with everything else, led the old Indian to believe that Villa's party was, if not starving, probably low on food. This was useful information to the Colonel, because he knew hungry men would not be in the best mood to put up a fight, if one became necessary.

And when the Colonel's troops arrived, the Indians brought out dinner for their new visitors. There were bowls of hot soup and tortillas and large trays of strange-looking batter-fried things that were especially tasty. After eating a handful, Crosswinds Charlie inquired what they were. Slim received a reply from the old Indian that they were eating butterflies.

"Butterflies!" Arthur exclaimed. "What kind of butterflies?" he asked.

"He says he doesn't know, but there are many of them in the mountains this time of year," Slim told him. Then the Indian added something else.

"He says the butterflies are the souls of their dead relatives."

"You mean he's serving us up old Grandma Juanita and Uncle Pablo?" asked Cowboy Bob.

"That's about the size of it," Slim said.

"They believe it puts a restorative into their bodies."

Butterflies, Arthur marveled, and damn tasty, too.

Meantime, Strucker had been examining the caves dug into the sides of a ridge and when he returned to camp pronounced the Indians "troglodytes."

"What's that?" Cowboy Bob asked.

"A lower form of life," the German informed him.

"From what?" Bob asked, not liking the German's answer. He always seemed aloof and snobbish and treated Bob, Slim, and the others like they were servants. Perhaps Strucker's idea of "a lower form of life."

"From ours, of course."

"Why? Because they don't have railroad trains or telephones?" Bob said. His distaste for the German grew from moment to moment.

"That's part of it. But they have no culture, either," Strucker shot back.

"Oh, they got a culture," Bob replied. "It's just different. Do you know that these people are descended from a civilization that's two thousand years old? Reason I know so is that back at El Paso they got a whole museum full of their pottery and things — you ought to visit it. Beautiful stuff."

"I'm sure," the German responded, "but

does it compare with Fokker or other of the great aircraft makers, or what the ancient Orientals were doing? I hardly think so."

"I dunno," said Bob, "but I sure thought it was pretty." He barely knew what Strucker was talking about, but wasn't about to let himself get outtalked.

"Pretty, perhaps, but if that's the pinnacle of their cultural advancement, I'd say it's fairly low on the scale."

"Yeah, maybe," Bob said. "I guess a higher advancement is what you people are doing to each other over there in Europe. What is it by now, two million killed just in France alone, last I read?"

Strucker gave a wave of dismissal and walked off. Bob felt like jerking him back into the woods and whipping his ass.

Later, by a low campfire, Bob resumed the conversation with Arthur that he'd left off earlier before they climbed the mountains.

"It must've been some shock when they took you out of that orphanage to the Colonel's place, huh?" Bob was wiping down his pistol with an oily rag.

"Big one," Arthur replied.

"So what was it like? Did he have a nice house?"

"Still does," Arthur said. He didn't so much mind the small talk, but he had other things to think about.

"You ever been to England?" Bob said.

"Several times, but only once on my own. London's an interesting city. Then I went to Ireland. Tried to look up my father's family, but there were so many Shaughnessys I didn't have much luck. We'd sort of lost touch with them."

"When did your people come over?" Bob asked. He offered Arthur the rag, and Arthur began wiping down his pistol, too.

"In 1861. My father's father came right when the Civil War broke out. But he really wasn't my grandfather. I don't know who I am," Arthur said. "I might be a Jew, for all I know." He thought about how much he disliked Strucker's unceasing remarks about the Jews. Bob must have been thinking the same thing, because he chuckled and patted his thigh.

"My grandfather came in 1868," said Bob. "Went to work when they were building the southern railroad. That's how we came to be out West. Our names are Sheen, so I reckon we're from the same race of people as yours."

"Same business, too," Arthur told him. He tossed another log on the fire.

"What's that?"

"The railroad business." Arthur smiled. Bob did, too.

"Do you ever see anybody from when you were at the orphanage?" Bob asked.

"No," Arthur said. He had been rolling that

thought around in his head for days, trying to make at least some sense of it. Earlier it came back to him, the time he'd seen Mick making up to his girl Betty on the Common. It hadn't struck him then as a betrayal; it wasn't as if he'd been in love with her or anything. At the orphanage he and Mick had shared practically everything. But looking back, he realized there most certainly had been a betrayal, and that Mick had been that kind of fellow all along. After Arthur's adoption, the Colonel had drummed into him all his notions of loyalty and honesty. "If everything else is stripped away," the Colonel said, "that's all you will have left, your honor, the most important thing in a man's life."

"Don't you ever wonder what happened to any of them?" Bob asked.

"No," Arthur told him. He also remembered the time he'd fixed Mick up with Harriet Quimby, and the strange and sudden cooling of their relationship. Something she'd said when he'd asked her about it began to make sense. It had been the day before the air show where she was killed, and Arthur was taking them all for lunch at a seaside place in Gloucester.

"Do you want me to see if Mick wants to come?" he'd asked.

Harriet started, and her lips pursed; she quickly shook her head, as if she were shaking off something malevolent or foul.

"Something go wrong between you two?" he'd said cheerfully.

"Not our sort of person," she replied icily. She'd said *our* sort, not *my* sort, which, looking back on it, conveyed an implication different from what he'd taken at the time. And there had also been that hardened expression in her eyes and voice that for a moment gave him a chill, but he'd brushed it off. Whatever had happened between Mick and Harriet Quimby, now, he expected no one would ever know.

"I reckon sometimes it's the best thing to put the past behind you," Bob was saying. Arthur handed him back his gun rag.

"Whenever possible," he said.

The next day, the weather suddenly turned pleasantly warm again, a kind of balmy Indian summer all knew wouldn't last. They moved out at daybreak with three Indian guides hired on to track Villa's band. From what the old Indian had told Slim, they knew Villa was headed for the canyons. The Indian guides traveled on foot but, being runners, soon outranged the Colonel's party.

Arthur sometimes would become an outrider, moving far to one side or the other of the main body, paralleling on the flank to scout for possible ambushes or other signs of danger. Arthur had begun to take a lively interest in the sights along the trail, the alpine meadows, the craggy mountain peaks, the tall firs and pines. Once he even spotted an eagle soaring thousands of feet above a steep, wooded valley; yet the eagle was still below Arthur, who was on an even higher ridge. For a while the view made him forget his feelings of gloom and anger over the children and Mick Martin, but presently it all returned with renewed fury. Arthur would let himself sink into the gloom and anger as if the moods were old friends, and got some kind of perverse satisfaction from them.

Three great things had happened in his life — being taken from the orphanage, his marriage to Xenia, and having the children — and he resolved never again to let anything stand in the way of those gifts. He couldn't help but think that the incident with Mick might never have happened if he had been more attentive, less reclusive, less occupied with the business; fewer days in Chicago. He wished he could have told Xenia that, but he couldn't, of course, and turned his horse and rode away.

Each evening the Rarámuri Indians returned with scouting reports, and everyone, Arthur, the Colonel, Bob, and Slim, was satisfied they were as close to Villa as they needed to be for the moment: far enough behind not to be discovered, but close enough to be ready for action if the occasion presented itself. Bob and Slim queried the

Indians each day on whether they thought a tactical advantage could come to the Colonel's party, based on terrain or other things, but the Indians had no opinions on that matter.

One morning Arthur invited Crosswinds Charlie to go outriding with him. The tall pines were enveloped in thick mist and the damp ground muffled the sounds of their horses' hooves. Even in the almost balmy weather, little patches of snow remained from a previous storm, unmelted in the shadows of the tall trees.

They'd been discussing flying, the perverse nature of air currents near mountains. As they plodded deeper into the forest, Charlie was expanding on the need for aviation to develop a reliable odometer-type device — something similar to a taffrail log on vessels — that accurately told the pilot how far he'd come, because, as weather and water currents can with ships, air currents can badly skew a pilot's positioning.

Suddenly Arthur held up his hand and reined in his horse. Charlie rose up in his stirrups and craned his neck forward. They were both hearing a strange sound, something like a rushing river or waterfall. Slowly, they crept along through the forest mists. Arthur stopped several more times, and each time the sound was louder. He turned to Charlie.

"Stay here and stay alert," he said. "Let me

go see what this is."

Arthur nudged his horse slowly forward until he disappeared into the mist. Charlie had been sitting there in his saddle for nearly twenty minutes when Arthur reappeared with a look of tremendous excitement on his face.

"What was it?" Charlie asked.

"Have you ever heard the sound of butterfly wings?" Arthur said, his eyes vivid with energy.

Charlie looked at him, puzzled.

"Millions of them," Arthur muttered under his breath. "Millions, I tell you, all over every tree! It's the great monarch migration some people have talked about but nobody's ever seen, as far as I know. At least not in these mountains. It's something you'll never witness again in your life. Come on!"

Charlie shrugged and nudged his horse after Arthur's. They rode through the misty pine forest for ten or fifteen minutes, the noise stronger and stronger — a thin, high-pitched beating of the air — and then Charlie began to see the butterflies. At first there were just a few of them, big orange, yellow, and black ones fluttering in the low bushes, and then more and more, until the trees nearly came to life. The butterflies thickly carpeted the forest floor, too, so much so that the horses couldn't step without setting foot upon them. The forest somehow reminded Charlie of a cathedral, with the trees forming

Gothic arches and the sunlight streaming in.

"Isn't it amazing?" Arthur gawked.

"It certainly is," replied Charlie. "I've never heard of anything like it."

"They're on their way south," continued Arthur, "some from as far north as Canada, I expect. The warm spell must have caused them to rest here. And then the cold came. Maybe they came too late, or somehow got off course. They're all freezing to death."

"Too bad we don't have a camera," Charlie said. His horse suddenly tossed its head and did a nervous little sidestep, as if it had picked up an unwelcome scent. Arthur's horse snorted and danced, too, and laid back its ears. He figured it was being spooked by the butterflies.

"A camera," said Arthur. "Exactly! Look, why don't you ride back and get one from Ah Dong and tell the others, too? I'll stay here."

Charlie nudged his horse off in the direction of the Colonel's caravan. Arthur turned and said happily, "God, it's the most beautiful thing I've ever seen." Charlie's horse neighed in the background and he could hear Charlie saying, "Whoa, there, whoa."

Arthur sat on his horse for a few minutes, then decided to amble through the butterflies. He had only ridden a dozen yards when he heard a wild and chilling roar and immediately the scream of his horse rising above it.

He wheeled around just in time to avoid the full brunt of a full-grown brown grizzly, which had charged out of a thicket, hell-bent on breaking the spine of his mount. The bear's enormous paw slashed the rump of Arthur's horse but couldn't bring enough force to break its back. The horse reared suddenly, and Arthur, taken totally by surprise, slid off the saddle and onto the ground; the horse, still screaming, took off through the forest.

The huge beast lunged after the horse for a moment and almost caught it, but, realizing the race was lost as the horse gained speed, the bear stopped and turned in Arthur's direction. He could see it clearly through the mist. He was standing in a clearing beside a large oak tree that was cloaked in butterflies, but Bob had told him bears climb a lot faster than humans. At least he had his pistol, but against something like this it was of dubious value. He drew it from the holster and pulled back the hammer, cocking it. The bear was coming at him slowly, inexorably, with horrible grunts and snarls.

About twenty feet away, the beast stopped and reared up so high it seemed to blot out the sun; the bear's neck was pushed forward toward Arthur, and its head was moving snakelike from one side to the other, studying him with its small glaring eyes.

Arthur fired twice, hitting the bear in the

chest, but instead of going down, it lunged forward. It was about halfway to Arthur when it faltered and lurched sideways into some thick brush. It made a few more grunts from the brush and then was quiet. Arthur stood stock-still and dumbfounded, with the pistol still pointing in the direction he had fired it, the whiff of gunpowder in the air. Right then, a party from the Colonel's group, including the Colonel himself, appeared out of the mist, coming on the double after encountering Arthur's bloody horse and then hearing the shots.

Cowboy Bob and Slim both had their rifles out and at the ready; Strucker, the Colonel, and Crosswinds Charlie brought up the rear. "I shot him twice but he still came at me," Arthur said shakily.

"It's a wonder he didn't eat you," Bob said. "You can't kill one of them things with a pistol."

"That weather must've got him out of hibernation," Slim said. "He was probably movin' kind of slow."

"Not when I saw him," Arthur said.

"*Gott!* Look there!" Strucker exclaimed.

In the swirling mist Arthur saw an enormous brown lump poking out of some bushes.

"I'll be damned," Bob said. He nudged his horse prudently toward the lump, rifle at the ready. He circled it at a distance, then dismounted and went up to it, the rifle at his shoulder, pointing. Satisfied the bear was dead, Bob grabbed his horse's reins and walked back toward the group that had gathered around Arthur.

"Partner," Bob said to Arthur, "you musta aimed right at his heart and hit it, 'cause that's the only way anybody's gonna drop one a these things with a pistol."

"Well," the Colonel said. "Well."

Arthur's fingers were clutching the pistol so tightly he felt his hands begin to cramp.

"I should have read the horses; they were spooked; they could smell it," Arthur said, to no one in particular.

"Ain't your fault," Slim said. "Could have happened to any of us, anytime. Still might."

"What's all this on the ground, here?" Crosswinds Slim asked.

"Butterflies," Arthur answered.

"There must be millions of them," the Colonel said.

"There are," Arthur told him. "It's a migration."

"But what are they doing way up here?" wondered the Colonel.

Arthur shook his head. "It's the place they come to breed, I think, but they're dying," he said, but he didn't feel like conversation.

"Got about as much business up here as we do, I reckon," Cowboy Bob said finally.

That night they camped near the rim of a canyon where they'd come onto a stream of fresh water cascading over the edge. The Rarámuri Indians had returned with news and a strange cargo.

The news was that Villa had indeed descended into the canyons and was about two days away, moving north. The strange cargo was the treasure seekers. The Colonel wanted to know from the Indians if there was some way to get ahead of Villa and come down on his flank or front, but since communication was limited, the best Slim could get out of them was that they didn't think so. The gold seekers were affable enough, and repeated their story about the lost mine of El Dorado.

"Yeah, I know about that," Slim said. "I looked for it myself for years. I think it's an old wives' tale. Somehow them things get started . . ."

"We saw a lot of the country, anyway," said the leader dejectedly.

The main thing everybody wanted to know, of course, was whether they had seen Villa and what about the children, but the leader claimed he hadn't seen Villa and nothing would shake him from his story. Arthur, for one, did not believe him. There was something in the offhand way he said it that made

Arthur think he was lying. He tried playing on the man's humanity, telling him how frightened he was for the children's lives; that they only wanted to reach Villa to pay him ransom. But the adventurer stuck to his story.

However, that night after dinner one of the others, a man named Moss, took Arthur aside.

"Look," he said, "we seen Villa, all right, but we didn't see no kids. He told us there'd be serious consequences if we told anybody we'd seen him. You could tell the man meant business and we just want to get out of here alive."

Arthur was appreciative and believed Moss when he said he hadn't seen the kids. After all, these people had only been there one night, and Villa had a big caravan. Nevertheless, he walked with Moss into a copse of trees and pumped him for information: How many men did Villa have with him? What kind of armaments? Machine guns? Cannon? Food supplies? Any hint of his intentions?

Moss did not have the answers to most of the questions. Near as he could recall, Villa had maybe fifty to a hundred men and a couple of small cannons. He hadn't seen any big artillery pieces, but there had been a wagon they passed by next morning that looked like it contained machine guns. He had plenty of food, too — a small herd of cattle brought up the rear — and spirits seemed high.

Arthur thanked Moss and went back to camp, where he called his father aside and gave him the information. This was useful stuff, good or bad, and the Colonel absorbed it and told Arthur to get some rest. They were striking out early the next day, and the Colonel himself was preparing to bed down when Strucker approached him.

"Do you remember when we talked about me going to Villa," Strucker began, "back as we were entering the mountains . . . ?"

"Yes, when that damn storm hit us," the Colonel said.

"Correct," replied the German. "And I said to you that if I could somehow get to Villa, he might accept me as a disinterested party. After all, I'm German and, frankly, we've been trying to establish good relations with the Mexicans."

"Are you on some kind of diplomatic mission?" Shaughnessy asked.

"*Gott,* no!" Strucker said. "It's just that I think I might be useful. You might find it difficult to subdue a military organization of Villa's strength, and my thought was that perhaps I could negotiate with him over the ransom, if that was what you had in mind."

"I did not have that in mind," Shaughnessy replied flatly, not wishing to go into the matter.

"Then in that case," the German said, "the

plan I mentioned to you earlier might be useful — to persuade Villa to attack the United
States and —"

"Wait a minute," Shaughnessy interrupted.
"Are you suggesting that I get the Mexicans
to start a war with my country?" The more
he'd thought about it afterward, the more
Strucker's notion seemed preposterous.

"No — not exactly — and yes, in a manner
of speaking. As I told you, my notion was to
convince Villa that if he attacked the United
States somewhere along the border, your
government would be compelled to send
troops into Mexico, would they not?"

"Yes, I imagine so," Shaughnessy said.

"And then Carranza and Villa's enemies in
Mexico City would be forced to fight the
United States to protect their border, right?"

"I imagine that, too."

"So what I want to persuade Villa is that
this would be in his best interests, because
while Carranza's people are fighting the
Americans, Villa would have a chance to
reinforce himself — especially since he could
recruit from men who found an American
invasion distasteful. At least that is what I
want him to believe."

"But how would that help me?" the Colonel
asked.

"Once Villa attacks, we get word to the
Americans where he is. He will no doubt have
retreated to hide, but you are right here on

his trail. And then suddenly he is confronted by a large force from your own army — one of the finest armies in the world. If you want an overwhelming force against him," Strucker said, "what could be better than that?"

"Then you *are* talking about starting a war — that's powerful stuff," Shaughnessy said.

"Well, you told me you tried to yourself when you attempted to persuade your President Wilson to send troops down, but he refused you."

"That's true," the Colonel conceded, "but that was strictly an American affair — Americans protecting American property and citizens. Not something the Germans were mixed up in."

"I was merely offering my help. I have no national interests in any of this," Strucker reminded him.

"I am sorry if I implied that, Strucker," Shaughnessy said. He didn't quite believe the German, but he would certainly have liked the American army to find a reason to come down into Mexico.

"If you wish," said the German, "I will say no more about it."

"No, no," replied the Colonel, "that isn't it. Perhaps you *can* be of help in some way like that. And it would certainly be useful to have a friend in Villa's camp, though I expect you know great dangers are involved."

"I'm aware of it," Strucker said. "But I

think when he hears my story he'll accept me as a friend. After all, he's supposed to have a somewhat international contingent riding with him now, does he not?"

"So I've heard," said the Colonel.

"Shall I go, then?"

"Well, the Indians are back here in camp now. I imagine at least one of them could take you close enough."

"Tomorrow?"

"Yes, they start out at daylight."

"Then, my friend, it's settled?"

"But how will you explain how you located him? It's going to look suspicious for you to just show up from out of nowhere, isn't it?"

"I don't think so. I'll say I went to Chihuahua City to look for him, but the battle had ended and he had already left, so I hired guides until I reached the canyons. I think that might actually impress him, that I, a lone man, would be so tenacious."

"And how will you get out?" Shaughnessy asked.

"I've considered that, too," Strucker said. "When I have done all I can, I'll take my leave, assuming he permits me, and hope to return to you and report everything I can. If I can figure out a way, I might even get the Indians to carry messages to you. We shall see. Naturally, my utmost dream would be to return with your grandchildren, but that might be to ask the impossible."

Colonel John Shaughnessy nodded and took Strucker's outstretched hand. Then the German took his leave to get himself ready. Shaughnessy sat down on a log and held his head in his hands. His head was throbbing and his back hurt. It had been a dangerous day, one that had almost cost Arthur his life. Back at San Juan Hill the Colonel had had men dying all around him, but he'd been younger then, and young men don't look at death quite like old ones do.

■ ■ ■ ■

PART FIVE:
THE *LOMAS*

■ ■ ■ ■

FORTY-FIVE

The snowstorm that caught Villa's party at the top of the mountains had also caught Bomba *in extremis.* His decision to abandon most of his clothes during the chase across the warm plains left him in bad straits when he reached the high altitudes. All this time he'd been shadowing Villa, trying to get close enough at least to glimpse the children, but so far the terrain hadn't allowed it and he took to hanging back two or three hours and hoping for a break.

First he caught a cold. He had managed to feed himself by taking squirrels and even once a deer, but he was weakened by the day, then by the hour. Worse, the wounds he'd suffered in the first encounter with Villa's men hadn't healed properly and were still oozing pus and blood. Gradually Bomba fell farther behind Villa's party and in a feverish haze simply let his horse wander on its own in the maze of highlands, canyons, and plateaus. He lost track of time and distance;

when the snow began to fall he thought he was freezing to death.

The horse had stumbled into a ravine and was plodding along a narrow stream when, faint and semi-delirious, Bomba smelled smoke. He only got a whiff of it, but the notion of fire and warmth was enough to revive him a little. He looked in all directions for the source of the smoke but saw nothing but the steep rocky walls of the ravine upon which dark shadows of night were approaching. Then as he glanced up toward the rim he finally saw a wisp of smoke. It was coming from a cavelike structure cut into the side of the cliff.

At first he couldn't tell how anyone could get up the side of the cliff but then he saw a narrow set of steps carved into the stone. A pair of burros grazed in shrubs as he dismounted and began climbing. The steps went one way, then the next, traversing the side of the cliff hundreds of feet skyward and it was painful and seemed to take forever.

Several times he reeled dizzily and rested, until he finally reached a ledge covered with a big rock overhang; beneath it was a man hovering over a flickering fire. Bomba made a sound that was no more than a grunt and the man looked up. Even in his fever-ravished stupor, Bomba was astonished to see the face of another black man like himself. He took several steps toward the man, who seemed even more startled than he, then collapsed to his knees. The man gaped at him for a few moments and then Bomba felt himself being lifted and dragged toward the warmth of the fire.

FORTY-SIX

Pancho Villa at last had reached the deep canyon bottoms and was slowly making his way north, confident he and his party were secure and undetected in the gigantic labyrinth spreading hundreds of miles though the mountain chain. Donita and the Americans — Katherine, Timmy, Mix, Reed, and even Bierce — were astonished that in contrast to the bleak and rugged cold at tops, the floors of the canyons were a semitropical paradise with shallow clear streams meandering down the centers.

Parrotlike birds and other bright avians squawked in bamboo breaks and there were wild bananas, lemons, oranges, mangoes, and figs for the picking. Wild orchids and a plant that might have been liana festooned tall hardwood trees, while up in the branches were hundreds of parakeets, doves, and occasionally a big yellow-beaked macaw-looking bird with brilliant red, green, and blue plumage.

They saw deer and rabbits, too, and at night there was a festive twinkling of fireflies. They also saw what looked like boa constrictors sunning themselves by the water's edge, and once just before dusk caught a glimpse of a full-grown jaguar, its yellow eyes gleaming in the faded light.

Katherine continued her evening chess matches with Pancho Villa, and sometimes during daytime breaks the general played checkers with Timmy, even letting him win on occasion. At each of these events, Katherine noticed Tom Mix hovering in the shadows. He always seemed to be doing something — leading his horse, looking for firewood — that brought him within sight whenever Villa was with Katherine.

Once, after Katherine had given Villa a particularly instructive lesson in chess, he had managed to take her castle and was moving toward her queen when she stopped him.

"Suppose you take my queen," she said, "and then I'm in check, right?"

"Yes, señorita," replied Villa. "And I will have you and the game."

"But not if I take your bishop here, because I have the next move; then *you* go into check, with no place to hide because you're in a box, and so I win the game."

Villa reflected on this for a long time, slowly tracing with his finger the moves she'd described.

"You are right, little señorita," Villa said finally. "You know, this chess," he went on, "is not unlike running an army. It's always the one thing you don't think of that does you in."

Katherine looked at him and smiled. She didn't know armies, but she did know chess, and Villa had been good to his word about keeping them in the clothes they needed.

"It's just a game," she said.

"So is everything else, little señorita. But sometime the stakes get higher."

Meanwhile, Timmy's spirits had improved immensely since he'd recovered from the gila monster bite. Sometimes Tom Mix would put him on his horse, seated in front of him, and let the boy take the reins while Pluto, the Mexican hairless, trotted alongside. Once, after they'd set up camp, Mix took Timmy down the canyon and let him shoot his pistol at oranges he'd picked up and lined across a log. He even taught him rope tricks. Mix kept reminding them that Villa had only taken them along for their own safety and when they got to a civilized place he would send them back to their parents. They were not placated by this and Donita Ollas pooh-poohed it as lies and deception.

But even though Katherine wasn't sure she believed Mix, she began more and more to like him. She especially liked the way he sometimes held her shoulders to help her down from her horse, and he was well skilled at conjuring delicious stews and soups at his campfire, while most everybody else was eating plain beans and beef. If they had to be captive, they could do worse than being under the care of Tom Mix.

During a break in chess games one evening, Villa asked Katherine to go for a walk with him. He was scrubbed clean and perfumed as usual and in the warmth of the canyons had removed his coat and hat as they strolled beside the streambed several hundred yards until they were out of earshot of the rest of the party.

"How old are you, little señorita?" Villa asked. He reached to tweak her cheek but she moved away.

"I will be thirteen soon," she said.

"Do you still think I am a terrible person?"

Katherine didn't know what to answer. If she said yes, it might anger him. If she said no, who knew what effect that might produce?

"I miss my mummy and papa," she replied. She saw Tom Mix, sitting on a rock above the stream, industriously cleaning his pistol. Villa never seemed to notice his artful glances their way.

"I can understand that," Villa said. He kicked a rock into the water and watched the ripples it made in the shallow stream. "Let's hope that soon you'll be with them."

"How soon?" Katherine asked.

"It will have to be after we get out of these barrancas," he said.

"And you'll let us go then?"

"I will let you go when it is safe. You wouldn't want me to turn you loose in Mexico with no protections, would you?"

"I don't know," Katherine said. "I think we could find our way home."

"There are dangerous men out there," the general replied. "There's no telling what they might do."

Katherine hung her head and looked into the water. She saw her reflection in the fading light. And then she saw Villa move close behind her, to one side, and reach out and put his arm around her shoulders. She smelled the perfume and below it the odor of perspiration he hadn't been able to scrub off. His fingers clutched her upper arm.

"You could do me a favor . . ."

"No," she said. "Please."

"Señorita, I'm not going to hurt you. Believe me. I —"

"I want my mother!" Katherine cried, moving away. "I want my father!"

Just then a gunshot cracked out across the canyon walls and a bullet ricocheted off a large stone in the stream. Its nasty pinging note hung in the air as a high-pitched shriek. Villa grabbed Katherine by the collar and snatched her almost off her feet while diving behind some large boulders. He lay flat in the sandy gravel, holding her down beside him by her head. He cursed himself for leaving his pistol back in camp and remained motionless until he could only feel the beating of his heart. Soon there were voices, and a number of his men rushed up, including Tom Mix, brandishing his pistol.

From his hiding place in the shrubbery of the canyon rim, Julio clenched his teeth. He'd had Villa straight in his sights, but Johnny's instruction had been to fire just to the side of him. It was not the time to kill the man. Julio remembered his own father, Buck, and wished he had put the bullet through Villa's heart, but knew he had to do what Johnny said. After all, Johnny was the leader, and it was his wife they were trying to rescue. The plan Johnny had designed, and Julio was to implement, was fairly simple: to get Villa nervous; let him know that over a period of days, or weeks even, that people were trying to kill him. Then Villa might panic, send out troops away from the main body, out of the *querencia,* leaving Donita lightly guarded, which was when Johnny would make his move. From behind, Julio felt a sudden tap on his shoulder and knew it was Gourd Woman, the signal to hightail it.

"A sniper!" Villa shouted, pointing ahead high into the trees. The men began pouring fire, and when they quit, a hush refilled the canyon. "Sniper" was a new expression for "sharpshooter." Market hunters who shot snipe were said to be the best shots. The British had coined the term on the Western Front in the big European war.

"Are you hurt, General?" somebody cried.

"No, I'm still here with the girl."

Men appeared around the rocks and formed a sort of human shield around Villa and Katherine.

"Did you see a flash?" one asked.

"No, nothing. Only heard a single shot. It missed me by several feet."

They continued the shield Villa and rushed him back to the campsite. It was dark by then and Villa's men pulled up some wagons to form a barricade, while others hastily gathered a posse and galloped off in the direction they had heard the gunshot come from. Katherine was taken by Mix back to his own campfire. She was shaken but tried to be calm.

"You've skinned your knees," Mix said. "Let's put some salve on them."

"I'm all right," Katherine said.

"What happened?" asked Timmy.

"I don't know, there was a shot. Just one. We hid behind rocks."

"Who was it?" Timmy said. He leaned over conspiratorially. "Do you think it was Grandpapa and Daddy?"

"I don't know," Katherine repeated. Mix

was rubbing the salve on her knees.

"Could have been anybody," he said, but he said it without conviction. Somebody had fired that shot, but he couldn't imagine who or why. The Federales would have ambushed them in force with machine guns. So would anybody else with a brain. A single shot, then nothing. Who knew what it meant?

Pancho Villa was thinking exactly the same thing, with one exception — Sanchez's ghost. A lone rifle shot that had missed, but was that the plan?

A warning?

If Sanchez had wanted him dead, why not kill him? He was a big target. Also, he thought, the shooter might be one of the remnants of the Apaches. It was said a few might still be roaming the canyons after all these years. Whatever or whoever it was, Villa understood there was a price on his head in Mexico City, and it was a cheerless feeling, knowing that so many people wanted to kill him.

It was nearly half an hour before Julio and Gourd Woman made their way back to Johnny Olla's place in the rear of the caravan. Rafael was already there and had related the confusion in Villa's camp when the shot was fired. Rafael had sidled past various soldiers in the outfit until he got close enough to Villa's tents to see what was going on. He didn't know that because Villa had taken the walk with Katherine he wasn't even there. Rafael hung around at the edges of the encampment, smoking and trying to look inconspicuous. When the shot rang out, almost everyone jumped to their feet, and there was a great commotion. In the faint light, Rafael could see Mix's campfire, with Donita and Timmy and several others around it. Everyone stood up, and several men ran off toward the sound, but Tom Mix didn't, as Johnny Ollas had hoped he would. When Julio and Gourd Woman reappeared, they, too, wanted to know what happened.

"They did not abandon her entirely," Rafael said. "The Americano moved in close with her and the little boy and he looked pretty wary."

"I could have killed him," Julio said of Villa. "It was just luck and the last of the light that let me find him alone — or out with the little girl."

"And they came after you?" Johnny asked.

"Oh, yes," said Julio. "First a bunch of soldiers came running to where Villa had hid himself and the girl behind rocks. Then they started shooting, and that's when we got out of there. But I could see they had got together a party to come after us on horseback. They rode up the canyon, probably close to where I'd been."

"He could have killed him, all right," Gourd

Woman said. "He had plenty of time."

"She's got good eyes," Julio said.

"I see what God wants me to see," Gourd Woman replied.

"For a moment, I had his back right in my sights," Julio said.

"Well, it's not what we want quite yet," said Johnny. "If we killed him, who knows what would happen? They might murder Donita on the spot. We need to be patient a little while longer."

FORTY-SEVEN

For several days it was uncertain whether Bomba was going to live or die, but hot soups and warm compresses slowly restored his health. He remained weak but was finally able to sit up near the edge of the cave and look out over the ravine. The man had dressed him in warm clothing made of the skins of animals he had killed for food — deer, rabbit, squirrel. In time Bomba managed to walk around and explore the cliff dwelling. To his astonishment it contained dozens of rooms in vast catacombs deep inside the cliff. Bats hung from the roofs and swarmed out at twilight.

A spring burbled from the rocks, providing water. Pieces of pottery, broken and whole, were everywhere — as was a great scattering of bones, animal and human. One cavernous room was covered in layers of ossified human feces; in another were stacks of mummies wrapped in clay. Strange pictures were carved into the walls that told a story Bomba understood — of a people who lived in the wild and worshipped many gods. It was a creepy place, especially for a man of Bomba's strong superstitions.

The man whose cave Bomba had stumbled on was named Henry O. Flipper, and in a land of strange stories, he had one of the strangest of all. He tried to convey it to Bomba over a period of several days, but wasn't sure how much got through. Flipper, it turned out, had been the first Negro graduate of the United States Military Academy at West Point.

He was born in Georgia, where his parents had been slaves before the Civil War. After he was commissioned a lieutenant, he was sent to Arizona to serve with the "Buffalo Soldiers" of the Tenth Cavalry regiment, chasing Indians. Five years later, while he was acting as commissary officer, several thousand dollars turned up missing, and Flipper was accused and court-martialed. The court acquitted him of embezzlement but found him guilty of "conduct unbecoming an officer," and he was kicked out of the army.

Humiliated, for the next twenty-five years Flipper used his West Point training to make a living as a surveyor and mining engineer, mostly in Mexico, where he was trusted and respected by the mine owners and managers. Now in his fifties, Flipper had been on what he decided was his last mining expedition when the Mexican Revolution exploded.

Recently Villa's people had swept through the gold, silver, copper, and tin mining towns in the sierras, driving out the gringos. A few weeks earlier they had murdered a dozen American mining engineers by shoving their train into a tunnel and then setting the tunnel on fire. Word of this quickly spread through the mining community, and scores of gringo miners scrambled best they could toward the border. Flipper himself had been trying to sneak toward Chihuahua City to catch a train north when he learned Villa was loose in the mountains. Since this was familiar terrain to him, he'd holed up in the cave of the mummies to await further developments.

When Bomba was able to convey what he was doing in this untamed wilderness, Flipper was amazed the man was still alive. Flipper felt lucky to be alive himself. He had stumbled on this particular cave by accident some weeks earlier, and considered himself especially fortunate to have come across it when it was almost winter.

"Pancho Villa and his ilk have even less liking of us than they do the white Americans," Flipper stated bluntly. "When they shoot us, they shoot us twice — once to kill us, and once to kill our ghost."

Bomba grunted. He had seen Villa's penchant for violence.

Flipper was impressed with Bomba's ability

to read the pictographs on the cave walls. Over the years Flipper had become an expert on native languages and learned to decipher ancient symbols, but Bomba picked it up so quickly Flipper decided he must be a genius. Once, however, he stopped Bomba from entering a large and uncharted chamber of the labyrinth. Treasure or not, Flipper had never darkened that forbidding portal because of an inscription etched over the door. When Bomba started to cross the opening, Flipper restrained him, pointing up at the inscription.

"It's a curse," Flipper said.

Bomba studied the writing but could make nothing of it. There were no pictures, only language-like symbols.

Flipper translated:

"As for the one who will violate this tomb, he shall be seized by Itzcoatl. He shall be for the flame of the Tepanec. He is an enemy and so is his son. May donkeys fuck him, may donkeys fuck his wife, may his wife fuck his son."

Bomba replied with a grunt.

"I don't much believe in curses myself," the old soldier said, "but this one seems sincere."

"Whose is it?" Bomba asked.

"Who knows?" Flipper answered. "And it may be a bunch of shit, too, but why take the chance?"

When he recovered sufficient strength, Bomba asked Flipper if he could help him find Pancho Villa and the children. The two men were sitting on rocks by the fire on the ledge of the cave.

"You must be out of your mind," Flipper responded. "Do you realize what he'll do to you if he catches you — me, too, for that matter?" A misty rain was falling and Flipper had cooked up some beans and corn, along with a rabbit he'd caught in a snare and was roasting slowly on a spit over hot coals.

Bomba tried to explain about Katherine and Timmy and the family, but Flipper was having none of it.

"I understand loyalty," he said. "Hell, I was the epitome of loyalty myself once — to an entire government — until that goverment turned on me and framed me and swept me back under the rug where they felt I belonged."

"Still mad?" Bomba asked.

"Damn right I am," said Flipper. "Besides, let me ask you this: Do you think that if Pancho Villa had captured *you,* instead — that this Colonel Shaughnessy or any of his people would come looking for you in these wild mountains? Hell, no, they wouldn't."

Bomba sat motionless, his eyes looking into

the eyes of his newfound friend. He knew about loyalty, too, though he couldn't really put a definition on it. For him, it was inborn. He received good food, shelter, clothing, money, but there was more than that. There was a bond between him and the Colonel in which Bomba felt he was a member of the family, as well as their guardian.

"Aw, c'mon, now," Flipper said. "You did all you could. You almost died protecting those people. You gotta let it go. Save yourself. These are perilous times. People are being murdered by the millions. What chance you think a couple of niggers like us got against the likes of Pancho Villa and his army?"

Bomba continued to look at Flipper. He knew he was asking a lot. Maybe more than a lot. But it was the Colonel's grandkids, whom he'd known since they were in swaddling clothes. What else could he do? How could he go back, assuming he got back, and face the Colonel?

"Hell, you'll never locate them out there in those canyons," Flipper continued. "It's a maze. I even get lost there myself, and I been working down here for twenty-five years. It's a crazy idea, simply insane."

"Rabbit cooked," Bomba said finally. He lifted the meat off the fire.

"Now, there's the spirit," Flipper said. "Let's eat a good supper, and tomorrow

you'll rethink all this and we can figure a way
to get ourselves back to the U.S. of A."

FORTY-EIGHT

Villa and his people had been moving through the canyons nearly a week when Reed and Bierce began arguing over whether or not Villa was a socialist. Reed insisted that he was. They were riding side by side down a desolate stretch of canyon so narrow that the sun only made it to the bottom a few minutes a day. All in all, it was a cool, pleasant morning.

"Look what he did when he had control of Northern Mexico," Reed said ardently. "He took over the railroads, mines, manufacturing, utilities, telephones, broke up the big landholdings, and redistributed the property among the people. He only left the rich Americans alone, and finally he's going for them, too."

"Yes, and all at the point of a gun," Bierce reminded him.

"There are times it's the only way, Mr. Robinson," Reed countered.

"And how much do you expect he will keep

for himself?"

Reed was silent on this question.

Bierce normally didn't converse with socialists, but he felt the need to talk to somebody, and Reed was one of the few respectable conversationalists in camp.

"And what about in America?" Bierce asked. "What will happen there?"

Reed squinted and looked skyward. "They'd tried it by the ballot, and look where it's got them," he said. The big industrialists had bought off voters with whiskey and cash, threatened their jobs, stuffed ballot boxes, and threw their organizers in prison. They couldn't even organize a union without fear of being beaten, shot, or jailed.

"The people won't stand for it much longer," he told Bierce.

Bierce had been irritable all morning because of a saddle sore on his buttock. At least talking might keep his mind off it.

"Are these *people* you're talking about the same ones who are presently blowing up buildings and assassinating our presidents?" Bierce asked.

Reed was actually enjoying the conversation; was grateful for it. And despite the fact that he and Bierce disagreed on almost everything, Reed had come to like the old gentleman "Jack Robinson," in spite of himself. The man was witty and informed and willing to listen. If there was to be a peaceful socialist revolution in America, Reed understood it was the Jack Robinsons of the nation who would have to be convinced. Once that was accomplished, the path was clear.

"You frighten me, Mr. Reed," Bierce said.

"Why is that?"

"Because according to your creed, you'd be willing to tear up the Constitution of the United States."

"It's a piece of paper," Reed said. "A good one, mind you," he added. "But a piece of paper nonetheless. Times change. Ideas change."

They rode awhile in silence as Bierce digested this last statement with mounting disgust. The sun was high and finally reaching the bottom of the canyon. He thought he felt a headache coming on.

"Where did you attend school, Mr. Reed?" Bierce inquired.

"Harvard."

"I thought so."

"And you, Mr. Robinson?"

"I didn't," Bierce said.

"I thought so."

The first sign Reed and Bierce noticed was a thin hum in the air. Then the blood bees swarmed. They weren't actually bees and they didn't actually sting — they bit. They bit hands and faces and also through clothes.

Others ahead and behind were having the same trouble. Horses began to buck and scream and plunge, and everyone was frantically swatting at themselves.

Reed and Bierce loosed their reins and spurred their horses after the others at a gallop. It took what seemed to be eternity, but after a while they slowed up and the blood bees had gone away.

In their way, two of the supply wagons had turned over and everybody in the party had nasty little stinging bites, which quickly began to itch. As people began righting the overturned wagons, Villa's doctor began dispensing ointments and poultices, and by afternoon everyone had at least several of these pressed on.

Reed was particularly put out because it had begun as such a fine day and to have his conversation interrupted this way seemed unfair.

He said to Tom Mix, who was applying poultices on Katherine and Timmy, "It was positively savage. They might have killed us if we were on foot."

"Them things have got a vengeful nature," Mix responded.

"So what do you think happened? Did somebody disturb their hive or something?"

"Who knows?" Mix told him. "It's a pretty chancy life out here."

"I'm curious," Bierce interjected. "With all

that clover you Harvard fellows must have been rolling in, didn't you ever encounter bees?"

"Different kind of clover, different kind of bees," Reed told him with a wry smile, figuring that their conversation had come to an end anyway.

That evening, instead of the chess game when Villa came by Mix's campfire, he asked Katherine again to take a walk with him. She was apprehensive and still aching from the bites, but dared not refuse. This time, instead of going outside the security of the encampment, Villa escorted her a short way to clearing in a grove of sycamore trees, out of earshot of the others, and at least didn't try to pinch her cheeks. She noticed that Mix had maneuvered himself to a stump in view of the clearing and was polishing his saddle in his lap with saddle soap.

"What I was trying to ask you the other evening was for a favor," Villa said. "But you misunderstood, and then we were interrupted."

"What favor?" Katherine asked.

"I want you to teach me how to read," he said, curtly, defensively.

"Read?"

"I can't read. I never learned how."

"In Spanish?" Katherine asked hesitantly. "I know French but I don't know Spanish."

"No. In English. English will be fine. Over time I've had to deal with communiqués from the Americans and I'm never sure if they are trying to trick me. Once I can read anything, I can read," he said.

"I've never tried to teach anybody how to read before. Why don't you ask Mr. Robinson or Mr. Reed?"

"Because I'm embarrassed," Villa told her bluntly. "It would be better for you to do it."

"But I don't have any books or anything," Katherine protested. "I learned to read from books. Our teacher —"

"I've seen teachers teach by writing on a blackboard," Villa countered. "Couldn't you just write lessons on a piece of paper?"

"Yes — I suppose so. When do you want to begin?"

"Is tomorrow too soon?"

"No, I guess not."

"How long will it take?" Villa asked.

"I don't know," Katherine said truthfully. "I suppose it depends on whether you apply yourself."

"I'll try, I promise. It's a necessary thing."

"Why?" she asked. "Is it because you want to be president, and presidents have to read? Is that what you're fighting a war for?"

"No, señorita. I'm not educated enough to be president. And it's not what I want. I'm fighting to keep somebody else from being president."

"Who?"

"For the moment, General Carranza. But that could change, too."

"What is wrong with General Carranza?" she asked. But Villa just shook his head.

"I want to know how to write, too," he told her.

"Oh," said Katherine. "Well, I guess the two go together. We'll see."

While Villa was asking Katherine his favor, Bierce sat down on a log away from everybody and took out his writing tablet.

Dear Miss Christiansen,
Villa lost the fight at Chihuahua City and we are now deep in the mountains. His men fight like devils but are reckless, undisciplined and there is much indiscriminate firing. Their behavior would not be tolerated in an American army. A few nights ago somebody took a potshot at the general himself, but he was not injured.

He includes in his caravan two young children, boy and girl, and a Mexican woman insisting they've been kidnapped. Villa claims he is only escorting them to safety, but I have my doubts. He's a ruthless man and kidnapping is not beneath him. He is furious at the administration in Washington for recognizing his enemy

Carranza as leader of Mexico, to his exclusion, and for closing the border to shipments of arms and supplies for his army.

The man Reed whom I mentioned in my last letter has revealed himself to me as a socialist. He's decent enough but his philosophy isn't right. It isn't even wrong. That's what's scary about it.

The weather agrees with me and even though the travel is rough and hard I feel hale for a man my age. Our diet is mainly beef and beans and onions and biscuits but I yearn for those good chicken dinners or a shad roe breakfast at the Willard.

Yours truly, A.B.

Bierce tore the paper from the tablet, sealed it in an envelope, and slipped it in his vest pocket next to the other unmailed letters he'd written to his secretary. He'd no sooner arrived back at the campfire than a gunshot rang out, zinging though the branches above and creating a little shower of leaves and twigs that floated down. Immediately there was the sound of machine guns and rifle fire ahead, where the sound of the shot had originated. In the camp there was shouting and confusion.

Villa himself had just returned from his conversation with Katherine and was standing over a kettle dishing up a plate of beans when the shot was fired. He fell flat to the ground and rolled toward the cover of a tree, cursing in Spanish.

From the canyon ahead, the shouting grew louder, and presently a group of horsemen appeared in the dim light, the lead rider dragging something behind him on a rope. It was the body of a man dressed in the white peasant uniform of one of Villa's soldiers. The rider dragged the body through the shallow stream and deposited it on a little spit of sand next to Villa's encampment.

"We got him sure, General," the rider cried excitedly. "He was right where you thought he'd be — up on that canyon rim there."

"Who is it?" Villa asked. Two men roughly turned the corpse over, but its face had been shot away by machine gun fire. There must have been a dozen holes in the blood-soaked clothing.

"Does anybody know this man?" Villa demanded. His lips were curled back in a snarl.

People shook their heads.

"Go through his pockets," Fierro ordered.

Another rider came up waving a rifle with a telescope sight. Fierro grabbed it.

"This is one of ours," he spat. He turned to one of his aides. "Go to the armory wagon and find out if one of our rifles is missing and how this happened."

"There is nothing in his clothing but a few

pesos," said one of the men examining the body. He held out several coins in his hand.

"All right," Villa told Fierro, "I want to scour this camp. Find out who's missing. Tell all the section leaders to assemble here in half an hour."

Fierro nodded and started to walk away; then, as an afterthought, he spun around and snatched the coins from the man who was still holding them out. Giving the man the once-over, Fierro spat, "Vamoose," and shoved the coins in his pocket as he stomped away.

Johnny Ollas and Rafael were waiting nervously with the cattle herd when Luis ran up breathless and white with shock.

"I think they killed Julio." He shuddered.

Johnny's breath caught in his throat. He'd heard the shot and then the machine gun fire and sensed it boded ill, coming so quickly after the shot. Still, he'd hoped for the best.

"I blinked the flashlight near Villa's camp," Luis said, "and when the shot was fired, I started coming back here. But then when I heard the other shots, I returned. They were dragging somebody behind a horse. From what I could tell, he was dead."

"Julio?" An animal wail came out of Johnny's throat. Julio, the youngest, whom he'd taught how to ride and rope.

"I think so," said Luis. "I couldn't get too close."

Just then Gourd Woman appeared out of the gloom.

"He was shot," she said.

"I think we'd better get out of here," said Johnny. He felt his voice crack.

Johnny's heart was beating so fast he thought it might jump outside his chest. There was nothing left to do but run. The plan might have worked. The ambush shots had gotten Villa edgy and he'd be looking for trouble ahead. Ahead and not behind, where Johnny had planned to come from next time, driving the herd straight through the camp, scattering people and confusing them, and then he would grab Donita in the uproar and they would disappear back down the canyons before anyone could figure out what had happened. But Villa had outsmarted him, laying a trap for his trap, and Julio was dead.

Johnny, Luis, and Rafael had just saddled their horses when Fierro and a party of a dozen soldiers burst into the clearing where the cattle were. The soldiers' rifles were drawn.

"Is one of your men missing?" Fierro demanded.

"I don't know," Johnny mumbled. "It's dark."

"How many do you have here with this herd?"

"Well, me and Luis and Rafael — and the woman."

"That's it?"

"Yes," Johnny fumbled.

"Say, amigo, why are your horses saddled?" Fierro asked suddenly. "You going someplace?"

"No . . . we've been out checking the beefs," said Johnny.

One of the soldiers was a sergeant who had a cigarette in his mouth. He puffed out a big cloud of smoke and said to Fierro, "General, I think there was five of them here. I used to come back with the orders for the beefs to be brought up. There was six when they came, including the woman. Then one of their guys was killed back before we got to the mountains. They cut his guts out, remember? That still left five."

"So how many are you?" Fierro said slowly, his suspicions aroused.

"Well, there is four of us. We had another guy, but I haven't seen him for a day or so."

"We can look at the roster and tell how many you are supposed to be," Fierro said, "but I think you all better come back with me and talk to the chief. He'll be interested in your story."

FORTY-NINE

Bomba and Henry Flipper learned at the Rarámuri Indian village that Villa had taken to the canyons. They also learned there was another party, too, following after them, but didn't know what to make of that. But after working the area for twenty-five years, Flipper was pretty sure where Villa would have gotten to by now, and he knew a shortcut.

Flipper cursed himself, and not always silently, for getting mixed up in a crazy thing such as this. He should have stayed put in the cave of the mummies. This was against every judgment he'd ever made, good or bad. But he also knew there was no way Bomba could possibly find Villa by himself and that he'd likely die out there alone. So he agreed to try to locate Villa. After that, Flipper would wash his hands of it and hightail it for the border, and Bomba would be on his own.

When he learned he'd been correct, and that the Indians had seen a young boy with Villa's troop, Flipper led Bomba and himself back down the way they had come and headed north on a course he calculated would parallel Villa's on the other side of the mountains. They'd make better time that way, and maybe make up for the time that was lost. Eventually they came to a mountain pass Flipper believed would intersect Villa's path through the canyons. They arrived just before dark in time to hear shots fired, and in the morning found themselves looking directly down into Villa's encampment. They were hidden on an outcropping that reached out over the canyon like a sharp tooth snagging the air. They could make out people, animals, and wagons.

"You see any children?" Flipper asked.

"Can't see that far," Bomba told him. They were behind low shrubbery, lying flat on their stomachs. The morning sun had risen behind, them but not high enough to shine down onto the canyon floor.

Flipper went back to one of the donkeys he'd tethered to a tree and returned with a spyglass. Bomba scanned the glass slowly across his field of vision. Something strange was going on. He saw no children, but there was an affair in one of the offshoot gullies, a little box canyon, that seemed a hive of activity. Bomba concentrated the spyglass on it. Dozens of men were gathered at one end of the gully, which was blocked off from the main canyon by a rockslide. Within the gully he could see a few men in motion, and they seemed to be moving around a bull.

"What is it?" Flipper asked.

Bomba handed him the glass. They could both make out a faint hum of human shouting that drummed up out of the canyon. Flipper studied the scene for a few moments, then put the spyglass down.

"What the hell is this?" he whispered. "That looks like . . . a bullfight going on down there!"

FIFTY

When they took Johnny Ollas to Pancho Villa, Johnny assumed his goose was cooked. The only slight chance was to convince Villa that Julio had somehow harbored a personal grudge against Villa and the decision to ambush was Julio's alone. It might have worked, until Donita saw Johnny being led into Villa's camp and rushed to him.

"Wait a minute!" Fierro said. "Say, this is that vaquero from back at that big ranch where we killed the fighting bull, isn't it? And this woman was his wife, right?"

Fierro was smirking at him sourly, as if he'd just eaten a pickle.

"So, Private Ollas," said Villa, "this is why you have come to join my army — to kill me, eh?" Dozens of people had gathered, including Bierce and Reed. Mix hurried Donita and the children away because he was pretty sure what was going to happen next.

"No," Johnny said, "to bring home my wife." He guessed it wouldn't do any good to lie now. They pretty much had him red-handed.

"Well, you tried to, didn't you?" Villa snapped. "Your man there was taking shots at me, wasn't he?" Villa motioned toward Julio's body, which still lay on the spit of sand. "Or were you with him, too?"

"No," Johnny said. "I . . . Julio was not trying to kill you, General."

"I suppose you wouldn't be the first man to lie," Villa informed him.

"No, General. We were merely trying to distract you."

"To what purpose?"

"I'm not a killer," Johnny said. "I am a bullfighter. The only way I knew how to fight you was like I fight the bulls. I tried to draw you out, see which way you hooked, correct it, if possible, and then make my move."

"Which was?"

"To run the herd through your camp and in the confusion rescue Donita. I just wanted to bring her home safely."

"Bullfighter, eh? You are a matador?"

"I am."

"And you had shots fired at me and were going to endanger my army by running a herd of stinking beefs through it!"

Johnny could see Villa was becoming worked up. It gave him a queasy feeling in his bowels. "Julio was not trying to hit you with the rifle," Johnny told him. "He could have, though, with the telescope sight. He was only trying to throw you off your guard."

"Off my guard!" Villa roared. "Are you stupid? Being shot at only put me *on* my guard! And look where it got your man there." He gestured again toward Julio's still form, the shirt and pants soaked in blood.

"He was my brother and my picador," Johnny said.

"Bullfighter!" Villa spat. "You're a fool, too."

"I know it," said Johnny, "but what was I supposed to do? You took my wife."

Villa considered this for a few moments. The silence was familiar to anyone who had known him long. The next words Villa uttered would seal Johnny's fate, of that much they were sure.

"And these people with you," Villa said, nodding to Rafael, Luis, and Gourd Woman. "What are their roles?"

"They are my cuadrilla," Johnny said. He started to say they were his brothers, too, but thought better of it. Guilt by relation might be even worse than guilt by association.

"The woman, too?" Villa seemed taken aback.

"No. She's just a peddler. She's not involved."

"Well, all right, Señor Matador," Villa said. "I'll tell you what. I'm going to give you a fighting chance, which is more than most men would receive who are assassins. So you fight the bull, huh? Well, I saw a big fighting bull back there with the herd. Is he still there?"

"He is," said Johnny hesitantly. "His name is Casa Grande and he's the grandson of the bull you killed at Señor Shaughnessy's ranch."

"And you, Señor Ollas, are going to fight him," Villa snorted, with the satisfaction of a man who had just divined a solution to a sticky problem.

"Fight him?" Johnny said.

"Yes — you claim to be a matador, right?"

"I am, but —"

"No 'buts.' I could have you shot right now, or in the morning you will fight this bull. Take your pick."

"But that's . . . I don't have my cuadrilla — there's just Rafael and Luis. And I don't have anything — no *muleto,* no *estoque,* no —"

"Oh, that is not for you to worry about." Villa rubbed his hands together warmly. "For a *muleto,* I think you can use the shirt of your companion there — your brother, you say." He pointed to Julio's body. "It will make a good cape — blood-red, eh?" And for an *es-toque,* well you can use one of our cavalry sabers. I'll have it especially sharpened up for you."

"But that's crazy," Johnny said nervously. "A saber is curved. It's not an *estoque.* There's no way to place it properly — it won't go in."

"Ah, but it is all we have, matador. Maybe you will plow new ground for bullfighting here — perhaps you can use the saber to cut off the bull's head."

"Or stick it up his ass," Fierro remarked.

"What do you think, General?" Villa asked Fierro. "We will have a bullfight, no?"

"It's murder — the animal will kill him," Fierro noted casually. "Still, our men have been without entertainment for some time."

"Good," Villa said. "The bullfight will begin when there's enough light to watch it."

"Would you mind," Johnny asked, "if I was with my wife tonight?"

"I don't see why not, señor. But you must also get some sleep. Tomorrow will be a big day for you," Villa replied.

At dawn next morning a remarkable apparition came riding into Villa's camp. He was tall and ramrod-stiff, with high polished riding boots and wearing a monocle. He guided his horse almost casually down the streambed that meandered through the canyon until he found someone to take him to Pancho Villa.

"Good morning, Herr General," Strucker said. Villa did not offer his hand. He had just returned from a clump of bushes behind which he'd performed his morning routine and was unhappy because his stomach was sour.

"Who the devil are *you*?" Villa asked, puzzled.

The German introduced himself and for once told the truth.

"I am representing His Imperial Majesty, the kaiser of the German Empire."

"Is that so?" Villa said. "Well, what do you want here?"

"I've been trying to find you since Chihuahua City," said Strucker. "It was an unfortunate reverse for you, I'm sure."

"We gave as good as we got," Villa told him curtly. "It didn't seem smart to hang around."

"No doubt," Strucker said. "I wonder if there is somewhere we can go and talk. I have come on official business."

"Are you hungry?" Villa said.

"Yes, I am," replied Strucker.

"Well, there's food on the fire. Someone will get you a plate. By the way, how in hell did you find me?"

"I have followed your trail from Chihuahua City," said the German.

"Are you a tracker?"

"No. I had guides to the Indian village you visited in the mountains. From there the Indians helped me. I'm sure I'd be wandering around out here for years without them."

"That's most likely true," Villa observed. "I should have killed those Indians before I left.

"Anyway," he continued, "there is a piece of entertainment this morning. There is going to be a bullfight. After that, you can state your business."

"A bullfight," Strucker remarked. "What an odd place to hold one."

"Yes, it is."

"Do you do it often?"

"No," Villa replied. "It's a special occasion."

FIFTY-ONE

The Rarámuri guides told Colonel Shaughnessy they were just a day behind Villa's party and might overtake him at any time. The Indians also informed him they were going home now. They had reached the limits of their range, they said, and the extent of their knowledge of the canyons. The Colonel didn't like this, but there wasn't much he could do about it. He was stewing over this late in the afternoon when catastrophe struck. The Colonel had been riding across a stream when his horse stumbled on a submerged log. The animal pitched forward, throwing the Colonel, and then, in a flailing scramble to get up, it kicked him in the leg.

Arthur and Slim witnessed the whole thing and were close enough to hear the *crack* when the leg broke, as if somebody had snapped a large stick in two. They got the Colonel out of the water and carried him to the sandy bank. Slim cut off the Colonel's trousers leg and was alarmed by what he saw.

The leg above the boot was already beginning to swell and had turned an ugly bright red.

"It's broke for sure," Slim said. "We need for somebody to go find Bob. He knows about these things." Bob was somewhere up ahead scouting. Arthur stayed with his father, who was in fierce pain.

"Tell Ah Dong to come up here," Arthur shouted. He knew the Chinaman had sedatives and other painkillers in the chuckwagon. By the time Ah Dong arrived, the Colonel was white-faced, grimacing. Taking only a quick look, the cook rushed back to his wagon.

"Papa, it's going to be all right," Arthur said. He was cradling his father's head in his lap. But he wasn't sure it would be all right. A broken leg under these conditions was no trifling matter. The Colonel looked at Arthur with pleading eyes but was speechless. Arthur knew the Old Man was fighting the urge to scream.

It didn't take long for Cowboy Bob to be located, and he returned at a gallop.

"It's broke," he said after examining the leg. "Just lucky the bone didn't poke out through the skin. Then we'd really have a problem."

"Can you set it?" Arthur asked.

"Set it? Me?" said Bob. "I ain't no doctor."

"Well, we have to do something," Arthur

replied. "What do we do?"

"Well, I reckon I'll have to try," said Bob, " 'cause it's gonna keep swellin', and then it'll be impossible. But I don't guarantee no results. If it don't set right, there's nothing more I can do."

Ah Dong came back with a bottle of laudanum, an opiate. It wasn't as good as chloroform or even ether for the process of setting the broken bone, but it would have to do. They put the bottle to the Colonel's lips and he managed to get some down. It took a while to get enough in him to take effect. By the time the Colonel was semiconscious, Bob was ready to do his work.

They sat the Colonel up so his legs were sticking out straight. Bob had used his hands to even out the sand so it was level. The break was in the tibia, just below the knee. It would have been good to remove the Colonel's boot, but Bob didn't want to disturb the leg any more than necessary. With Arthur, Slim, and Ah Dong holding the Colonel up straight, Bob began to slowly pull and turn on the leg. The Colonel let out a moan. Obviously the laudanum had not killed all the pain. Using both hands, Bob felt for the break, trying to align the tibia and the fibula with the femur and the ankle bones, too, so the leg looked as normal as possible. Then he told Arthur and Slim to pull one way while he turned the other. The Colonel groaned pitifully.

"I think I got it," Bob said, running his hands along both sides of the leg. "I don't know how good, but it looks about as straight as I can tell. I helped a guy to do this during a rodeo once, but the feller always walked with a limp after that. Now we got to fix up some kind of cast to put it in. Otherwise, it'll just separate again."

Ah Dong produced some muslin from his wagon and fashioned a sort of loose stocking to go over the leg. Then he packed it with sand from the riverbank. They made some splints by pulling plank pieces out of one of the wagons and lashed them together around the leg with rope and pieces of a spare bridle. It was a crude affair, and when they were done the Colonel looked as if he'd stepped into a tall wooden garbage can. The laudanum had finally put him into a restive sleep. There was nothing else to do but camp there for the night, falling farther behind.

"Well, now what?" Arthur asked as they sat around the fire. "I guess we'd better get him to some kind of hospital." His head was spinning at the complications — his children, his father — this threw the whole plan out of whack. They'd come all this way and now a silly horse accident had put the thing into serious jeopardy.

"Now, how you gonna do that?" Bob said. "There ain't no hospitals unless we climb back across those mountains, and it's gonna be snow and ice and God only knows what else before we get back down the other side. I don't know that we could make it. Only other thing I can think is keep on going the way we are. Sooner or later we're gonna run out of these canyons and be where there's some civilization."

"But what about Father?" Arthur said. "He needs medical attention."

"Ain't none," Bob said. "Look, don't worry, Arthur. I know he's your old man, but people been breakin' legs out here for thousands of years. He's luckier than most — we was here to set it, such as it is, and he's got a wagon to ride in. It's a sure thing he can't ride no horse. But he's a tough old bird. He'll make it."

"You think Villa's got a doctor with him?" Arthur asked. "The man must have some compassion in him, doesn't he? This is an old man who's badly hurt."

"What would you say to him? We come after you with a bunch of gunmen to get back those kidnapped kids and now you gotta help us with a doctor? I hardly think so," Bob said.

"You don't know Villa like I do," Bob continued. "Sure, maybe he'll lend you his doctor and even help carry the Colonel to safety. On the other hand, he might just murder us all. Depends on whether he's having a good day or not. You want to take the chance?"

"It was a thought," Arthur in a low voice. He walked off a distance, kicking stones in the sand, mad at himself for not thinking clearly. It was the one thing he needed to do now. Who knew what would happen? The Colonel had been the glue that held everything together, as he had been all of Arthur's life. Some of the things he did were crazy, but he'd always been the one in charge. Now they were deep in a place so wild and remote that all of them could be killed to the last man and probably nobody would ever find their bones or know what had happened to them.

Cowboy Bob was a good man, but in the end he was a hired hand with no stake in the outcome. So somebody had to take charge and mean it, and Arthur understood who that had to be. After all, it wasn't anybody else's kids, and out here you played the hand you were dealt.

Arthur stood by himself in the canyon looking up at the hard bright stars that were beginning to appear in the late autumn sky. A shiver ran through him. Despite everything else, he and Xenia had raised two good children and had become a family that, like the millions of other families when all was said and done, was alone in the world, like a little island adrift.

For all his preoccupation with the trials of the railroad company and the search for profits and security, during these last long days on the trail Arthur had begun to understand with devastating clarity that the most valuable thing a human can do is commit to another human, or humans — in this case, his family. The bleak despondence he sank into after Xenia told him about Mick Martin had turned to black despair when the children were kidnapped. Until this moment he hadn't been able to shake it off, but now something different was happening.

There was a stone in front of him and he kicked it so hard his toe stung. All his life Arthur had never really hated anybody, not even the bully Hawkins who tormented him at Groton. But suddenly there began to well up in him such a hatred of Pancho Villa and Mick Martin that he thought his head would blow off. For others who over the years had treated him poorly, Arthur had felt either fear or apathy, but never hatred. Yet that's what he was experiencing now, raw and undiluted, so that it actually pushed out the anxiety and despair. From childhood he'd been taught the difference between good and evil, but just knowing what evil was didn't protect you from it. He considered that if Katherine and Timmy were somehow free and he came upon Villa face-to-face, he'd willingly sacrifice his own life just for the satisfaction of snuffing out that cruel, wicked son-of-a-bitch. In this last, he was responding to an instinct he didn't quite comprehend, but one that he suddenly trusted unconditionally.

Finally he walked back to the fire.

"Okay, we go on," he said. "We've lost time with this and we'll probably lose more with my father and his condition. So I think we'd best get moving right after we fix some dinner. At least the canyons are easy to navigate, even at night. From now on, we'll break for sleep four hours a day and keep on pushing."

Slim glanced at Bob, who said to Arthur, "So what happens when we catch up to Villa?"

"I don't know yet," Arthur said. "I guess I'll figure it out when I see the lay of the land. Any more questions?"

"Nope, boss. No questions. I'll tell the men," Bob said.

FIFTY-TWO

Johnny Ollas sat staring into the low flames of the campfire and contemplating his fate. Donita was next to him, hugging his arm. Rafael and Luis were nearby perched on logs, and Gourd Woman squatted in the shadows. Mix hadn't put on any extra guards; there was no need to. Where could they go if they escaped?

Johnny had talked it over with Luis and Rafael earlier. He was badly handicapped from having his cuadrilla cut in half by the deaths of Julio and Rigaz. Besides, he was pretty sure Villa wasn't going to let Luis and Rafael ride horses in the fight, if he even let them in the ring in the first place. Actually, Johnny had tried to persuade them not to fight at all — the little band of brothers was already reduced enough as it was. But it appeared Villa would shoot them otherwise, so they might as well go down fighting. Villa had not said what he would do if Casa Grande was killed and they survived, but at least he *hadn't* said they would face the firing squad anyway.

"What were you thinking, coming after us like this?" Donita said. After they had taken Johnny to her, she was so glad to see him that she'd thought of nothing but embraces and gratitude. Finally the grave truth of his predicament had sunk in.

"I had to do something. I couldn't just sit around and wait."

"Better than this," Donita said. She knew enough about the bullring to understand the desperate situation Johnny was facing. Since people began recording the history of bullfighting about half of all matadors had ended their careers by being crippled or gored to death — and that happened in regular rings with a fair fight.

"Well, whatever I do in the morning, I guess it will have to be pretty quick," Johnny observed. "I'm not going to be out there trying to please the crowd."

There was no sleeping that night for Johnny Ollas and the others. Dawn arrived above the canyon rim with a hellish glow that quickly turned to gray. Exotic birds began to squawk high in the trees, while all around was the din of Villa's soldiers awakening — low muffled curses, the snorting of horses, the rattle of utensils, the sounds of hawking, spitting, pissing, and coughing — a strange and mournful cacophony to greet another day.

Except that it wasn't just another day for Johnny Ollas. His was to be a trial by fire, or, rather, trial by *el toro.*

"Maybe Casa Grande will recognize you," Rafael had encouraged him the night before. "If he does, he'll have that little uncertainty — just a moment or two . . . who knows? It would give you a better chance."

"I doubt it," Johnny had replied. "When they get him away from those steers and he sees me alone, there'll be only one thing on his mind."

Fierro suddenly appeared, with the usual sarcastic sneer on his face. Lieutenant Crucia was with him, the necklace of noses dangling about his chest.

"Well, matador, are you ready to fight the bull?"

"I wouldn't want to keep him waiting," Johnny said mildly.

"You wouldn't want to keep the chief waiting, either," Fierro added. "Lieutenant Crucia has your gear." Crucia produced the neatly folded bloody shirt that had been Julio's and a gleaming cavalry saber. In revulsion, Johnny dropped the still-damp shirt on the ground. He fingered the saber and found it sharp as promised but totally unsuited to the type of sword he needed. To kill the bull it was necessary to plunge the blade deep into the muscle hump on its neck and sever its spinal chord, but the cavalry saber was honed only on one side and designed for slashing, not sticking.

"I'll have to have more of these," Johnny said flatly.

"More sabers? What for?"

"Sometimes they break. Sometimes one doesn't get the job done."

"Well, that's all we can spare, so you better be careful. I'm sorry we couldn't come up with a *traje de luces* for you," Fierro added nicely.

"It doesn't matter what kind of clothes I wear," Johnny said. "What about my cuadrilla?"

"Cuadrilla? I only see two men here," Fierro said mockingly.

"Well, they'll have to do," Johnny replied.

"The general made no mention of others."

"Don't you want it to be a bullfight?" Johnny asked. "Or just for me to go out there and get killed?"

"Well, there are time considerations. We have to be on our way. But I'll see what I can do. Can they use knives, or do they need lances, too?"

"Can they use horses?" Johnny asked hopefully.

"I think that would be out of the question," said Fierro. "We need all our horses. The chief would be displeased to see any of our animals killed."

"But we brought our horses with us when

we joined up. We own the horses." Johnny thought this was a good point, and fair.

"Not anymore," Fierro told him. "They are the property of the Grand Army of the North."

"Then knives will have to do," Johnny said resignedly.

"So," said Fierro, "shall we go?"

Gourd Woman had been hovering nearby and she sidled up to Johnny and slipped something in his pocket.

"What's that?" Fierro wanted to know.

"A good-luck charm," Gourd Woman answered.

"So, you think I'll need it, huh?" Johnny asked cheerlessly. "What is it — one of your bones?"

"Yes," she said, "it will make you invisible."

Johnny laughed in spite of himself. "Can any of you see me now?"

"No, but we know where you are," Fierro told him. "Let's go."

They had set up the bullfight in a little offshoot box canyon a few hundred yards ahead of the encampment. It was smaller than a regular bullring but not by much, which Johnny Ollas was quick to see. It had a narrow entrance that was marked by a collapsed debris of rocks that Villa's men arranged so they could pile them up again fairly quickly once Casa Grande entered the arena.

This would more or less form a ring, though any respectable fighting bull could climb up the rock pile and out of it, if it was so inclined.

Getting Casa Grande into the ring was no small problem. Fighting bulls are loaded through chutes from corrals into the arenas, but there were no chutes here. Fierro had sent Luis and Rafael under heavy escort to bring Casa Grande, since they were the only ones who knew how to control him with the trained steers.

But as they escorted Johnny to the ring, he could see no Casa Grande and wondered, like the condemned, when his executioner would turn up.

Oddly, Johnny wasn't feeling much fear just then. That would come when Casa Grande came thundering out. He only hoped he could control the fear. All matadors are frightened by the bulls; being able to overcome fear was what mattered. Almost always after finishing a bullfight Johnny would go behind a wall and throw up; then the shakes would come. A stiff cup of brandy cured them.

If Casa Grande hadn't been the bull he was, Johnny would have felt he had a better chance. Matadors can always refuse a bull before the fight, but there was no refusing this one, and Casa Grande was *el toro supremo*. He was of perfect fighting age, descended from one of the great strains of fighting bulls in Mexico, and Johnny knew him well. He was big, fast, brave, agile as a cat, and smart to boot.

Suddenly there was a commotion from the men at the entrance end of the canyon. Johnny could see them standing up on the rock pile and waving hats and hands. Then he saw coming through the little entrance several of the steers, and he could also see Luis and Rafael on horseback. More steers entered and Johnny could make out amid them the great hump and horns of Casa Grande. Rafael and Luis began herding the steers back outside the canyon and, when they were done, Casa Grande stood alone near the entrance, which Johnny figured would become his *querencia,* if the thing ever got that far.

Death and glory often come together, but Johnny was thinking about it differently. Today they became disassociated. He didn't give a damn about glory right now; and death, if it was to be his, seemed very unfair this way. He watched Villa's soldiers piling big logs across the narrow entrance to the canyon. They also piled some logs for a small *barrera,* behind which Johnny, Luis, and Rafael could take refuge during various stages of the fight. Casa Grande hulked nearby, pawing the ground and snorting, tossing his massive head. If Johnny stayed still, he wouldn't charge. It was when Johnny moved that things would get dicey.

Villa decreed that the procedure would be as in all bullfights: The first *tercio* would be the *tercio de varas,* in which Casa Grande was introduced. Johnny would perform some *capeos* to move Casa Grande around; test him, get a feel for him and which way he hooked — but not expose himself to the bull's horns.

Then Luis would enter with his pics. Normally, Luis would have his pics at the ends of eight-foot lances, or *varas.* Luis would stab them at the back of Casa Grande's hump, or *morillo,* so as to make him lower his head. This was important because a bull with a raised head is hard to kill, and can kill you instead. But there were no *varas* today and Luis would have to do his work crudely and alone, with knives. At least Fierro had compromised and let them use one of their horses; they would have to share it.

Next came the *tercio de banderillas,* in which Rafael would approach Casa Grande with what, in a fair fight, would be two-and-a-half-foot banderillas with small iron barbs on the ends. He would use them to "correct" Casa Grande's posture; if the bull was hooking the wrong way, this could generally be fixed. Except that today, like Luis, Rafael had only knives to work with and no other banderillero to help him out.

Finally there would come the *tercio de*

muerte, the "third of death," in which Johnny would fight Casa Grande to the finish. In a fair fight a professional matador would not have much trouble killing his bull if it was just a matter of sticking in the sword. The trick was to kill him while at the same time entertaining the fans by putting himself in harm's way with the bull's horns. Cowardly matadors were immediately detected by bullfighting aficionados and, in addition to the booing, often as not got pelted out of the ring with flying objects.

With Villa watching, Johnny knew he could not fight a cowardly fight today; if he was to go, he decided, he'd go with his own head held high. If the crowd was entertained by that, so be it, he decided.

One of Villa's soldiers blew some kind of fanfare on a bugle, which was the signal to get started, and Johnny picked up and un-furled Julio's bloody shirt for a cape and began walking toward Casa Grande, who im-mediately charged. The first pass nearly did Johnny in, because the shirt was nowhere near as big as a regular *muleta* and he was able to dance out of the way only by inches as the bull thundered past. He thought he looked ridiculous — the way he had to fight with the damned shirt — sticking his butt out and leaning over cranelike — but unless he wanted to die on the spot, he had to do it. He goaded Casa Grande into a few more passes before waving for Luis to come on with his knives.

Luis dashed out as Casa Grande completed a swipe at Johnny and, just as the bull turned, reached over his horse's shoulder and stuck one of his knives in the bull's hump. He would have stuck both of them in, like a banderillero, but he couldn't reach that high. The enraged Casa Grande turned on him and made a charge that Luis dodged, just as Johnny came up with the bloody shirt to distract him.

When he thought it was relatively safe, Luis ran at the bull again and plunged in the other knife. He took an instant too long, unfamiliar as he was in the new art of fighting bulls with knives, and Casa Grande jerked his head up in an explosion of fury that caught the horse in its chest, and it stumbled down on its knees. Another lunge caught Luis's leg in the stirrup and lifted him eight feet into the air. Johnny's heart stuck in his throat when he saw Luis crash to earth.

He must have broken something, because he was dragging along the ground on his hands when Casa Grande bore down him again, this time plunging an eighteen-inch horn all the way to the hilt under the armpit; then, with a ferocious toss of the head, the bull flung Luis again into the air.

Luis was dead before he hit the ground, but Casa Grande was not yet satisfied and continued to butt and trample and nudge him along until Luis became a limp, filthy mass on the ground covered in dirt and blood and entrails. Johnny was almost paralyzed at the horror of what he was watching. He wanted somebody to shoot the bull immediately so he could to rush to Luis, but even as that was going through his mind Johnny ran up behind Casa Grande and seized his tail, giving it a yank to distract him. It was not a matadorlike thing to do but, being shorthanded, he couldn't think of anything else.

Casa Grande let out a grotesque bellow and turned on Johnny, who eluded him several more times before retiring behind the *barrera* they'd erected at the entrance to the canyon. Sweat poured into his eyes and he was trembling from head to toe. He felt like he wanted to be sick. Now it was Rafael's turn with the banderillas. He looked sick, too. Luis had been the brother closest to him, only a year apart in age, gored and trampled now to jelly.

"He's hooking left," Johnny panted, "and his horns still aren't down." Rafael had seen that, too, and nodded. They entered the ring side by side, saying nothing further because there was nothing left to say. There was a lot of yelling from the men watching from atop the rocks, and while Johnny couldn't make out what they were chanting, he had a sense they were enjoying the spectacle.

To put in his banderillas, now that the horse was down, Rafael would have to stand on his toes, legs together, body tall and straight, and, with both arms raised, plunge the knives into Casa Grande's hump in the right spot to correct the hook.

He did this just a little to the left of the bull as it came at him, but right when he made the downward thrust, Casa Grande hooked left, as Johnny had warned. The big head was lowered now, but that wasn't a good thing in this instance, since the horn caught Rafael in the groin, spilling his guts out when the bull whipped his neck around and the bloody horn pulled out. Rafael sank to his knees, trying to hold himself in with both hands and with a look of stricken terror on his face.

Johnny rushed up with the bloody shirt, flicked it into Casa Grande's eyes, temporarily blinding him but enraging him even further. The bull brushed the shirt aside and trotted to the part of the ring by the entrance; just as Johnny predicted, it was to be his *querencia.* Only one of Rafael's knives had sunk in and Johnny didn't know if it would correct the hook or not, so he decided to fight Casa Grande from the right side.

This would be difficult if the bull was still hooking left, because if he hooked he would take the target of the hump away from Johnny and make it harder to kill him. Casa Grande must have been tiring by now, because he stayed in his *querencia* snorting and pawing but not charging. His nostrils were bubbling froth and his eyes were crazed. Johnny welcomed the respite — but not for long. Rafael, disemboweled, was beginning to cry and scream, and it was a distraction. He was still on his knees, one hand holding on to his entrails and the other hand gesturing, beckoning for Johnny to come to him. Both knew that was impossible; the situation was more than distracting, it was horrifying. The sun had begun to come into the little box canyon by now, lighting up Rafael's face as a pathetic mask of dread. Then, without a further sound, he toppled forward and lay facedown and still.

If he'd had time, Johnny would have tried to pick up the knife Rafael hadn't managed to stick into Casa Grande and finish the job, but he realized this wouldn't work. So, in his authority as matador he declared the first two *tercios* to be finished and the final one, the *tercio* of death, to begin. The custom was for the matador to then present himself to the *juez* of the bullfight — the judge, who in this case was Villa himself. Ordinarily, after receiving a nod to proceed, Johnny would "dedicate" the bull to someone.

Under other circumstances it would have been Donita, as he'd done in the past, but he was thankful that, by her own request, she

595

wouldn't be here, and so there was no need for a charade. He merely stood before Villa, who was conspicuous atop the rocks with Fierro and others of his staff — including an odd-looking character in a dark suit wearing a monocle — and bowed. Villa returned the gesture with a nod of his own.

Despite the bottomless pain and remorse Johnny felt at the loss of his brothers, he thought of Donita and felt sad that she would probably have to witness his burial. He hoped that if something grave happened, Villa would just leave him there as crow bait and move on. He wished he'd brought the matter up before the bullfight.

There was a cruel little smile on Villa's lips, but otherwise the general's face remained impassive. Johnny tried to overcome his horror by thinking of Donita. It all suddenly rushed back to him that he'd been unfair to her and brusque and impatient when she'd wanted him to give up bullfighting and concentrate on getting the ranch manager's job; and was arrogant in his ways, too, and often not caring of someone who loved him so. In the few remaining moments he had to himself, he dedicated the bull to her. Maybe it would bring him luck.

Reed had never seen a bullfight before and was perfectly ignorant of what could happen. He turned away disgusted at the first sight of blood even before Luis was dead. Bierce, who had seen some fights in Tijuana during his California newspapering days, stayed, but he was revolted, too. During the short break in the action he was standing next to Strucker, the newcomer in Villa's entourage.

"This is almost prehistoric, don't you think?" the German asked him, apparently enraptured with the goings-on down in the little canyon.

"No. In fact, it's utterly consistent with this gruesome century," Bierce responded. "It may be a pity, but it's true. I thought the last century was horrid, but it's nothing compared to what this one's going to be."

Strucker digested that answer for a moment, but wasn't satisfied with it. "Yes, but here is man against beast; a marvelous anachrony. It carries us all back to barbarism, don't you think?"

"We've never left it," retorted Bierce. "Look what's going on in Europe — or down here in Mexico, for that matter. If that's civilized, I'll kiss your ass."

Startled by this uncouth response, Strucker nodded with a grunt, never taking his eyes off the gory spectacle unfolding before him. By now, Johnny Ollas had walked back out to face Casa Grande.

"You, sir, I take it, are an American?" Strucker said.

"You take it right. Are you a Dutchman?"

"German," Strucker replied.

"In the war, they were all the same to us," said Bierce. A great many German emigrants had fought for the North and were referred to by boths sides as "Dutchmen" — as in, *Sprechen Sie deutsch?*

"Your Civil War, I expect?" he said, having noted Bierce's age. "Well, we aren't. The Dutch are a silly little people who wear wooden shoes and build windmills and live in swamps."

"For a while they ruled the seas and the continents," Bierce reminded him. He felt like leaving the bullfight but thought it would be cowardly. If the third man was to be killed, he might as well bear witness to it as the only reluctant spectator of the bunch. When he saw the German Strucker come into camp that morning, with all his pomp and bearing, Bierce thought he might turn out to be some peculiar voice of civility or rectitude or decency.

Now he understood otherwise. The human race was still headed to hell in a handbasket, just like it always had been, he thought.

Tom Mix was standing nearby and had overheard Bierce and Strucker. He didn't know what to make of the German, but had to give him credit for following them all the way out here alone. Mix squinted down into the bullring. He could see Johnny assuming a profiled stance to receive Casa Grande's charge. Poor brave fellow, Mix thought. He had left Donita and the children under the guard of several of his men and told her he would come straight back and tell her what had happened. Now, as he watched the grisly panorama, Mix sensed that Johnny was going to die in a very few minutes — in the full glory of his life and without ever catching on to the lie that he was going live forever — a textbook case of no way out.

Johnny Ollas felt the ground beneath him tremble as Casa Grande thundered toward him. A second later Johnny turned daintily to avoid the horn and managed to slash out with the saber at Casa Grande's left eye. The blow struck home and the animal let out a bellow and began madly tossing his head. Johnny could see blood pouring from the eye and suddenly saw a ray of hope. If he could slash the other eye, the bull would be blinded. But Casa Grande was hooking left again — not a good sign.

His good eye was on the opposite side of his head, where Johnny couldn't get at it, but he could actually feel the steamy breath as the bull nudged the bloody shirt and went past. Johnny was consciously trying to keep his feet still — avoiding the little pitty-pat mouse feet that were the sign of fear and cowardice. If this was to be his last fight, he could at least not show he was scared.

Casa Grande trotted a dozen yards away and turned, hooves pawing, head shaking. His hide shining wet with blood from the knives of Luis and Rafael, and his face covered with gore from the sabered eye.

"Ayiii, toro!" Johnny exclaimed, jiggling the shirt. The bull snorted and came at him again — and again Johnny eluded him with some fancy cape work. From the crowd of spectators he heard someone shout, *"Olé!"* Johnny knew he had to get on the side with the good eye.

On the next charge others took up the cry, until the little box canyon swelled with their approval. Johnny was inciting Casa Grande with a series of veronicas, maneuvers in which he stood with his feet planted, sweeping the shirt out ahead of the bull's face just as he was about to gore, hoping he would turn the blind eye to the side. This further inspired the enthusiasm of the crowd, because they'd noticed that Johnny's feet were still and firmly planted, as if he were nailed to the ground.

It was not so hard for a matador to run or jump out of the bull's way, but performing veronicas took courage not to get the little mouse-feet. Knowledgeable spectators appreciated that.

Johnny had managed to put the fates of Luis and Rafael temporarily behind him and was feeling more confident. His heart actually beat with the satisfaction that he hadn't turned coward. He finished one pass with a *mariposa* — a butterfly — stepping in so close that Casa Grande turned in on himself so sharply that it actually brought the bull to his knees. The crowd now began to shout, "Bravo! Bravo! Bravo!"

If the bastards had flowers they would be throwing them at me, Johnny thought bitterly.

The bull was tiring quickly now and had returned to his *querencia* and wouldn't come out. It was the most dangerous part of the *tercio* of death because the matador has to enter the bull's terrain to lure him out. Casa Grande seemed instinctively to know not to expose his uninjured eye to Johnny, who was closing in. Johnny decided it might be a good time to forget about the eye and go for the kill.

Johnny got down on his knees and began to provoke Casa Grande with the bloody shirt. The bull pawed and snorted and tossed his head once, but did not charge. The tossing of the head was a bad sign, too. Johnny inched closer on his knees, playing the shirt slightly in his left hand, his right clutching the cavalry saber. It was a far cry from the Seville steel of a matador's *estoque.*

"Hey, *toro!*" Johnny cried.

Casa Grande backed up a few steps until he literally bumped into the logs the soldiers had piled for a *barrera* and this obviously startled him, because all at once Casa Grande rushed at Johnny with a ferocious charge, head lowered. Johnny sprang to his feet and with a clear, swift motion raised the saber over his head to plunge it in. The bull unexpectedly swerved right, throwing Johnny off balance as he tried to gain position; then the two of them, man and beast, collided.

Johnny was tossed over the bull's horns, plunging the saber into Casa Grande's hump; he could feel it slide through flesh and then something more solid — not the bone of the spinal cord but the pad that connected the bones, thus severing the spine, while at the same instant Casa Grande jerked his head upward, goring Johnny clean through his thigh and lifting him into the air with a mighty toss. Before Johnny even hit the ground, Casa Grande was dead. The bull took two wobbly steps, then keeled over, all four legs in the air.

Johnny knew he, himself, was hurt but not how badly; he was still in shock from what had happened to his brothers, and from the collision with Casa Grande. But he'd won the fight. He heard yelling and cheering. Men rushed down from the rock pile and surrounded him. Someone cut away his pants and there was a groan from the bystanders. The horn had gone clean through the leg and cut the femoral artery, leaving a ragged hole nearly three inches wide that was spurting blood like a pump.

After he watched the final act, Mix ran back to the encampment to fetch Donita. He didn't know how badly Johnny was hurt, but figured that if the wound was fatal, at least the couple deserved some last words. Johnny lay on his back with his head raised, trying to see the wound. He saw only his life spilling out on the bare dirt of the canyon floor. He felt dizzy and sick but there was no pain. Hovering over him were the faces of Villa, Fierro, and a few others he recognized, including Gourd Woman, whose face was ashen and her teeth bared; the pain that Johnny didn't feel was all in her eyes. Men knelt beside him, and one whom Johnny recognized as Villa's doctor was doing something to his leg and talking excitedly.

"You fought a brave fight, matador," he heard Villa say, as if from a distance.

It was the last thing Johnny Ollas remembered.

FIFTY-THREE

From their hiding place on the canyon rim, Bomba and Henry Flipper had been passing the spyglass between them, quiet as mice. They saw the deaths of Luis and Rafael and the goring of Johnny and the collapse of Casa Grande. It was a mystifying spectacle.

Finally Flipper whispered, "I wonder where they got that bull."

"Still don't see the children," Bomba said.

"Well, it's a big camp. You can't see everybody."

"You think something happened to them?"

"I can't believe they would have brought a fighting bull all the way down in these canyons," Flipper said. "These people might do anything."

By now the crowd had begun to drift back to their campfires. The smell of food cooking wafted up to the top of the bluffs. Flipper scanned the box canyon again. He saw the dead bull, the still bodies of two men, and hovering over the third appeared to be a woman. Bomba took the glass and crept away down the bluff to get a better view. After a long while he came back, disgusted, and shook his head.

"No children. Looks like they finished breakfast and they all leaving now," he said. Flipper had already seen Villa's advance guard riding out up the canyon and the wagons and others moving behind them.

"Well, at least you've found Villa," Flipper told him. "I hope you're satisfied. Now what do you propose to do?"

"Go after," said Bomba.

"How can you possibly do anything to get out those kids, in these canyons?" Flipper said under his breath, exasperated. "There's no room for maneuver. There's no place to go."

"Have to try," Bomba replied.

"You're a fool," Flipper told him. "They're headed north. They'll be out of the canyons in another day or so. Maybe then there'll be an opportunity."

"Maybe," Bomba said. He put the spyglass to his eye again and swung it down along the caravan. Suddenly he stopped and swung back.

"There," he said. "Children."

Flipper took a look. He saw the boy and girl surrounded by a dozen or so riders. They were moving past the little box canyon where the bullfight had been held. There was a woman on a horse someone was leading by the reins. She was shaking her head violently and waving her arms, and the sounds of her screaming drifted up out of the canyon and echoed on its walls.

"See, what did I tell you?" Flipper said. "How do you think you can get through that to take those kids — and still live?"

"The people they left behind," Bomba said, meaning the downed matador and the woman kneeling next to him. "Maybe they know something."

"Might be," Flipper said. "But I'm going to take my time before I go down there."

FIFTY-FOUR

Arthur, Cowboy Bob, and Slim were riding in the shallow streambed of the canyon. Arthur was feeling strangely in control since he'd taken over the expedition, and actually, as wretched as the experience had been, had felt supremely confident ever since killing the grizzly, back on the mountain. His hands were now tough and callused, his face tanned, and the fare along the trail had left him without an ounce of fat. As he rode along, he practiced snapping at rocks and sticks with his bullwhip, and tried out his fast draw, too — but of course didn't fire, since they were getting closer to Villa.

Colonel Shaughnessy was strapped down in a two-wheeled, burro-drawn wagon that previously had contained sacks of beans and was led by one of Ah Dong's helpers. He was in pain but held his silence. For a day and a half the laudanum kept him in and out of consciousness and he looked pale and old and his teeth were often bared in a grimace.

At least this morning he'd been able to get down a little breakfast, and Ah Dong was trying to wean him off the sedative.

"I'm working on a plan," Arthur announced, "but first I need to know where Villa's going."

"If we had some ham, we could have some ham and eggs," Bob observed. "If we had some eggs."

Arthur ignored that and went on. "There's nothing we can do while he's still here in these canyons. We know that. But we'll be out of them in a day or so, right?"

"I think so," Slim said. "Seems as if we've been going as much east as north."

"And assuming we're able to slip in at some point and take the children, what would happen?"

"Villa's people would most likely ride us down and murder us all," said Bob.

"Precisely," replied Arthur. "But what if there was an aeroplane waiting for the children nearby? If we could get them to it, they're free, and we can all sort of scatter."

"An aeroplane?" Bob exclaimed. "Where in hell would we find an aeroplane?"

"I have one," Arthur answered. "It's back in El Paso in a boxcar on the train."

"A lot of good that does us," Bob said.

"An aeroplane riding the train — if that don't beat all," remarked Slim.

"Seriously," Arthur told them. "Look,

Crosswinds Charlie knows how to fly a plane. If I can get him back to El Paso, he can assemble it and get it ready and we can arrange some sort of rendezvous. He could land somewhere just about dusk, while they're bedding down. I doubt anybody would notice it. He could land behind trees or something."

"Trees — there might not be no trees to speak of once we're out of here," Slim said.

"Well, a ridge, then, or some piece of terrain where they can't see him."

"And what about Villa?" Bob asked. "You think he's just gonna stand there with his thing in his hand and watch us do it?"

"No," Arthur continued. "But he won't be expecting it, either. We'll have the element of surprise."

"What's Crosswinds Charlie have to say about all this?" Bob asked. "Is he ready to get himself shot full of holes?" To Bob it seemed like a harebrained scheme.

"I haven't mentioned it to him yet," said Arthur. "But he's a seat-of-the-pants aviator. He'd trade a brick of gold just to get into the air."

"But how could anybody flying an aeroplane ever find Villa — or us, for that matter?" Slim asked.

"That's the problem I was talking about," said Arthur. "When we get out of these canyons there'll be some sort of civilization, won't there?"

"Yup," said Slim. "There's a few villages don't amount to much, but we oughta start runnin' into them."

"Well, if we knew where Villa was headed, then I could send Crosswinds over to the nearest railroad and on to El Paso."

"If we had some bread, we could make us a sow's-ear sandwich, if we had some sow's ears," Bob remarked.

Arthur let this pass, too; he didn't want to get bogged down in useless conversation. "Once Crosswinds got there, it wouldn't take a day to get the plane ready. He could be back in this area that same afternoon if he took some extra gas with him. Once we're in the open and if the weather holds, it shouldn't be much trouble finding us from the air — or Villa, either, for that matter."

"Yeah, but who knows where Villa's headed?" asked Bob. "He could do anything. He might decide to stop and hole up before we run out of canyons. He might keep on goin' north or he might turn east or west. He might even double back and run straight into us. There's no tellin'."

"Somebody might be able to intersect him," Arthur said. "What if somebody he's on friendly terms with just happens to wander into his camp? I was hoping Strucker might get some word back to us, but then the Indians quit, so now that's out. But if somebody Villa knows joins up with him, they

610

might be able to find out something."

"Who?" Bob asked. Arthur looked at him, and the truth suddenly dawned.

"Aw, hell, Arthur," Bob replied, "that man's dangerous. I feel lucky to come away in one piece every time I get near him."

"Well, it was just a thought," Arthur said with a hint of scorn.

They let the conversation drop as Slim began whistling a tune that set the birds in the trees to singing. Arthur noticed half a dozen butterflies floating around a bush with yellow flowers. He identified them as Frickstone's white skippers, a rare type, but forced himself to quit thinking of butterflies as he rode past them.

After a while Bob said, "I imagine he'll be stopping in one of them villages. His men'll want to get drunk and get up with whores; they been out here a long time."

Arthur said nothing. This was the man who had taught him everything along the trail; good old brave Bob. Could Arthur blame him for wanting nothing to do with being near Villa? Bob knew as well as anyone how dangerous Villa could be; he had seen it back in the village near the tin mines. Still, Arthur had hoped Bob would rise to the occasion anyway. But he couldn't blame him if he didn't.

"I reckon I might arrange to be there ahead of them, maybe. But how in hell I'm gonna find out what Villa's plans are is somethin' else. I ain't exactly a confidant of his, you know."

"We've got to make a move sooner or later," Arthur said. "Otherwise we might as well just go on home."

FIFTY-FIVE

It was midmorning by the time Bomba and Henry Flipper made their way down to where the bullfight had taken place. They had waited on the bluff until Villa's soldiers disappeared behind a bend, and then some. They climbed the rock pile at the entrance to the little box canyon and beheld the grim theater. The bodies of Luis, Rafael, and Casa Grande lay where they were killed, drying and shriveling in the sun like dead fish. Gourd Woman had propped Johnny's head up on a rock and was kneeling over him, trying to give him some shade. She noticed them when they began climbing over the *barrera* of logs.

"Is he still with us, sister?" Flipper asked when they were within talking distance.

"No thanks to you," she said, stroking Johnny's face.

"What happened? Did the bull get him?" He was just trying to open a conversation.

"As if you didn't know," she replied. Nearby

her was a box with some sort of food — beans, peppers, flour, dried corn. "They send you back to finish the job?"

"We ain't with them," said Flipper. "We just watched this bullfight thing from up there." He indicated the top of the canyon.

"Then what are you doing here?" she asked, examining them closely for the first time. "Are you lost?"

"Looking for children," Bomba told her.

"Well, everybody's looking for somebody, I guess — he was looking for his wife," she said, nodding at Johnny, who appeared to be asleep, but his chest rose and fell in labored breathing.

"We saw the bullfight," Flipper said again. "What was that all about?"

"A way of killing somebody without having to waste bullets," she answered. "Big man, this Pancho Villa — said Johnny was lucky to be alive, and that was that."

Flipper bent over and peered at the bandaged leg. "Cut through the blood vessel?" he asked.

Gourd Woman nodded. "They had the doctor look at it. He did what he could but it wasn't much. Said if he moved him it would most likely kill him. Villa said they couldn't wait around, so he gave us a little food and left us here to die."

"It still bleeding?" asked Flipper.

"No, The doctor tied it off. Said he'll lose

the leg anyway but Villa didn't give him time to saw it off. So I guess we just wait here until it rots," she said angrily.

"Harsh treatment," Flipper remarked, noting that the lower leg had already turned a bloated ghastly purple. He knew something about gangrene; they'd had a brief training course on wounds when he was at West Point. "Why was he bullfighting?" he asked.

Gourd Woman explained what had happened. "These two are his brothers," she said, "and another one is back there a little ways. All dead. Actually they're not his real brothers. He was an orphan. He was born in a ditch."

"Well, he fought a pretty good fight, far as I could tell from up there," Flipper said.

"I wouldn't know," Gourd Woman said. "I've never seen one till now. It looked pretty disgusting to me."

"At least it seems they could have taken off that leg. It might've given him a fighting chance."

"They're fiends," she told him. "I don't care what they say about giving back property to the people. What's the use if the people are all dead anyway?"

"I'm sorry there's nothing we can do," Flipper told her.

"If you've got a shovel you might could dig him a grave. This ground's pretty hard to dig with your hands."

"How come they left you here with him? You his kin or something?"

"No," she said. "I sell brooms."

Flipper felt a sudden admiration for this Johnny Ollas; he had indeed fought a good fight, an honorable fight, and now he was going to die for it, way out here in the desolation.

FIFTY-SIX

Death Valley Slim, who'd been scouting ahead, came riding back to Arthur's party to say he'd discovered the corpse of one of Villa's soldiers lying on a sand spit not far down the canyon.

"From the look of him, it was an execution," Slim said.

"Let's hope he keeps it up," said Arthur. "Maybe he'll whittle himself down to our size."

Soon they came on the sandbar and Julio's body. Several buzzards were picking over the flesh. They flapped their big wings and flew away, leaving the canyon in a ghoulish quiet; the only sound was of flies buzzing on Julio's blood. From the holes Arthur and the others could see in the skin, it looked to be an execution for sure. Arthur nudged his horse and moved on, leading his party away. Then Bob, forward again, held up his hand to halt and be quiet. He rode back to Arthur and Slim quietly as possible.

"There's still people here," he said. "Couple of pack donkeys up ahead." Just then they all saw a man emerge from behind a pile of rocks that sealed up a little box canyon.

"Hey!" the man hollered, waving.

"Who the hell is that?" Arthur said.

"Beats me," Bob replied. "He ain't dressed like one of Villa's men, though."

"It could be a trap," said Slim.

"If they knew we was here, we'd already been trapped," Bob said. The man continued to wave and holler.

"You two stay here," Bob told them. "I'll go see what this is about." He rode cautiously toward the man, scanning the canyon from floor to rim for signs of others. He was amazed, as he got closer, to see that it was a black man hailing them. The man began to climb down off the rocks and come toward him.

"Who are you?" Bob said when he got nearer. "Prospecting?" He had noted Flipper's khaki clothing, which a lot of miners and engineers wore.

"Hell, no," Flipper said. "We been . . ." He stopped. He couldn't think how to explain it.

"I can't believe this — we're all out in this godforsaken place for the same reason?" Bob exclaimed. Arthur, Slim, and some of the others had come up to the rock pile, and Flipper had been trying to tell them what he was doing, and about Bomba and the children. Bob almost felt like laughing — it sounded crazy. Suddenly there was a cry from atop the rock pile and Bomba appeared, huge and backlit by the fading sun, a spade in his hand. He'd recognized Arthur and scrambled down toward him.

Arthur could hardly believe his eyes. He leaped off the horse and ran toward Bomba, and they embraced, close to tears. Bob, Slim, and Flipper gaped in astonishment. It took a little while to get the whole story unraveled. By that time Colonel Shaughnessy's wagon had arrived and another reunion was in order. Bomba looked as if he were going to weep at the sight of the Old Man, not just because of his condition, but because he was so glad to see him. Instead, he tried to explain about the children.

"I understand," said the Colonel, "don't worry about that. It wasn't your fault."

"They shot me," Bomba said. "Took a while to get well."

"I know," Shaughnessy replied. "You did everything you could."

"He's a tough sombitch," Flipper chimed in. "When he got to me he was half naked, near froze, and had pneumonia."

"Put on your war paint, did you, Bomba?" The Colonel chuckled. It was the first time he'd laughed since his leg had been broken.

"Saw children this morning — they all

right," said the Samoan. "Maybe eight, maybe nine hours." He pointed north down the canyon.

"Bless your heart," Arthur told him. He didn't know quite what yet, but with Bomba here, he felt he had a better chance to do something. Bomba had always been there since Arthur was a little boy; Arthur always felt protected when he was around; in fact, Arthur had once thought that if Bomba had stayed there with him at Groton, nothing bad would have happened. In any case, in Arthur's mind, Bomba now added up to major reinforcements.

"How many men you got?" Flipper asked.

"Two dozen," Arthur said, "more or less."

"Well, Villa's got himself a couple of mounted companies — maybe more — plus some cavalry. I expect you'd have trouble in a fight."

"You got any idea where he's headed?" Arthur said.

"No, but from the look of it he'll be out of the canyons pretty soon," Flipper said, "and I'd expect he'll be trying to link up with the rest of his army — provided it hasn't disintegrated. Say, you boys don't have any morphine or something, do you? There's a boy over behind them rocks got pretty bad hurt in a bullfight this morning. He's gonna die, but it might ease his pain."

"A *what,* did you say?" Bob asked.

"That's another long story," Flipper answered.

Some of the men removed the barricade of logs that led to the box canyon entrance and the Shaughnessy party circled up inside. It was sort of cozy and gave them a little break from a chilly wind that had begun to blow down the main canyon. It was the first cold they'd felt since they'd left the mountaintops and started north. Before dark Bomba and some others had dug graves for Luis, Raphael, and Julio. Casa Grande's carcass they left for the *zopilotes*.

They had parked the Colonel's ambulance wagon not far from Ah Dong's kitchen, and presently four men appeared with a flat board that they were using for a stretcher. They laid it gently on the ground a few yards from the Colonel, and when he saw who was on the stretcher it rendered him momentarily speechless.

Ah Dong was examining Johnny's leg, along with Cowboy Bob and Henry Flipper. Gourd Woman was mopping Johnny's brow with a damp cloth.

"That boy there, do you know who that is?" the Colonel finally exclaimed.

"Who?" Arthur said, alarmed.

"That's Johnny Ollas. Arthur, you met him years ago when you were kids and you came down to the ranch. Buck Callahan raised him. He's like a son to me." Gourd Woman looked up at him strangely.

Arthur vaguely remembered: the little boy at Valle del Sol with the bright personality and dark shining eyes who'd taught him a little Spanish.

"He's gonna die for sure if that leg don't come off," Flipper said. "It's startin' to fester already."

"The leg — what happened?" asked the Colonel. Arthur told him.

Ah Dong had carefully removed Johnny's bandage and was studying the wound. "I think maybe I can," he said.

"Can what?" Arthur asked.

"Cut leg," the Chinaman replied.

"Amputate it?"

"Only way. We don't, he die, huh?"

"My God," murmured the Colonel.

"How're you gonna amputate a leg?" Arthur asked.

"I have meat saw. It cut through beef and pork bones. I have needle and string to sew up chickens and turkeys. Maybe it work — maybe not."

"Well, one thing's for sure. He won't live with that leg on," Bob said.

"It's his only chance?" asked Arthur.

Ah Dong nodded. Cowboy Bob and Gourd Woman voiced their agreement. The Colonel put his hands to his head and took a breath. They took his silence for an affirmation.

"All right," Arthur said, "let's get some light here. We've got a battery light in the wagon, too." Ah Dong poured water into a kettle and put it on the fire, then went to get his saw.

"Well," Slim remarked, "I heard of doctors that become butchers, but never a butcher that become a doctor."

Ah Dong performed the operation by lanterns and flashlights beneath a three-quarter silver moon that also helped to illuminate the little canyon. Villa's doctor had already performed the most delicate and dangerous task by tying off Johnny's artery. Sawing off the leg took no longer than sawing off a dead steer's leg. The sawing made a harsh grating sound, like chalk scraping a blackboard, that gave chills to everybody near enough to hear it. Ah Dong made sure he'd peeled back enough extra skin to sew over the stump. He told Gourd Woman to wash the wound carefully and put disinfectants on it, since he was sure the bull's horn had been dirty. When the cook finished his suturing, Johnny Ollas was alive and breathing, but he'd fought his last bull.

Bomba carried Johnny's leg out to the grave he'd dug for him earlier and buried it there, next to Luis, Julio, and Rafael.

Everybody drifted back to their various encampments except for Gourd Woman, who stayed around to help Ah Dong clean up. She seemed exceedingly grateful to him.

"Now, I don't understand what a woman is doing out in this wild territory," remarked the Colonel. "How did you end up with Johnny?"

She told him her story and the Colonel told her his. Ah Dong kept his fire going brightly and they basked in its warmth and light. Shaughnessy was glad to have the company of a woman, even if she was a Mexican. His own leg had stopped hurting as much, now that they were off the jolts and jostles of the trail. He explained who he was and why he was here, but Gourd Woman seemed remarkably unsurprised. He got an odd feeling that she already knew. She told him about selling brooms and how she had met Johnny and his brothers, and then about following after Villa and joining his army, and about Rigaz being killed and the failed rescue attempt.

Still, Shaughnessy had a haunting intuition that he knew her from someplace. From a campfire not far away rang out the melodious sounds of a guitar and Death Valley Slim's pure, high-pitched warble, singing "Oh Bury Me Not on the Lone Prairie." The sad musical notes danced around the canyon's walls as though it were an opera house.

"You really feel something for that boy." She made it a statement instead of a question.

"Of course I do. He's like my own."

"He ought to be." There was a funny tone

in her voice when she said it.

"Well, he was found on my place. Wasn't much more than a day old. Born in a ditch, they said. We took him in."

"You should have," she told him.

"Of course we did. The only proper thing to do. Buck and Rosalita Callahan raised him like their own."

"I thought you said he was like *your* own." Something in the way she said it made the Colonel uncomfortable.

"I did," he replied.

"Well, he is."

"Is what?"

"He's your own. But you know that already, don't you?"

"I don't."

"Yes, you do, Señor Shaughnessy." She said it so flatly that he was shocked.

"What makes you say something like that?" he asked uneasily. There was something . . .

"Because there was a woman at your Valle del Sol, a long time ago. A young girl. Just after you bought the property. You and she —"

"No," cried Shaughnessy. The eyes, the voice, suddenly came together. "Lurie? Lurie? But how can this be? I thought . . . ?"

She looked at him intently from beneath her rebozo. Suddenly she swept it back from her head and smiled, while the firelight flickered softly on her face, the handsome nose, the piercing eyes, the full lips, the full lustrous hair.

"Lurie Ollas," he gasped under his breath.

"After my parents found out, they disowned me and I went to live in a little hut out on the llanos. It was okay. There was a stream and I could pick corn from your fields down in the valley." She spoke deliberately and in a faraway voice. "That was where it happened, one day after I was coming back with a basket of corn and there was no time. Just like that, he came. And then the rain began and a big windstorm came up and I got down with him into the ditch. Señor Callahan found me there that afternoon."

"But Buck told me you were dead," he said in an intense whisper.

"It's what I asked him to say. You see, they took me in and let us stay there with them. For a while I wasn't well, and Señora Callahan, she was so good with him. I hadn't even named him — they did that afterward. I was just eighteen, and what future could I give him? So what was I going to do? No place, no home for the little one. All I could do was steal corn and beg. They offered to take him in as one of theirs."

"And after all these years. It would have been 1890 . . ."

"I went south to Zacatecas, then Jalisco, and worked as a maid for a while. But it wasn't so nice. Then I got a job selling apples on the street. That was better than a maid. Then I just sort of wandered around. Time really goes fast, doesn't it?"

"Lurie."

"I tried to keep up with him," she continued. "Señora Callahan would write me from time to time. When I learned he had gone into bullfighting, sometimes I went to the arenas if they were near. I wouldn't go in to watch, though, because I was frightened for him. But I could see through the gates when they came in. I was so proud of him, but I hate killing. I always read the newspaper accounts afterward. That time when he was gored . . ."

"Lurie," he said. He reached out and she came over to him and let him stroke her face. "I'm sorry, oh, I'm really so very sorry." She was surprised to see tears well up in his eyes.

"I would have taken him back to the States with me, you know. I considered it."

"You don't have to explain," she said gently, touching his side. "He's gonna live now, I think. And that's all that's important. Your cook did a pretty good job, far as I can tell. Sewed him up like a goose." The moon had dipped over the canyon rim but still washed the walls in a thin patina of light. Colonel Shaughnessy was gnawing on his thumb and trying to keep control of himself. Strange things had happened today.

She took something out of her dress pocket

and handed it to him. "Hold on to this tonight, it will make you sleep well."

"What is it?" He held the object up for a better look.

"It'll make you invisible," she said.

FIFTY-SEVEN

"General, Señor Reed tells me you are a socialist," Bierce said. "Is that true?" Four days had passed since the bullfight and they were riding abreast in the late afternoon along a broad stretch of canyon rimmed by dark green trees. Earlier Villa held a powwow with his leading officers and, shortly after that, Fierro took a small party and rode on ahead. The German Strucker was on Villa's left, erect and superior-looking on a horse that he informed everyone was named Blucher. Reed was riding on Bierce's right.

"How could I be a socialist?" Villa replied. "I have just accepted an offer of ten million German marks from this man's government, which is one of the great imperialist governments of the world. Does a socialist do business with capitalist-imperialists?" Strucker was so startled Villa would reveal their transaction that he barely caught his monocle as it fell out.

"My appreciation of socialists," Bierce

responded, "is that they'll do business with the devil himself if it accomplishes their ends."

"Not me, Señor Robinson. It's been said I am a man of low character and no morals, but that's not entirely true. I have morals when it comes to who I take money from." Villa seemed remarkably cheerful.

"Would you accept money from the Americans, if they offered it?" Reed asked.

"Not anymore. They betrayed me. I don't need their stinking money."

"This money that Herr Strucker here has offered — what's it for?" Bierce asked.

"To make war on your country," Villa answered bluntly.

"On the United States?" Reed was aghast. "Whatever for?"

"Ask Señor Strucker," Villa told him.

Strucker was completely nonplussed at what he was hearing. He'd assumed the agreements made between him and Villa were top-secret.

"My country was simply making an offer to assist General Villa in his revolution," Strucker said, flustered.

"You told me it would be in my best interests to attack the United States, at El Paso or some other place, didn't you?"

"I don't believe it is in your best interest, or mine, to discuss our private conversations with these two Americans," Strucker said.

"Why not? They're friends. They been with me a long time. I trust them, why shouldn't you?"

"Nationalism does not make good bedfellows," said Strucker, "at least not in my experience."

"Señor Reed here is a socialist," Bierce interjected. "They'll get in bed with anybody."

"Well, I won't," said Villa. "And Señor Strucker has promised that these ten million marks are going to be placed in a bank of my choosing, in gold, within two weeks. And he is of course going to remain with me until I can go and retrieve them, isn't that correct, señor?"

"Well, yes, of course," Strucker said. He suddenly seemed further shaken. "But first I must communicate with my government. And I don't know how long it will take to get the money transferred. These are hard times for all of us, and banking routes are interrupted."

"Oh, we'll get you to a telegraph depot pretty soon. But you did tell me in two weeks, didn't you?" Villa asked. "Surely the imperial government of Germany that wages big wars all over the world can accomplish something as easy as this."

"I believe so," Strucker said darkly. His mouth went dry and he felt himself starting to break out in a sweat.

"You better be right," Villa informed him. "I don't like to be delayed or go out of my way over false promises from a bagman."

Scheisse! Strucker realized; he wanted to slap his forehead. I am kidnapped, too.

"So where are we headed now, General?" Bierce inquired. "I understand we're about to get out of these wastelands."

"We are," Villa said. "And we're going to a stinking Federale outpost at a town called Agua Prieta and wipe it out. I have already sent General Fierro to bring up the rest of the army."

"Where is that?" Reed asked.

"Right across from your American border," Villa said. "So they can get a good look at how Mexicans fight."

"How far is it?" asked Bierce.

"A few days away if we rode straight there. I told you I was going to be a pesky horsefly, didn't I? Well, let's see how long that bastard Carranza can keep putting out fires I start all over this territory. Pretty soon I'll have him running around like a chicken with his head cut off."

Reed was trying to digest the news he'd just heard and fit it into a story he would write. But Bierce had gone beyond that, apprehending that by revealing the information, Villa had already decided that neither of them was going to be given any opportunity to file stories.

"This town Agua Prieta," Bierce said. "*Agua* is water. What —"

"In your language, señor, it means, 'Dirty Water,'" Villa said.

When they camped that night, Katherine continued the reading lessons she'd begun with Villa. She had written out an alphabet for him to memorize and was amazed when he'd learned it in a single day. For his first writing lesson she told him to copy it down several times. Now she was working him through some simple sentences, such as "This is a cat" and "See the cat run." She wished she had an English-language dictionary, and Villa had promised to send somebody to find one when they got close to the border.

Since he hadn't wished for others to know what they were up to, Villa insisted that the lessons be done in private, and the routine was that after supper they would go off where they could be alone and Katherine would pull out the papers and pencils Villa had provided.

Invariably Tom Mix would find an occasion to pass by or pretend to do something in the distance, just keeping an eye on things. She couldn't help being drawn to Mix: he was so handsome, and there was an almost childlike aura about him; almost everything was a happy surprise to him. Sometimes Katherine thought Villa sat too close to her, but he made no move to touch her. Once when it looked about to happen Mix suddenly materialized to ask the chief an inane question, and the look in Mix's eyes told Katherine he was being watchful over her.

Actually, she was softening a little toward Villa, as well. He seemed very tired, she thought, and worried. But he exerted his best efforts in the reading-and-writing endeavor and she was impressed. They were getting places.

"I been observing you, señorita," Villa said when they took a little break. There was a fine chill in the air and Villa stuck his hands in his pockets. "You are a good rider and have adapted yourself to the trail. That's tough to do."

"I do what I have to. For myself and my brother."

"He beat me at checkers yesterday," Villa said.

"You let him win. I thought that was a nice thing to do."

"How do you know he didn't beat me fair and square?"

"I watched."

"You watch good," Villa said.

"We'd better get back to the lessons," Katherine told him. "We're running out of light."

"I think I am going to set you free," Villa said suddenly. Katherine looked at him, not believing what she'd heard.

"First I have to go to a bank and get some of that German's money. Then we are going up to your American border, and after I defeat my enemies there, I'll take you across the river and deliver you to the gringo soldiers on the other side."

"You'll do it!" Katherine gasped.

"I will," Villa told her. "If I get my German money and I destroy those people at the border."

"But what if you don't?" she asked. "What happens to us then?"

"I don't know," he told her. "You better say your prayers."

She put her hands to her mouth and, somewhere between elation and fear, she began to cry. Villa stepped to her and took her in his arms. It was a fatherly embrace, and she could smell his cheap perfume mixed with sweat and the stench of cigars.

"Let's get back to the reading, little señorita," Villa said. "Like you said, time's running short."

Timmy had been curled up with Pluto when Katherine arrived back with the news. At first he seemed hesitant.

"When?" Timmy asked.

"Soon as he gets to the border and fights his enemies," Katherine said.

"When is that?"

"He didn't say."

"He's a bloodthirsty liar," said Donita Ollas. "All along he's been telling people we're not kidnapped, but we are. What kind of man would refuse me even to see my dying husband? He's a monster!" Ever since the bullfight in the box canyon she had refused to speak to anyone, until now. Katherine took her anger as a good sign.

"But how long will it be?" Timmy asked.

Mix had been whittling on a stick and listening. "A week, maybe two," he said. "Maybe less." Mix was surprised at the news and wasn't quite sure what to make of it. If Villa had said that to Katherine, he obviously had a reason. But Mix wasn't sure what to make of his own feelings about this, either, assuming it was true. On the one hand, he'd be relieved to get shut of the responsibility of babysitting, and maybe even be able to get away from there. On the other, he'd grown fond of the kids and even enjoyed the company of Donita on those infrequent occasions when she chose to be pleasant.

"Who are these enemies he talks about?" Katherine asked.

"General Carranza," Mix replied.

"I know that. What I meant was, who are his enemies at the border?"

"Carranza has a Federal post there — about fifteen hundred troops."

"But if they are there, why doesn't General Villa just go somewhere else?"

"The general commands an army, missy. Armies only have one reason to exist, and that's to fight."

"But why?" she asked.

"Who knows?" Mix told her. "These people been fighting each other so long they've forgot what they're fighting about."

Just before they bedded down for the night, Katherine went to Mix and excused herself to go into the bushes. It was the most humiliating part of her experience in Villa's company, but she'd had to get used to it. Pluto was barking at something in the darkness when Katherine walked out of camp. The canyon floor was broad and open, and she had to find some low scrub near a little rivulet that cascaded down from the side of the bluffs.

She had just pulled down her pants and squatted when she heard a noise that sounded like a large piece of furniture being moved. She didn't give it much thought until she heard it again. A quarter moon gave off just enough light to see a bit, once the eyes adjusted. Suddenly she had the cold, breathless feeling that something was lurking. When she heard the noise again, Katherine thought it sounded like a large animal. She could feel its presence, its heavy breathing, like a dragon in a fairy tale. Immediately she straightened up and began backing away slowly toward the camp. Then in the faint light of the moon she saw its eyes, bright, wild, yellow.

Mix heard the scream and bolted from his

blanket bootless and wearing only pants. He grabbed his pistol and the end of a burning log from the fire and dashed toward the sounds. He spotted Katherine in the moonlight, slowly backing through the scrub, and then he saw the jaguar, too. It was a huge cat, two or three hundred pounds, and looked like it was seven feet long, teeth to tail. It was stalking her, crouched, from about twenty feet away; with each step she took backward, the jaguar would take one of its own.

Mix arrived at her side, brandishing the burning log, and the cat halted and hissed. Its fangs were bared and ferocious-looking, and its quick breath made little white clouds in the chill air.

"Get on behind me," Mix told her under his breath, "but for heaven's sake don't run."

Katherine backed farther away. Mix was backing, too, but the jaguar was moving in on him now. Mix turned a moment to see where Katherine was, and as he did he stumbled over something and lost his balance. He caught himself from falling with a hand on the ground, but the cat sensed a kill and sprang at him. Mix managed to hit it in the face with the glowing log and the jaguar recoiled, screaming. Others in the camp heard this and dashed toward the scene. The cat recovered and was about to spring again when Mix shot it straight in the eye with his pistol. The creature spun five feet in the air, twisting and shrieking, hit the ground, and keeled over, finally still. Mix was trembling, and a shiver ran up his spine. The smoke from his revolver hung in the air and his ears rang from the shot.

Half a dozen armed men rushed up to Mix, who was about to squeeze off another round into the thing to make sure it was dead. He'd killed men before, but this . . .

"*Jesús,* Capitán!" one man exclaimed. "You killed a *tigre*?"

"If he's dead," Mix replied. He took a few steps to pick up the glowing log and tentatively approached the creature with it. The others followed with cocked guns.

"*Sí,* he is dead, Capitán," one man observed.

"That's a big one," another remarked. "I never seen a *tigre* that big!"

"You ought to get the cooks to skin him for you," somebody said. "Make a good blanket — or a rug."

"Not a bad idea," Mix said. He turned and walked back toward the camp. He realized his feet were cut and scuffed up from running across the rocky ground barefoot. Katherine was waiting for him by the fire with a blanket around her shoulders.

"What was it?" she asked, still trembling, "a mountain lion?"

"A jaguar," he said, "worse than a mountain lion. The Mexicans call 'em *tigres*. Only thing bigger or meaner than a jaguar is an African lion or a tiger from India." Mix sat down and looked at his feet. They were bleeding and he reached for his shirt to wipe them off, but Katherine said, "No, wait — I have some clean cloths in my bag." She dipped a cloth in a pot of water they'd boiled earlier for coffee and gently began wiping off Mix's feet.

"There's some salve in my kit," he told her. Katherine got it and applied this, too.

"Did you . . . kill it?" she asked.

"I did," Mix told her. "Otherwise, you'd likely be cat food by now."

Her mother had always admonished her, "Darling, before you do anything, always ask yourself first, where is this leading me?" She'd remembered that starkly on the day she'd been captured; and had ground it into her mind ever since. But that night, against her better judgment, Katherine began to have very changed feelings about Tom Mix.

FIFTY-EIGHT

Two days later, Villa's troops were out of the canyons and entered a terrain of grassy valleys and rolling hills surrounded by lilac-hued mountains that could have been the subject of a Chinese watercolor. At last there were signs of civilization: wagon tracks, pepper trees, fruit groves, sheep and goats. Hungry for sheep meat, the soldiers stole and slaughtered a dozen of these.

They traveled most of the day beside a clear rocky stream until at dusk they came to the outskirts of a village. Along a dusty road they passed miserable hovels and filthy, naked children playing in the dirt among chickens or the occasional pig. Here the stream ran a murky yellowish brown and stank of sewage and the children's eyes were hollow, filled only with hunger and sadness. When Villa's riders approached, some of the women gathered their children inside and closed their doors. A sinister atmosphere reeked over everything.

Such as it was, the town consisted of half a dozen low adobe buildings and a morose two-story frame structure that was both the cantina and the whorehouse. There they stopped and tethered their horses. Despite the breathtaking poverty, preparations for a fiesta were in progress. Bright banners had been strung along the street and a small grandstand had been erected. Inside the cantina a handful of peons were drinking pulque served by a scrawny saloon-keep who had one of the most unattractive faces you could find outside of an ape house. In the corner a drunk Mexican was trying to negotiate a tune out of a piano as Villa led the way in, followed by his officers and entourage.

"What is this place?" Villa asked of the saloon-keep.

"Reyes," replied the man.

"Never heard of it," the general said.

When the man did not respond, Villa sat down and requested a lemonade.

"No tengo," the man told him.

"What?" Villa said. "You got no lemons?"

"No."

"Oranges?" Villa said. "I'll take an orange-ade."

"No tengo."

"Do you know who I am?" he asked.

"No, señor."

"I am General Villa."

"Sí."

642

"Now do you know who I am?"

"*Sí*, you are General Villa," the man said stupidly.

"Well, if you know what's good for you, you'll find me some lemons and make a lemonade."

"Peaches," the man said. "That's all I got."

"Hell with it, then," Villa grumbled. "All right, squeeze me some peaches and I'll have a peachade — with plenty of sugar." What Villa really craved was ice cream, but he realized that was out of the question.

The man nodded and disappeared into a back room. The drunk at the piano had gotten a load of Villa's conversation with the saloon-keep and wisely slunk out of the room.

Bierce, Reed, and Strucker had sat down with Villa. After Villa got his peachade, Reed and Bierce ordered themselves beer, while Strucker uncharacteristically asked for water because his stomach was cramped with indigestion.

"What a wretched place," Reed remarked. "The people almost seem like prisoners." Reed had foolishly hoped that when they finally got out of the canyons they would come upon a quaint, lovely town where he could get a hot bath and soft bed. Instead he got a repulsive shithole.

"They probably are," Villa said. "Somewhere around here there's going to be a big fancy hacienda, and all these poor bastards work on it. They get paid a few centavos a day and if they get caught so much as taking home one ear of the corn they picked, they'll get horsewhipped. That's their only future, and their children's future, too. I lived in a place like this myself once."

Suddenly the silhouette of a large man appeared in the doorway. Villa had seated himself to face the door and squinted at the stranger, who said:

"Well, what a surprise to find you here, General."

It was Cowboy Bob. It took Villa a moment to recognize him, then he broke out in a grin.

"As I live and breathe!" Villa exuded. "What in hell are you doing here?"

Cowboy Bob had left Arthur's party the day before and picked his way all night past Villa's troop, swinging wide so that he entered the village from the north end.

"Passin' through," Bob replied. "I just needed a place to stay for the night. Say! Ain't that Mr. Jack Robinson there?"

"It is," Bierce said. "Fancy seeing you here, Bob."

Bob said, "I thought you would've got your taste of this country and gone on home by now."

"Maybe I should have," Bierce told him, "but I'm gonna stick around a little while longer. General Villa needs my advice."

"All of Mexico needs Señor Robinson's

advice," Villa said sarcastically, motioning for Cowboy Bob to take a seat. "He'll take his last breath for Mexico."

Bierce took a swallow of his beer. "That's not so. If I owned Mexico and hell both, I'd rent out Mexico and live in hell," he said, borrowing a line from William T. Sherman.

"You're very witty today," Villa told him.

"No, I'm not," Bierce said calmly. "It only sounds that way."

Strucker had not yet been served his water and became impatient. "What do I have to do to get some water in this dump?" he demanded.

"Why don't you try setting yourself on fire?" Bierce suggested.

Strucker was not amused and began banging on the table to attract attention. He was in a predicament he'd never counted on: Villa was not an honorable man in any sense, contrary to what he'd been told. The Mexican apparently had no intention of attacking the United States, yet now insisted on the ten million marks anyway as a condition of Strucker's survival. It would be difficult for Strucker to explain to his superiors back in Berlin, but if the money did not arrive, no explanations or anything else would be forthcoming from Strucker anyway.

Bob had ridden past the big Mission-style hacienda that Villa had alluded to earlier and been impressed. He even saw a motorcar in

the courtyard. Therefore, Bob was unpleas-
antly surprised when he encountered the
squalor of the village. Like Reed, he'd hoped
for amenities.

"So, General, where you headed?" Bob
asked, suddenly deciding to tackle the question straightforward.

"What's it to you?" Villa answered.

"Just trying to make a conversation." Bob
smiled, trying not to seem nervous.

"And you," Villa said. "Where are you coming from?"

"El Paso," Bob lied.

"And where are you going?"

"West," Bob said. "I'm thinking about going to California to get in the movies."

"Aren't you a little old for that?" Villa said,
more as a statement than a question.

"Maybe, but I'd like to give it a try before I
cash in."

"Why didn't you just take the train?" Villa
asked suspiciously. "Sort of out of your way,
isn't it? Being this far south?"

"Not a'tall," Bob said. "I figured I'd come
down here first to get some work. Maybe
punch some cows or even get a job as a foreman. You can't go to Hollywood without any
money. I don't even have train fare."

"Any luck?"

"Not yet, but there's a big hacienda up
across them hills there. I thought I'd ask
around in the morning."

Villa seemed satisfied with that explanation. His troopers had now filled the saloon and were marching single-file up the stairs to the whores like a line of termites climbing a dead limb. Bob decided he'd played the only card he could in asking about Villa's plans. If the man wasn't going to tell him, Bob figured it wasn't worth persisting and getting shot or hung. Nevertheless, he decided to try one more gambit.

"So how long you gonna hang around here?" he asked pleasantly.

"Not long," Villa told him. "We got things to do. But there's some kind of fiesta tomorrow and the men need a little relaxation. I expect we'll stay here a couple of days — maybe more. The men'll need to sober up after the fiesta and get their strength back after the whores."

FIFTY-NINE

It wasn't much, but at least it was a chance, provided Bob could get word back to Arthur in time. He said his good nights, telling Villa that he'd best get some sleep before job-hunting next day. Then he went outside, desperate to get a line on the whereabouts of the children. Just being in Villa's company gave him the heebie-jeebies. As luck would have it, he spotted Tom Mix herding Katherine, Timmy, and Donita Ollas into a little encampment at the far end of town. Bob dismounted and hung around for a while to study the setup, carefully avoiding Mix's attention. There seemed to be four or five men assisting Mix, and they had all set up under a big oak away from the stench of the hovels. Bob calculated the approaches. There were other encampments, but he saw a possible avenue if Arthur and his people could swing in on the north side of town like he had earlier, then go west to a pecan grove where they could hide their horses. A drainage ditch would provide cover. To make sure he had it exactly right, Bob sketched the site on a pad, then mounted his horse and rode away into the night.

He wheeled wide around the town through a lettuce field, until he came upon the same road Villa had ridden in on. It would be a lot shorter going back that way than the circuitous overland route he'd had to take the night before. There wasn't much, but by starlight he was able to scout out some spots where a plane might land, as well as the possible escape paths for Arthur's raiders. When Bob finally ran into Arthur's party on the road after sunup, he'd had no sleep in twenty-four hours.

"You're about half a day away," he told him. "The good thing is that they'll be a lot of drunks from the fiesta and the town itself provides pretty good cover. There's a lot of coming and going. You might just pull it off."

Arthur took a deep breath and nodded. "If we're going to do it, looks like now's the time," he said. Arthur summoned Crosswinds Charlie and Bob briefed him on his reconnaissance.

"There's a spot I rode through in a lettuce patch," Bob said. "It's dry, at least, and level, and it's behind a big knoll. I think you can land the plane there. They'll probably hear your motor, but I doubt they'll see you. Even if they do, maybe they'll just think it's something to do with the fiesta."

"A lettuce patch?" Charlie asked. "Are there lettuces growing on it?"

"Yep," Bob said. "Big ones, too. But they're in rows; maybe you can put your wheels in between 'em."

Charlie turned to Arthur. "I ain't never landed in a lettuce field before," he said.

"Well, do you think you can?" Arthur asked.

"I landed in a tree once," Charlie told him. "I can try."

"All right, that's it, then," Arthur said. "We won't make our move till you're on the ground and we're sure you can take off again." Crosswinds Charlie already had a letter Arthur had written to the rail authorities giving permission for him to put together the Luft-Verkehrs, and also his handwritten letter of credit to provide Charlie any funds he needed. He crossed his fingers that there'd be enough in the NE&P coffers to cover it. According to Cowboy Bob the train Charlie had to catch to El Paso was thirty miles away, and Arthur put an arm around his shoulder.

"This is going to be a tight-run business," Arthur told him, "so you'd best ride like the wind."

"Suppose I can't find nobody to help me get the thing assembled?" Charlie asked.

"You will," Arthur said confidently, echoing his father. "They can do anything in El Paso."

Sixty

The fiesta in Reyes began the next day with a three-person mariachi band playing a gay tune leading a procession of bedraggled men naked from the waist up with big crucifix crosses strapped to their backs. Next came some Mexican cowboys, *charros,* on horseback with fancy silver-and-turquoise saddles. When the fancy *charros* rode past the crowd, all the men spectators took off their sombreros and the women lowered their eyes and bowed. There were a couple of dancing acts with women twirling in full colored skirts, and then the children of the village appeared in one large and unseemly mob. The children were partly naked and just as filthy as when Villa's people had ridden into town the day before.

The grandstand was filled with about a dozen well-dressed men, women, and children, and all the paraders paid them some kind of deference as they passed. The men carrying the crucifixes bowed and scraped, the *charros* on horseback waved and reared their horses. When the village children came to the grandstand, they got on the ground and groveled while a short fat man in a sequined suit threw coins at them.

Villa and his staff were watching from the boardwalk in front of the cantina. They had bought some tortillas from a woman who was frying them in a huge iron cauldron of boiling grease. The cantina saloon-keep was standing in his doorway when Villa addressed him.

"Who are those people in the seats there?" he asked, indicating the grandstand.

"El Padrino and his family," replied the man.

"The Godfather, huh?" Villa spat. "And I bet he's the one with the big hacienda around here, too?"

"That is right," the man said. "If it was not for El Padrino, everyone would starve."

"Looks to me like you're starving anyway!" Villa told him. "Can't you see that? Look at those children!"

"El Padrino is good to us, Señor General," the barkeep said. "All this land belongs to him. He lets us live on it and work for him. What would we do otherwise?"

"That fat *cabrón* is wringing the lifeblood from you, and you kiss his ass," Villa snorted. The saloon-keep said nothing.

They stood in the street with their backs to

El Padrino and his entourage, while a tall gaunt man wearing polished boots and a black outfit strode down the street toward them. He had a red bandanna tied around his head and was carrying a bullwhip. A priest who had been sitting in the stands got down and began administering the Communion sacraments to the crucifix men.

When he had finished, the man with the bullwhip began his work. He lashed out at the naked backs of the men, tearing flesh with an awful cracking sound. The crosses the men were carrying provided some protection but not enough. Somehow the whipper managed to get to the skin anyway. The whipped men stood ramrod-stiff and did not cry out. Soon all the crucifix men's backs and shoulders were bloody.

This was enough for Villa. He pulled out his pistol and fired it into the air, penetrating the crowd with great strides until he got in front of the grandstand. Tom Mix herded the children and Donita Ollas back to their camp.

"Arrest him!" Villa cried, pointing to the flogger. Half a dozen soldiers surrounded the man, relieving him of his whip. Then Villa turned to the startled occupants in the grandstand.

"So you're supposed to be El Padrino, huh?" he said to the fat man in the sequined suit. "Well, I say you're an asshole."

"I am Señor Reyes, but they call me El

Padrino," the man said, standing. His face was ashen and the muscles of his jaw seemed to click. "And who, please, are you?"

"Pancho Villa."

"I have heard of you, señor. What is it you want? We're having a fiesta."

"It's not like any fiesta I've ever seen," Villa replied. "You don't whip men and have little children grovel in the dirt at fiestas."

"It has been this way here since before I was born. My father and my grandfather, and his —"

"Shut up you stinking *gachupín*!" Villa flared up again. "You and your thieving ancestors made slaves of these people and this is only your way of keeping them in line. Why were you whipping those men? Did they do something wrong?"

"It is not me, it's the Church," El Padrino replied. "They are doing penitence."

Villa asked the priest, "Is that so, Padre?" He was an old man with a red face blotched with spiderwebs of veins from drinking too much wine.

"It is," the padre said. "It has been this way in Reyes since well before I came here. It's a tradition every year," he said, with an air of wonderment that anyone would even ask such a question, "because they are Jews."

"Jews?" Villa queried, confused.

"That is correct, General. These people are some of the Marrano Jews whose ancestors

654

came with the Cortés conquest more than three hundred years ago. We understand that their ancestors signed up for the expedition to avoid the Spanish Inquisition. We don't know how or why, but somehow they broke off from Cortés and settled here. Their descendants inhabit much of the town, except for Señor Reyes and his family. They go to church, of course, but some of them still burn a candle and wash their hands on Friday nights."

"Well, what in hell are you beating them for?" Villa demanded. "What's wrong with Jews?"

"As I said, General, it's a tradition. It has been so for hundreds of years. They expect it; it's part of their lives."

"Bullshit!" Villa stormed. He was working himself up. He felt his neck muscles swell and his head became light and disembodied, as though somebody else were doing the talking. He jabbed his finger savagely at the priest while addressing the crowd of peons.

"These priests feed off of you like lice!" he shouted. "You go into church dressed in rags every day to be confronted with the stinking collection boxes at every door saying, 'Alms for the dead!' For prayers for the dead — bullshit!" Villa repeated. "Do you think you can buy the souls out of purgatory? Do you believe you can buy any prayers for the dead that will do the dead any good? It all goes to these stinking people who call themselves priests. And now they whip you because they say you are Jews. Are you?"

One man who was struggling to stand up under the weight of his crucifix answered. His face was flushed from the beating, and sweat poured from his brow, so that he had to keep blinking his eyes to see.

"They say so, señor."

"And do you do these rituals on Fridays?"

"We always have, señor," the man replied. "But we go to church, too."

Villa was now in a white-hot rage. He turned on the priest. "I ought to take this man's whip and flog you to shreds!" he screamed. "Now get out of here, before I do it!" The priest hurried off and went out of sight behind a building.

"And when I am finished with you," Villa said to the bullwhip man, "you won't be doing any more whipping!" He addressed the soldiers, who flung the man to the ground and began pulling off his boots. Next it was El Padrino's turn.

"As for you, señor, you have held your last fiesta." He motioned for his men to grab El Padrino. "Get a rope!" Villa bellowed.

"Please, señor," El Padrino cried, "do not hang me!"

"Hang you? Why not?" Villa said indignantly. "Why, you've given me an idea!" The men in El Padrino's party were on their feet with dismayed looks and the women began to moan and wail.

"Over here!" Villa ordered. The soldiers shoved El Padrino through the crowd of peons to the boardwalk in front of the cantina. "Tie his hands! Rope his feet!" the general cried. While his men were carrying out these orders, Villa spoke to the soldiers who had the bullwhip man on the ground. He was thrashing and squealing as they sliced the skin off of his bared feet with sharp knives.

"Now run him through the fields!" Villa told them. The soldiers hauled the man to his feet and one of them kicked him in the ass. Then they began merrily chasing him, shooting at the ground beneath his bloody feet with their pistols so that when he ran he left his bloody footprints in the street.

Now roped per instructions, El Padrino watched all of this in terror.

"No, please! I will give you money," El Padrino begged.

"Up there!" Villa barked. He pointed to one of the beams supporting the second-story balcony above the boardwalk that served as a reviewing stand for the whores who were watching the fiesta. It was directly above the enormous iron cooking pot of boiling grease that the old woman had been frying her tortillas in. The men tossed up the rope, looping it over the beam.

"Hoist him up," Villa ordered.

The soldiers pulled until El Padrino was hanging upside down, kicking.

"Now, you miserable scum, you will find out what revolution is all about!" Villa hollered. "In front of God and everybody else, do you give all your lands to these people?"

"Señor . . . please . . ." El Padrino whined.

"Do you!" Villa was almost beside himself.

"*Sí.*"

"Even if they are Jews?"

"*Sí* . . . please, señor . . ."

"Good," Villa proclaimed. "And all of you heard this, right?"

There was a murmur from the crowd.

"Now put him in it," Villa exclaimed to the soldiers holding the end of the rope. They began dropping El Padrino down toward the smoking, seething cauldron of grease.

"No! No!" El Padrino pleaded.

Reed, Bierce, and Strucker remained, watching the spectacle. El Padrino suddenly reminded Reed of an unwilling participant in one of Houdini's magic acts, but none of them, not even Bierce, actually expected Villa to go through with it.

When the soldiers lowered El Padrino kicking and screaming, his head disappeared into the vat of grease. He writhed for a few moments and then became still. The members of his family in the grandstand were paralyzed with horror. When Villa was satisfied that El

Padrino was well done, he nodded for them to raise the rope, and what emerged was a hideous sight. El Padrino's skin had become translucent and almost glowing, like a wax dummy in a department store window. His eyeballs had been burned out; on his face was an abominable grimace and his tongue was gray and shriveled.

Reed had watched the village children standing mute and wide-eyed. He thought it odd when they didn't scream or otherwise react, until he decided they'd probably been subjected to such brutality all their lives. Bierce was standing next to him, biting his lip, but managed to say, "Don't look so sick, Mr. Reed, I'm sure your General Villa means well."

Both Reed and Bierce thought at almost exactly the same moment how pitilessly, how savagely, this violence could come, even while they stood there watching. It was shocking, the macabre display of revolutionary politics. Each had different views of the overall philosophy, but it was nevertheless shocking.

"Tie him off," Villa roared, intending to let El Padrino hang there as an instructive lesson in revolutionary zeal. He turned to the crucifix men, who remained standing in the street, agog.

"Why don't you throw down those crosses and join my army!" Villa told them. "When we're finished with our business, you can come home and work your own lands." Some of the men began unburdening themselves of the crucifixes. Villa addressed the crowd again.

"Well, go on with your fiesta!" he shouted. "Let's have some music." The mariachi band began to play erratically and the people came slowly to life with a low collective murmur. The dancing women began to dance again under Villa's watchful eye, and the children went to the little food stands to get treats. Villa had been holding his pistol in his hand the entire time and he finally holstered it.

"I've got a headache," he said to nobody in particular, and went into the cantina to get a peachade.

SIXTY-ONE

Crosswinds Charlie Blake was making good time until his horse, running fast, caught its foot between two sharp narrow rocks. When it pulled out the whole hoof came off, leaving only a bloody stump. It was a completely freak accident that, surprisingly, didn't throw Charlie, but the shocked horse lurched and then tried to hobble on three legs. Charlie got down and surveyed the situation. The horse was standing with its mangled left rear leg cocked up so as not to touch the ground. Of all times, this would have to be his luck. Charlie took out his pistol, put it behind the horse's ear, and pulled the trigger. The horse recoiled, sank to its knees, and rolled over. Charlie shook his head sadly. Now he was in a fine fix.

He had ridden all day across the valley and over a mountain pass toward where the El Paso railroad ought to have been. He knew roughly which way the railroad tracks ran and if he kept on going, he couldn't help but run into them. But now, afoot, it would take longer. He was pretty certain the tracks weren't far off, but when he looked into the distance he could see no signs. He left the horse, saddle and all, except for the saddlebags, and started walking, with the sun low behind him. He walked all night, but still no rail tracks. In the morning, as the sun came up, he spied a clump of adobe houses out in the middle of nowhere, not a tree or shrub around them.

When he got there he discovered that the houses were empty but not abandoned. There was a pot of beans still warm on the fire in one of them, and Charlie helped himself. Then he sat down in the doorway and scratched his head. Was he sure he was going in the right direction? The sun came up in the east and the rail tracks at this point ought to run north and south. He was headed into the sun, but no tracks were in sight. He calculated he must have gone at least thirty miles before the horse broke down. He picked up his bags and moved out.

He'd only gone a few miles when to his amazement he came upon the railroad tracks. They were low behind a big rise in the ground, which was why he couldn't see the telegraph poles. Charlie sat down and waited. The trains ran along this route three or four times a day, and he didn't have to wait long. He felt the train before he saw it, a kind of thin tremor in the steel track he was sitting on. Next he heard a whistle, and then he saw smoke and the train came rolling into sight around a bend. Charlie stood in the middle of the tracks and began waving the saddlebags over his head to hail the train. Trains often stopped for people out in the plains like that, but this one didn't, and he had to jump out of the way to keep from getting run over. As it went past, the engineer shouted something at him in Mexican that sounded like an oath. Fortunately, it was a long train and not making much time, and Charlie was barely able to grab an iron rung of a ladder on a boxcar in the rear and hoist himself aboard. He climbed to the top of the car and sat down. Screw 'em, he thought, at least I won't have to pay for no ticket.

Xenia had been beside herself in El Paso through all the long days and nights since she and Beatie had escaped from Valle del Sol. When they finally healed up enough from the car crash to take the train back across the border, they were greeted with letters both from Arthur and his father telling them they'd gone after Pancho Villa and not to worry, they would bring the children home.

Not to worry? It was one of the craziest notions Xenia could imagine — a couple of Bostonians going after a cold-blooded murderer who ran a Mexican army. She and

Beatie remained at the Toltec Hotel, trying to pick up any tidbit through the newspapers or on the streets as to Villa's whereabouts, but they got no further than the general speculation he was in the mountains and would come out when he was good and ready. There was no word from the rescue expedition, so Xenia didn't even know if the children were dead or alive — or, for that matter, her husband and her father-in-law.

Xenia had gotten to know both General Pershing and his aide, Lieutenant George Patton, who were also staying at the Toltec and were entirely sympathetic with her plight after the Hearst papers inconsiderately broke the story that Villa had kidnapped her children.

"I'd like to go down there and put a bullet through his thick head," Patton said of Villa. "These Mexicans are treating us with about as much respect as you'd show to a cockroach, and right now there's nothing we can do but take it."

"Well, George, I expect he'll make a mistake one of these days," Pershing said, "and then maybe you'll get your chance." Pershing seemed comfortable around Patton — more so than with his senior staff. One reason was that after the deaths of Pershing's wife and children in a fire, Patton introduced the general to his sister and they had started up an intense and romantic exchange of letters.

"He's already made his mistake," Xenia snapped, "by kidnapping my family. A man will not be forgiven for that, by God or anybody else."

"I believe you may be right," Pershing told her. "Whatever sympathy there was for Villa in the United States has certainly evaporated since these stories began being published."

That conversation had taken place several weeks earlier. Then, four days ago, Xenia had received wonderful news.

Patton had gone to the movie theater where they were playing the new Ben Turpin film. Before the main feature they showed the latest Black's Movie News of the World that contained the footage of Pancho Villa. It had the shots of Villa preparing to attack at Chihuahua, Villa leading his troops at daylight, his defeat there, the retreat, and finally the footage the movie men had filmed in the mountains before they departed. Villa was quoted in the subtitles saying that he was not washed up yet and would return with an even larger army to defeat his enemies. The film showed Tom Mix doing horse and rope tricks, and then for a few moments the camera panned in on a lovely blond girl who Patton believed might be the age of Katherine Shaughnessy, and moments later a boy about the age of Timmy. He returned to the hotel immediately to get Xenia.

He escorted her to the cinema, where both

of them tried to persuade the projectionist to rerun the Black's Movie News of the World clip, but he spoke no English. Exasperated, they waited in a restaurant until the Ben Turpin film was over and returned to seat themselves in the theater for the Black's newsreel. Xenia was almost beside herself as the film rolled on. In the moment after Tom finished his rope tricks, Xenia's left hand flew to her throat and her right grabbed Patton's arm so hard that he nearly jumped out of his seat.

"It's them!" Xenia cried, pointing at the screen.

"You're sure."

"Of course. My children! They're alive."

"I thought it would be them," Patton said.

Other spectators in the theater turned around in their seats, and several of them said, "Shussssh." Patton growled at them.

By now the newsreel had moved on to Reed's interview with Villa.

"Can they show it again?" Xenia asked fervidly.

"If they won't, I'll have my men confiscate the film," Patton told her. They went to see the theater manager, who agreed that after the show they could come back and he'd run the newsreel again for them. He had the projectionist show the part with the kids a dozen times and ran the whole reel over again until they were satisfied there was no more information to be gleaned. All the newsreel said was that Villa had taken to the sierras, "where," he was quoted as saying, "I will live off roots, if necessary."

Xenia returned to the hotel elated, and managed to get connected to the Hollywood offices of Black's Movie News of the World. She told them she wished to speak directly with the people who took the film of Villa but was informed they were away on assignment in the North Sea, filming British ships hunting German submarines. Nobody at Black's Movie News had any information about exactly where the final Pancho Villa footage had been shot.

She got another shock two days later when the telephone rang in her room and the desk clerk told Xenia a gentleman was downstairs asking to see her. She went into the lobby, and standing there beside a big potted palm was Mick Martin.

Xenia felt her face flush crimson. She started to turn and rush back upstairs but Mick stopped her.

"Just give me a moment, please," he said.

"What are you doing here?" was all she could manage.

"I came to see if I could help," he told her.

"You!" she said, horrified.

"Please, Xenia, just give me a moment."

Xenia was so dumbfounded, her feet suddenly seemed rooted in place. Her heart thumped wildly, and for a moment her mind raced in thoughts almost incoherently. It was like coming upon a huge snake in the woods. But a moment was all Mick needed.

He explained to Xenia that he had read about the kidnappings in the Hearst papers and that he'd found out from the Colonel's office that she was staying in El Paso. The papers also had told of Arthur's and the Colonel's expedition to go after Villa. Then, two days ago when he himself watched the same release of Black's Movie News of the World, he'd decided to come down and see what he could do.

"It's my line of business," Mick told her, "I've had to deal with kidnappings. Most of the time the kidnappers don't want to hurt anybody, they just want money. The secret is to get them to feel secure, as though you're actually trying to help them. They're always suspicious of trickery."

Xenia remained aghast and said nothing. She felt dirty just being in his presence. Her stomach churned, as though with cramps.

"It entered my mind," Mick continued, "that the Colonel — grand old man that he is — would probably not be the best person to deal with somebody who's kidnapped his family. He's pretty hotheaded, as we all know. And Arthur . . ."

She was not looking at him, but heard the words. Above all, she wanted to flee up the stairs, but remained rooted in place.

"And Arthur," Mick said, "well, it's his children, and I just don't know if he would be up to this. Sometimes it's better to have a disinterested party."

"I don't know why you dared to come here," Xenia blurted finally.

"Please, Xenia, listen to reason. I need this for myself, too. I need to make it up."

"You can never make it up." She was beginning to regain some measure of composure.

"I need to try," Mick said. "For Katherine and Timmy's sake. All I ask is your blessing to try to negotiate with Villa. If I have that, I won't trouble you further."

She had to look away because she was confused by what she felt. Didn't he even know she was carrying his child? Well, she wasn't showing yet; it had scarcely been three months. The very thought of him revolted and frightened her. But there were other considerations now. She knew his reputation. Arthur had spoken of it, too. She shook her head.

"If you wish, do what you can. That's all I will say."

The problem, of course, was that nobody knew where Villa was. Mick had assumed that, famous as Villa was, he wouldn't be hard to find, but all the information he received while in El Paso convinced him otherwise. He'd decided to stay another day or so and see if he could pick more information before

plunging into Mexico when Crosswinds
Charlie turned up to see Xenia, carrying with
him a letter from Arthur.

The letter described what had happened on
the manhunt: the ascent into the mountains,
the encounter with Indian village, the attack
of grizzly bear, and the descent into the
canyons. It told of the Colonel's broken leg
and of finding Bomba and said that they were
now poised to attempt a rescue, with Crosswinds Charlie flying Arthur's plane.

Xenia didn't know whether to be happy or
sick. On the one hand, she was grateful to
know Arthur and his father were alive; on the
other, she seriously doubted his ability to
execute anything so difficult as an attack on
Pancho Villa's army. Yet there was something
in the tone of the letter that gave her re-
assurance.

It took all morning, but she finally summoned up her courage and phoned Mick
Martin's room and told him of the letter. She
felt uncomfortable, even guilty about it, and
positively sick to hear his voice answer the
telephone. How would Arthur feel, if he knew
she had shown Mick his letter? In any case,
she met him downstairs, and after Mick read
it, he dispelled her hopes.

"Xenia," he told her, "I don't know exactly
what he's trying to do here, but I'd say it's
nuts. Why do this? Why not just go to Villa
and see if you can pay him off? It's a lot bet-

ter than risking everybody's lives. Frankly, I can't believe this is Arthur talking."

"It's not the Arthur I know," she said. "He's sounding like his father."

"Let me suggest this," Mick said. "I will go out with this Charlie fellow in the aeroplane. Maybe I can persuade Arthur to let me have a crack at Villa before he does something rash."

"If you do, I want you to take him a letter from me," Xenia said. Her mouth was dry and she still couldn't bring herself to actually look at him. But who else was there to get what she wanted to say to Arthur? She went to her room as soon as possible and washed her hands and face.

Butcher Fierro had also arrived in El Paso. Actually he'd arrived in Juárez, just across the river, where he'd begun preparation by telegraph and riders delivering messages to re-form and organize part of Villa's army to join him for the attack on Agua Prieta, some two hundred miles west of El Paso. Meantime, he decided to cross the border into El Paso with a specific motive in mind. He wanted to purchase a rifle.

Not just any rifle; Fierro wanted to buy one of the new American Springfield rifles the United States Army had equipped itself with. He'd heard good things about this weapon. It was a bolt-action repeater rumored to have an accurate killing range of five hundred yards or better. Fierro liked nothing more than to shoot men at a great distance and determined to get one of these rifles and see for himself. One morning, shortly after he'd arrived in Juárez, Fierro rode across the international bridge that linked the two cities and presented himself at a gun shop where he'd been told the rifle could be bought.

When someone of the stature of General Rudolfo Fierro entered the United States in a city like El Paso, it was bound to stir up interest. If few people knew Fierro by sight, most knew him by reputation, and word quickly spread that the infamous "butcher" was now in their town. Among the recipients of the news was Lieutenant George Patton, who decided to get a look at the ruthless warrior for himself.

A crowd of onlookers had gathered outside the shop where Fierro went to buy the Springfield, and Patton followed the Mexican inside. When he came through the door, Fierro ignored him despite the fact that Patton was dressed in the spit-and-polish uniform of an American officer. Even from ten feet away Fierro's aroma was enough to knock a wolf off a gutwagon, so Patton kept his distance for the time being.

"What is your pleasure, Señor General?" asked the proprietor of the gun shop.

"My pleasure is fucking, drinking whiskey,

and killing gringos," Fierro replied, evidently for Patton's edification, "but what I came here for was to buy a rifle." He was feeling particularly mean that morning.

The general pointed to the Springfield, and the store owner, somewhat unnerved by Fierro's brazen response, handed it to him across the counter.

"Every time I leave this country I tell myself it's for the last time," Fierro said by way of conversation, "yet every time I leave, I return like a dog who returns to its vomit." He began sighting the rifle to and fro and working the bolt action.

"It's the finest infantry weapon in the world," the proprietor told him proudly.

"It's too short for me," Fierro said.

"I can put a pad on it for you," the owner offered.

"You don't need a pad," Patton interjected. "It's supposed to be a little short. The reason is that when you fight in cold weather, as they're doing in Europe, your clothing will make up the difference."

"I don't want it to fight in cold weather. And this is not Europe," Fierro snapped.

"Suit yourself," Patton told him, moving closer. "But I want to ask you a question. Your General Villa has kidnapped the children of somebody I know. What do they have to do to get them back?"

"I don't know anything about that," Fierro

replied. "What General Villa does is his own business."

"Well, I've got a lady here in El Paso who's the mother of those children, and she just wants to know where General Villa is so she can talk to him," Patton said. "If there's ransom involved, maybe it can be arranged."

"Tell her to arrange it with General Villa," said Fierro. "He'll turn up sooner or later."

"And you don't know his whereabouts?"

"If I did, I certainly wouldn't tell *you*," Fierro replied. He was examining the rifle closely, looking down the barrel and checking the sights. "How much is it?" he asked the owner.

"Just a minute," Patton said. He had bellied closer to the counter and was looking at Fierro eyeball to eyeball. "Are you expecting this man to sell you this rifle so you can use it to kill American soldiers?"

"No," Fierro said calmly. "I want it to kill jaguars in the canyons. For killing American soldiers, I use a stick."

"Are you always this pleasant?" Patton inquired.

"Only when I'm in a good mood," Fierro answered.

The two remained locked in a fiery gaze until Patton finally broke out in a sardonic grin.

"Okay, General — buy the rifle. I'd be interested to learn how well you can actually shoot it."

"If you do, it'll be the last thing you ever find out," Fierro told him.

Crosswinds Charlie Blake had been at work all night putting Arthur's airplane together. First he hired half a dozen men to move it piece by piece from the railcar where Arthur had stored it to a hangar at the flying field on the outskirts of town. The hangar had no electric lights, so Charlie borrowed railroad lanterns to illuminate his task. By dawn he was prepared to see if the thing worked. Three spins of the propeller, and the Luft-Verkehrs sputtered, then caught. Charlie revved the throttle and the engine roared. He shut it off. Now there was nothing to do but wait. His landing needed to be timed with dusk.

Charlie had been skeptical about taking Mick Martin along, but Xenia's voice couldn't be ignored. The problem was that Mick's added weight meant Charlie couldn't take along an extra three cans of gasoline. He already had two spare cans, but had wanted the other three to be on the safe side in case he had trouble finding his landing spot. He also knew Mick would be stuck in Mexico once they landed, for better or for worse. For the return trip, there was no room in the plane for anyone but the children.

He found a shady piece of grass near the

flying shack and lay down to grab a nap after being up all night. Charlie had been crushed when the aerial circus had moved on and left him behind. And now to be given a mission of the most delicate gravity — this was something Charlie could only have dreamed about. In his mind, he was the right man, in the right place, at the right time.

At two p.m. Mick Martin showed up in cavalry-twill pants and a mohair jacket, wearing a .38 revolver strapped to his waist. At two-fifteen they were in the air, flying into a white-hot Mexican sun.

SIXTY-TWO

Arthur had selected five men to go with him on the rescue: Cowboy Bob, Death Valley Slim, two of the Mexican teamsters for their knowledge of the language, and Bomba. At noon they rode forward, and four hours later were in hiding positions in a drainage ditch at the edge of the lettuce field. Meantime, Bob had ridden back into the town for a last-minute reconnaissance. He returned vexed; Villa was no longer there.

Following the fiesta, Villa had sent a party of troops to boot out El Padrino's remaining family from their hacienda, which he then took over for his headquarters. For the rescue, it was a setback but not a catastrophe, as Bob explained after scouting the hacienda. Even though much of his original plan would have to be scrapped, the way the hacienda was situated might work to their advantage. There were more and better escape routes for after Villa's captives were rescued. If his previous experience was an indicator, Bob figured Villa would most likely open up the hacienda's wine cellar to the soldiers, who would waste no time becoming even drunker than they'd already gotten during the fiesta, if such a thing was possible. All in all, Bob didn't think the new circumstances were going to be any more difficult than the original plan to grab the kids from the soldiers' camp in town, which was to say that he would have been surprised if any of them escaped with their lives. As he rode into town, he'd observed the horrid spectacle of El Padrino's waxen body hanging upside down above the grease pot. At almost the same moment he decided not to mention it when he got back to the group. Everybody was jumpy enough as it was.

The way Arthur had worked things out, while the rescue party went about their mission the others, including his father and Johnny Ollas, would head east toward the railroad and then on to El Paso. Johnny was now conscious enough from his amputation to give them some useful information, including the fact that the kids and Donita were being kept by Tom Mix and usually remained close by Villa's headquarters.

Arthur had to tell Johnny there was no room in the plane for Donita, and though Johnny was naturally disappointed, he understood. The Colonel promised that after the children were safe he would see what he could do to negotiate a ransom for her. He swore to Johnny she'd be rescued. Johnny took the Colonel by the hand and gripped it tightly, his eyes glistening. "Please," he said. "Okay?"

"I promise you, son, it will all come out right," said Colonel Shaughnessy.

The sun was going down and was casting long shadows across the lettuce field when Arthur's men first heard the thin drone of an airplane. Earlier they had sneaked out and pulled up six rows of lettuce to make a smoother landing strip for Crosswinds Charlie. The plane came over the field from behind them so low and sudden that they were all startled; then it swooped upward in a sharp turn, banking east, and disappeared behind some trees. When they saw it again, the plane was leveling in from the south, headed right for the landing area they had cleared. Within half a minute it was on the ground, and in a few more moments was turned around and pointing back down the cleared strip for a takeoff.

Charlie cut the throttle immediately and a hard silence fell back over the farmlands, broken occasionally by the distant lowing of a cow. Everybody was surprised to see a second passenger in Charlie's plane.

When Arthur recognized the passenger as

Mick Martin, he felt the hair on his neck stand up and his body solidified into a wooden block that would not turn. He could only glare as Mick Martin and Charlie walked toward him across the lettuce field. Cowboy Bob had risen out of the ditch and was waving his hat to motion them over, but he needn't have bothered, since Charlie had already seen them from the air.

Arthur was standing at the rim of the ditch when Mick and Charlie came walking up. Mick stuck out his hand. Arthur hit him hard as he could in the mouth, knocking him to the ground. Mick tasted blood on his lip and reflexively reached up to wipe it off, when Arthur kicked him in the side of the head and Mick slid down into the ditch. The others were startled and frozen by this behavior. Mick pushed himself to his feet but Arthur jumped down into the ditch in front of him and hit him again, this time in the nose, but he didn't go down. Neither did he try to fight back, but instead stood with his arms by his sides, waiting for the next blow. Arthur realized what Mick was doing and didn't hit him anymore. He would have shot him, but the noise might have attracted unwanted attention.

Arthur scrambled out of the ditch and said to the perplexed Crosswinds Charlie, "There's been a little change in plans but your job's the same. It's going to be later than

I hoped when we get back here after we rescue the children and I don't know what the visibility's going to be like after it gets dark. If there isn't enough for you to see, you better post torches along the strip; that ought to get you into the air."

Bob, Slim, and the others were frowning down at Mick, who was still standing in the ditch. Whatever he'd done to provoke Arthur's wrath must have been serious, because they all liked Arthur and knew he was an even-tempered fellow. Bomba was more mystified than anyone, since he'd known Mick as Arthur's friend since the Christmas Day he'd brought him to the Shaughnessy home from the orphanage.

Charlie finally spoke: "It was your wife that told me to bring him along, Arthur. I didn't know y'all wasn't friends."

"Arthur, I need to talk to you," Mick said, climbing out of the ditch and dusting himself off.

"No, you don't. I don't have time for you now. Best thing you can do is start walking east and away from here."

"I know what you're trying to do," Mick said. "I came to try to talk you out of it. Let me try something. This is my specialty." Arthur gave him a steely glare. The silence between them was vast and stony. Then Arthur spoke:

"You're not talking anyone out of anything," he said furiously. "We have a plan and we're going to stick to it, so shut up and get going. There's a railroad about twenty or thirty miles east from here."

"Look, I don't know what Xenia has told you. But it wasn't what you think . . ." Mick took out the letter Xenia had given him and tried to hand it to Arthur.

Arthur hit him again.

At the hacienda of El Padrino, a celebration was in progress. Villa had opened the wine cellar to his soldiers and they were sprawled all over the ground or reeling among one another with wine bottles in their hands. Inside the main house, Villa had ordered a great feast to be prepared: roasted chickens and ducks with tomatoes, peppers, and cheese; lamb chops and mint jelly; broiled calves' liver with rice and fresh spinach; baked ham with cabbage and sautéed onions; and, of course, fine wines. This nearly cleaned out the pantries and larders of the hacienda, but Villa wasn't concerned because he had plans for the house, too. Having ordered all this, Villa retired with the headache that had nagged him since the incident at the fiesta that morning. Finally he got his lemonade.

The meal was served bacchanal-style over the course of many hours. In the dining room, Bierce, Reed, Fierro, Strucker, and a host of others, including Donita Ollas and the children, sat at an enormous table made from ponderosa pine. The food was a delicious change from the beans and beef of the trail. Pluto, the Mexican hairless, sat under the table gobbling chunks of meat that Timmy fed him. In a corner, the mariachi band from the fiesta played gay tunes, including, at Fierro's insistence, "La Cucaracha," and there was noisy singing amid a blue pall of cigar smoke from El Padrino's private stock.

During a break in the courses, Katherine excused herself and walked outside for some air. Tom Mix saw her and motioned for her to come with him onto a secluded lawn away from the drunken soldiers.

"Those men have been out in the wild for a long time," he told her, "and when they get a bellyful of drinking, sometimes unpleasant things can happen."

"Do you know what day this is?" Katherine asked him. They sat down on a stone bench in a corner of the lawn that was framed with flowering bushes.

Mix was somewhat baffled. In fact he didn't know what day it was, though for some reason he thought it might be Tuesday. But out here, Tuesdays were pretty much the same as Mondays, or Wednesdays or Thursdays, or even Sundays, for that matter.

"Tuesday?" he offered.

"No, silly, not what day of the week. But

what day," she said.

Earlier Katherine had luxuriated in her first real bath since her capture. Upstairs in the hacienda was a huge commode room with mosaic tiled floors and a white marble tub; the servants had been told to bring buckets of hot water. She scrubbed herself with perfumed soaps and washed her hair for nearly half an hour. It had actually become matted in places. Since Mix told them to take or use anything they wished at the hacienda, Katherine managed to find a nice lace dress in somebody's room. It had been a grown-up's room, and she was a little surprised when the dress actually fit her. When she looked in the mirror, she sensed that she had grown, not just taller, but in other places, too. Katherine looked at herself for a long time and was pleased she was still pretty.

"Well, they were having a fiesta," Mix said. "Are you asking if it is some saint's day?"

"No, not that," she said coyly.

"What, then? I don't know," Mix replied.

"It's my birthday," she told him.

"Is it really?" Mix said, genuinely surprised.

"I'm thirteen."

"That's nice and grown-up," he said. "I remember the day when I was thirteen."

"What did you do?"

"I went down to the river with some friends and we caught crawfish, and my ma boiled them up for us with corn and potatoes. It's still my favorite dish to eat."

"Did you know I'm teaching General Villa to read?" she asked.

"I wasn't sure what you two were up to, but I kind of expected it might be something like that."

"He's my first student, and a good one, too."

"The general's a smart man," Mix said.

"Are you always going to stay with him?" Katherine asked.

Mix looked at her. She seemed somehow changed, and not just because of the dress she was wearing. It ran across his mind that she was going to be quite a beautiful woman. But suddenly she didn't seem to be so much a child anymore, either; there was a difference in her attitude that made him a little uneasy, the way he usually got when he was in the presence of beautiful women.

"Truth is, I ain't sure what I'm going to do," Mix said. "This war can't last forever — although it's got a pretty good start on it."

"So then what?" The bright sunlight made her blue eyes sparkle, and it caused Mix to feel protective of her.

"Who knows? Sometimes I think about going out to California."

"Whatever for?" Katherine asked. Mix sensed disappointment in her voice.

"To be in the movies, maybe."

"The movies! Really? Do you think you can?"

"I don't know why not," he said. "I reckon I'm just as good a cowboy as the next feller. And I hope I'm not any worse-lookin', either."

"Worse-looking! Why, you're the most handsome man I've ever met." She'd blurted it out before thinking and caught her breath when she realized what she'd just said.

"Why, that's . . . mighty nice of you to tell me that," Mix replied uncomfortably.

Katherine felt herself beginning to flush, and she gulped. She hadn't intended to say anything to Mix that was so forward, but now that she had, she decided to go on.

"Maybe my grandfather can help you," Katherine told him, "to get in the movies."

"How's that?"

"Well, he knows *everybody,* you know. I mean, he can just call up the president of the United States whenever he wants to."

"Anybody can do that," Mix replied.

"They can't, either."

"Sure they can. But it don't mean he'll answer the phone, though."

"Well, he talks to Grandpapa."

"I appreciate it, young lady," Mix told her. He was beginning to feel fidgety with the conversation. Here he was, charged with holding these people hostage, and now one of them, a child, was offering him help to get into show business.

"Can you read?" Katherine asked.

"Sure I can read. Read all the time."

"I've never seen you."

"That's because I don't have anything to read. There ain't exactly any libraries out here."

"I'll teach you, too, if you can't," she said.

"Well, I can. But thanks for the offer anyway."

"Can you dance?" Katherine asked.

"Me, dance? Sure."

"What kind of dance?"

"Whatever kind. I've been to dances."

"I don't mean like square dances or those western things. I mean real dancing."

"You mean toe-dancing, like in a ballet or something?"

"Of course not, silly, I mean waltzes, where they have an orchestra."

"Well, I don't know about that. I never heard an orchestra before except over the Victrola."

"Grandpapa has orchestras for his parties at Cornwall."

Mix asked what that was.

"His cottage. It's in Newport."

"Sounds kinda peculiar, having an orchestra in a cottage."

"Oh, it's not actually a cottage. They just call it that. It's real big and it looks out over the ocean."

"I never saw the ocean," Mix replied.

"Never saw the ocean!" Katherine exclaimed. "I don't believe that."

"Well, now, where would I have ever seen the ocean?"

"It's all over the world," Katherine informed him.

"Look, I was raised in the state of Arizona and there ain't no ocean anywheres near there." Mix was getting annoyed. He wondered if she was trying to make a fool of him.

"If you come to Cornwall sometime," she said, "I'll show you the ocean. There's a special place along the cliffs and I'm the only one who knows about it." Katherine began forming the picture in her mind. Tom might have been a rude cowboy, but there was something else in him that she saw. She saw possibilities.

Mix stood up. "I reckon we better go on back inside the house," he said. "I think I smell those chickens roastin'."

SIXTY-THREE

It was nearly dark, and Arthur was studying the hacienda through field glasses. Bob, Slim, and Bomba were by his side in a clump of bushes about a hundred yards away from the main house. The two Mexican teamsters had been sent into the encampment to see what they could find out. Arthur scanned across the lawns littered with soldiers whose drunken cries filled the air. He swung around to the house, and through the open doors could see people milling in the foyer, and through the windows he saw others eating and drinking. It seemed like every light in the house was burning. Then his heart caught. Two people were walking up the broad steps to the hacienda: an American-looking cowboy and a young girl.

Arthur had in his pocket the letter from Xenia that Mick had tried to hand to him earlier. He'd picked it up off the ground. The letter had nearly unnerved him when he read it, but he'd managed to collect himself and proceed with his scheme.

Xenia was earnestly frightened for the children's safety by Arthur's proposal to try to rescue them. Had he thought of the seriousness of the consequences if he failed? It had struck a note with Arthur and made him wonder if he had. All these days he'd been working himself up to do this, letting the anger and the rage push the notion of failure out of his mind. But reading Xenia's letter, he realized he was now holding reality in his hands.

"I cannot even imagine how you must feel right now," she wrote, *"but I agreed to let Mick go out and try his skill at releasing the children. Whatever else he might be, he is known as an expert in this dreadful business. I can't believe that if this man Villa is confronted with an offer from the mother of her children to be paid money for their release, that he will not listen to reason."*

What money? Arthur had closed his eyes when he read the line. Yes, it was conceivable that Mick could negotiate Villa down to some workable sum, but what would that be? By borrowing and selling off what he could, Arthur might be able to raise fifty or sixty thousand. But Villa had demanded a million. And what if Villa refused to negotiate, which he probably would? Even getting Mick into Villa's camp would be problematic; they couldn't just send him marching up tonight out of the blue; they would have to concoct some additional scheme for that. And all the while the opportunity they had been waiting and planning for would slip away. No, Arthur decided. They were here. The plane was here. The children were here. And Villa suspected nothing.

Arthur had folded the letter, put it in his pocket, and had shaken his head.

"I'm going on. What time is it?" he said absently, barely looking at Mick, who'd been waiting for an answer.

"Arthur, you really must listen to me. Negotiation is the only safe way. Anything else will be putting your kids' life on the line."

"Don't you think I know that?" Arthur snapped savagely.

"But then why?"

"Because there's nothing to negotiate. We don't have any money. Father's broke and so is the company."

"What?" Mick had said, stunned.

"Look, I don't have time to go into it. You'd better start walking like I said, because chances are, when we get back here they'll be coming after us, and there aren't any spare horses. If they catch you, they'll kill you."

Mick had stood on the edge of the lettuce field and watched Arthur and the others ride away. He'd felt his heart sink, not just for the children and for Arthur and Xenia, but for himself, too, because he'd somehow hoped that if he could pull this off, he'd be forgiven. At least he'd hoped so, until he'd felt the loathing and disgust in Arthur's voice and eyes, which had hit him harder than Arthur's fists.

The Mexican teamsters returned with the news that they'd seen a young boy through the dining room window of the hacienda. And they'd seen the girl, too, with an Americano. It looked as though the only guards posted were two by the front door.

Arthur told one of the teamsters to go back and see if he could find enough articles of clothing among any of the passed-out soldiers to make himself fit in, and then to get positioned in such a way as to keep an eye on the children. They all believed the children were being kept in the house, probably upstairs, and would most likely be put to bed soon. When the festivities died down enough, Bomba would deal with the guards, and Arthur and Bob would sneak to the house and make the rescue. Slim would remain at the hiding place with the other teamster, who was holding the horses.

Arthur had a deep gash on his right knuckle from hitting Mick in the teeth. Unfortunately, the wound was on his trigger finger, and the finger was getting stiff. Arthur shook his head. If it came down to gunplay, would this trip him up in the rescue? So many things were hammering through his mind he had trouble concentrating.

Cowboy Bob had been in some tough scrapes in his life, but nothing quite like this. He thought about some of them while they were waiting for the festivities to quiet down. He'd been trampled in a stampede, all but drowned in a river, nearly burned up in a prairie fire, and almost frozen to death on the range one winter and had to eat his horse. He'd been shot at, knifed, and once thrown in jail for beating a man to death in a fight. The man had deserved it.

Without a woman in his life, there wasn't much to do except hang out around saloons and sign on with the drives or go out on the ranges punching cattle.

When he'd been thirty years old he decided to go back to El Paso and try to find a woman to keep him straight.

He'd found one, all right, but in hindsight he'd made a hasty choice. She was just a saloon girl, but Bob thought she had possibilities. They'd gotten married by taking out a certificate at city hall, and Bob spent his savings on a little shack and about sixty acres, where he intended to raise a few breed cows. It wasn't much, but to him it was the prettiest place on earth. He plowed to plant feed corn and to his disgust had to fence most of it in, the days of the open range having all but vanished. In the space of six weeks a blue norther came through and killed half the cattle, rains washed out all the corn he'd planted, and his wife ran off with a pots-and-pans salesman. After that, Bob sold the cows that were left and the land, too, and as a parting gesture set fire to the shack and watched it burn. He vowed then and there he'd never own another thing in his life he couldn't carry with him on a horse, including a woman. In fact, he decided, if he could find a shoe store that would agree to it, he'd even rent his boots.

"Some of them lights are going out upstairs," Slim said. Arthur looked at his watch; it was just after ten. A lot of the singing and shouting from the drunken soldiers had died away and many of their fires had gone low.

"Well, boys, I guess it won't do to wait till the sun comes up," Arthur said.

Bob nodded. They might as well get on with it. For some reason he felt hungry. It occurred to him suddenly to wonder if he had eaten his last breakfast.

"There's one last thing I've been thinking about," Arthur continued. "I want you guys to be absolutely certain that you still want to go through with this."

They all looked at each other, and finally Bob broke out in a nervous chuckle under his breath.

"I think that's the question that's been on

our minds to ask *you*."

"Let's do it," Arthur told them.

Arthur, Bob, and Bomba stood up, and checked their guns. "Good luck," Slim said.

The three men walked slowly, casually, toward the hacienda. There were still a few loud voices coming from inside, but the mariachi band had stopped playing. When they got to the edge of the lawn, Bomba, carrying his blowgun, split off and maneuvered himself into some shrubs alongside the house by the door. This time Bomba had put enough frog poison on his darts to ensure that the guards would not wake up.

Arthur and Bob waited for several minutes and saw one of the guards slap at his neck and then keel over. The other guard went to him and bent down to look but quickly slapped at himself, too, and collapsed on top of the first. Arthur and Bob went forward between the campfires of passed-out, snoring soldiers until they reached the big steps to the house. Bob waited on the lawn while Arthur stepped up to the portals of the house. Suddenly from bushes beside the gallery a hushed voice said, "Psssssst!"

It was the Mexican teamster. He had found a set of cross bandoliers and was wearing the big sombrero of one of Villa's men. Arthur didn't start, but turned slowly and sat down on a stone wall that framed the steps.

"Señor," the teamster whispered, "they took the children upstairs, as you thought. I follow them."

"Where?" Arthur said quietly.

"Up to the top, then you turn right. Fourth door, I think."

"Muchas gracias," Arthur told him under his breath. He sat there for a few moments longer, then nodded for Bob to come forward. When he joined him, Arthur nodded to go inside. He had decided not to take Bomba into the house, since his presence would obviously be noticeable. Passed-out Mexicans lay all over the foyer, on the sofas and benches and the floor. Someone in the dining room was making a toast: slow, drunk, and, from the sound of it, vulgar. Arthur and Bob went by the open double doors unnoticed. The stairs creaked and they walked up slowly, hands in their pockets, trying to look at home. At the top Arthur turned right and counted four doors. He tried the handle but it was locked. He looked at Bob.

Bob shrugged. He didn't know what to do next. He motioned to Arthur with his leg, to suggest kicking it in, but Arthur shook his head violently. One false move now, and it would all be over. They'd come too far for that.

Arthur signaled he was going downstairs to find some kind of jimmy. Bob looked at him and let out a breath of resigned exasperation.

He was fairly certain they'd overstayed their welcome already. Arthur waved him off and started back down the stairs. He'd only gotten halfway down when a man began staggering up from the other direction. He was dressed in the uniform of a lieutenant and wore an odd necklace made of shriveled things that looked peculiar. He held on to the balcony with one hand and grinned drunkenly. Just as Arthur was passing him, the man stopped him with an arm.

"Who are you, señor?" he demanded.

Arthur tried to act drunk, too, and swayed and smiled, then started back down the stairs again. The man grabbed him by the collar.

"You! You answer me!" the man slurred.

That was enough for Bob, who'd been watching nervously from above. He turned and kicked in the door to the room with one huge crash. The door flew open and Bob rushed in. It was dark and he saw nothing at first. Suddenly a dog began barking.

Arthur heard the noise, looked up, and saw what had happened. He whipped out his pistol and cracked the lieutenant on his head, and the man tumbled down the staircase. Then Arthur rushed back up toward the room.

Bob was emerging with a wild-eyed Timmy in his arms and Katherine by the wrist and a hairless dog snapping at his leg. When Katherine saw Arthur, she started to shout, but

Arthur put his finger to his lips. Timmy saw this, too, and was silent, but the dog wasn't. It began to bark frantically and went for Arthur's leg the moment he approached them. Arthur waved his arms for somebody to shut the dog up, but nobody knew how.

"Pluto, no!" Timmy hissed, but the dog continued to bark. Arthur grabbed Katherine by the arm and began pulling her toward the staircase. Bob followed with Timmy; the dog continued its furious barking that was certain to wake people up. They had just reached the upstairs landing when another of the doors opened and Tom Mix appeared in the hallway in his long johns. He ducked back into his room as the rescue party fled down the stairs. They had just gotten to the dining room when they heard shots fired. Mix had retrieved his pistol and sounded the alarm, and was rushing down the stairs after them. Suddenly the doorway was blocked by soldiers, dumb and sleepy-eyed, but there nonetheless.

Arthur turned off into the dining room, startling a dozen Mexicans who were still celebrating with toasts.

Bob saw an open window and made for it. He hoisted himself to the sill, still carrying Tim, and let himself through. Arthur followed, lifting Katherine to the window and letting her down before scrambling through it himself. Outside, somebody was shouting in Spanish, "Stop them, stop them!"

It was hopeless. Scores of soldiers were jumping up, grabbing guns, squinting into the dim light. Arthur, Bob, Tim, and Katherine had landed in bushes beneath the window, but there was no way out beyond this; the Mexicans were rushing toward them. Bomba had come up, too, and took both children in his arms. But Arthur made a split-second decision.

He hugged Katherine and Timmy for an instant and said, "I'm sorry, stay here. We'll be back." Then he, Bob, and Bomba ran off into the darkness, with rifle shots ringing and splintering in trees all around them. If they had tried to take the children with them, they would have all been killed.

"Goddamn dog!" Bob wheezed as they ran. "We had 'em! We almost had 'em!" Behind, they could hear shouting and the sounds of more shots. Slim and the Mexican teamster who'd been holding the horses were waiting when they came up. The other teamster was there, too, after drifting back from the hacienda.

"Let's get out of here now!" Arthur said. His heart was still pounding but he knew it was over. At least the children were still unharmed, and for the moment, so were he and his companions. There wasn't time for second thoughts.

The original plan had been to take the children back to the lettuce patch, put them on the plane, then scatter in different directions, meeting up later at the railroad tracks to the east. Now they had to return to the patch to tell Charlie to take off empty-handed. When they got there the place was lit up with torches Charlie had set out; the plane's engine was running and Charlie was sitting in it. In the glare of the torches Arthur saw Mick Martin was still there, too. They galloped up to the plane.

"Didn't work," Arthur said, "and they'll be right behind us. Dammit! I told you to get going!" he spat to Mick.

"I thought I might be able to help here," Mick replied.

"You get back in that damn plane and go with Charlie!" Arthur ordered.

"Look, Arthur. If I can ride double with one of you guys, I might still —"

"Get in the plane now!" Arthur screamed. Just then shots began singing around them. The plane's engine was so loud they couldn't hear most of them, but they could actually *feel* them whiz by. Mick clambered into the rear seat of the plane. Charlie gave a thumbs-up and throttled high, and the plane began to move.

"Let's go!" Arthur shouted. As planned, they split out in five different directions. As Arthur galloped through a large open cow pasture, he glanced back in time to see the Luft-Verkehrs lift into the air, its shiny red underbelly lit by the burning torches. Arthur cursed himself, not just over the children, but because he hadn't had the guts to leave Mick Martin to Villa's tender mercy.

Sixty-Four

Villa got everyone moving at dawn and they had been on the trail all day, headed north toward Agua Prieta. He himself was furious.

"It seems like everybody in Mexico is after me," he remarked to Bierce and Reed, who were riding with him at the head of the column. "I've never had so much trouble kidnapping people in my life. I get sniped at, my drovers are murdered, guards get killed, people start breaking into my quarters."

Lieutenant Crucia had led the interrogation of Katherine and Timmy after he recovered from the bump on his head from Arthur's pistol. He was even angrier than Villa, but got nothing from the children. Katherine had made Timmy swear not to tell that it was their father who had come to get them. All anyone knew was that it was somebody with an airplane and that the plan appeared to have been well thought out. Tom Mix received some of the blame, although no one was sure exactly why.

Bierce had been irritable ever since Villa decided to burn down the hacienda of El Padrino. It had made a spectacular fire after being drenched in coal oil by the soldiers, and after they left they could still see the smoke from miles away. Finally Bierce asked him about it.

"Why did you find it necessary to destroy that beautiful home?" he said. "It must date back to colonial times." It was not the opportune moment to ask such a question.

"So what, Señor Robinson? The people can rebuild it if they want to."

"Rebuild what it took centuries to build?" Bierce asked.

"Who cares how long it took?" Villa growled. "It was constructed by stinking Spaniards who enslaved my people."

"Doesn't history matter to you?" said Bierce.

"We're making history now, señor."

"No matter who it hurts?"

"War's no tea party, Señor Robinson."

"Yes, I think I used that line once myself," Bierce told him.

"I think the general has a point," Reed chimed in. "This El Padrino ruled that valley like a feudal serfdom and lived in splendor while the people were famished." Reed didn't object to the immolation of the hacienda, but he did have second thoughts about Villa's treatment of El Padrino himself. Under the revolutionary rules Reed understood, El Padrino would have been given a trial, then shot or hung if found guilty.

"It seems to me," Bierce said, "that a revolution ought to be orderly. Not going around indiscriminately burning things down and killing people." Bierce hated disorder, and anarchy certainly didn't suit him. He needed the things in his life to be meticulous because, he'd decided, his mind was so chaotic that if his surroundings were, too, it would probably drive him insane.

Villa told him, "The very nature of revolution is disorderly."

"Not ours," Bierce retorted. "We enlisted an army and fought the British man to man. If anybody burned down buildings, it was them."

"Maybe you should have tried it, too," Villa said. "Might have shortened the war."

"But they were our own buildings," Bierce countered.

"Listen, Señor Robinson, the English antagonized your country with taxes and so you rebelled with your tea party. But that was child's play compared with what the stinking Spanish have done to us for three hundred years. And their stinking descendants and associates still control ninety-five percent of all the land and wealth in Mexico. We're going to put a stop to it, and if killing's necessary, it won't stand in our way."

"Sometimes the best intentions give way to murder," Bierce remarked.

"Why give them a second chance?" Villa said. "Then their sons will come after you. This time there'll be no going back."

Villa was getting angry and felt the hairs on his neck begin to stand up, but it was too soon to go into another rage. Rages gave him headaches. He wished he'd never brought this old coot with him; who needed a ration of shit from some worn-out gringo? Señor Jack Robinson was insubordinate and, like everyone had predicted, had seriously begun to get on Villa's nerves. He began to wonder if Sanchez's ghost had somehow transformed itself into this hoary old man.

Katherine and Timmy were still trying to comprehend what had happened the night before. Their father! She had known someone would come, but had never expected *him*. It had happened so suddenly that when she woke up this morning, she thought it had been a dream. Timmy wasn't even sure that it wasn't. He'd been half asleep the whole time. And also, they hadn't been able to talk about it much between themselves because they hadn't been alone all day.

"Seems like you have got friends trying to help you out," Mix told her, trying to make conversation.

"Maybe they weren't friends, maybe they

were enemies," Katherine said deceptively.

"Why would you two have any enemies?" They were riding now in a strange new terrain. The green of El Padrino's valley now turned into a dusty wasteland of low scrub and volcanic rocks. To the west a yellowish sunset framed a row of huge black mesas that stretched as far as the eye could see. They reminded Timmy of a fleet of steaming dreadnoughts he'd once seen in a picture.

"Maybe they were just more kidnappers, like you are," she replied.

Ever since she woke up, Katherine had been confused about her feelings for Mix. Yesterday it had been wonderful talking with him in the garden. She sensed kindness, and vulnerability, too. She'd pictured the two of them walking along the cliffs at Newport and going down the path to the little secret place she had, a small cave with a ledge where they could sit on rocks and watch the ocean swells crash below. He would be a movie star by then and wealthy, and would waltz with her that night at the Colonel's ball.

Reality had struck Katherine when Mix joined Lieutenant Crucia in the interrogation later in the morning. Mix had been more gentle and seemed to believe her when she said she didn't know who the intruders were. But then, Mix hadn't been knocked in the head by a gun butt like Crucia had, which had raised a large lump. Still, it came back

706

with undeniable clarity that she was his prisoner and there wasn't any way to argue herself out of that.

"Whoever they were," Mix said, "it was the most foolhardy thing I've ever heard of."

"Maybe it was brave," she countered.

"Maybe, but it was stupid, too."

She had to bite her lip to keep from retorting.

"You still want to teach me to dance?" he asked.

"I don't know," she answered after a long pause.

"You'd have to grow about a foot to make us even," he told her.

"Maybe I won't grow," she said. "Maybe this is as tall as I'll get."

"That might come true, if you don't stop pouting."

"I'm not pouting, I'm thinking."

"What about?"

"About my father — and my mother," she said.

"You think your father had something to do with what happened last night?"

"No," she said. "Father's not a kidnapper."

"He might be if it was his own kids," Mix said.

To that she had no reply.

"I'd kinda like to see that ocean you talked about," Mix told her, increasingly embarrassed.

"Maybe someday you will, if you set us free."

"Yep, maybe someday I will," he said.

Arthur found the rest of his party without too much trouble. Bob, Slim, and the Mexican teamsters were already there. An hour later, Bomba turned up. They had hidden in a stand of woods off the road that led to the mountain pass, discussing options.

"I expect Villa's gonna follow along this river here," Slim said. He had taken out his map. "He's gotta water his horses, and if he keeps headed north, that's the only water there is."

"I think what we do now," Arthur said, "is to have Mr. Flipper take Father and Johnny Ollas and the lady here," he said, referring to Gourd Woman, "over to where they can meet the Chihuahua railroad and go on to El Paso. The rest of us will follow after Villa. With some luck there'll be another chance."

"I'm not going to El Paso or anyplace else until those children are safe," the Colonel said. Both he and Johnny were sitting up in the little cart wagon on a wooden brace Ah Dong had built. Ah Dong had also made a sort of pallet for them out of some material he had stuffed with leaves and sewn up.

"Colonel, it's out of the question. You'd slow us down," Arthur said. This was the first time in his life he had addressed his father as

"Colonel," but Arthur felt it somehow lent authority to his own sense of command.

"My word, who's in charge here?" the Colonel cried indignantly.

"I am," Arthur told him.

The Colonel considered this for a moment. "Well, in that case I tell you respectfully that I would not slow you down," he barked. "We can make time just as well as Villa can, with all his wagons and baggage and artillery and so on."

"Both of you need medical attention," Arthur said.

"We'll get it at an appropriate time," the Colonel retorted. "Johnny and I have talked it over. It's his wife they've got, too. He wants to go on."

"That so, Johnny?" Arthur asked. Johnny nodded.

"Well, Mr. Flipper, I guess it's up to you to escort the lady here."

"Lady's going with you, too," said Gourd Woman. "I come too far to quit now."

Arthur shook his head in resignation and turned to Flipper. "I guess you'll have to make do with your own company, then."

"If it's all the same to you, I suppose I'll come along, too," Flipper told him. "I'd kind of like to see how this thing turns out."

Xenia was overwrought when Mick Martin broke the news. He and Crosswinds Charlie were seated in chairs in the lobby of the Toltec and Xenia was on a sofa with a handkerchief to her lips.

"He could have gotten them all killed," she cried. She was appalled at Mick's busted-up face, but when she asked him about it he shook his head and was silent. She more or less guessed what might have happened.

"No, ma'am, ever'body's safe as they was before. At least that was good luck," said Crosswinds Charlie.

"With your permission," Mick said, "I'd like to try it myself now, if Charlie will agree to fly me out there again."

"What's Arthur going to do now?" Xenia wondered.

"I dunno," Charlie offered. "There wadn't no other plan except for that one."

"Far as I can tell, he's got two choices," Mick said. "Either he'll give up and come back here to El Paso or he'll keep going after Villa to give it another try. Mood he seems to be in now, my guess is he'll keep on."

"What must he be thinking of, endangering the children this way?" Xenia said.

"Charlie, do you think you can find Pancho Villa and land me near him?" Mick asked.

"Depends on what he does," Charlie replied. "If he's kept going north, that's fairly open country. There's some mountains here and there, but I expect he'll be following along a river. But if he goes back to hole up in them canyons, it'd be pretty dicey."

"Would you give it a try?" Mick asked.

"I reckon," Charlie said. "I ain't got nothin' better to do."

That afternoon and evening, Mick was on the phone to Boston raising money. He'd started with ten thousand of his own, then went to the leaders of the gangs he represented and managed to raise forty thousand more. He explained that it would be good public relations and they'd probably get their names in the newspapers for performing a good deed. Next day the money was wired to a bank in El Paso and Mick tucked it all into a fat satchel in hundred-dollar bills. In Mick's experience, most kidnappers were willing to settle for something like ten cents on the dollar, if it came to negotiation, and there was nothing like green money in the bag to help that happen. He figured it was worth a try.

SIXTY-FIVE

Strucker had to concentrate to keep his hand from shaking as he wrote out the telegram to the first secretary of the Imperial German Foreign Service in Berlin. Villa watched over him, standing beside a desk in the dinky telegraph depot in the little town of Cabullona, about a day's march from the Federal outpost at Agua Prieta.

The way Villa had decreed it, first the money was to be transferred, in gold, to a bank in Juárez, and as soon as Villa received a telegram saying it had arrived, he would attack the Americans somewhere along the border. Strucker had come to the conclusion that Villa had little intention of doing this, and that the money would be little more than ransom, but he didn't see any choice in the matter.

All day vast pillars of smoke had boiled up toward them out of the desert from the arriving troop trains of Villa's main army. Fierro had managed to get them all assembled and moved out of Coahuila, and now they came, rugged, bearded, gaunt, and filthy, crammed on the tops of the boxcars inside of which were the horses, wagons, rations, artillery, and other equipment necessary for the battle. The men were all singing "La Cucaracha."

Reed and Bierce were astonished at the excitement building up in everyone. Villa had put on his worn American-made businessman's suit and his eyes were red from poring over battle maps. Fierro was rushing around barking orders and slapping people on the back. Almost all the men had a cornhusk cigarette dangling from their mouths. It took the entire day to organize everybody into an army again. The artillery pieces were unloaded and hitched to teams, rations and ammunition were issued, first-aid facilities were set up, roll calls taken, and the shouting never ceased.

Villa had been developing and refining his plans for attack during the long days on the trail. It was a plan of amazing simplicity, just the way he used to do it in the old days. His intelligence network had informed him that there were twelve hundred Federal troops manning the garrison at Agua Prieta. To overrun them, Villa had assembled four thousand men of his own. It would be a night attack and, he hoped, a complete surprise. Artillery would open up first. Then the soldiers would march forward, breaching the Federal lines.

Next the cavalry would dash in and exploit the gaps and the rest of the army would simply steamroll over the garrison.

The "pesky horsefly" strategy had been born of necessity because of his losses at Chihuahua City and elsewhere, but now Villa saw renewed hope. When word got out that Agua Prieta had fallen, Carranza would naturally rush an army there to attack Villa. But by then he intended to be gone, after resupplying himself from the Federals' own garrison. And whatever garrison the Federal army had come from, that was where he would go, popping up like a jack-in-the-box in front of the understrength ranks before they could be reinforced.

At supper that night, Bierce was entertaining everyone with a discourse on ghouls, which was one of his favorite topics.

"In 1640, a Father Secchi saw one in a cemetery near Florence and frightened it away with the sign of the cross. He said it had many heads and he saw it in more than one place at a time," Bierce informed them. "On another occasion, a ghoul was caught by some peasants in a churchyard near Sudbury and ducked into a horse pond. The water at once turned to blood."

"May I suggest, Señor Robinson," Strucker said, "that El Padrino was a ghoul?"

"That I don't know, Herr Strucker," Bierce

told him, "but there's one more account that might shed some light on the subject. At the beginning of the fourteenth century a ghoul was cornered in a crypt of the Amiens Cathedral and the whole population surrounded the place. Twenty armed men, with a priest at their head, captured the ghoul, which, thinking to escape by a trick, had transformed itself into the figure of a well-known citizen of the town. It was nevertheless hanged, drawn, and quartered."

"Sounds like it served him right," Strucker remarked.

"Yes, I suppose," Bierce continued. "But the citizen whose shape the ghoul had assumed was said to be so affected by the experience he never again showed his face in Amiens and his fate remains a mystery."

Everyone laughed except Villa, who decided the gibe had been aimed at him. Here he was, general of an army that was to attack the enemy any day now, and getting needled by a cynical old gringo.

Late in the afternoon next day, Villa's army was entrenched behind a low rise in the desert overlooking Agua Prieta when a startling sight appeared in the sky. First they heard a high-pitched mosquitolike hum, and when they looked up they saw an airplane. It circled once, then began to spiral down until it came in for a landing not two hundred yards from where Villa's whole force was hidden. Villa was concerned that it might spoil his surprise attack.

Agua Prieta was a huddle of gaunt adobe buildings in the windswept desert just yards from the American border town of Douglas. From the look of it, Agua Prieta was aptly named: a filthy little river ran through the town. Villa had positioned his artillery east and west to keep from throwing shells across the border and starting an incident. A little earlier, he had crawled atop the rise and studied the garrison through field glasses. He was surprised to find that the Federals had strung barbed wire in many rows in front of the garrison. That would make things more difficult because his artillery now had to open up sooner than he wanted, so as to cut the wire. Bierce advised him against attacking at all, but Villa was in no mood to listen to that kind of talk.

"Señor Robinson, we have been up against barbed wire before and succeeded," he said patiently, as if talking to a child.

"You didn't succeed at Chihuahua City," Bierce reminded him. "I was there, remember?"

"I wish you hadn't been," Villa said. "All you have done in the past weeks is make unwelcome remarks to me."

"I'm sorry if you see it that way, General Villa," Bierce replied. "I thought you'd requested my advice, and so I gave it."

"Well, stop giving it," Villa told him. "It's causing me a headache."

A passenger emerged from the plane. The pilot then turned it around and took off.

Mick was a little disoriented by the landing. He had seen Villa's people from the air when he and Charlie had circled, but he was surprised there were so many. He'd only expected a troop. But Charlie had recognized the distinctive flags and simply told him that, whatever the case, this was Villa's army. Now on the ground, Mick at first began walking the wrong way before several men shouted to him to come to the little rise they were on. He was stumbling over rocks when he saw a big rattlesnake flinch out from under a little scrub bush in front of him and slither off without rattling. It nearly startled him to death. Mick had never liked snakes; they gave him the willies. He stumbled to the top of the rise, where people pulled him down and escorted him to the general, who was sitting in a field chair peeling an apple. He looked angry when Mick was presented to him. Mick began to say something, but Villa cut him off.

"I don't care who you are or what you want," Villa spat. "You may have ruined our whole plan!"

"I'm here to talk about the two children

you're holding," Mick said. "I'm an attorney and am authorized to work something out."

Villa gaped at him. "You came here about that! On the eve of a battle! You must be loco!"

"I didn't know anything about a battle," Mick said. "The parents of those kids are worried sick. And I went to a lot of trouble to come see you. I nearly got bit by a god-damn snake just a minute ago."

Fierro, sitting beside Villa, took patriotic exception. "A serpent is part of our national emblem," he told Mick. "We don't need any gringos running it down."

"It's going to have to wait until this fight is finished," Villa said. "And you better pray to whatever god you pray to that your coming here didn't upset my plan."

SIXTY-SIX

Villa's artillery opened up at midnight. The attack began an hour later and was a total disaster. Villa's soldiers surged forward toward Agua Prieta, when suddenly their ranks were illuminated by huge searchlights. At once a hail of fire from dozens of machine guns in the Federal garrison broke out. For Bierce, Reed, Strucker, and the others who'd stayed behind, it sounded like a roomful of people furiously typing away on typewriters. Villa's men dropped dead in their tracks in windrows twenty feet apart. He ordered more troops sent in; the same thing happened. Rifle and machine gun fire hit them, too, sounding like the tearing of a giant canvas.

From what Villa could tell, the searchlights were coming from the American side of the border at Douglas, where a detachment of the U.S. Army was located. Green flashes of illumination shells from Villa's artillery lit up the garrison, and from this, he believed he could count many more guns firing at his men than he'd ever expected. Thousands of little flashes of gunfire were coming from irrigation ditches outside Agua Prieta. His men were not only blinded by the illumination from the searchlights, but those few of them who actually reached the barbed wire were horrified when they discovered the wire had been electrified. Villa finally understood, with ratlike realism, that he'd been led into a trap.

Daybreak revealed a pitiless carnage on the desert sands. Villa's soldiers lay in grotesque positions where they had fallen in their ranks. Officers' horses, broken and mutilated, lay among them. In less than two hours more than six hundred of his men had perished.

Villa now went into one of his towering rages. Two things he knew: the American searchlights had ruined the attack, and either there were a lot more Federal troops in the Agua Prieta garrison than there were supposed to be or the Americans had joined in the fight. He pulled the remnants of his army away from Agua Prieta not long after sunup and headed east toward El Paso. Along the way he spotted an open motorcar and a contingent of American soldiers leaning on the wire fence that marked the international border. Villa rode up to them and singled out a young lieutenant who was chewing on a piece of straw.

It was Patton.

"You people turned your searchlights on us

last night. That was an act of war."

"I don't know a thing about that, General," Patton told him.

"Like hell you don't," Villa replied. "You're a liar like the rest of your stinking race."

"Why don't you climb over this fence and say that again," Patton told him, "and I'll throw your fat ass in jail."

"Why don't you climb over it yourself on this side, and I'll shoot you so full of holes you'll look like a side of Swiss cheese," Villa retorted.

"Those are bold words for a man who's just got his butt handed to him in a battle," Patton said.

"Yes, and only because you gringos joined in without even a declaration of war."

"We joined in nothing, General," Patton said. "That was your own countrymen you were fighting."

"There were supposed to be twelve hundred. It had to be five times that many."

"I'd suggest you ask General Obregón about it," Patton told him.

"What's Obregón got to do with it?"

"He talked to our General Pershing at El Paso last week and asked if he could use our rail lines to transport some of his troops out of Coahuila to Agua Prieta. The general told him yes, so long as it was to make a fool of you."

Villa's hand dropped to his waist where his

pistol was, but when he did it, half a dozen American soldiers drew up their rifles and the sound of clicking safeties told Villa this wasn't the time.

"So what you are telling me is that your General Pershing allowed Obregón's soldiers to cross over to here on American soil and on American railroads to defeat me?"

"That's about the size of it, General," Patton said. "You got a beef, you can take it up with President Wilson."

"Okay, Lieutenant, so now I know. And I pity any of you gringos that comes in my way from now on."

"You might ingratiate yourself with my country if you release those American children you're holding," Patton said. "They're pretty important to some good people. The whole country would be impressed by such a gesture."

"I'm not releasing anybody," Villa told him. "You gringos have laid down with the dogs, now you'll get up with fleas."

"I'm just making a recommendation," Patton said. "The mother of those children is in El Paso right now, worried to death about them. It's cruel of you not to turn them loose."

"You haven't seen cruelty yet, Lieutenant," Villa replied. "There are worse things than murder, in case you don't know it." He wheeled his horse and galloped off across the dusty desert to join his passing army.

To Strucker's utter amazement, a telegram came to Pancho Villa in Cabullona two days later informing him that the money from Germany had arrived and was being held for him at the bank in Juárez. For Villa it meant he could pay his army, or what remained of it.

"So, Señor Strucker, now you will get your wish," Villa told him a day afterward. "I would have attacked them even without the money, after what happened at Agua Prieta." They were in one of the dusky little adobe buildings in an unnamed village that Villa had commandeered for his headquarters.

"I don't think you'll regret it, General," Strucker said. "The Americans no doubt will come after you, and when they do, your enemies here will be forced to fight them. American soldiers on Mexican soil will be intolerable. It will present you with a perfect opportunity."

"You'll be coming along with us, of course," Villa announced.

"Into the United States?" Strucker said.

"Don't you want to see how your money's being spent?"

"Well, yes, but it puts me in a delicate position, you see. I am a German national. If something should happen, if I should be captured . . ."

"Surely you wouldn't want to miss this," Villa responded. "In fact, I'm gonna insist on it."

Strucker was thoroughly nonplussed at this development, and felt suddenly sick to his stomach.

"Well, General," he managed, "if you put it that way, I suppose I've got no choice. But afterward, I'd like to take my leave and go back to Germany. Will that be possible?"

"Certainly," Villa said. "As a matter of fact, the train runs not far from Columbus. If you want to, get on it and go."

"Where did you say?" Strucker asked.

"Columbus, New Mexico," Villa told him. "It's where I am going to attack the American army."

"Why there?" Strucker had never heard of the place.

"Because they are there and I can beat them," Villa said.

Villa didn't know what the reaction would be when he attacked the American outpost at Columbus but he didn't think it could hurt anything. After all, it was a small outpost and he figured he'd have no trouble overrunning it. If the Americans reacted by crossing over the border as Strucker predicted, then Villa was pretty sure, like the German said, Carranza's government would have no choice but to fight them, buying Villa time against Carranza fighting him. If they didn't, nothing much would be lost anyway and he still had the German gold in the bank.

Finally, after supper, he summoned Mick Martin for an audience.

"So now what's this about those children?" he inquired.

"I came at the behest of their family. I'm an attorney and I want to negotiate for their release."

"Negotiate?" Villa snapped. "I don't negotiate, I dictate. Do you have the million dollars?"

"Well, no, frankly," Mick said. "We think that's excessive."

"I don't give a damn what you think. I set the price and expect it to be paid."

"The children's family don't have a million dollars."

"Do you actually want me to believe that?" Villa retorted.

"It's the truth," Mick said. "I didn't believe it at first when I heard it, either."

"Then maybe it's not the truth," Villa said. "This Colonel Shaughnessy, he owns an American railroad, doesn't he, as well as the property he stole from us down here?"

"The railroad is broke," Mick told him. "So is the Colonel."

"That's his problem. I just want the money for keeping these children safe. I've gone to a lot of trouble to make sure nothing happens to them."

"May I see them?" Mick asked.

"No," Villa replied. "It might upset them." Actually, he wasn't sure what he was going to do with the children. He'd promised Katherine they'd be let go if he got his gold and won the battle at Agua Prieta, but only half of that had come true. It wouldn't hurt, he thought, to keep them a little longer and see what developed.

"General Villa, I don't like saying this, but that's hatefully cruel," Mick said. "I've known those kids since they were babies. They'd welcome seeing me."

"Don't you tell me about cruel!" Villa shouted. "That's all you stinking gringos seem to talk about. You ruined my attack on Agua Prieta and much of my army is dead on the field! And by the way, I've been meaning to ask you, isn't that plane you came in the same one that those people used to attack me back in that valley?" Someone had told Villa that a red plane had been seen in the vicinity before the aborted rescue mission.

"I don't know about that," Mick said. "I chartered it in El Paso."

"You're a liar!" Villa growled. "My men tell me it's the same one. They saw it."

"Like I said, General —"

"How many red flying machines are there in this part of the country?" Villa asked angrily. "I don't like being lied at by some goddamn Philadelphia lawyer."

"I told you, General, I don't know. And I'm from Boston." This was not going at all as Mick had planned. In the dozens of kidnap negotiations he'd been involved with, the atmosphere had at least been civil. Villa hadn't even invited him to sit down.

Just then Fierro entered the room, glowering and sour-faced. It had been his men who'd borne the brunt of the battle losses. He sulked in the shadows of a corner, leaning against the wall.

"I have raised fifty thousand dollars for the release of the children," Mick stated.

Villa choked out a malevolent laugh and spat on the floor. "You people take me for a joke. First you betray me by letting that swine Obregón bring his troops across your country to thwart me, then you turn your searchlights on helpless soldiers, sending them to their deaths! I would rather lose to a Chinaman than to that traitor Obregón!" he added.

"General, I don't understand why I'm being blamed —"

"Shut up!" Villa shouted. "And now you come and insult me with a handful of centavos and expect me to do what you want. Well, I won't." He turned to Fierro.

"General, lock this son-of-a-bitch up until I can decide what to do with him."

Fierro stuck his head out the door and said

something to one of the guards. A few moments later four soldiers came into the room and marched Mick Martin outside.

"What do you think I should do with that gringo?" Villa asked Fierro. He was having another of his headaches and his mood was pitch-black.

"Do you think he brought the fifty thousand with him?" Fierro asked sensibly.

"How would I know? Have your men searched his baggage?"

"Suppose he did?" Fierro asked.

"Then take the money and distribute it to the men. As for him, I don't care what happens. Use your own judgment. He's no friend of ours."

Villa's army was on the move at first light and two days later were poised in a little village called Los Palomas, only a stone's throw from Columbus. They were just a day's march from El Paso, too, where Pershing kept a good portion of the twenty thousand troops he commanded. But at Columbus there was only a small garrison.

When Bierce found out Villa was planning to kill Americans, it was too much for the old Civil War soldier. He approached Villa in his headquarters tent.

"General, I'm an old man and I've seen a lot in my life, including killing on a scale that is probably unimaginable to you. After that I devoted my entire life to making idiots feel uncomfortable. Therefore I feel perfectly secure in telling you that what you are contemplating is the most idiotic thing I have ever heard of. Not only that, it is sinful, wicked, and unlawful."

Bierce was poised to go on, but Villa cut him off. Like a fire that had been creeping up behind walls and beneath floors, Villa's rage suddenly exploded in full fury.

"That will be enough from you, Señor Robinson! You've spoken your last criticism of me. If you have a wish for death, consider it fulfilled."

Villa ordered the guards to arrest Bierce on the spot, and hold him until a firing squad could be organized. Even as he made his decision, Villa felt a rare tinge of remorse. In a way, he actually had become fond of the old buzzard and was going to miss having him around.

When Reed found out what had happened, he immediately went to Bierce, who was seated on a bench in a small adobe house guarded by two soldiers.

"You've got to apologize," Reed told him.

"I won't do it. He's wrong and he knows it."

"What does it matter?" Reed countered. "He'll shoot you, you know."

"I expect he will."

"And that doesn't bother you?"

"Of course it does. Nobody likes to die," Bierce told him.

"Then why not apologize?"

"Because I'm right."

"So, what," Reed exclaimed. "are you doing this merely out of pride?"

"Principle," Bierce informed him. He had clenched his jaws and pursed his lips so that he looked like he had just eaten something sour.

"Please," Reed pleaded, "don't do this."

Bierce said nothing in reply. So far he'd enjoyed most of his adventure with Villa, but the notion of being any part of killing Americans was the end of it, as far as he was concerned. He could apologize, as Reed suggested, and maybe Villa would let him go off to America. But he didn't want to do that. He'd left America for good, and there wasn't any other place he wanted to go; he'd already been just about everywhere else. Plus there was the fact that he'd never apologized to anyone in his life and didn't want to start now, just because he was about to be shot.

Lieutenant Crucia was chosen to command the firing squad. He came to see Bierce.

"Señor Robinson, we will be ready in about twenty minutes. Do you want some lunch?"

"No, thank you," Bierce said. He didn't like it that Crucia was going to be the one to do him in. He considered the lieutenant an inferior species and wondered if the man would cut off his nose afterward to add to the necklace.

"I wish you'd change your mind," Reed told him. "Please just consider it."

"Thank you," Bierce said. "It's been interesting getting to know you, Reed. I only wish I had more time to turn you away from Bolshevism. It's a repugnant philosophy."

Reed momentarily considered offering to renounce his beliefs if only Bierce would apologize and save his life, but he realized he couldn't do it. Thereby Reed learned something about the "principles" whereof Bierce had spoken. He shook Bierce's hand and asked if he could take any last message to anyone.

"No," Bierce told him. "But in my bag is a notebook with some letters I have written to a Miss Christiansen in Washington City. They're all addressed and stamped. I'd appreciate it if you'd mail them to her, without comment."

Reed nodded, then walked away sadly.

They marched Bierce to a whitewashed wall in the village and lined him up facing the firing squad, his hands tied behind his back. Bierce counted seven of them, including Crucia, who'd found a sword and a gold sash someplace to give the occasion formality. Villa was there, too, as was Fierro. They offered Bierce a blindfold but he refused. Crucia gave the orders.

"Ready!" The firing squad raised their guns and locked the shells in their chambers.

"Aim!" The squad pointed their rifles at Bierce.

"Wait a minute!" Bierce said. "Don't I get a last request?"

Crucia seemed uncertain and glanced at Villa, who nodded his head.

"What is it?" Crucia wanted to know.

"I'd like a cigar," Bierce told him. There was a small ironic smile on his lips, which showed through his beard, which was beginning to go white, since a week ago he had run out of the shoe polish he'd been dyeing it with. But his voice was steady and his eyes steely.

"Here's one already lit for you," Fierro said, taking his cigar out of his mouth and handing it to Crucia, who walked over and stuck it in Bierce's mouth. The firing squad was still poised with their rifles at the ready.

"There's something else," Bierce said. Crucia was getting annoyed.

"What?" he asked.

"I'm told it is the custom in your army to give condemned men the opportunity to signal for the execution to be performed."

"It is," Villa said.

"Well, I'd like to do that."

"Okay," Villa told him, "if it's what you want."

"Right when the ash falls off the end of the cigar," Bierce told them, "before it hits the ground — do it then."

Crucia looked to Villa for guidance. The sun was hot and he was ready to get on with it, but Villa shrugged and nodded his head again. He didn't see how it could hurt anything.

The soldiers were still poised with their rifles shouldered. The sun beat down. Only the noise of their breathing could be heard.

The ash on the cigar was not a very large one at first, maybe a quarter inch. Bierce was relieved that it was a good make of cigar, because well-made cigars tend to have long-lasting ashes, especially when they are smoked right. Bierce always enjoyed a good cigar. He made sure to puff very gently. The sunshine was so bright it dazzled the eyes. Bierce could see the sweat begin to seep through the shirts of the firing squad, some of whose rifles were beginning to wobble noticeably.

Minutes passed, five, seven, nine. The firing squad stood with knees locked, which restricted the flow of blood. Suddenly the silence was shattered by the clatter of a rifle hitting the dirt. The man who had held it followed, passed out from leg-lock and sunstroke. The others held their places. Bierce took an imperceptible puff on the cigar. The ash was now more than half an inch long.

Villa was wondering how this was going to

turn out. He was feeling a little queasy himself and shifted around on his feet. Lieutenant Crucia remained at ramrod-straight attention, the sword poised in his right hand ready to drop the instant the ash fell off the cigar. A little wisp of smoke continued to curl up around the cigar. A bumblebee suddenly appeared and began to buzz around Bierce's beard. He wanted to bite his lip to keep still but couldn't, with the cigar in his mouth. He kept still anyway. The sun beat down.

Two of the firing squad men could not keep their weapons at the ready any longer. The rifles weighed about ten pounds, and keeping them locked up to the shoulder still and straight for this length of time was excruciating. Crucia motioned for the two to retire. It was a long-standing custom of firing squads that if for any reason a man could not continue, such as if he became queasy about his duty, nauseated, uneasy, then he must leave the squad in disgrace. Crucia was now down to three men. Bierce guessed that the ash at this point amounted to nearly an inch, and that more than fifteen minutes had passed. In a perverse way, he was actually enjoying himself.

The bee landed in Bierce's beard. He could feel it crawling around and wondered if it would sting him. That would pose a major problem and he steeled himself for it. How

perfectly ironic, it crossed Bierce's mind, to
be done in after all by an insect. He had
hoped the smoke from the cigar would drive
the bee away, but it hadn't. Two more of the
firing squad could not hold their weapons up
any longer and retired in odium. Lieutenant
Crucia was drenched with sweat and Bierce
could see, in his glare of hatred mixed with
fear, that he was afraid he would screw up
his task in front of his boss. The sun beat
down. The last member of the firing squad
dropped his rifle and sank to his knees.

Crucia was beside himself. There were no
regulations governing this kind of thing. If
he'd thought to bring his pistol, he could have
drawn it and performed the execution himself. But all he had was the sword and he
wasn't sure if Villa would want it done that
way. Finally the general himself solved the
problem.

"Okay," he said to Crucia. "Take your men
and go away."

"*Sí, sí,* General," Crucia said in a mixture
of confusion, anger, fear, and utter humiliation.

The ash on the cigar was still burning,
longer than ever. Villa walked up to him.

"Well, Señor Jack Robinson," he said, "so
you have made fools of our young lieutenant
and his men. I hope you enjoyed your re-
prieve."

Bierce grunted. He still didn't want to lose

the ash on the cigar. Villa reached into his pocket and pulled out the little ivory-handled, nickel-plated derringer that Bierce had given him as a gift on that long-ago day when he had joined Villa's army.

"You remember this, don't you?" Villa asked nicely, towering over Bierce.

Bierce grunted again. He didn't really feel unkindly toward Villa; in fact, he thought he understood him, at least until the decision to attack Americans. He thought of apologizing and maybe shaking hands and going on back home anyway. A vision came upon him, as visions often do at such times, and it began to reveal the mystery of himself. He was a writer, a thinker, and his writings moved the minds of others. There might still be words he could write that would make a difference to people, almost like those of a teacher.

Villa bent forward, pursed his lips, and blew on the cigar ash. It glowed orange for an instant, almost like it was breathing itself, and then dropped noiselessly to the ground. Villa smiled.

"Do you know why you are doomed, Señor Robinson?"

Bierce shook his head. In fact, he had begun to believe he hadn't been doomed.

"If a man is born under the wrong star," said Pancho Villa, "it will shine on his ass always — even when he is seated."

Bierce was pondering this when Villa stuck

the derringer between Bierce's eyes and
pulled the trigger.

SIXTY-SEVEN

Mick Martin got his wish to see the children anyway. After the battle at Agua Prieta General Fierro had told Tom Mix to take charge of Mick in his guard of prisoners and captives. Katherine and Timmy were delirious to see him.

"Your mummy wanted me to try to negotiate for your release so you can go home," he told them.

"General Villa said he's going to let us go," Katherine told him.

Mick was surprised. That wasn't the way it had sounded to him.

"When did he tell you that?"

"A week or so ago," Katherine said. "He said that if he got some money from somebody, I think it was Germans, and won the battle, he'd turn us loose."

"Well, he didn't win the battle," Mick said. "I don't know about the money."

"Do you think he'll let us go anyway?" Timmy asked.

"Yes, I'm certain he will," Mick told them. "I have faith in it."

They were riding in one of the wagons and Katherine knew the teamster driving it didn't understand English.

"Do you know that Papa came and tried to rescue us?" she asked.

"Yes. I was there when he returned. It would have been a blessing if he had been successful, but I thought it was a dangerous thing to do."

"Is that how you got your face hurt, Uncle Mick?" Timmy said.

"Yes. There was a big fight, but your father's safe and sound."

"Is Mummy scared for us?" Katherine asked.

"Of course, but she's being very brave. She's in El Paso, waiting for you."

They asked about everybody and Mick told them what he knew.

"Your grandfather broke his leg, but he's going to be all right. And Bomba was fine, too, last time I saw him."

"Are they back at El Paso?" Katherine wondered.

"I don't know, but I'm sure they will be shortly. Now I want to know about you. Have they treated you well?"

They told Mick about Timmy's gila monster bite and about the jaguar, about going through the mountains and canyons, and

Katherine described how she was teaching Villa to read and she also talked a little about Tom Mix.

"He's really quite nice," she said, "although I think he's made a big mistake. He's not like these people at all."

"I'm sure," Mick said. From what he'd seen of Mix so far, he was just another adventuring fool looking to earn a reputation for himself.

"Well, I don't want you to worry anymore," he told them. "Uncle Mick's here now and we'll all be going home." Nervous and worried as he was, Mick felt better trying to reassure the children — as though in some small way he could make it right, no matter what might happen.

They traveled for nearly a week across the prairies, or llanos, to Mick's growing concern about their ultimate fate. Mick was shocked that Villa seemed to have no interest whatever in negotiating anything. It was unlike any of his previous experience, and thus he began to look for some other way out. He noticed that in the late evening a small black Ford truck appeared toward the end of the caravan and off-loaded what probably was food to the commissary wagon; the driver then spent the night and left again in the late morning, after breakfast. By his own estimate, Mick figured they could not be more than twenty or thirty miles from the U.S. border. If he could somehow get hold of that truck by surprise, and put the kids in it, he ought to be able to outrun men on horseback. It was chancy, but being among these killers all day was chancier, Mick decided.

Working in his favor was the fact that the cowboy Tom Mix who had been taking care of the children and the Mexican woman Donita had been sent ahead for a day or so to scout. Someone had put Lieutenant Crucia in charge of the hostages. Mix had been nearly constantly with them, seeing to their food and other needs; but Crucia's directive had simply been to guard the prisoners, and when he quickly realized there was no place for them to go, he ceased being a presence in the entourage except in the morning and evening, when he stopped by to count noses, so to speak.

Mick sprang the plan on his fellow captives the following evening. Next morning, Mick said, after Crucia's routine visit, he would drift back toward the commissary wagon and hijack the truck. The only rub would be whether or not the key would be left in the truck; the plan would be ruined if it wasn't, but Mick figured there'd be no reason for the driver to remove it. After all, who would steal a truck out here? He was familiar with this particular vehicle; Ford had made them by the tens of thousands. Luckily, a year or two earlier Ford had replaced the awkward — and attention-calling — hand crank with an ignition starter button on the floor next to the clutch pedal. Provided the ignition caught quickly, Mick figured he could wheel the truck along the column of men at maximum speed, slam on brakes to gather up Timmy, Katherine, Donita Ollas, and the dog, and speed north across the open prairie toward the U.S. border, outdistancing any pursuers on horseback.

Shortly after sunup, Lieutenant Crucia arrived for roll call, and then rode off to some other occupation. After positioning the kids and Donita near a small shrub, Mick sneaked down the column with his hat pulled low. The truck was parked casually about ten yards from the commissary wagon, near the reata where the horses were tethered. That would provide good cover. He could see the soldiers and others at their breakfasts.

From behind one of the chuckwagons, Mick strided into the open and quickly put himself between the reata and the truck. From there the coast was clear and he loped across to the vehicle and ducked into the cab. Immediately he saw the key was in place — as he'd guessed, the driver hadn't bothered to lock the steering column. Mick put the gear in neutral, took a deep breath, and hit the starter button. The engine groaned and turned over but failed to catch. He exhaled, waited a moment, and tried again. Same result. Another deep breath. The starter whined and strained, as if the battery might be low. He held it down for what seemed an eternity, when suddenly the motor caught, sputtered, caught and sputtered again, and then caught for good. Mick was in the process of putting the vehicle in first gear when he felt the cold steel of a pistol barrel hard behind his left ear. He froze in midmotion, then let off the clutch and slowly raised his hands. The pistol barrel was removed and Mick slowly — slowly — turned his head to meet the grimly smirking face of Lieutenant Crucia, standing in front of the driver of the truck, who had heard his engine being started.

"You were planning a drive in the country, señor?" Crucia said nicely.

"It was on my mind," said Mick.

Claus Strucker had helped Reed bury Bierce following the execution.

"I enjoyed knowing Mr. Robinson," the German told Reed. "He was a cultivated man and deserved better than this."

They had found a coffin in Los Palomas that was waiting for an old woman to die and persuaded the family to accept ten dollars for it. Reed and Strucker took turns shoveling out a grave in a little desert plot of ground that was covered with pretty orange flowers the shape of violets, as well as some spiny cactus plants.

"He was a fool, too," Reed said bitterly. "He might have saved himself."

Reed wasn't as angry or disgusted with Bierce as it sounded. He was feeling a heavy weight in his chest from the death. The two of them had come through a lot together and Reed had grown fonder than he'd realized of the old man, even though he disagreed with practically everything he said. In a way they were perfect companions: opposites attracting each other, each with a keen, witty mind and the capacity to argue without fighting.

"Well, he died a brave man," Strucker replied. "I think facing a firing squad must take more courage than any other way of going."

"He committed suicide, you know," Reed told him.

"They said he died defiantly. Did you hear what he did?"

"Yes," Reed said. "Now I wish I'd been there. To at least have been a friendly face he could recognize at the end."

"Are you going on this raid tonight?" Strucker asked.

"No, I couldn't do that," Reed replied, "and Robinson was right, of course. This is a stupid plan and Villa will regret it." He stopped digging and leaned on his shovel.

"I am going," Strucker told him. "It's a command performance."

"Well, it was your idea in the first place, wasn't it?"

"Listen, my country is fighting for its life and yours is aiding our enemies. It isn't that I have anything against Americans."

"Your nation will reap the whirlwind," Reed informed him, "and so will England and France and everybody else mixed up in that thing, including the USA, if it goes in. And it serves them right. The only thing that'll be left when it's over is a brotherhood of man which will demand an end to war and injustice. This time, they'll get it."

"You might be right, Mr. Reed," Strucker said. "I just hope there are enough of us left who've put our money in safe places so we can live our lives out in respectability."

Reed nodded and resumed his shoveling. He might as well have been addressing one of the cacti.

Strucker had been issued a rifle and a pistol to take along on the raid. He felt uncomfortable about that, but took them anyway. He'd seen firsthand what happened to people who didn't do what they were told. Villa's raiding party got into Columbus without a hitch. First, half the troops attacked the American garrison, shooting it up so that in the dark it sounded like a display of fireworks was being set off. Strucker's group rode into the town proper and things quickly turned into confusion. Since the town wasn't lighted, the riders had trouble finding the stores and banks they were looking for. One of the soldiers got the bright idea to set fire to some buildings so they could see what they were doing.

At about the same time, some of the American machine guns began to open up and there was pandemonium in the streets. People rushed from houses that had been set fire, some shooting, some just running, women in nightclothes, barefoot men in long johns, children. In the center of the main street, standing alone in his nightclothes and crying, was a little boy. He couldn't have been more than two or three years old, and Strucker was sure he'd be shot or run down by the galloping horses if he remained there. In an unusual moment of compassion, Strucker rode out to pick the little boy up, but as he did he felt machine gun bullets slap into his horse, which collapsed on its side. Strucker managed to scramble out from under the horse and was in the process of grabbing the child when bullets struck him in the chest. He had only a few moments to consider what life had been like. Curiously, his starring role at age nine in his gymnasium class tableau was the last thing Strucker would ever remember on this earth. He'd played Tristan.

The attack on Columbus produced the precise outcome that Strucker had intended, at least at first. Newspapers all over the United States began screaming for an invasion of Mexico and at once President Wilson ordered General Pershing to form a military expedition to find and punish Pancho Villa. But first the diplomats went to work and the consequences of that were the opposite of the German's hopes. The Americans went to the Carranza government and actually got permission to invade Mexico. The agreed-on rules were that the Americans were not allowed to use the Mexican railroads for resupply, nor enter any city, and they were confined to roads that led only north and south. The war Strucker hoped would ensue had not developed and never would.

Pershing was confused by the orders he received from President Wilson and phoned him to say so.

"Mr. President, are you telling me you want the United States to make war on one man?"

"He's the one causing the trouble, isn't he?" Wilson replied testily.

"Well, suppose he should get into a train and go to Guatemala; are you prepared for me to go after him?" Pershing inquired.

"Well, no, I am not."

"So what you really want is to have his band captured or destroyed," Pershing suggested.

"Yes, that is what I really want," Wilson replied.

At least it clarified things for Pershing and

satisfied him yet again that civilians such as Wilson had no business telling the military what to do.

The story of Villa's attack was big news all over the country, and nowhere was it bigger than in El Paso, where four thousand American troops were preparing for the hunt. Xenia immediately went to Patton.

"I would like to come with you," she said.

"Oh, madam, that's hardly possible," Patton replied. "We are going after a vicious desperado."

"I have already crossed the state of Chihuahua without a military escort," she said. "I expect I can do it again."

"Alone?" Patton asked.

"No, that is why I want to come along with you. Don't you consider yourselves safe?"

"Of course, but we don't have any place for women. They have special needs."

"I'm confident I can conform to anything your army requires," Xenia told him. "I will have my own car and driver." Then she smiled at Patton and hoped to play on his sympathy.

"If only I can get near him," she said, "and explain to him personally about the children. I don't think he would murder a woman."

"There are worse things than murder," Patton said. "He told me that himself."

"All these weeks I've been praying our

government would enter Mexico and that I would have the chance to go with them and plead my case to General Villa. And now . . ." Tears formed in Xenia's eyes. She daubed at them with a handkerchief.

"Now, now," Patton said.

"I just can't believe you won't let me come along!" She put her hands to her face and burst into tears.

"Well, please don't cry, Mrs. Shaughnessy. Let me talk to the general. He recently lost his wife and children in a fire. Perhaps he'll be willing to listen."

Xenia was grateful, and so confident that she went back to the hotel to pack. Crosswinds Charlie had described locating Villa and depositing Mick Martin with his army, and that, of course, was as far as his knowledge went. But it had been days ago and no word had come from Mick, though Xenia asked at the hotel telegraph desk several times a day. Either Villa was unwilling to negotiate or the negotiations were taking an exceptionally long time, which did not bode well — there was just so much that could be negotiated. She thought about having Charlie fly her out to Villa's army, but the word had come that the army had now dispersed, and once more no one knew where Villa was.

Fierro was delighted to find that Mick actually brought fifty thousand dollars with him.

He considered stuffing five thousand or so into his own saddlebags but reconsidered when he remembered that Villa knew the figure Mick had proposed. After all, he still had the gold bars he'd withheld from Colonel Shaughnessy's estancia. He turned the whole amount over to Villa's quartermaster and set out to deal with Mick. For this Fierro had a treat in mind.

Fierro enjoyed tormenting people. If the condemned asked to be shot instead of hanged, he hung them. If he learned they were afraid of heights, he threw them off a cliff. If he knew somebody couldn't swim, it delighted him to dispatch them by drowning. For Mick, who had disparaged the Mexican national emblem, he'd concocted a special surprise.

The evening after Mick's aborted escape in the truck, Fierro visited him in his holding room in one of the adobe houses in a small village where they had stopped for the day. With him was Crucia, holding a burlap sack, inside of which something seemed to be moving.

"Well, Señor Martin, you are not enjoying your visit with us?"

"Oh, course I am. Who told you that?" Mick asked hesitantly. He looked uneasily at the burlap bag.

"Captain Mix did. Said you complained that General Villa will not deal with you."

"I did say something like that, but it wasn't in the nature of a complaint."

"General Villa didn't see it that way," Fierro replied. "He thinks you have been ungrateful for his hospitality."

"Do you call it hospitality to keep me captive? If the general doesn't want to negotiate, that's one thing. But to make me a prisoner is something else. I came in good faith. Why wouldn't he let me go so I can see if more money can be raised?"

"General Villa negotiates on his own terms," Fierro told him. "And because your initial offering was so low as to be insulting, he has decided you are unworthy of consideration."

"What's that mean?" Mick asked nervously, again eyeing the burlap sack.

"It means that you are to have a trial," Fierro said, "but not the sort of trial you are used to as an attorney. It's the type of trial the stinking Spaniards put us through," he went on, "in the days of the Inquisition. If you survived it, you were presumed innocent and set free. Are you ready?"

"Ready for what?" Mick asked.

Fierro motioned to Crucia, who flung the burlap sack against the wall, and a large rattlesnake plopped out on the dirt floor. It was waving its bloody chopped-off tail, momentarily stunned from being thrown against the wall. Fierro and Crucia made a quick exit, slamming the door shut. The windows had already been boarded up to serve for a jail.

Normally rattlesnakes attacked only when they felt threatened, but the snake was in a wild rage because its tail had been cut off. There was a moment of silent menace as the snake slithered around the room, then came straight for Mick. He leaped up on the sill of a boarded-up window, but as he did, the snake struck his leg and he heard himself scream as the fangs went in. He didn't know if it would hurt a lot when a snake bit you. It did. It felt like being stabbed by an ice pick. The snake struck again, missed, then it continued working all over the room, stopping every so often to get its bearings. After a few minutes the snake came for Mick again. He felt his heartbeat rising and was dizzy. The snake struck several times and missed; the loss of its tail was apparently throwing the snake off its mark, but it was persistent.

Mick tried to stand up on the window ledge instead of squatting on it, but when he moved the snake struck at him and he lost his balance and fell to the floor. The snake struck at his neck. He grabbed the reptile and flung it against the wall, but it bounced off and came at him again. Mick made for the sill again, but the snake bit him in the back of his leg. He tried kicking it, but it was too quick and got him on the foot. He managed to get up on the windowsill again. The snake remained right below him and every time he even twitched it would launch another strike just beneath his feet. Mick began to feel as though something were squeezing his neck, choking him; he couldn't seem to get air; stinging perspiration poured into his eyes.

He held on to the windowsill for dear life, trying to clear his head. Damnable luck, to have fallen in with these dreadful people, Mick thought; everybody he knew up to this point, including murderous gangsters — all could be dealt with. They were at least rational. Villa's people were instead maniacs, he thought. He wondered if Xenia and Arthur would ever find out what had happened to him, and why. He hoped at least for that — that they would one day know why.

Mick began to focus on the tiny dust motes in the air that were illuminated by thin rays of sunshine coming in through cracks in the boards that covered the window. His fingers began to cramp and his vision became blurred. At some point he felt himself falling.

Next morning, Fierro was seated in a chair outside his tent having a cup of coffee in the sunshine when Lieutenant Crucia passed by.

"Say, Crucia, shouldn't someone go and warn this Señor Martin that there may be a dangerous snake in his quarters?"

"He already knows," Crucia said.

SIXTY-EIGHT

Arthur's party had lagged behind Villa at a respectful distance after they saw that his army had reunited near Agua Prieta. It was frustrating, since there was nothing to do now but hang back and wait.

"What was it like, getting took in by the Colonel after you'd growed up in an orphanage?" Bob asked. It had been on Bob's mind ever since Arthur had first told him.

"It was a dream come true, I guess," Arthur told him. "We all dreamed of that." He, Bob, and Slim were riding across the desert far in front of everyone, following the tracks of some of Villa's horsemen, who by then had already reached Columbus and staged the raid.

"You guess?" Bob said. "You were living in an orphanage and suddenly you got everything you always wanted, and you still ain't sure?"

"Pretty much. But I suppose it had its drawbacks," Arthur said.

"How's that?"

"For one thing, I was always a little scared it would end, you know? Like a dream."

"You mean that they'd kick you out?" Slim asked.

"Something like that. It was just always a little thing in the back of your mind."

"Does the Colonel have his own railroad car?" Bob asked.

"Yes, it's in El Paso now."

"I seen pictures of those, but I never been in one."

"Well, when all this is over I'll take you both for a ride," Arthur told them.

"Closest I ever come to anything fancy was when I went to Denver once. I stayed in the Brown Palace. Every single room had its own toilet," said Bob.

"Why were you there?"

"Went to pick up some stock for a feller from Dallas. He wanted to breed some a them old range mustangs to his thoroughbreds to make polo ponies out of."

"Did it work?"

"Hell, no," Bob said. "What they got was stupid, mean, and wild. Last I heard, he'd sold 'em for dog food."

"You know, I've never been to Denver," Arthur said.

"I can't go back," Bob remarked.

"Why's that?"

"I got in trouble there. A fight."

"Must've been a serious one," said Slim.

"It was."

"What was it over?" Arthur asked.

"He was beatin' up a woman in the hotel room next door. I knocked on the wall, and when it kept on goin' I busted his door in. He came at me with a shoe and he was kickin' an' bitin' me, and so I grabbed a lamp and hit him with it. I didn't mean to, but it killed him dead. They throwed me in jail."

"In Texas they'd've probably given you a medal," Slim remarked.

"In Colorado they liked to gave me a rope."

"So what did you do?" Arthur asked.

"The guy I was pickin' up the horses for got me a lawyer and he posted a bail the guy had given him. I was supposed to stay around for the trial, but the feller that was killed turned out to be a senator in the Colorado legislature. And it was his own wife he was beatin' up. I decided I didn't like the odds on that one."

"So you're a wanted man, huh?" Arthur said.

"Prob'ly. I ain't seen my picture in no post offices, though, and it's been fourteen years ago. I hope they forgot about it by now. Took me three years just to earn enough money to pay back the guy from Dallas that posted my bail."

"Hell with Colorado," Slim declared, "ain't nothing there but the Rocky Mountains and the whores of Denver."

"I'll second the motion," said Bob.

"Hey, look there." Arthur pointed to a big cloud of dust that was moving across the desert away from them to the east.

"That's a lot of horses or cows or somethin'," Slim observed.

"That's Pancho Villa's army," Bob said.

Later that afternoon they came into Los Palomas. Bob had scouted it out and found no one there but its residents, from whom he learned that Villa had used it for his headquarters during the raid across the border.

A cantina-keeper finally came out and explained what had happened. Almost everybody had shut themselves up in their houses during Villa's visit. One man had been executed by a firing squad and another had a snake sicced on him and was lying dead in an adobe hut they had boarded up for a jail. The man said both the dead were Americanos.

They bought some dinner at a filthy hovel that served for the cantina and were sitting around a table drinking warm beer and pondering over what the Mexican had said.

"If he's crossed over the border, there's gonna be hell to pay," Bob said. A piece of meat he was eating was so chewy he pulled it out of his mouth and put it back on his plate. Arthur wondered if he was going to eat it later. It reminded him for some reason of his first Christmas Day at the Colonel and Beatie's when Mick had spit out the artichoke. Mick, he thought. He suddenly wasn't hungry anymore.

"I reckon the army will have to do something about it now," Slim said. "If he's killed Americans, they can't just sit by and watch."

"I wonder who the two were who he killed here," Bob said. "If he's started killing Americans, it might pose a problem."

Arthur knew what Bob was getting at. At least the dead had been grown men. After they'd eaten, they walked out into the street and found the spot where Bierce had been buried. A little wooden cross had been erected on the grave, etched with the name "Jack Robinson."

"That's a unlikely name," Slim remarked.

"These are unlikely times," Bob replied.

"Say, do you think that the other man might be Strucker?" Arthur asked.

They looked at each other. "I guess we ought to find out," Arthur told them.

They went back to the cantina and asked the owner where the adobe hut was. He pointed it out to them at the end of town but warned that the snake might still be inside. They walked down to it and Bob pushed open the door. They saw no snake, but Arthur discovered Mick Martin lying on the dirt floor. Mick's eyes were open and his face was a grimace. There were purple-bruised fang marks all over his face and hands, and his body had turned a pale shade of gray. His arms were folded across his chest and his legs were together, almost as if he'd been laid out in a funeral parlor. Arthur stumbled back outside and was sick, there in the dust of the street. When he was finished, Bob said:

"You reckon we ought to bury him?"

Arthur nodded. Slim and Bob carried Mick up to a little rise covered with the orange flowers shaped like violets. They borrowed a shovel and dug a grave next to Jack Robinson's. The late December sun was nearly set and threw a burnished hue over the grave site and beyond, so that the desert seemed as if it had been painted in deep oranges and browns set against a sky that was azure-blue. A thin sliver of moon hung in the sky, while Venus shone brilliantly on the eastern horizon. Slim and Bob looked to Arthur to say some words after they had lowered Mick into the ground. After all, even if he and Arthur had hated each other, at least Arthur had known him, while they hadn't.

Arthur stood at the foot of the grave and spoke:

"The Lord giveth and the Lord taketh away. Amen," was all he said.

"You want us to make a marker with his name on it like they done for this other feller?" Slim asked.

Arthur shook his head. "It wouldn't mean anything. He didn't have any family."

One piece of good news they did learn from the cantina-keeper was that Villa had not gone with his army but had ridden separately back south with a small mounted guard, apparently for the mountains again, but in a more easterly direction. He had only left a few hours earlier, and the Mexican said he saw two children and a woman with him. Arthur decided to wait and let the Colonel and the rest of his party catch up. Arthur, Slim, and Bob would leave at daybreak.

They made a small camp in the desert within sight of Mick Martin's burial place and sat around a fire waiting for Flipper to bring up the others. Slim and Bob gathered some wood for the fire. After a while, Bob said:

"You don't mind me asking, Arthur, who was that feller we just buried?"

Arthur stared into the fire and didn't answer. Pieces of orange ashes were floating skyward, like little fireflies.

"Must've been some bad blood between you two," Slim offered. He wanted to know, too.

"I've known him all my life," Arthur finally answered. "We grew up together in the orphanage."

"But you wasn't friends, I take it," Slim said.

"We were for a long time. Then he invaded my wife's privacy."

Bob wasn't sure what Arthur had meant, but the way he'd said it made Bob think it was something more than reading somebody else's mail.

Arthur suddenly wanted to blurt it all out, tell them about the rape, about Xenia carrying Mick's child. All this time he had kept it to himself. He couldn't tell the Colonel; he couldn't tell anybody. But for a moment he thought that if he unburdened himself now, the secret would be kept with these two cowboys. In the end, though, he just kept quiet.

"Well, it sounds like he's got what he deserved, then," Slim said.

"I wouldn't have wished that on him," Arthur said after a pause.

No, Arthur thought, Mick hadn't deserved to die that way. Arthur would have rather done it himself. At least then there would have been a final understanding between them. He tried not to imagine Mick's last, terrifying moments, but couldn't help himself.

"It's an old Indian torture," Bob told him. "Cut off a rattler's tail and he'll go crazy, bite anything."

After Arthur left Mick's death cell, Bob had

found the snake twisted onto itself in a corner, bled to death. It looked like it had been biting at pieces of wood. "I heard stories they used to do it as punishment for a man who offended another man's wife," Bob said. "Put him in a pit and then throw one of them things down there with him. They say they'd give the man a rock to defend himself, but the snake invariably won."

Actually, Bob had made up the part of the story about the other man's wife, thinking it might make Arthur feel better.

"Whatever else, he came here to help me," Arthur said wearily. "And got killed for it." Arthur remembered when Mick had come to his defense at Groton. He'd asked nothing for it. He'd done it out of friendship, and then the friendship grew even stronger. Arthur had often told him whatever he had was his.

"He must've done somethin' to piss Villa off bad," Slim said. "Villa's a killer, but I've never known him to do it without a reason, even if it's a bad one."

"Unless he's just decided to start killing Americans," Bob told him. "In Villa's book, that could be reason enough."

"Let's hope not," Arthur said. He knew they couldn't just keep shadowing Villa forever, and the graves behind them told him negotiation wasn't going to work, either. Night had come, and Venus was outshining everything in heaven. "Either of you know what day this is?" Arthur asked.

"Yeah, it must be Sunday," Slim said. "All them Mexican's was in church."

"You're wrong," Arthur told them. "For what it's worth, it's Christmas Eve."

Arthur went to sleep and dreamed a familiar dream, one of a dark reverie wrought of frustration and visions of killing Pancho Villa. He woke briefly and saw the glowing sparks from the fire wafting into the dark desert night. He slept again, and dreamed again, this time of himself roped to a boulder in the canyon where the bullfight had taken place, and what he heard was his own maddening screams echoing down the endless canyon walls.

John Reed was no longer with Villa's entourage. After the Columbus raid and the death of the old man Robinson, he said his good-byes and headed for the border. His heart wasn't in it anymore, at least not with Villa's army.

Before he left, he said to Villa, "General, I'm close to home now and I think my work is done. I'd like your permission to move on."

"Is it because of Señor Robinson?" Villa asked.

"Partly," he said evasively. "But I think my publishers will want me to start writing my story now. I've been out of touch for a long time."

"Will you write nice things about me?" Villa asked.

"I've seen nothing to move me otherwise," Reed told him, knowing full well that was only partly true.

"What do you suppose is going to happen to us?" Villa asked.

"Why, I don't know," Reed said, unprepared for such a question.

"Well, my army has just about evaporated. Carranza has fifty thousand men at his disposal to hunt me down, and I suppose the American army will march on me, too."

"I don't understand why you attacked Columbus," Reed said. "Was it because of Strucker, or because of what the Americans did at Agua Prieta?"

"A little of all that," Villa replied. "You see, Mexico is a strange place. The things we do don't always make sense to you Americanos, but that's not the important thing. The important thing is that they make sense to *us.*"

"And attacking Columbus made sense to you?"

"It did at the time," Villa told him, with a pithiness that Reed never forgot. "The difference between you and us, Señor Reed, is that you are just playing with all this, and we are living it."

■ ■ ■ ■

Katherine knew what day it was. Christmas morning she presented Tom Mix with a gift she'd been working on.

From some of the worn out clothing she'd won from Villa in the chess matches, Katherine selected four colored squares — blue, red, green, and white — that she stitched together into a neckerchief, which she understood as an ascot. On the white square she'd embroidered "Tom Mix" with red thread.

"Every time you ask me what day it is, I get embarrassed," Mix complained sheepishly. "Birthdays, Christmases, and I never have any present to give you back."

Mix was delighted with the neckerchief and put it on then and there.

Afterward, he sneaked off to see Villa.

"Did you know this was Christmas, Chief?"

"Well, what is that to me?" Villa grumbled. He'd been feeling blue about killing Robinson, and about Reed's leaving, too — and even about Strucker's bad luck. Worse, last night he believed he'd seen Sanchez's ghost again, out in the desert. As he was squinting at it just before it disappeared, it seemed for a moment to transform itself into Robinson. He'd had Sanchez hung at Christmastime.

"What I mean," Mix went on, "is the children. I expect they'll be missing their mama and papa, and I just thought we might do something for them."

"Like what?" Villa asked.

"A piñata,"

"A piñata?" Villa asked. "Where in hell would we get a piñata?"

"Make one," Mix told him. "We've got some big water *ollas* in the wagons. We could use one of those for the piñata. And the men, I mean, I guess everybody might put something in it, just a little things, to fill it up. If they wanted to."

Villa digested this suggestion. "Okay, Capitán Mix, have your piñata. Tell everybody I said so; that might make your gift-collecting a little easier."

SIXTY-NINE

The chilly, open desert felt refreshing to Xenia after being cooped up in El Paso all this time. She'd hired a big convertible Oldsmobile motorcar to accompany Pershing's expedition into Mexico. The general had been warm and understanding when she went to him after her conversation with Patton. He told her that she must keep out of harm's way, but that he was confident his army was quite strong enough to protect her.

They were deep into Chihuahua by now, and Xenia was thinking of the children and wondering what, if anything, they were doing for Christmas. She longed for them to all be back home and out of this terrible place, with a blazing fire, a tree, gifts, a fat Christmas turkey, and Katherine singing and playing for them. Of course, for all she knew, they might be on their way to El Paso with Mick at this very moment, but deep down she doubted it.

That afternoon the expedition was following south along the railroad tracks and sending scouting parties to the east and west. When they stopped for a short break, Xenia noticed Patton standing beside his Packard, a polished boot up on the running board as he stared pensively at the sky.

"Are you thinking of home, too, Lieutenant Patton?" Xenia asked.

"No, ma'am, I'm thinking about catching that shameless bandit and punishing him."

"Doesn't the army permit you to think about home on Christmas Day?" she asked.

"It does, but I won't. First, it doesn't do any good, and second, I don't want to. It distracts me."

Just then a rider appeared and galloped up to them. The rider was a staff sergeant.

"Lieutenant, some of our scouts saw a band of men that might be Villa."

"Where?" Patton cried. "Somebody get the maps out!"

"It's not too far from here," the sergeant said. "About eight or ten miles." He got down from his horse and looked at the maps Patton had ordered spread out on the hood of his Packard.

"You see this road that we're on?" the sergeant said. "Well, if we take it and turn off down this other road here, there's this little rise. But there's a river here, you see. The scouts spotted them on the other side of the river."

"How many men?"

"They counted about twenty, maybe twenty-five," the sergeant told him.

"That's all?"

"Yessir. That's all they could see. One of them Mexicans we've got with us looked through a spyglass and thought he recognized Pancho Villa."

"Well, let's get going!" Patton said. "There's no time for horses, pile everybody into these cars." He turned to Xenia. "Ma'am, I'm going to have to commandeer your automobile," he said. "We need all the transportation we can get."

"As long as I'm in it, as well," Xenia replied.

"Now, Mrs. Shaughnessy — Xenia," Patton said. "That wasn't your agreement with General Pershing. He said to keep you strictly out of harm's way."

"I won't be in harm's way, Lieutenant Patton," she told him calmly. "I'll be with you."

"Ma'am, please!" But Xenia opened the car door, stepped into the backseat, and sat with arms folded, chin high, looking forward.

"Oh, to hell with it," Patton muttered. "Some of you men come and get in this automobile." They started out in a westwardly direction, with Patton riding on the running board and holding on to the windshield. After about five miles they were out of the desert and on some rolling plains where stands of trees began to appear and the land was covered in waving sedge grass.

■ ■ ■ ■

Earlier that morning Arthur ran fresh out of patience. He'd discussed his decision with his father and the others after they'd come into the camp with Henry Flipper in the lead. It had been nearly a week and both the Colonel and Johnny Ollas had recuperated enough to be on horseback, though Johnny had to be strapped into his saddle. Riding was painful, but little more so than bouncing around in the back of Ah Dong's infernal wagon. Ah Dong had made crutches for both of them so they could hobble around.

"We can't keep on following him all over Mexico," Arthur said. "I'm going to make my move."

He told them he was going to ride ahead with Bob and Slim and confront Villa personally, and alone.

"Not so long as I can still sit a horse," the Colonel told him. "I've come too far and been through too much to squat on the sidelines now." Johnny Ollas insisted on coming, too. "It's my wife," he told Arthur. By the time it was over, all of them said they were going — even Flipper, who, against his better judgment, refused to be left behind. By late afternoon, they had caught up with Villa's party, who had camped in a grove of trees.

Some kind of celebration was in progress. Through his field glasses Arthur could see that they had strung a large object from a tree branch and somebody was swatting at it clumsily with a stick. From the distance faint sounds of laughter wafted back toward them. Arthur motioned them forward at a slow, even pace so they wouldn't be taken for attackers.

Timmy had been swatting at the piñata for nearly ten minutes, blindfolded, as was the Mexican custom. He'd only hit it once or twice, and it remained intact. When it was Katherine's turn she, too, stumbled around swiping thin air, but finally with a lucky strike whacked it solid, and the piñata burst open, showering them with the little gifts Tom Mix had collected from the men. There wasn't much of real value, but everybody had contributed something. There were centavo coins and some little paper Mexican flags, and someone had even thrown in some used pencils.

There was a faded picture of a soldier and his wife, and a pair of shoelaces, and some brass cartridge casings that had been hammered into tiny candlesticks, as if for an altar. Also a number of good-luck charms — rabbits' feet, bear claws, buckeyes, and other jujus. Someone had coughed up a tooled leather belt, and the mess men had baked a lot of cookies and cakes, in fact used up nearly all their sugar. Villa himself had even whittled a couple of his little wooden animals, one in the shape of the jaguar that Katherine had had her run-in with. He'd also considered carving a gila monster but thought better of it.

The soldiers surrounded Katherine and Timmy, laughing and drinking coffee, and pointing as they examined their tender treasures being found. There were more smiles than anyone had seen in months. Just then came a cry from one of the guards.

"Vaqueros!"

They all turned toward the party of people riding slowly toward them. Villa thought he recognized the woman who hobbled behind on foot. As they got closer, he recognized Johnny Ollas, too, minus a leg. He shook his head. Who was going to turn up next — that old gringo Jack Robinson? Villa's men had mounted and now rode out to the edge of the woods to meet them, rifles at the ready.

Arthur had put on his most somber expression and his mood matched it. Far as he was concerned, it had come down to live or die. Mick's death still lay heavily upon him. It was as if, by dying to help save Arthur's children, Mick had somehow cheated him out of vengeance. Arthur no longer felt angry with Mick; he didn't feel sorrow, either; instead there was just an awful sad weight that nagged in his mind.

"Buenas tardes," Villa said. Katherine had a pincer grip on her brother's arm to keep him from shouting out. She wasn't sure what the plan was, but didn't want to spoil anything.

"I recognize Señor Ollas here," Villa said. "I'm glad he survived his ordeal. And I'm surprised to see old Bob, and Slim, too, as well as this woman. So I suppose I can guess you must be Shaughnessy."

"That would be me. I am Arthur Shaughnessy, and I've come for my children."

"Then I expect you have come here to kill me, huh?" Villa's eyes were narrowed. A little smile began to curl beneath his mustache, but his hands remained by his sides.

"Whoever says that is a liar," Arthur said.

"I believe it is so," the general replied.

"Why?"

"Because everybody says it is so. They believe that you were responsible for the attack on my headquarters back at Reyes."

"Do you always believe what everybody says?" Arthur asked. He leaned back in the saddle and crooked his leg over the pommel so that he was sitting brazenly and impertinently, almost sidesaddle.

"Of course I do," Villa answered. He spat on the ground.

"Well, General," Arthur continued, "do you always believe what everybody says about *you?*

"What do they say about me?"

"That you're a lying, thieving, kidnapping, no-good son-of-a-bitch."

Villa looked puzzled for a moment. He squinted even harder and turned his head slightly to the left, as though he hadn't heard correctly. From the blue sky behind Pancho Villa, unexpectedly there emerged a small butterfly that fluttered about his hat. It was a white-darted yellowheart, an extremely rare species Arthur had seen in picture books but had not yet collected, or even seen. In fact, the only known collected specimen had been lost in a fire.

"They say this about me?" the general asked.

"I'm saying it," Arthur replied, and with an almost noiseless motion, so deft and smooth and sudden even the ferocious Fierro did not detect it in time, Arthur whipped his revolver out of its holster so that in a flash it was cocked and leveled at Pancho Villa.

"And," Arthur continued, "if you don't return my children right now, I'll blow your greasy head off."

Villa looked as though his feelings were hurt. Behind them, Colonel Shaughnessy cleared his throat, plainly not approving of the way the conversation was developing.

Villa looked back at his men, who had by this time raised up their weapons. Then he turned to Fierro and asked something in

Spanish.

"Greasy," the butcher replied. "You know — *greasy.*" He tapped his head. "He called you 'greasy,' " Fierro said.

Pancho Villa began to scowl and turned icily on Arthur's little band. "I wasn't sure I heard you right," he told Arthur.

The white-darted yellowheart butterfly continued to flit around Villa's head, rare and beautiful as the Hope diamond. Arthur couldn't help imagining how impressive it would look pinned in a special case in his collection on the wall of his study back in Boston, and the thought of a net fleetingly crossed his mind. At almost the same moment an irony occurred to him: that he was actually in one of those famous Mexican standoffs he'd read about.

"I apologize for any offense," Arthur said. "I just want my children back."

Villa couldn't tell exactly where this was headed. Of course, his men could blow Arthur to rags, but he doubted they could do it before Arthur put a hole through him first.

"You sent a man to negotiate a ransom," Villa said.

"And you murdered him in a despicable way."

"So why can't you and I negotiate something? Just us two parties."

"I'm negotiating right now," Arthur said. "Your life for my children. Take your pick."

He was hoping Villa would blink, but it occurred to him they could also stay here all night and somebody would get tired or mad and call his bluff.

But Villa saw something in Arthur Shaughnessy's eyes he didn't like, and the way the words rolled off Arthur's tongue sent chilling reverberations through his body.

"I don't like holding people's children," Villa informed him. "I'd much rather go for bigger game."

"What might that be?"

"You."

"Why? I don't have any money."

"You own a railroad, don't you?"

"No. My father does, but it's broke, anyway."

"Is that a fact? What's wrong with it?"

"It's in debt. There's more money going out than coming in."

"Railroads have property, don't they? Cash some in and I'll give you back these kids."

Arthur heard his father clear his throat again. "I think the person you want to ransom is me," the Colonel said.

"You? Who are you?"

"I am Colonel Shaughnessy. I own the railroad."

"I have met you before, señor. You've aged."

"So have you, but it's beside the point. Why don't you turn those children loose and take me instead? I'm the only one who can raise a ransom." Arthur wanted to turn and look at his father, but knew if he did Villa's riflemen could blow him and everybody else to Kingdom Come.

"You've injured yourself, señor," Villa observed.

"I broke my leg trying to find you. Release these children and take me in their place. I'll see what I can do. They can't get you any money, but I can."

Villa considered this for a moment. He didn't want to waste time, seeing as how a gun barrel was pointed at his heart, and might even go off accidentally.

"Colonel —" Arthur began. He hadn't taken his steely glare off of Villa, but his father cut him short.

"Don't contradict me, son," the Colonel growled.

"You'd better to do it, Chief." These tense words belonged to Tom Mix, who'd been watching from the crowd.

"Who asked you?" Villa snapped. "I don't take orders from capitanes."

Mix went on. "I've been the one responsible for taking care of those kids and they don't belong out here; too many things can happen."

Villa mulled this over, too. He wanted to get this over with and not have a gun pointing at him. "Those kids have been a burden to me," he said finally. "Besides, they need to be in school."

"What about my wife?" Johnny Ollas asked.

"I'll throw her in for good measure. She's rude to me and calls me names," Villa told him.

The Colonel nudged his horse forward. "Somebody'll have to help me down," he said. Villa motioned for some soldiers to assist the Colonel.

Arthur felt completely undone by what was happening. It wasn't supposed to have gone this way, but he could see the perfect sense in his father's argument. The children would be free, and at least the Old Man might be able to hold his own with someone like Villa. Still, he was torn by the idea that now his father would have to survive in the hands of such a creature. Would it never end? He could think of nothing to say, and while he was saying nothing Villa told Mix to bring the children.

"What's to keep you from killing us all once I take this gun off you?" Arthur asked prudently.

"My word says so," Villa responded.

"All right, I'll take it," Arthur said. "But before I put this back in its holster, I also want your word that you'll keep open some kind of line of communication with us. Keep us informed about my father. We're going back to El Paso. The telegraph depot will know how to reach us."

"Done," Villa said.

Katherine and Timmy were standing in front of Arthur's horse. Donita Ollas had already swung up behind Johnny. Arthur took Katherine, and Cowboy Bob pulled Timmy up in the saddle in front of him.

"I hope you're a man of your word," Arthur said to Villa.

"Ask around," the general told him.

With deep reservation as well as great relief, Arthur eased the hammer down on his revolver and put it away. He looked down at his father.

"Papa, I don't know what to say to you except that this is the most generous and honorable thing I've ever heard of."

"We're a generous and honorable family, son," the Old Man replied. "And don't worry about me, I enjoy adventures and General Villa and I can get to renew our acquaintance."

Arthur nodded. When he looked into his father's pale eyes, he saw a different man; for the first time he seemed much older and frail. But there was nothing left to say, so he turned the horse and rode off east, toward the railroad. They'd gone a long way before he unclenched his teeth and let his muscles relax. They topped a rise and could see the river. Arthur's heart lifted; they were almost there.

SEVENTY

Villa invited the Colonel to enjoy the remainder of the piñata celebration with him. Villa's men had long since eaten up all the cattle Villa had rustled from Valle del Sol, but they'd stolen others at Reyes. The men enjoyed a feast of flank steak barbecued in an open pit, yet the too-familiar smell of beans and peppers offended the Colonel.

Villa wanted to know how they came to locate him, and Colonel Shaughnessy proudly obliged, describing their trek across the desert from the train tracks and recounting their ordeals in the mountains with storms, bears, cold, and so forth. Villa was amazed to hear they'd trailed him across half of Mexico.

"You are persistent people," he told the Colonel.

"It's a splendid trait of my nation," Shaughnessy replied. "It's why we're a great people, where others fail."

"There may be something to that," Villa said, offering the Colonel a cigar. "With my country, it's always mañana."

"Why did your soldiers destroy the village near the tin mines?" Shaughnessy asked. "You killed your own people, and left a ruin of sad women and orphans."

Villa was surprised to learn of the massacre and denied it was his men, even after Shaughnessy described the slaughter to him in detail.

"But they all said it was," the Colonel told him.

"Then I'll conduct an investigation," Villa replied. "I'm not going to kill any more of my countrymen. It pains me." Great God, Villa thought, this fool is worse than Jack Robinson.

Colonel Shaughnessy wanted to know about Strucker, and Villa told him what had happened. Strucker, he lied, had been most anxious to go on the raid.

"That's shocking. The man was a decent sort and had a family back in Germany," said the Colonel.

"I'm sorry we didn't have time to bring him back for a burial," Villa said, "but things were getting close.

"And that lawyer you sent to negotiate with us, a snake bit him."

"So I heard," Shaughnessy said. "He was a nice boy." Arthur had not told the Colonel about Mick Martin's crime.

"Bad things happen to nice boys, too," Villa replied. "The offer he made in your name was insulting, and it would have taken too many men to watch over him as we marched. Women and children are one thing. A grown man is another."

Just then two riders appeared over the rise, galloping hell-for-leather. They were escorted to Villa's headquarters.

"Generale," one said, "the American soldiers are coming our way!"

Villa asked for details and was told that a dozen automobiles full of soldiers had pulled up at the edge of the river less than a mile away and the party was looking for a place to ford.

"I'll go take a look, Chief," Fierro said. He began barking orders, and presently a dozen men were saddled and ready to ride.

"Take care of yourself, General," Villa cautioned him. "Fighting Americans likely won't be like fighting that stinking scum Carranza."

Fierro nodded and went on his way, hoping he'd get a chance to kill gringos on Mexican soil.

Arthur's party reached the river just as Patton's detachment pulled up on the other side. At first Patton thought they were Villa's men, but a quick look through the field glasses told him otherwise. "That's Americans of some description," Patton announced, "and they've got children riding with them."

"May I see, please?" Xenia asked. Patton handed her the glasses.

"It's them!" she cried in a high, choked whisper. She stood up in the back of the car.

Henry Flipper was familiar with this river. He'd once prospected not far from here looking for a nonexistent silver vein, and was apprehensive when Arthur went down to cross. There was quicksand in the river bottom and they would have to be careful, so he cautioned them to wait while he cut a long branch to test the route. Meantime, Xenia, Patton, and all his soldiers were waving and shouting at them from the other side.

Flipper found a safe crossing, and they waded the horses into the river. It was muddy brown from rains upriver, and the current was running strong and high as they picked their way to the other side, with Flipper and Slim in the lead. Arthur, Bob, and Johnny Ollas waited with their precious cargoes until the others had gotten over; they'd come too far to make mistakes now.

The conversation between the two groups was so animated, it didn't make much sense for a few minutes. Patton finally ascertained what had happened and that indeed Villa and his band were near at hand. The problem was that the river was just high enough with the flood that their cars couldn't cross and he didn't want to lead his men on foot against armed horsemen. After all, he was a cavalry officer.

Katherine and Timmy were hugging Xenia, who was sobbing with joy, while Arthur looked on. Flipper, Bob, and Slim were standing with Patton over the hood of his Packard, trying to pinpoint Villa's location on the map. About that time Fierro's bunch arrived on the other side of the river. The Butcher pulled out his field glasses and eventually swung them onto the group huddled around the car. Immediately he recognized the insolent young American officer who'd insulted him back in El Paso.

So now, Fierro thought, that stinking gringo lieutenant is finally in Mexico and still wonders how well I can shoot. He remembered telling Patton that if he ever found out, it would be the last thing he'd ever know. But he realized that the shot right now was too far for accuracy, even with the American Springfield rifle, so he'd have to get closer until only the river was between them. Fierro told his posse to wait and rode his horse to the river's edge, but the distance was still a bit too far. He waded his horse out in the muddy current, a hundred, two hundred, three hundred feet, almost to the middle. Now he had the range.

Some of Patton's soldiers were shouting about Mexicans and that a Mexican horseman was in the water, but Patton was preoccupied with the maps where he'd been told the main body of Mexican troops would be, and waved them off. Fierro raised the rifle in a deliberate and careful way and adjusted the sights and windage. He put the bead directly on Patton's chest, but in that same instant Patton raised his head and turned to say something to his sergeant. When Fierro squeezed the trigger, the rifle recoiled, and by the time he was able to get his bearings again, Fierro saw a tall blondish man in a red cowboy shirt topple over the hood of the car.

Fierro's bullet had hit Cowboy Bob in the chest. Bob didn't have much time to consider it, though for an instant it flickered in Bob's mind that he had a few things he wanted to say. Flipper and Slim caught him before he could fall and laid him gently onto the ground. Patton yelled for his men to shoot the horseman, but they needn't have bothered. Fierro had nudged his horse one step too many, and the quicksand had him. At least it got his horse, and the animal was sinking quickly. It took Fierro a moment to realize what was happening, but he managed to dismount, taking the rifle with him in the rushing current. Immediately he discovered the gun was dragging him down and he let go of it.

Then he felt something else dragging him down. All these long days Fierro had carried with him the bars of gold he'd personally stolen from Colonel Shaughnessy's safe at Valle del Sol. He'd sewn them into the seams of his duster, and now the gold was pulling him under in the quicksand just as if a heavy hand had seized him by the legs. Fierro struggled to get the duster off, but it was too late.

Lieutenant Crucia saw his boss in trouble and bolted out into the stream. He put his horse alongside Fierro and snatched up a piece of his duster to pull him to safety. Then he realized that his own horse was being pulled into the quicksand.

Fierro felt the water pour into his lungs when he tried to come up for air, and he choked to spit it out but instead took in another gulp. The water was only four feet deep, but the quicksand was sucking at his feet and down he went, despite Crucia's efforts. He didn't even have time for last words.

Arthur had rushed to Bob when he realized what had happened. Patton's men were firing furiously across the river at Villa's soldiers, who had come to the riverbank and were milling back and forth on their horses at the sight of their commander going under. But at the shots, they quickly hightailed it back toward Villa's camp. By then both Fierro and his horse had disappeared under the swift, growling water. Lieutenant Crucia's horse was dragged down also, and he had slid off and was still futilely holding on to some part Fierro's duster under the water. Without any gold to drag him down, however, Crucia could still float.

"Aw, hell, Arthur, I don't believe somebody shot me," Bob croaked. Arthur could see the pallor starting in Bob's face and noticed his eyes were beginning to dim.

"Bob, please hold on. There's a medic here."

"I don't think so," Bob said weakly. "I don't feel good. My wages . . . would you give 'em to . . ."

"Yes, who, Bob?" Arthur bit his lip so hard he bit a hole in it. Bob couldn't get the word out because he was blowing out little bubbles of blood, but managed to point feebly at Slim.

Arthur looked to Patton pleadingly, but the lieutenant shook his head. There was no medic and it wouldn't have helped anyway. Cowboy Bob was gone.

Arthur rose up in a rage and stormed toward the river with his pistol in his hand and began firing into the water where Fierro had sunk and Crucia was floating until the chambers were empty, then kept snapping the trigger until the clicking sound became a monotonous reverberation that was almost obscene. He must have hit Crucia several times, and the rebel lieutenant floated lifelessly downstream along with his grisly necklace.

Patton walked toward Arthur and several of his troops followed him. By then Arthur had returned his aim to the spot where Fierro had sunk, and continued his futile trigger-snapping of the empty gun until one of the enlisted men finally said, "Sir, that man was drownded."

They went back to Bob, who was lying in the grass beside Patton's car. Bob's eyes were still open and the last light from the setting sun had transfixed them into a wistful gaze that for a strange and horrid instant reminded Arthur of the old elephant the Colonel had shot in Africa years before, when Arthur had been a boy.

Slim was standing by Patton's car, holding on to the door and shaking his head with shock and grief.

Arthur knelt down. By that time Xenia was there. Arthur took Bob's head in his hands and cradled it. He began to choke up quietly.

"Darling, please," Xenia said, but she had never seen him like this. As she walked back to the children, Xenia realized that life was likely to be different from now on.

Slim and Ah Dong finally had to draw Arthur away from Bob's corpse. Xenia shielded the children from the sight. Arthur's eyes were stinging and not clear. After all those days on the trail, he'd thought he might almost have found the big brother he'd always wanted, or the friend of a lifetime, but now that was gone forever as the sun went down over a cold Christmas Day.

Meantime, at the third car, Patton was having a conversation with Henry Flipper.

"I've heard of you," Patton told him. "You were the one who got court-martialed, is that right?"

"They did it, yes," Flipper told him.

"Well, all that's behind you now. You've made something of yourself. You've got a reputation all over this part of the world."

Flipper didn't know whether to thank him or not. It didn't sound like much of a compliment, even if Patton had meant it as one.

"You know this country pretty well, don't you?" Patton asked.

"Yes," Flipper said.

"Well, I believe I'm authorized to hire you in the name of the United States Army as a scout. We need to find Villa."

Flipper looked at him numbly. "No, thank you," he said.

"No?"

"That's what I said."

Seventy-One

Patton was thoughtful enough to lend one of the army automobiles to carry Bob's remains back to El Paso, where they went to the best funeral home in town. Since Bob wasn't known to any of the few churches in the area, Arthur arranged a meeting with a young Episcopal priest and described to him what he knew of Bob's life.

The first night, when they got back to the Toltec Hotel, Arthur had gone down to the bar to get a bottle of rye to take back to his room. He hadn't had a proper drink in quite a while, and was startled to find the grimy old prospector they had met in the sierras standing at the counter, drinking tequila.

"Did you ever find what you were after?" the man asked him.

"Yes," Arthur said, "we did."

"You found Pancho Villa?"

"And more," Arthur told him.

"I'd say you were lucky to escape out of Mexico," said the prospector. "These are perilous times over there."

"What are you doing on Wednesday?" Arthur asked. The man seemed nonplussed.

"Because I want you to come to a funeral," Arthur told him.

The funeral service was in a fine small chapel not far from the hotel. An organist was playing the old Episcopal hymn "The Prayer of Thanksgiving." Arthur had been worried there wouldn't be many people there, but a lot more showed up than expected; in fact, he needn't have invited the prospector at all. It seemed Bob had made a lot of friends among the stockyard and saloon crowd in El Paso, who had found out what had happened from the newspapers. The priest went through the traditional funeral service. Then he said:

"I did not know Bob Braswell personally but I am told he led an exemplary life. He was orphaned at the age of nine and forced to work his way through the world. He survived the Indian wars, miscarriages of justice, and the rough life of a plainsman, only to perish at the cruel hands of a killer while helping rescue children from harm. Greater love hath no man than this, that he lay down his life for a friend." The organist concluded the service by playing the old gospel hymn "Going Home" as pallbearers from Bob's old haunts in the saloons and stockyards slowly moved Bob's casket out the door and on to the local boot hill.

It was an emotional moment and Arthur felt a tear coming, which he brushed away. It was a much nicer service than he'd expected. He, Xenia, Katherine and Timmy, Beatie, Slim, Henry Flipper, Ah Dong, Bomba, Johnny and Donita Ollas, Gourd Woman, and Crosswinds Charlie sat in the front pews like family — after what they'd all been through, they all *were* family in a way. Even the old prospector turned up and had seated himself in the back of the church. Afterward, as they were walking down the steps of the church, a man approached Arthur.

"Mr. Shaughnessy," he said, "my name is John Reed, and I've heard of your ordeal. You might remember that I helped you back before all this, to get you gasoline for your plane in the desert. I want you to know that I was with Pancho Villa while he held your children captive."

"Why?" Arthur asked him.

"Well, like I told you then, I'm reporting on the revolution for the *New York World.*"

"Revolution?" Arthur repeated the word slowly, deliberately, so that it came out in four distinct syllables. "Is that what you call a revolution?"

"The process takes many forms," Reed responded, but felt a little uncomfortable saying it. "I lost a friend there myself," he added.

Arthur said nothing, but there was something icy in his gaze that almost frightened Reed.

"I'd like to interview you for a story," Reed said.

"No, thank you," Arthur told him.

"No?"

"I'm tired right now," Arthur said.

"But you rescued your children from Pancho Villa," Reed said incredulously. "That's a story the whole world will want to hear. It's front-page stuff."

"Who cares?" Arthur replied. "I'm not in the newspaper business."

After they left the cemetery, Arthur was leading his party back to the hotel for a farewell luncheon. For most of them, he figured, it would probably be the last time they saw each other. Just then, the train out of Mexico was arriving. Its bell was clanging and steam was hissing as it pulled into the station, blocking their way. Arthur began to lead them around it when from out of the coal tender behind the engine a disheveled figure emerged, hobbling on a crutch. He was black with coal dust from head to toe, hair wild and eyes wide, and for all the world looked like a man in the circus who'd just been shot out of a cannon. For a moment Arthur didn't recognized him.

It was the Colonel.

"Papa!" Arthur shouted, and rushed to him.

The Old Man was grinning from ear to ear and gave Arthur a hug. Ah Dong, Bomba, Flipper — with Gourd Woman and Johnny Ollas hobbling after — had followed Arthur and were dancing around the Colonel; there was so much excitement that it took a while to get the story out.

"I swapped myself for *The City of Hartford*!" the Colonel howled.

"Your train car?" Arthur cried.

"I hope you all don't mind riding back to Boston in the coaches," the Colonel said, chortling.

"But how did you do it?" Arthur asked.

The Colonel rubbed his hands merrily as he told them. "Old Villa wanted to know if I had my own car, and so I described it to him. When he learned it was right here in El Paso, we worked out a deal. He took me to a telegraph and I ordered the thing sent down toward Chihuahua. Villa says he's gonna retire and move it onto a ranch and live in it! After a couple of days he began saying I was more of a pain to him than the children, that I was disagreeable and talked too much. He turned me loose near the railroad tracks, but since I didn't have any money for a ticket, they let me ride in the coal car."

"I'll be a son-of-a-bitch!" Arthur cried gleefully.

"No, you won't, and never will," the Colonel told him soberly. "And don't ever say that again."

Beatie, Xenia, and the children had also seen the creature emerge from the coal car but, like Arthur, didn't recognize him immediately. When they realized who it was, they, too, rushed down the train platform, including Slim and Crosswinds Charlie. Everybody was talking and chattering and hugging and kissing the Colonel or clapping him on the back and pumping his hand. Arthur felt so glad that everybody was happy and together again. Between that and the hissing and clanging of the steam engine, the noise became a din, as if he'd stepped out into the rail yard in Chicago, or put his ear to a seashell. He tried to tell his father about Bob but the racket was too loud. He finally gave up. That could be later. For now, family, to him, was all that mattered.

"Mexico," the Colonel cried. "The hell with it."

"It ain't that bad for some people," said Death Valley Slim, "once you get used to it."

Epilogue

The doctors pronounced that the mending of both the Colonel and Johnny Ollas was going as well as could be expected, considering the circumstances. In fact, one doctor said he'd never seen a severed limb sewn up so nicely as the job Ah Dong had done on Johnny. As for the Colonel, the doctor was astonished that his leg had been set almost perfectly by Cowboy Bob and he probably wouldn't even have a limp.

They remained in El Paso for a few days more, which didn't seem to bother anyone; the reunion was bracing in itself. Arthur had to get the *Grendel* biplane taken apart again and put into a boxcar for shipment home.

The morning they were to leave, Colonel Shaughnessy had a private meeting with Gourd Woman in his rooms at the Toltec. She'd asked to see him, and he suspected he knew why.

"I suppose this is about Johnny," the Colonel said.

"No, it's about you," she told him.

"Me, Lurie? What about me?"

"I know you've been struggling with it," she said.

"With what?"

"To tell him or not."

"You're right, I have. It's difficult. Why don't you do it?"

"He should hear it from you."

"Well, I don't know why. You're his mother, aren't you? I'd take it as a kindness."

"Yes, but it would mean more to him if it was from you. After all, what could I give him? I barely make a living selling brooms."

Colonel Shaughnessy reflected on that for a long moment, then said:

"You're right again, Lurie. I was planning to bring him back to Boston with me anyway, him and his wife. Mexico's no place for Johnny with all these lunatics on the loose, and he can't fight bulls anymore, that's for sure."

"But were you going to tell him?" she asked.

"I hadn't made up my mind. After all, if I do, I'll have to tell my wife, too."

"Why?"

"Because I don't want him to have to live a lie. If he knows, after all this time, and then has to hide it as a secret, it wouldn't be right."

"That will cause you trouble, won't it?"

"Of course, but I still like to think I'm an honorable man, even if I've done some things

797

that everyone else, including my wife, might think weren't right."

"You are honorable, John Shaughnessy. You're one of the most honorable men I know."

"Say," he said, "why don't you come along, too? Mexico's no good for you anymore, either."

"And do what?"

"Something better than selling brooms, I imagine."

The following year, when America entered the European war, the New England & Pacific Railroad at last got the profitable war contracts the Colonel had sought after, and Arthur finally convinced him that the only way to save the company in the long run was to take it public. When they did, the Old Man's greatest fears were realized.

First the new board of directors ordered him to sell *Ajax,* on grounds it was an extravagance, although they did let him order another private railcar, which he named *The City of El Paso,* even though his trains didn't run within a thousand miles of there. Then they began reorganizing the company. Soon, speculating robber barons began moving in on the enterprise, driving up stock, trying to take it over. In the end they succeeded, and just as the Colonel had predicted, they tossed him and Arthur out on their ears — though fortunately with enough money to keep them comfortable for the rest of their lives. The Colonel wasn't really bitter about it. "I'd have done the same thing myself, if I'd been in their shoes," he said.

Johnny Ollas and Donita stayed around Boston long enough for him to get fitted with a cork leg. When he could dance as well as he used to bullfight, the Colonel gave him a job at the railroad, but he wasn't really suited to it, and the weather didn't much agree with the leg. Then, out of the blue, Donita wrote to Tom Mix out in Hollywood and he sent them an invitation to come out and visit. When they arrived, Mix set them up running a Mexican restaurant, one of the first fancy ones in Southern California, and it soon became the talk of the town.

Crosswinds Charlie also became a success story — one for the books. After America got into the world war, he joined up with the U.S. Army Flying Corps. He went to France and became an ace pilot, with rows of medals on his chest after shooting down fourteen German planes. He became a colonel and was on the short list for general, but got out of the service to become the president of a large airline company.

As for Slim, the Colonel gave him enough money to start his own musical band: Death Valley Slim and the Ghost Riders. They got a big record hit out on the radio in the 1920s — a pretty waltz called "I Love You More Than Yesterday," in which Slim got to show off his Irish tenor and false-soprano yodel. Beatie invited him to play at one of the dances at Cornwall that she'd designed as a western theme party, complete with hay bales, western two-step dancing, and a few horses snorting around outside.

By then, Tom Mix had become the biggest cowboy star in Hollywood, and to everyone's surprise — and Katherine's breathless delight — he accepted an invitation to come to Newport for Beatie's big western party featuring Slim's band. When he arrived that afternoon, Mix immediately visited Timmy and Katherine, and what was said between them has remained a secret from that day to this.

Duly impressed by Cornwall, Mix informed the Colonel and Arthur that he left Pancho Villa right after the kids were rescued, figuring that one day it was "going to come down to Villa and me, and I reckoned it would probably be Villa," so he sneaked off. He said he'd rather have done it another way, but the way it was done would just have to be good enough.

Tom brought a lady friend with him, however, which almost broke Katherine's heart. She'd never quite lost the crush she'd developed, and for a while it became more ardent when he began appearing in movies. She told her mother later that she noticed when he arrived he was wearing the little four-colored ascot-neckerchief she'd sewn for him. He didn't mention it, she supposed, because the lady friend was present most of the time.

However, at the western party that night Tom asked Katherine to dance — she had just turned seventeen — when Slim played his theme song, "I Love You More Than Yesterday." She was radiantly beautiful in a white crinoline dress and he looked fine himself in a dark blue western-style suit with a cowboy-trimmed shirt and white silk tie. They made such a handsome couple waltzing around the floor that the other dancers not only cleared a path for them, but pretty soon couples left the dance floor entirely and stood on the sidelines to watch the famous movie star and the beautiful granddaughter of the host and hostess glide faultlessly along the dance floor, smiling and looking into each other's eyes.

They wound up in front of Slim's bandstand as he sang the concluding melodic lyrics:

This is how I love you,
Forever and a year.
I love you more than yesterday,
And less than tomorrow, dear.

Mix and Katherine exchanged bows and salutations with Death Valley Slim, who was all smiles and had grown a little mustache, and was resplendent in his fancy cowboy suit that glimmered with red sequins. Everyone at the party was applauding except for Mix's lady friend, who remained at her table keeping a wary eye on things. As Mix escorted Katherine off the floor, he whispered to her, "Well, missy, I reckon I've finally saw the ocean."

"Yes," she said, "and much more, I'm sure."

"If you ever come out to California I'll show you something special," he told her.

"What's that, Tom?" Katherine asked.

"You remember that big cat that got after you?"

"The jaguar," she gasped, putting a hand to her throat, stopping just short of the family table where the lady friend sat.

"Now he's a rug in my office," Mix told her. "I had him skinned, tanned, and stuffed, head an' all."

"Oh, my," Katherine said. "A rug?"

"I wouldn't have let him hurt you, missy," Mix told her. "I became very fond of you two."

"I know that," Katherine said. "And thank you for it." She leaned up and gave him a quick kiss on the cheek. " 'Bye Tom," Katherine said, and fluttered off toward some friends from her school. There was still something there, barely definable, but suddenly it wasn't a crush anymore. Katherine was certain of it. It was a kind of gratitude mixed with — oh, she'd figure it out another time.

Beatie passed away in 1938 and the Colonel died the following year, but from the day she and the Colonel got back from El Paso till the day she died, she was a different woman. Maybe it was because the Colonel was a different man, too. They traveled to Europe and the South of France, and even went on African safaris. The last years were good to both of them.

Bomba had stayed on for a while as the Colonel's chauffeur until he proposed marriage to Lurie, the Gourd Woman. Colonel Shaughnessy set him up in a chauffeuring business in Hartford, where he acquired a fleet of big cars to haul the state's crooked politicians around, and made a handsome living while Lurie ran the office side of the business.

Xenia had Mick's baby and she and Arthur adored him from the outset. Officially, he became Arthur Shaughnessy, Jr., but they called him Cowboy. Like his grandfather, he finished Harvard, but just in time for World War II. In 1943, he was killed in the South Pacific as a captain in the U.S. Marine Corps.

After the railroad fiasco, Arthur did not

return to Boston. Instead, with money from the sale of the NE&P, he and Xenia went down to El Paso and started an orphanage. Arthur asked around and found the same little piece of property northwest of the city that Cowboy Bob had once owned with the runaway wife. Bob's description of it had been so charming that Arthur had pictured it in his mind as a golden place. He bought that and much more, in the shadows of the Franklin Mountains.

There they built the orphanage of adobe buildings and put in trees amid the big cacti, and flowers, a lake, a school, a chapel, a hospital, fields for farming, riding trails, and livestock operations. There were baseball and football fields, a fully enclosed basketball court, as well as clay tennis courts and an eighteen-hole golf course. It was a first-class orphanage. They named it the Bob Braswell Children's Academy, and opened it to any orphan, regardless of race, creed, or gender. For a while they took in a lot of Mexican kids whose parents had died in the revolution.

There was a grassy spot with some cottonwood trees next to the horse corral where Arthur had commissioned a larger-than-life-sized bronze monument modeled on a Frederic Remington sculpture. It was of a cowboy riding a bucking bronco, waving his hat in his hand, and at the base was an inscription from what the priest had said at

Bob's funeral: "Greater Love Hath No Man Than This, That He Lay Down His Life For A Friend."

The children liked the monument because it was a place to gather around, but also because it represented action and toughness, and bravery and loyalty — what people like to think of as the old cowboy creed; the children went there during their lunch recesses. The birds liked the monument, too, and after a few years, with rains, baking heat, cold blue northers, and the birds, it took on a special patina that, if you caught it just right in the El Paso sunsets, made it glow "like an old iron skillet that's been left too long on a fire," the Colonel once said.

Timmy — Tim now — finished at Groton, and went on to Harvard, graduating summa cum laude. Taught to fly by his father, he stayed in El Paso, where he started a flying school that the army used during World War II to train pilots. He survived the war himself, flying P-38 fighters in the Pacific, and became involved in the orphanage. But he spent much of his time in adventurous traveling, too — hiking in the Alps and Urals, diving in the South Pacific, mountain climbing in South America, sailing in Australia. At one point, for a lark, he even led a gold prospecting expedition in Mexico's high sierras.

Katherine's fate, however, was tragic. She had just graduated from Miss Porter's School at Farmington when Arthur and Xenia moved to El Paso, and she went with them for the summer. Tall, beautiful, smart, and poised, she was teaching equestrian jumping to some of the older orphans when her horse nicked the high bar; a fluke. It stumbled, couldn't recover, and she went over the top. She only lived for a few minutes after that, but Arthur and Xenia managed to rush to her. Her last words were, "Papa, I'm cold . . ."

They buried Katherine in the corner of the field near Cowboy Bob's monument. More than twenty years afterward, Tom Mix stopped by while traveling for promotion of his Wild West show. He was a little old by then, and somewhat bent, but people, including Arthur and Xenia, remembered that at one point he went down on a knee before the stone and hung his head for a long while.

As he walked away, children from the orphanage, scores of them, swarmed around wanting autographs. They presented pads of lined paper from school, backs of church bulletins, paper napkins, brown lunch bags, and scraps of paper of all description. Mix put on his signature smile and signed his name, as he'd done thousands of times before.

Arthur, gray-haired now and a bit portlier, had been watching from the shade of a long open corridor between buildings, and after a while walked out to where Mix was finishing up his signing, not far from Katherine's grave.

"You understand," Mix said, "that I never wanted to keep those children. I said so at the time, but was overruled."

"That's what Katherine told us," Arthur said. "You know, she developed a serious crush on you," he added.

"I kind of thought so," Mix replied. "At that time, though, I never had anybody have a crush on me. Didn't really know what one was."

"I've always wondered," Arthur said, "why you got mixed up with Pancho Villa in the first place." The great red-orange sun was setting low between a gap in the mountains and cast cathedral-like rays of light on the school and its yards, as if they were filtered in stained glass.

"Well," Mix said, "I've thought a lot about that myself. What comes up to me is that there's a difference between dreams and lies, and while I was with those people, I think I might've got it confused."

Arthur nodded. "El Paso," he said.

"What?"

"A lot of people come to El Paso hoping for a break, and then jump the wrong way."

"That was me, I guess," Mix said. "I went there to get in the movies and wound up in Mexico."

"You've had quite a career, haven't you?" Arthur remarked.

"It was a privilege, sir, to have known your

son and daughter," Mix said earnestly.

"I wonder," Arthur said, "if you see your way to coming back here sometime. You're such a big star to the children."

"Mr. Shaughnessy," said Tom Mix, "I will bring the whole show with me. And I'll do it every year. It'll be a pleasure, sir. Why, you have a whole family here."

AFTERWORD

Casualty figures during the Mexican Revolution are sketchy, but millions are estimated to have perished. Students of the period will notice that I have occasionally tampered with the evidence. Some of the terrain has been altered and some historical events described happened at slightly different times than those fancied in the plot and have occasionally been condensed to suit the story line. I hope it will be forgiven, since this is a novel, not a history, and not even a "historical novel" in any conventional sense.

Of the actual, historical characters depicted in this tale:

◇ Tom Mix went on, of course, to become the most famous cowboy movie star of his era. He later owned a traveling western circus and died peacefully in his sleep in 1940.

◇ John Reed returned to the U.S. and wrote a popular book on Pancho Villa and the Mexican Revolution. He also founded the American Communist Labor Party and in 1919, facing a charge of sedition by the federal government, he fled to Russia, where he wrote his famous book about the Bolshevik Revolution, *Ten Days That Shook the World,* then contracted typhus and died in Moscow in 1920. He is buried in Red Square, near the tombs of other famous Communists.

◊ In 1929, *The Treasure of the Sierra Madre,* about an old prospector in the Mexican sierras, was published, and in 1948 was made into a movie classic directed by John Huston. Its author, B. Traven, disappeared south of the border during the 1930s. His fate remains unknown.

◊ Pancho Villa's archenemy, General Venustiano Carranza, was ousted from the Mexican presidency in 1920 by Villa's other nemesis, General Obregón, after Carranza began the wholesale murder of political prisoners, including fifteen generals. Carranza tried to flee the country with millions in government gold. He almost made it, but was caught heading for the port of Veracruz and executed on the spot.

◊ In 1919, Henry O. Flipper was hired as translator for Mexican affairs in the Senate Foreign Relations Committee and later served as an assistant to Interior

Secretary Albert Fall. He retired in 1930 to his native Georgia and devoted the rest of his life to clearing his name. He died in 1940, the same year as Tom Mix. In 1999, President Clinton granted Flipper a full pardon for his court-martial conviction for "conduct unbecoming a gentleman."

◊ Pancho Villa was also granted a pardon, in 1920, by the government of Mexican president Adolfo de la Huerta and went on to become a peaceful farmer in Parral, where it was reported he was learning how to type. In 1923 he was assassinated by people believed to be associated with the wealthy Herrera family, four members of whom Villa had murdered during the revolution. He was forty-five years old.

◊ General Rudolfo Fierro was leading his soldiers to the Battle of Agua Prieta when they came to a body of water the men did not want to cross. Leading by example, Fierro rode out in the stream and was caught in quicksand. It was said he might have escaped but for a load of stolen gold he was carrying, which weighted him down and drowned him.

◊ Ambrose Bierce vanished in Mexico after being rumored to have joined Villa's army as an observer. His fate has never been determined, despite the efforts of numerous biographers and historians.

◊ General Pershing became commander-in-chief of the American Expeditionary Forces in France during World War I. Under him, George Patton rose to the rank of colonel and went on to fame and fortune in the next world war. During the American invasion of Mexico in 1916, riding on the running board of a car, he personally shot and killed the top aide to Pancho Villa.

◊ Toward the end of his last term in office, President Woodrow Wilson suffered a stroke from which he never recovered. He died in 1924.

◊ The figure upon which the character of Claus Strucker is based was a German agent in Mexico named Franz von Rintelen. His attempts to draw America into a full-scale war with Mexico proved futile and he left the country in 1917 after discovery and publication of the infamous Zimmerman Telegram, in which the Germans offered to assist in the return to the Mexican government of the states of California, Texas, New Mexico, and Arizona in exchange for a declaration of war on the U.S.

◊ The American owners of the huge estates and industrial holdings in Northern Mexico lost their land and their money when a series of Mexican revolutionary governments nationalized their property. The Mexican government subsequently decreed that foreigners could not own any property in Mexico — down to and including private residences — a restriction that has applied in one fashion or another until this day. C. V. "Sonny" Whitney, however, litigated the confiscation of his property through the Mexican courts and in 1927 was awarded $250,000, a fraction of its worth. He used the money to finance an aviation enterprise that became Pan American World Airways.

As to the research necessary for any book of this kind, I relied on several biographies of Ambrose Bierce, especially Roy Morris, Jr.'s fine work *Ambrose Bierce: Alone in Bad Company.* Quite a lot has been written about Pancho Villa and his lieutenants, much of it fantasy. Most recently and most notably, Friedrich Katz's monumental biography *The Life and Times of Pancho Villa* is a worthy analysis. For the bullfighting sequences, no study in the English language has ever been more comprehensive on the subject than Ernest Hemingway's *Death in the Afternoon.* I am deeply grateful to these authors, and many others, for their insights and illuminations.

ABOUT THE AUTHOR

Winston Groom is the celebrated author of twenty books, including the cultural phenomenon *Forrest Gump*. His other novels include *Gump & Co., Better Times Than These, Only, Gone the Sun, Such a Pretty, Pretty Girl,* and the award-winning *As Summers Die.* In addition, Groom has established himself as an acclaimed historian with books such as *Conversations With the Enemy* (nominated for a Pulitzer Prize), *Kearny's March, Shiloh, 1862, Vicksburg, 1863,* and more recently, *The Aviators* and *The Generals.*

Groom grew up in Mobile, Alabama, where he went to University Military School, and graduated with a degree in English literature from the University of Alabama. He served as a lieutenant in the U.S. army, completing a tour of duty in Vietnam with the First Brigade of the Fourth Infantry Division (1966–1967), which would inspire much of his work. Discharged with the rank of captain, he was a journalist for nine years for the

Washington Star, after which he spent ten years in the Hamptons and in New York City writing novels.

Recipient of the prestigious Harper Lee Award and several honorary Ph.D. degrees, Groom regularly gives lectures on his novels and history books. He lives in Point Clear, Alabama, with his wife, Susan, and daughter, Carolina. Find him online at winstongroom .com.

The employees of Thorndike Press hope you have enjoyed this Large Print book. All our Thorndike, Wheeler, and Kennebec Large Print titles are designed for easy reading, and all our books are made to last. Other Thorndike Press Large Print books are available at your library, through selected bookstores, or directly from us.

For information about titles, please call:
(800) 223-1244

or visit our Web site at:
http://gale.cengage.com/thorndike

To share your comments, please write:
Publisher
Thorndike Press
10 Water St., Suite 310
Waterville, ME 04901